SUSPECT

SCOTT TUROW

Swift

SWIFT PRESS

This paperback edition first published by Swift Press 2023

First published in Great Britain by Swift Press 2022
First published in the United States of America by Grand Central,
a division of Hachette Book Group 2022

1 3 5 7 9 10 8 6 4 2

Offset by Tetragon, London
Printed and bound in Great Britain by CPI Group (UK) Ltd, Croydon, CR0 4YY

A CIP catalogue record for this book is available from the British Library

ISBN: 9781800751705
eISBN: 9781800751699

For Julian and Stacee

SUSPECT

verb

\sə'spekt\

1. to believe something is probable without certain proof

//I suspect she is telling the truth

2. to doubt or distrust

//I suspect his motives

noun

\'səs‚pekt\

a person thought to be possibly guilty of wrongdoing

//She is a suspect in the investigation

adjective

\'səs‚pekt\

doubtful or questionable

//His explanation is suspect

SUSPECT

1. SOMETHING WEIRD

"There is something weird with the dude next door to me," I tell Rik. Across the conference room table, his small, weary eyes rise reluctantly from the file he's reviewing. His brain seems to chase after my words for a second, then he hits me with a sneaky little grin.

"Oh, I get it," I say. "'Look who's talking,' right? But he's weird. Maybe not me-weird, but he's strange."

"You mean he doesn't have a nail through his nose?"

"Ha," I answer. It isn't even in today. And it isn't even real, just old Goth jewelry I bought used, the head and blunted point of a framing nail worn as separate studs on each side. It's been kind of my trademark look for years now. But Rik says I might as well hang one of those road signs around my neck that warns, 'Sharp Curve Ahead.' Before I started here two years ago as the investigator in his law office, I promised to ghost the nail when I'm doing interviews or meeting clients. In fact, because Rik is so stressed about this case, I've put on one of my three dresses, a shapeless blue sheath whose long sleeves hide some of my most outrageous ink.

"You can mock me," I say, "but something's up with this guy. He moved in like a month ago and he doesn't talk to anybody. He has no visitors. He doesn't go to work. The inside walls in that building are like those Japanese screens, but it's been weeks since I heard anything from next door. It's like he's one of those silent monks—no voices, no phone, no music. He doesn't own a car, as far as I can see. And he's never even cleaned out his mailbox from the prior tenant. The post lady has to dump his mail on the floor, and he walks right over it. Just a very weird dude."

Rik says, "He sounds like a guy who wants to be left alone. Which means you should leave him alone."

"I have a creepy feeling about him," I answer.

Rik holds up a soft hand.

"Pinky, please," he says. "We've got ten minutes before our first real meeting with this client. Let's make a good impression."

The case has been breaking the Internet—days of headlines in various papers and even a few national hits on the gossipy TV shows. Our client, the chief of police here in Highland Isle, has been accused by three officers of demanding sex in exchange for promotions on the force—'sextortion' as a couple grocery-store tabloids have labeled it. A complaint before the local Police and Fire Commission, 'P&F' as it's called, is asking for Chief Gomez to be fired. Worse, the United States Attorney has launched a federal grand jury investigation, which could even mean jail time. The Chief is in deep.

As Rik is rereading the file, I say, "I just can't figure this dude. I mean, he goes out once every day around noon with his gym bag. And he grabs some carryout at dinner. Seven days a week, same same. So what's his deal? Is he stalking somebody? Is he in witness protection?"

Glancing up again, Rik clearly can't even remember what I'm

talking about. You might call Rik and me family, depending on how you're counting. His dear dead mom, Helen, married Pops, my grandfather Sandy Stern, not long after I was born. As I remember Rik from my childhood, he was this uber-nerdy chubby college student, still super messed-up after his parents' divorce, who managed to flunk out of Easton College by not attending a single class for forty-nine straight days. Even when he got it together enough to go back, he drifted through college and barely made it into law school.

Now, about twenty-five years later, he's got the shape of an autumn gourd. His little remaining mouse-colored hair looks like dirty soapsuds that will blow away any second. Still, I sometimes think it would be okay to end up like him, a person who learned from his troubles back in the day and, as a result, is kind to everyone.

After playing rewind in his head, Rik is frowning about me going off again about my neighbor.

"Pinky, your imagination must be one of the most interesting places on earth. It's like living in 4-D. All this stuff that never could happen, and you're running it as the feature attraction."

"Hey, I have great instincts, right? Don't you say like sometimes I have ESP?"

"Sometimes ESP," he says. "And sometimes PES."

I take a second. "PES?"

"Piles of Erroneous Shit." Teasing me is one of Rik's favorite office pastimes. Since I was little, being the object of a joke starts a near-riot close to my heart, but with Rik I can mostly ride with it. He is the best boss ever and gets his biggest chuckles at his own expense (like how in high school he decided to drop the c in 'Rick,' actually hoping that axing one little letter would make him cool). Plus him and Helen always seemed to like me better than most people in my own family.

"Let's stay on task," he says. "I don't want the Chief changing her mind. You know what this case could do around here."

Rik doesn't do much legal work that attracts big attention. I was a paralegal in my grandfather's law office before Pops closed shop. He and my aunt represented all the richest crooks in the Tri-Cities, and our space had the quiet atmosphere and heavy furnishings of a bank lobby. With Rik, I'm kind of in the working class of the legal world. Our office, in a recovering part of Highland Isle, is cramped, with the same cheap paneled walls people put up in their basements. We do a lot of worker's comp and quick-hitting personal injury cases to keep the electricity flowing in the sockets. Rik would love to handle headline defenses like Pops, but most of the criminal cases that come through the door here are rumdum misdemeanors—bar fights and first-time DUIs and drunken stunts by teenagers. At fifty-two, Rik thinks Chief Gomez's case might help him finally step up.

"I thought you'd been retained," I say.

"We had a get-together at a coffee shop for about ten minutes before the Chief went on vacation. But Mr. Green has not arrived." He's referring to a retainer. In criminal, you have to get paid up front, since clients don't send many checks from prison. "Supposedly, we'll see it today."

His attention returns for a second to the P&F complaint, then he suddenly stops cold and squints at me.

"How's he look?" Rik says.

"Who?"

"Your wacky neighbor. You've been keeping quite an eye on him. What's he *look* like?"

"I don't know," I say. "Asian."

"He's going to the gym two hours a day, so he must be in good shape, right?"

The man is definitely lean and fit, but what's most striking is his skin, a rich shade I've never seen before, close to what was called 'ochre' in my crayon box but with a more lustrous undertone. He's tall too, around six foot three.

"Point?" I ask.

"Point is maybe you're a little hot for him."

"Nah," I say. "This guy's maybe forty-five. You know my story, Rik—older women, younger men."

"Pinky," he says, "it's none of my business, but your story seems to be anybody born human."

"Ha," I say again, although he's probably right.

Nomi, Rik's assistant, peeks around the door.

"Chief Gomez is here," Nomi says.

Not the kind to wait, Lucia Gomez-Barrera sweeps in with a burst of positive energy that fills the room. She immediately opens her arms to Rik for a hug.

2. THE CHIEF

As Rik tells it, the Chief and him were tight in high school. She was one of those superhot chicks who left a lot of the guys in heat just by walking down the hall, and Rik was her assigned lab partner in Bio who was basically no threat. (Besides, he had already pretty much bonded for life with Marnie, his wife, a fact that, frankly, makes my head explode. At thirty-three, I still regard one person forever as impossible, let alone coupling up before you're old enough to drive.)

Rik introduces me as his 'ace investigator' and the Chief offers her hand. Even today, many police brass have no taste for people like me, inked from neck to ankle and with a magenta Mohawk (and a blue undercut on one side). But Chief Gomez comes on warm as a kindergarten teacher, with a smile that's 100,000 lumens of pure light, and—get this—dimples. A police chief with *dimples*!

I have a kinda/sorta ex who never unfriended me and was on the job in HI last I checked. Just to give myself some cred, I ask about her, Tonya Eo.

"Tonya's the Real Police," the Chief says, which is top praise. "Just made detective sergeant. Friend?"

"We were cadets in the Kindle County Academy together."

"Back more than a decade? Did you get sworn?"

"No, I fucked up," I say. I flamed out on a drug test, the last week. "Story of my life."

I receive a sweet, sympathetic smile. I'm getting a positive feel about Chief Gomez, which is kind of a surprise. I don't really like most people to start, and they definitely don't like me. I tend to get up in their grills almost as soon as we say hello. It took me a while—and a therapist or two—to realize I'm still basically a kid, scared of strangers.

First thing, she slides an envelope over to Rik.

"I took a second on my house, Ricky. I hope you're worth it, man."

The Chief is in her dress uniform in Highland Isle's puke-worthy shade of blue green, which I would call Sick Teal. The long jacket, which is probably covering her weapon, has gold braiding on each shoulder and double-breasted rows of brass buttons, and her actual police star, also gold, over the left breast. The light in here is not what they would choose at the beauty counter: harsh fluorescents and no windows. Even so, in the flesh, Lucia Gomez is prettier than she appears on TV, although, just saying, there is a fair amount of flesh. I make her as five two and maybe 150 pounds. She has a round face with movie-star cheekbones, huge dark eyes and great skin, 'Warm Beige,' as they call the shade at Sephora.

Just to get rolling, Rik starts by going over her biographical details. After high school, they pretty much lost touch, and even once they found each other again here in Highland Isle, their contacts have generally been limited to lunch every now and then. Still, given what most cops think of defense lawyers, Rik isn't surprised that in the current crisis she's turned to someone she's known forever.

As for her background, the Chief grew up in Highland Isle, with six brothers and sisters in a three-bedroom bungalow with one bath. Dad was a welder, Ecuadorian, Mom Mexican, and both are gone now. The Chief enlisted in the Army a month after high school graduation, because she figured the GI Bill was the only way she'd get to college. After surviving Desert Storm, she enrolled at Greenwood County JC, which was where she heard about the veterans' preference on law-enforcement hiring. The Kindle County Unified Police Force offered her space in the academy.

"I never made you for a cop," Rik says.

"Me neither. But I loved it from the start—except riding with the Ritz, who was my first training officer. But I felt like this is what I was meant to do, something where you could make a difference every day. I took the time to listen to everyone—the victims, the witnesses, even the dude in cuffs."

She kept going to school at night, got a BA in criminology, then a master's, and made detective in Kindle County in less than six years.

"They were looking for women by then." She offers a humble shrug.

She married another detective, but the fact that she was moving up faster than Danny created issues. Hoping to save things, she left Kindle for Highland Isle, where the marriage cratered anyway, while her career continued to boom. She reached commander, number two in the department, in record time.

When the old chief, Stanley Sicilino, got the boot twelve years ago from Highland Isle's first reform mayor, Amity DeFranco Nieves, the Chief became the consensus choice to replace him. Latinx. Raised in HI. Strong educational credentials. By now, she says, she's made her share of enemies, but that's how it goes.

With that soft start, Rik turns to the real business, the P&F complaint. Pops used to tell me that clients come in two flavors: the ones who can't talk about their cases enough and the others who will do anything to avoid the subject. You might think the talkers are innocent and outraged, but Pops said a lot of bad guys think the next best thing to not having done the crime is to make somebody else believe that. By contrast, the wrongly accused—a smaller group, frankly—are often struggling to get a grip.

The Chief definitely has not been looking forward to this conversation. Once she hired Rik, she took off two weeks for her older daughter's wedding and promised not to think about any of this, and clearly meant it. Rik says he had to call her four times to get her to come in.

For me, though, it's easy to see why she'd be having a hard time dealing with the charges, which have seemed totally sketchy to me since Rik first explained them.

'Why's that a crime?' I asked him. 'Hooking up? What's the US Attorney investigating?'

'Because she's a public official,' Rik said.

'Because she's a woman, Boss. Men still hate it when a female does what she wants with her body. These dudes' stories make no sense. Yeah, okay, men can get raped or assaulted, but not usually when they're carrying a .38. Not to mention the basics: If winky-dink doesn't want to come out to play, there's no game. So how'd she force them?'

'They say they didn't want to.' Rik shrugged.

At that point—the day Rik met the Chief for coffee a month ago—all we knew were the few details that had been leaked to the *Tribune*. Even so, it was clear that somebody canny about election-year politics was involved. The P&F complaint, which was filed a few days later, was clearly timed to put maximum pressure on Mayor Nieves, who's running again, to fire the Chief. Instead, the mayor, who's learned how to swerve after twelve years in office, said she would leave it all up to the Police and Fire Commission. Rather than give in, the Chief declined to take a leave.

"This is all horse hockey," the Chief says now. "I wanna see those jokers up there testifying to this crap, that I supposedly said, 'Sex or else.' This is just typical police department baloney. Cops think the worst of everybody, especially half the officers they work with, and are always making up shit about them."

"Okay," says Rik. "Okay." He nods several times, clearly trying to determine how safe it is to probe. "But all three of these guys got promoted, right?"

"Sure. And I signed off. But there was a good reason in each case."

Rik asks her for a thumbnail on the three men accusing her, 'the allegators' as Rik calls them in the typical grim humor of the world of criminal defense.

"Well, two of them," she says, "Primo DeGrassi and Walter Cornish, were in Narcotics together for years, until I moved them out. Cornish retired last year, and DeGrassi left about twelve months before. I can tell you right now, if you dig around"—she points straight at me—"they're both connected to the Ritz. He's behind this."

That's the second time she's said 'the Ritz.' Part of what freaks me out about other people is how often I can't follow them or make the connections everybody else sees as obvious. I can remember watching TV when I was a kid and being so baffled about what was happening with the characters that I'd ask my younger brother, Johnny, to explain. 'Why did she just say she hates him? I thought she liked him.' 'She does like him. That's why she said she hates him. Because she's real disappointed.' Even now, I often find myself feeling lost and a little panicked.

"The Ritz?" I ask, although Rik prefers I just listen. "Like the hotel?"

She smiles, nicely. "It's a nickname for a really bad guy."

Rik lifts a hand so he can continue to direct the conversation. He wants her to tell us first about the third officer in the complaint.

"Blanco?" she asks. "We call him Frito around the station. He's the big mystery. Former altar boy and Eagle Scout. Bronze Star in Afghanistan. Quiet. Never gets excited. A coppers' cop. And I been *so* good to him. I got no idea why he's making up this shit."

Rik jots another note and then says, "Okay, I'm with Pinky. Who's the Ritz?"

The Chief responds with a bitter laugh.

"Everybody around here knows who the Ritz is. Moritz Vojczek?" Voy-check.

"The property guy?" I ask, proving her point. Vojczek's name is all over. His company seems to manage every apartment building in town, including mine. He owns the biggest real estate brokerage in Highland Isle and is clearly the busiest developer. If you see a hole in the ground in HI, odds are there's a sign in front that says 'Vojczek.' Definitely a local power.

"I read in the *Trib* last year," says the Chief, "that the Ritz is worth about 300 million dollars. And he owes it all to me."

"To you?" Rik asks.

"Cause I fired his ass from the police force as soon as I became Chief. Well, not fired. Suggested he resign."

"Didn't you say you rode with the Ritz in Kindle County?" I'm still confused.

"Right," she says. "We both started out there. I could take all afternoon telling you stories about the two of us, but the long short is simple: He'll spit on the ground I've walked on because I canned him. Not to mention that I still have my eye on all the dirty shit he's got going around here."

"What kind of dirty shit does a real estate mogul have going?" Rik asks.

"A lot. When the Ritz was in Narcotics, everybody knew he was dealing himself. He's better insulated now, but he's not changing his spots. Fentanyl's the money drug right now, so he's probably got some angle there. I mean, I'd be happy to testify about all the bad blood between us."

Rik spends some time shaking his head.

"Lucy," he says, "you're not going anywhere near a witness stand for a while."

Rik details the odd procedural footing of the P&F case. Because of the political heat, the city attorney, who acts as the prosecutor, has agreed to convene the hearing so the three accusers can tell their stories in public. But because of the Fifth Amendment, the Chief won't present a defense until the US Attorney has cleared her.

"Which is the best of both worlds for us," says Rik. "We chew holes in these guys' stories, using all the great stuff Pinky is developing." He shoots me a smile, and I know better than to gulp. "Once the Feds decline to prosecute, if the City hasn't dismissed the case already, then you get on the stand and say, 'This is all bull-pucky, I never had sex with any of these guys.'"

The Chief takes a long time, but the dimples are gone.

"Well, maybe that's not exactly what I'd say," she finally answers.

"Oh," says Rik eventually.

The Chief studies her watch and says, "Let's put a pin in this."

Rik asks me to walk her out. He's still at the conference room table, massaging his temples, when I return. His eyes rise to me.

"Clients," he says.

3. THE WEIRD GUY NEXT DOOR

My job with Rik is probably the first time in my life I've headed for work in the morning without feeling like I'm going to prison. (Hanging around with Pops was always cool, but my job there was an eight-hour day inside a fortress of paper.)

Years before, I had been pumped at the thought of being a cop. I was sure I could be less of a jerk than the guys who'd harassed me when I was in my super-druggy phase, right after I broke my back and had to give up competitive boarding. And the squinty-eyed distrusting way cops look at other people is, frankly, pretty close to my basic attitude toward everyone. Crashing and burning at the academy left me feeling for a long time like I'd missed the chance to be myself.

Becoming a private investigator never occurred to me. It was my grandfather who thought I might have a talent for it. When Pops and my aunt, who were law partners, decided to retire, they offered to pay for a PI training course for me as outplacement. I was like, 'Why not, okay,' but I had no clue how much I'd get into it.

Yet here's the truth—I love to snoop and pry. I get a

butt-tightening thrill out of it. Maybe some of that has to do with how often I miss signals. Investigating is like being the Invisible Man—not the one from the book I had to read in high school, but the old movie, somebody who can drift around and look in on people without ever really being seen. Oh, I think often, oh, so *that's* this chick's deal.

And when I'm being a PI, I can do stuff that's hard for me ordinarily. I don't have to grope for the words with strangers, because I'm there to ask, 'What do you know about Joe Blow or Clown Brown?' I don't care about the usual judgy thoughts people have about Crazy Pinky, because I've got a job to do.

At night, I spend hours watching YouTube and visiting obscure sites, trying to master what I call the P.I. BOT. The PIBOT has nothing to do with algorithms or robots. It means the Private Investigator's Bag of Tricks. That started with a concealed carry permit, training included in my PI course. Now I'm always reading about and practicing skills—surveillance techniques, disguises, clever ruses to get people to talk.

But none of that has helped me learn much about the weird guy next door. I've taken to scribbling notes, guesses and whatnot, so I can review every little detail and put together two and two, but so far nothing is really adding up.

Tonight, after our meeting with the Chief, as I approach the apartment building, The Weird One (or TWO, as I've started calling him in my own brain) is in the old tiled foyer, on his way out. He is a creature of unvarying habit. Judging from the yellow plastic bag he comes back with every night, he's on his way to Ruben's, a little Mexican storefront two blocks away, where the whole family cooks.

TWO has got manners, I'll say that, since he holds the door open as he sees me headed up the walk. Then again, it gives him something to hide behind. He's literally shielded by the beveled glass panes of the old entry door as I pass by.

"Hey," I say. He doesn't answer, doesn't smile. Not even a nod. He's gone as soon as I skinny past.

Through the so-called wall, substantial as a communion wafer, that separates our units, I thought I heard voices not long after he moved in around March 1, and I immediately decided to eavesdrop. The old tricks from 1930s movies—a glass against the wall or a stethoscope—do pretty well, but they have nothing on today's amplification apps, which both increase the sound and cancel extraneous noises. They are also purely illegal, which means I've never told Rik about them. In PI school, they always reminded us that your employer can be held responsible for whatever you do. Which led me to adopt what I regard as the PI's Golden Rules. One: Don't tell your boss more than he needs to know. Two: Above all, never get caught.

But listening in on TWO, I have learned next to nothing. Most of the time, I can't even make out his shoes on the floor or the hardwood creaking. It's like he's over there meditating or practicing how long he can hold his breath. I hear the plumbing now and then. My two biggest discoveries are that he has hay fever, because he sneezes loudly on occasion, and that he likes the History Channel, especially shows about old wars, which is what the voices I thought I'd heard turned out to be. Otherwise, zero. If he's typing on a computer keyboard, he has it silenced. And he must have started listening to his TV with headphones, since in the last several weeks I haven't even heard that.

Yet my Spidey-sense tells me this guy is up to something strange or dangerous. What if he's building a bomb and my last thought, as the building and I become a million pieces of debris, is, I knew it, I fucking knew it? And so, after I watch TWO turn the corner,

I decide the way I decide most things, without thinking about it much, to follow him to Ruben's. This isn't completely odd, because I stop in there at least once a week, although usually closer to closing time at nine.

Ruben opened this place after the worst of the pandemic. He had lost his job, like so many other restaurant people, as establishments closed. That left a lot of vacant restaurant space here on the edge of downtown Highland Isle, and Mayor Amity used some of the federal COVID money to fund a loan program, basically begging people to give it another try.

Ruben's is doing really well, because the food is absolutely banging. The carnitas in particular rival a G-spot orgasm. Ruben uses pulled meat—no ground beef here—and spices you can see them grinding in the kitchen.

Three generations toil there in sight of the tiny dining room. The younger teenagers are chopping up the veggies to make salsa. The big hit in the online reviews is Grandma, who sits over a hot stone oven in a corner flipping tortillas. The pretty daughter, who is in college, and whose English is way better than her parents', works out front to greet the customers and take the carryout orders. If there's any lull, she goes back to her books. She told me once she wants to be a pediatrician.

"Usual?" she asks when I'm halfway from the door, and I answer, "You know it." I follow her toward the cash register and tap the credit card gizmo with my phone. Mr. Weird, who I caught sight of as I came in, is sitting at a tiny table not ten feet behind me and waiting for his food.

Once I've ordered, I turn and do the whole what-a-surprise thing. "Hey," I say, all warm and friendly, a mode I am not especially good at. He's reading a newspaper. There are folks, like me, who can be so shy it hurts, and if that was his story, I'd let him be. But it takes one to know one, and TWO is not that kind of person. Nobody scares him. His narrow black eyes are hard as marbles. He says nothing as he glances back to the paper.

I am really bad about taking 'Fuck you' for an answer.

"Okay if I sit with you while I'm waiting?" I ask.

His mouth sours. I can see that if he could bring himself to say it, he would answer, 'Go away,' but he knows that if he pisses me off, I can start banging heavy metal at three a.m. Instead, he waves a hand, sort of like 'I can't stop you,' and I plop down in the molded chair on the other side of the two-top. There's a total of ten tables in here, a couple rows with red-checked paper tablecloths, lined up between the store window and the kitchen. Colorful woven hangings with simple figures are on the walls.

TWO continues studying the paper, with an intensity that is clearly faked. Fact is I've never seen a newspaper in the trash or recycling bins for our floor, which we share and which I've examined periodically, hoping futilely for signs of what TWO is up to. My guess is he either grabbed what he's reading off the table or else bought it for a special reason. There are two other customers waiting for their orders, but they're doing the standard thing, thumbing through their phones.

"So like what's the weather?" I ask him. I mean, could I do any worse? When I say I'm lame with other people, I am lame. "Do you think climate change is real?" I add. That is maybe even stupider than my first remark, and so in total shame I find myself babbling. "Cause like I'm a snowboarder, I was anyway, before I broke my back doing it, and, you know, I like had a professional interest in snow, and I mean I can see that it's different, we get ass-little here anymore. I mean, maybe I don't have to tell you that. Are you from here?"

He sits over there with his bullet eyes, calculating whether he needs to answer at all.

"This paper doesn't do the weather," he says. These are the first words I've ever heard him utter. His voice is wispy and he's got just the faintest accent, like he grew up with another language besides English.

I lean a little closer to see the facing pages of what he's been reading.

"Is that the *Wall Street Journal*?" I ask.

He glances at the top of the page, as if he's not sure himself, then makes a sound to say yes.

"Oh, so you're like in finance?" I ask.

"No."

"Just an investor?"

"It's something to read," he says.

I think about asking him what he ordered, and aren't the carnitas epic, but I sense he's on the verge of changing tables. The paper remains raised as a barrier. In the kitchen, the family chatters in high-rpm Spanish, shouting occasionally to be heard over the ranchera music that booms out for the benefit of the customers.

It's just my luck that my order comes up before TWO's. Ruben himself emerges from the kitchen in his apron and plastic gloves, holding the yellow bag.

"Clarence," he says, "su comida." For carryout or other places where you need to give a name, I've lately started saying 'Clarice,' which I was christened with. Partly it's because nobody ever gets 'Pinky.' I'm called Stinky, or Peeky, or Penny, which is super annoying. Also, sometimes I like to pretend a little. Actually, I like pretending a lot—another great thing about being a PI, since I often have to act out some off-the-hook cover stories to hide what I'm up to.

Calling myself Clarice is different, naturally, but it's still a way to kind of pretend, as if I'd been born into a different family, or at a different time, or with a different mom. My mother's mother's name was Clara, and Clara stuffed a rag in the tailpipe of her Cadillac and suicided herself in her garage about six months before I was born. In memory of her, I was named Clarice, but my mom, still overcome with grief, found herself choking on a name so much like her mother's. As a result, she accepted it when my dad started referring to me as Pinky. He thought he was a complete stitch, because his demented grandmother couldn't remember 'Clarice' and just said, 'Hello, Pinky' whenever she looked at rosy little me down in the bassinet.

But Ruben doesn't get 'Clarice.' He's been calling me Clarence since the first time I came in here. I've stopped trying to correct him and just take the yellow bag.

I return to His Weirdness at the table and say, "You heading back? I'll wait."

He won't answer for a second, then says, "I'm going to eat here. Take care." Again, the look that goes with this remark is about as friendly as a pointed weapon.

"Sure, okay." I stall a second longer and go out the door, feeling humiliated and terminally stupid. That was some ace investigative work. I know nothing more about TWO, except he's kind of a dick, and he's sure now the inked-up chick next door is a complete creeper.

I've strolled a block when I suddenly reverse and go south to a little convenience store on the corner, where I ask whether they still have some of this morning's papers. The South Asian guy behind the counter just points. I find today's *Wall Street Journal* and pay for it.

I walk an indirect route home, taking my time to look in

windows and stopping twice to check my phone. As I get close
to our building, I see just what I expected, TWO heading in, his
yellow bag and dinner at his side. Like I said—creature of habit.
I stifle the urge to sprint up and say something to embarrass him,
because it would be counterproductive to let him know I didn't
buy his act.

Instead, I lay back until he is inside. Spring or not, it's a chilly
night, and I'm wearing a puffy coat with my shorts. In this part
of the country, April is a write-off, often damp-cold and gloomy,
even a little snow sometimes.

Our building has a brass nameplate on the front that's been
there for more than a century and says, 'The Archer.' The sign is
not a slick marketing move—we're on Archer Avenue. I guess a
hundred years ago, buildings were given names because street ad-
dresses were just starting to be used. Anyway, it's a big buff-brick
three-flat, solid as a castle and constructed in a U, the projecting
wings creating a nice landscaped courtyard out front. I trudge up
to the third floor.

I guess when the Archer was first built, my place and Weirdo's
next door were a single apartment, probably crowded with one
of the large families of European immigrants who were flooding
Highland Isle. On my side now, there's a galley kitchen with a
minuscule living room and a small bedroom. The old bathroom
was split in half, leaving me with the claw-foot tub, outfitted with
a ring shower. When I was searching for rentals, I also looked
at TWO's apartment. It's bigger, but not worth the extra three
hundred bucks the Vojczek leasing agent was asking.

My little hand-me-down dog, Gomer III—Gomer the Turd, as
a woman I was hanging out with called him—peps up and then
sags at the sight of me. He is always hoping against hope that
it will be Helen, Rik's mom, Gomer's original owner, coming

through the door. When Pops moved to assisted living, I got
the dog by default since Rik's younger daughter is allergic. Out
of mutual gratitude, I was offered first dibs on Pops's furniture.
Most of what him and Helen owned was too big for this place,
but I did take a small table that seats four, wicker with a glass top,
that doubles as my desk, and a nice blue tweed love seat that I've
made a mess of by eating there as I watch TV.

Tonight I spread out the newspaper on the table even before
I unwrap my dinner. I can honestly say I've never opened the
Wall Street Journal in my life. The only news I really care about is
sports, and I get that from Twitter and *The Athletic*. The reason
I recognized what Weird was reading was because the paper was
delivered every day to the reception area at Pops's law firm.

Anyway, I turn the big pages one by one, looking for the
story that was facing me as I sat there at Ruben's, with a photo
of the newest wreckage in Ukraine. On the side TWO was
looking at, I don't find much, just a bunch of four-inch articles,
mostly about quarterly financial results of various corporations.
For me, they could just as well be written in Etruscan, with
terms like 'fiscal first quarter net' and 'EBITDA,' requiring me
to fight the lifelong habit to just quit reading. But I force myself to continue until I finally hit pay dirt, or what might be pay
dirt, a squib about Northern Direct, Highland Isle's biggest
employer.

When Amity Nieves beat the so-called Mayor for Life, Lorenzo
DeLoria, twelve years ago, while he was under federal indictment,
her number one campaign promise was serious redevelopment
in Highland Isle. With the help of our US senator, she brought
in a ton of federal money. The city center is nicer now, which
has attracted a lot of obnoxious hipsters to my part of town.
Amity's other big project, a so-called Tech Park in the blighted,

half-deserted neighborhood of Anglia right under the interstate, has had mixed results. In fact, it's the main issue this year in Amity's race against Steven DeLoria, Lorenzo's son, who is kind of his dad with better tailoring and speech classes.

In some senses, the Tech Park worked out well. A few local companies moved in there, including an educational software developer and two 'green' manufacturers—one that makes a switch that strengthens your Internet signal, and another that produces veterinary pharmaceuticals. But about 70 percent of the space set aside for the first phase of the Tech Park was awarded to Northern Direct, a huge defense contractor, which builds guidance systems here for missiles and planes. It's a scary-looking place, a one-story building with these radar dishes on top and no windows, surrounded by chain link and razor wire, and security guys who carry AK-47s.

Direct brought with it nearly a thousand jobs—and a shitstorm. The uber liberals, who hate the military to start with, joined forces with local civil rights organizations and sued to block the tax breaks Amity gave Direct, which are supposedly keeping the City from honoring all the promises it made to the displaced residents. That halted the second stage of development, which is a problem for local businesspeople, like Rik, who bought our office building, anticipating big demand. Now he can't get the rents he expected, which is why we're stuck in the dingiest space in the place.

Anyway, the *WSJ* article says that Northern Direct just won a $92,646,787 cost-plus fixed-fee contract from the Defense Department for a cybersecurity component that will protect air guidance systems from hacking. The paper says other details about the agreement are limited due to national security concerns, including where the equipment will be assembled.

It's possible TWO was reading about Direct simply because it's a company with a large local presence. Or because he seems to be a war guy who figures to be fascinated by weapons systems. Assuming the new security component will be built here, TWO, for all I know about him, may even see a job opportunity for himself. There are a lot of innocent explanations. But there are some sinister ones, too, that rush to mind as soon as you say 'national security.' Maybe TWO's a peacenik intent on sabotaging Direct. Or a patent thief who wants to steal this new technology and sell it to someone else. I could probably conjure a dozen bad possibilities.

But this is my first solid clue. I point a finger at the wall we share and murmur, "Dude, I got my eye on you."

4. TONYA

Rik has had an office in Highland Isle for more than twenty years. He's very loyal to the place and is kind of Mr. Google, sharing little factoids whether or not I've asked. I now know that the population of HI has grown since the last census and is about 120,000 and that the city is an actual island in the River Kindle, which I, trapped on Planet Pinky, had never noticed. To the west, a skinny little tributary, not much more than a ditch beneath the roads, separates Highland Isle from the fancy West Bank suburbs where I grew up in eternal misery. To the east, across about a thousand yards of water, lies Kindle County and the North End of Kewahnee. Since the time of the first settlers, a busy port has operated over there, with freighters lined up carrying prime Midwestern cargo like iron ore and coal and wheat to the rest of the country.

In the 1880s, the poorest of the port workers, mostly Italian and Irish immigrants, became the first residents of HI. In the old-timey brown photos from the period, the island is just an unpromising pile of sand and shale in the middle of the water. The men would row to work in dinghies, except in the winter, when the Kindle iced over and they'd walk, meaning that in the dark some poor bastard was always stepping through a soft spot and drowning. From the start, Highland Isle was grim and tough— and full of crime.

By the 1920s, the mob had taken over, ensuring that the only crimes happening were the ones they were in charge of, especially bootlegging, with crates of illegal liquor boated around the Tri-Cities at night. They also controlled the city government, which was why Highland Isle never got absorbed into Kindle County.

In the 1960s, the white people headed for the nearby suburbs, and Latinos—mostly Puerto Ricans and Mexicans—moved into the blocks of solid brick tenements that are mixed in with rows of small bungalows that always remind me of fat toads. The mob still managed to run the city until a dozen years ago, when Mayor Lorenzo was nailed by the Feds for passing out city contracts to his sons and his brother-in-law and several cousins. Sixteen DeLorias in all got all-expenses-paid vacations in various federal correctional institutions. Steven, this year's mayoral candidate, was the only close relative of Lorenzo's who didn't get indicted, and that was just because he was too young.

From my place in Highland Isle, it's about a ten-minute drive to Mike's, Kindle County's busiest cop bar, which is situated on the edge of the bungalow belt across the river in Kewahnee at the foot of a highway cloverleaf. Mike's is definitely no-frills. The bar occupies a freestanding storefront that could easily be mistaken for somebody's garage, a flat-roofed one-story building with shingle siding around the door and a black window. Inside, it's knotty pine with neon beer signs, including the one I've always loved, featuring a twinkling waterfall. Civilians come in here, too, but they are generally ignored.

Mike's is the place players tend to head after the Monday and Thursday night Fraternal Order of Police Softball League games, now that things are kind of back to normal after COVID. (Since cops always want to appear fearless and don't care much for rules applied to them, masks were always a rare sight in here.) League rules require each team to have two women on the field at all times, and I was all-conference in high school for three years, so after I flunked out at the academy, my teammates at the Shakespeare Street station found some discretionary fund that continues to pay my FOP dues. On the roster, I'm listed as 'Regular Female,' which I don't hear many other places.

My postgame stops here are pretty much what passes for my social life during the season, which extends from the current mittens weather in April to late October. This is a no-judgment place. Guys get wasted and tell all kinds of lies, strange stories from the street that they heard years ago and repeat as something that happened to them last night. Over time, I have heard three different cops claim to have found an intact human kidney in a Ziploc bag. This is about as comfortable as I will ever be in a crowd. No one seems to look long at my nail or my haircut (although now and then somebody tuning me will whisper, 'UC, right?' as they're handing me a beer, thinking I work undercover and that my ink is something that will wash off in the shower).

It's 7 p.m., between the after-work crowd and the folks who drift in for a nightcap. We had beautiful weather for our first game last week, but tonight, leaving aside the smokers, it's too cold to sit out in the so-called beer garden, which is nothing more than a yard with picnic benches and views of the empty lot next door, full of busted concrete from some construction project, and the rushing highway overhead. It's an indoors night, with the jukebox gunning heavy metal, and the yeasty smell of spilled beer heavy in the air.

I figured this would be neutral turf for a meetup with me and Tonya Eo. No one she cares about will see us, since most HI cops never visit, inasmuch as the Kindle County officers always treat the HI police like they are six-year-olds with plastic stars. I climb up on a wooden stool next to a high-top and wait. I figure it's fifty-fifty Tonya will show. I messaged her on Facebook that I wanted to talk offline about police business, and she answered 'ok,' but ours wasn't a good breakup, and if it were me, I'd probably decide against being zombied. Aside from a couple innocuous comments about posts, Tonya—'Toy' I sometimes called her— and me haven't had a real conversation in a dozen years.

But about ten minutes later, here she is, in civvies with a belted trench coat, which she quickly throws over a stool. I haven't spent much time on her feed, and I'm glad for her sake about how good she looks.

"Girl," I say, "you're all glo'd up."

She gives me an itsy-bitsy smile in spite of herself.

"Said bye to a few LBs," she answers.

She is wearing makeup, which she never used to, and a short blunt cut with a part to one side. In her black fashion jeans, she has a waist now. She's definitely gone femme.

"Still Lite?" I ask. She likes that I remember, and I signal Dutch, the bartender, for the beer. "How's the fam?"

"Same same. Dad's got some stuff with his kidneys."

"You ever come out to them?"

She rears back a tad and shoots me a tentative look. I can tell she's not sure she wants to get personal, but she finally answers.

"Couple years back," she says.

"And?"

"And just screaming and yelling and crying, and then finally they decided, you know, 'You're gonna change your mind.' That's where they are, waiting for me to change my mind. Like I'm gonna drive up in a minivan full of kids with my husband any day now."

"That's tough."

"You know, it makes me feel better that I did it, but I shouldn't have been surprised. My mother's brother in Manila? He's in fashion, and a sweetheart. I love him to pieces, I swear, but the guy is *so* gay, and nobody in the family can see it. 'Uncle Eo? He's just different.' He's sixty and my mom refers to him as a bachelor, like he'll be next on the TV show."

I laugh. She's funny. She's always been funny. She didn't usually say much, but that sense of humor was always kind of lying in wait.

"What's up with you?" she asks. "Still hate your mom?"

"Forever," I say. "Dad's still a washout, but it looks better on him now that he's old enough to be retired. You remember my grandfather?" Sitting here, I recall taking her over once to meet Sandy and Helen. "I'd been living in his house, helping out, but he's in assisted living now. So I've got my own place. It's in HI, actually."

I know she also lives in town, because the cops have residency requirements, and the way she perks up when I say that makes me instantly afraid that I've sent the wrong signal, as I so often do. I take a sharp left and head for the safety of business.

"I work as an investigator for Rik Dudek. Do you know who that is?" I ask.

"He's represented the bad guy on a couple of my cases. Not the usual slimebag."

"He's a good guy."

"He's a lawyer," says Tonya.

"Well, he's the Chief's lawyer. What do you think of her?"

"I think she's crushing it. She promoted me." No smile. Very Tonya. Her main act is tough. Quiet. Blank faced. Straight ahead. When I was just getting to know her, years before, catching on to her deadpan was the first thing that made me realize there was more to her than met the eye. "I actually took the HI offer," Tonya says, "when I graduated from the academy, instead of Kindle, because the Chief had just been appointed. I figured any department run by a woman was a better bet. Kindle County back then, a female cop was either a mother, a bitch or a whore—those were the only ways they'd see you."

In the academy, most of the cadets stayed the hell away from me. I was an inked-up queerdo who, given my whole vibe, was destined for failure. Eventually word spread that I had once been sort-of/kind-of on my way to the Olympic trials, which bought me something, along with the fact that I kicked ass in physical training, stuff like our morning run, where I beat all the boys.

Still, I noticed when Tonya seemed to make a point of sitting down next to me during the middle of the day when we were doing academic classes, like criminal procedure. She kept to herself so much that she clearly wasn't there for conversation, meaning I got a feeling pretty soon about what was up. I wasn't completely sure, because her family had emigrated when she was a kid, and now and then there were cultural nuances that seemed to go past her, so I wasn't positive she intended the messages she seemed to be sending. That's me too, of course. Once in a while, some person who is getting to know me, say in a bar, will ask me in a super-nice way, 'Did you grow up here?'

I did not necessarily find her attractive. She was pretty lumberjack, which is not my thing. She's got kind of a squinched-up face, and her skin looked like it had been really bad when she was a teen, and she was thicker physically. Then again, she was interesting, secretly funny, and not quite like anybody else I'd met. All I knew about Filipinos was that some racist kid in high school once said they eat dogs, which I didn't imagine was actually true. Her family was from one of the outer islands, and all the rest of them—her father, her mother, her two sisters—worked as caregivers for older people. I asked her once why so many Filipinos seemed to do that, at least around Kindle County, and she said, 'We respect our elders.'

"She says you slay, by the way," I tell her. "The Chief?"

"Oh yeah? How do you know that?" She's suspicious, as I expected her to be.

"I mentioned your name, you know, when I met her. As someone I knew in her department."

"Okay."

"How you feel about the charges against her with P&F? You know the allegations, right?"

She smirks. "Of course."

"And what do you think?"

She makes a face and says, "I think that's what you get when you mess around with men."

This may be meant as a kind of a put-down of me, but I won't go there. Truth is she always had an edge about guys, like they're all just waiting out there to rape or beat you. Me, I basically like men. The most reliable people in my life are male—my dad, Pops, Rik. I start out giving a guy the benefit of the doubt and let him show me that he's a jerk, which, to be honest, a lot of them do. But Tonya's attitude gives me a way to work her.

"Yeah," I say, "but don't you think it's insane bullshit? You believe there's a man in the world, let alone three of them, who is going to let a woman tell him what to do with his thing? I mean, guys, men, that piece of meat is who they are. They'd give her a smack, commanding officer or not. Don't you think?"

"Definitely," she answers. "No, you're right," she says. She sits back to take my measure. "We just spillin tea or what?"

"Rik—and the Chief—are counting on me to come up with stuff to shoot holes in the three HI cops' stories, and so far I don't have much ammunition. For obvious reasons, the Chief can't ask around. I need background on these guys. Anything will help. It can all be on the DL. I won't write anything down."

"Background? Well, how about the foreground? Not throwin shade, but have you had a look at those dudes? Even Frito," she says, meaning Blanco. "He's younger and a good guy, but he could stand a full season in the gym. The other two, Cornish and DeGrassi? Old fucks, if you don't mind."

"There's got to be mountains about these guys I'd like to know."

"I'll tell you right now, with Frito, I don't see him lying. He'd think God would strike him dead. The other two? You know, when I came on, they were already the usual cop burnouts, turned into sad shits twenty years ago when they figured out the job wasn't a television show. I worked a little with both of them. On the street, they're okay. They'd have your back if something went down. But they're not worth much anywhere else." She drops her voice a couple octaves in imitation. "'You write the report, okay?'" She shakes her head. "They hang together a whole lot."

Twelve years on the street has made her a different person, so much more confident it's hard to recognize her in a way. I'm glad for her, and wonder for a second what the badge would have done for me.

"Family guys?" I ask.

"Hardly. Fucked their way out of their marriages from what I hear. Both of them. Well, maybe Primo's wife is still holding on. You know, they're the kind of dudes, half the guys who come in here are that way—get drunk and hook up with whoever they can. They don't even have to be that drunk. I know Cornish's ex better than him, to tell you the truth."

"She a cop, too?"

"No. I know her from church."

"*Church?*" I keep myself from saying anything else. Tonya has definitely been through some changes.

"It feels good. The whole vibe, you know. Mass. The community. And I like the priest."

"Hip young dude who's cool with lesbians?"

"Hip old dude. But yeah, he couldn't care less. God made me, too, you know."

God on top of everything else. This is why, when I was younger, I promised myself that I would never become a so-called adult and end up just accepting things that deep down have never made sense to me.

"Could you see if she'd talk to me? Mrs. Cornish?"

"Paulette." She doesn't think long, before shaking her head. "I can't get in the middle of this. I'm all for the Chief, but you know, I've got a long time left out there. I don't want to be on anybody's team. That shit, his faction and her faction, it's bad for the department. And me."

"Understand," I say, "but I bet Paulette's got no love lost with her ex, given the way he fucked around on her. I wouldn't want her to make anything up. Maybe you could just ask her? Tell her I'm good people and won't screw her over. Then just step out of the way."

She hitches a shoulder, noncommittal. We sit there looking at each other. With every passing second, the past is beginning to take up a lot more space.

In the academy, after a while, I kind of gave in and hung out with Tonya on a few weekends. The cadets were housed in this dilapidated old dorm at the U. We each had roommates but mine drove home when classes ended on Fridays.

With sex, starting with my so-called boyfriends in junior high, I have never been very good at saying no to anyone who seems to genuinely want me. One Friday night we ended up in my room on the crummy mattress, the old bed frame sort of singing along with us as we rolled around. Cadets were supposed to bring their own sheets, but that was the kind of thing I never could remember, and I recall laying there with her on the blue-and-white-striped ticking after the first time. She was crying like she'd lost something. I was clearly a lot more experienced.

'I just know what I'm doing,' I said.

'I'll say,' she answered. 'And you enjoy it so much.'

'I always do,' I told her, and that is the truth. I can almost always cut loose, especially with someone like Tonya, who is basically kind.

Now, across the high-top, I ask Tonya, "You ever hear any of the three talk about Moritz Vojczek?"

"Sure. He's like the yeti. Everybody talks about him. Dude goes from the job to gazillionaire? What do you think?"

"But these guys specifically? They have any tie to Vojczek you know of?"

"They could. Word is the Ritz employs a lot of ex-cops or guys looking for a side hustle after hours. I mean, Primo and Walter, Vojczek was their lieutenant when he was on the job. The Chief was reorganizing the Narcotics Bureau when I started. She got rid of Ritz somehow and split up Cornish and DeGrassi. Some strange shit going down supposedly. Money and drugs disappearing during busts. You know, my heart won't break for a dealer. But still. Chief straightened that out."

I nod several times, just to show I am seeing things her way.

"Either of them, Cornish or DeGrassi, have any, you know, kind of enemies on the force or guys who don't like them?" I ask.

"I don't know. DeGrassi, he's kind of a clown really, lots of laughs. Cornish has some edges. I don't think he gets along with some of the Black officers. He had a fight a couple years ago with a cop named Emmitt LaTreaux about something LaTreaux thought was racist."

I write 'LaTreaux' on a napkin, then say, "I could use your help on a couple things." I keep going before she can say no. "You Facebook friends with any of the three?"

"Blanco, yeah."

"Could you friend the other two?"

"I guess."

"I just want to see their feed. Photos. Profile. A screen grab here and there, if you could. Just print them out and mail it to me at the office in an envelope without a return address. No questions asked."

Her lips rumple up. "I'll think about it."

"Great. Thanks. Thanks. It could really help the Chief."

She looks at me across her beer. Her eyes, as I remembered, are so black. Dead stars.

"You happy?" she asks me. There's a lot lingering in that question, but I decide to play it straight.

" 'Happy?' " I'm not really sure what that means. I've had a lot of thrills in my life, boarding especially, that moment where oh-fuck meets the will to live and you have a split second to keep control.

Landing was always such an amazing rush, such a triumph, your body—your ability—triumphing over chaos and gravity. When I broke my back, and the doctors canceled jumping again, that was the hardest part—knowing that moment was gone for good. "I'm not sure 'happy' is ever gonna be a Pinky state of being," I tell Tonya. "I figure I'm aiming more for 'okay,' Toy. Like I just want to be okay. And I pretty much am. I love this gig, being an investigator. I think all the time, Don't fuck this up, the way you did the academy. That just laid waste to me for years."

"You got fucked over on that," she says. We'd had our bad breakup by the time I was dismissed, so she never heard the whole story. In the first couple months, quite a few recruits peeled off every week, mostly because they were failing the written tests, but in the last month, we all felt we were on a glide path. Around then, my jaw began to feel like it was breaking, and I ended up at an oral surgeon who said I had to get my wisdom teeth out. He gave me a letter for the lieutenant, saying I would need Vicodin for the pain afterwards, and the lieutenant said I could skip my drop that week—we peed in the bottle every Friday.

After the extractions, thinking I had a freebie, I got some X and also had a little smoke, mostly just because I could. Then the lieutenant told me that the commandant had overruled him and decided I should drop anyway. Like I say, cops are always suspicious. I had a history of juvenile adjustments for drugs. State law said they couldn't keep me out of the academy for underage offenses, but the commandant had an eye on me all along and never liked my look. I was gone by Monday.

"Story of my life," I say to Tonya. "But I always think, What if." She sort of seesaws her head.

"I don't know, Pinky," she says. "I realize you loved the thought of being a cop, but in reality, you might have decided it sucked. There are rules, double-dumbshit stuff you have to do. You would never have put up with that."

"I'm a little different now."

"You're never gonna be that different. I bet as an investigator you just go off and do whatever the fuck you think will work, right?"

"Pretty much."

"Well, that's not being a cop. Not a good cop. I love most of it and accept what I don't love. But I'm cut out for that. You know, my parents brought me up to think of obedience as a virtue."

I know she means well by saying all of this. But hearing it casts me down into the dungeon of gloom where I end up now and then, remembering how often I fucked up, and the heavy price I seemed to pay almost every time. I wiped out on a 1080 I'd completed a dozen times in the half-pipe, destroying my back and my future, because I was obsessing on a nasty remark my mom had passed that morning. And now that I'm in this mood, the memory returns full force of how I screwed over Tonya, a nice person with a heart that had been pretty much unscarred until I stomped on it.

"Gotta bounce," I say, standing abruptly. "Thanks for coming out. Think about that stuff, okay?"

I get out fast, feeling sick, not of Tonya, but myself.

5. ANOTHER STRANGE THING

Every few days, I clock another strange detail about my next-door neighbor. For example: All these brick tenements in the Tri-Cities metro area were constructed the same way a century ago. Instead of iron fire escapes, the buildings have flights of carpenter's stairs, built along the unfaced bricks at the rear. On every floor, there is a good-sized landing outside the kitchen door of each apartment. Some of my neighbors even park lawn chairs out there to take the air on summer evenings. For reasons I have yet to understand, both the stairways and the porches throughout Kindle County and the nearby towns are always painted in this heavy gray enamel, the color of pigeons.

Since our apartments were carved from what was once one home, TWO and I share the rear porch. Not long after he moved in, I heard the boards out there squeaking around two a.m. and realized, even in my sleep, that there was a human weight behind the sound. I bolted up. Peering around my shade, I saw a man and was already heading for the biometric gun safe under my bed when I realized who it was. My cell service has recently gone completely to shit—it was never great to start—and my first thought was that he was awake to call someone in Asia and was outside looking for a signal. Then I saw the orange ember: He was sneaking a cigarette.

Our whole building is no-smoking, including the porches, where I suspect the goal is to keep people from barbecuing on the landings and maybe burning the whole place down. I was a smoker for years and still will bum a cigarette sometimes when I'm hammered.

Having been there, I knew that this had to be a bitch for TWO—waiting until the middle of the night to get his little fix, just to be sure Arturo, the janitor, doesn't see him and the neighbors can't tell where the smell is coming from. But as I wrote in my notes, *'There are still rentals in Highland Isle with smoking wings or first-floor smoking lounges. Why move in here?'*

I also realized eventually that it was strange I could see so little when he was out there. I checked the light fixture between our back doors that's supposed to stay on all night in case of fire. The bulb had been loosened. I screwed it back in. But by the end of the week, the fixture seemed to have shorted out.

I'm frequently in my apartment during the day. Even before COVID, Rik was okay with me doing my written stuff—interview reports or document summaries—at home, where there are fewer distractions. Given a choice, I always prefer to be alone anyway.

That means I'm often around when TWO heads out with his gym bag. That gives me a couple hours to snoop. Several times I've gone to the back porch to try to sneak a peek through his kitchen window, but he seems to have installed a shade, which I slowly recognized is always drawn. Each week, I paw through his trash and recycling but learn nothing.

A few days after my drink with Tonya, while I'm at home in

the late afternoon doing some Internet research about the three
guys who are going to testify against the Chief, I hear El Weirdo
moving around inside his place. This doesn't happen much, and
I freeze. Then his front door slams. I hustle to my own door and
make out his footfalls as he heads downstairs. About ten minutes
later, I hear him coming back up.

The following day it's the same deal, and I creep out about
thirty seconds behind him. I wonder if maybe he's visiting another
tenant, but as I peer down between the railings, I catch sight of
him using his key to enter the first-floor door to the basement.
I go down there myself sometimes to talk to Arturo, but I can
hear the janitor working outside now, hauling the trash cans to
the alley for garbage pickup tomorrow. Eventually, I realize TWO
must be visiting the little storage coop which each tenant has.

The next afternoon, as soon as he has departed with his gym
bag, I scurry down. TWO's cage, like his apartment, is next to
mine, and he's secured it with a heavy-duty padlock. Inside the
chain link, he's stored only a single item, a kind of trunk that
I think is called an ATA case, used by roadies to haul around
expensive musical equipment like amps. It's black vinyl with
riveted aluminum on the seams, thick stainless-steel handles on
two sides, and small casters that allow it to roll.

I open my own coop and step in to get a closer look. Even
though the coop is padlocked, he's applied another lock to secure
the center latch on the case, meaning he's taking a lot of precautions to protect what's in there. Without a car, TWO had to
ship the case here, but he's removed any baggage or freight tags.
I store my skis in my cage—I still go every winter with my dad
for a day or two—and now I extend an aluminum pole between
the openings in the chain link and prod TWO's trunk. It won't
budge, meaning he's got something pretty heavy stored inside.

The succeeding day, it's the same, he makes two trips down and up. *'Best guess, he's got something in that case that he's using and then storing again. But what kind of shit can't you keep in your own apartment?'* I decide I've got to get a look inside.

One piece of PIBOT know-how I've had in mind to learn is lock picking, and TWO's storage cage presents a teachable moment. Believe it or not, there are several instructional videos on YouTube. The one I like best is from England and makes the whole operation look pretty simple. Two tiny tools are required. One is a little L-shaped piece of metal called a tension wrench that goes through the opening for the key and then relieves the pressure of the springs that normally fix the pins in place to keep the barrel from turning. The second thing you need is a pick, which functions more or less the way your key does, slowly lifting the pins to the heights that open the mechanism.

I order the tools online and take cell phone photos of TWO's padlocks. Both are a brand called Superlock. I locate those online, too. Everything arrives in a day, and I practice that night until I can open each lock in less than thirty seconds.

By definition, what I'm going to do—picking my way into TWO's cage and opening his trunk—is illegal, trespassing at best, probably breaking and entering, which is a felony. If someone— Arturo or another tenant or even, God forbid, TWO—sees me in there, I'll say I saw the padlocks hanging open and curiosity got the best of me. Lame, but probably good enough not to get busted.

My plan requires occupying Arturo, who has an office of sorts in what is basically a closet in the basement. A heavyset guy with a bad leg he's always dragging behind him, Arturo is probably the only thing about this building that is genuinely superior. He is one of those people who does his supposedly menial job like he's handling the nuclear codes. The common areas gleam. I barely put the phone down after telling him something's broken, when he's at my door. The basement smells strongly of the disinfectant he uses to conduct his ongoing campaign against mold.

I find him in his office, just finishing lunch—I'm always touched by the tender way he unwraps the tortillas his wife packs. I tell him I'm on my way out but ask if he would mind checking my apartment, because I think I heard squirrels in the walls. This conversation, like most I have with Arturo, is conducted in my broken Spanish, but I blank on the word for squirrels and have to do a little pantomime to explain what I mean by "como una rata con cola peluda." (Like a rat with a bushy tail.) Once he gets it, though, his heavy face with his thick black mustache assumes an indignant look. He gets right to it and heads up with his tool-box. With his bad leg, it will take him a bit longer to get upstairs, and then he'll go around knocking on the walls while he listens. Overall, I should get at least ten minutes.

Once I'm alone, I have the heavy-duty padlock on TWO's cage door open in less than thirty seconds, and I quietly move inside. I grab the trunk's handle, hoping to nudge it a little so I can get to the other lock, which is up against the concrete wall. At that point, I recognize a mistake, which worries me immediately that I've made others. The reason the case wouldn't move when I poked it was because the casters are locked. Once I turn the switches, the trunk slides around like it's on ice.

I grab hold of the second padlock and fit the tension wrench inside easily, but I have to apply more force to the pick this time. The lock clicks open. But at the same instant, the pick breaks in my hand. It happens so quickly that it seems as if the tool was designed to snap. A jagged little piece of black metal protrudes from the key slot.

"Oh, fuck me," I say under my breath. I can't just leave it there, because TWO will know someone has been in here. Same problem if I steal the lock outright. And if I run back to my apartment for a pair of pliers, Arturo's going to expect me to hang out while he finishes his inspection. Having no other choice, I get down on my knees and lift the padlock to my mouth.

We are now at a quintessential Pinky moment. I have done something really stupid, ignoring the possible consequences, and have been forced into a maneuver destined by some eternal law worse than Murphy's to go completely to shit. I'll cut my gum and bleed all over, or break a tooth. My worthless ass will get arrested, I'll lose my PI license and my job, and to top it all, I'll have to endure that old look on my mother's face. But there is no retreating now. I catch the edge of what's left of the pick between my front teeth and bite hard. To my amazement the piece slides out smoothly on the first try.

I am about to pop the latches when it dawns on me that TWO might have set some kind of alarm. I use the flashlight on my phone to see if there's anything visible, like a tiny wire. There isn't, but I'm not completely convinced. I take a deep breath and can feel my heart beating all the way to my fingertips as I lift the stainless-steel catches and then the lid. I am so freaked by what I'm doing that it takes a second or two to believe what I see.

There is nothing.

The inside of TWO's case is lined in heavy black rubber, roughly an inch thick. He had something fragile in here. But the trunk is empty now. No dust, not even a stray thread or a screw left behind. Completely fucking empty.

'I cannot figure this out. I must have gotten to the trunk on the wrong side of the cycle. He must be removing something from his apartment for about ten minutes and storing it downstairs. But what is it he can't keep around? The next time I hear him leave, I'll rush out to see what he's carrying.'

Two mornings later, around 10:30, I hear him striding out and the thump of his door. I throw open my own door and charge to the stairs.

That's when I see him from the corner of my eye as I rush past. I revolve in panic. TWO is standing in the recess for his front door with a hard look that can't fully conceal his amusement.

"Clarence," he says.

My heart is slamming. With some effort, I manufacture a cheery smile.

"I was trying to catch you," I say.

"Oh yes? Why?"

"I've been thinking we should get coffee sometime. You know, just the neighbor thing."

I can see immediately that like so often I have said the wrong thing. The amused look is still skating around in his eyes, but now he's actually showing a little wrinkle of a hipped-up smile. He thinks he's on to me: When I sat down with him at the diner I was tuning him, and now I'm taking the next step. Lonely girl next door seeks convenient dick. It's all I can do to keep from laughing and saying, 'No, not sex, I have no trouble finding that.'

"Sometime maybe," he answers and turns back to his door, key in hand. Even though I'm pretty close to busted, I can't resist edging forward another couple inches in the hope of glimpsing something inside, but he's like a mouse and seems to slip through an impossibly narrow opening.

Before he's completely across the threshold, I blurt, "And what's your name?"

He stops, looks back, takes a beat, then says, "Clarence," before shutting the door.

Afterwards, I am so depleted by fright and frustration that I have to lie down on my bed. This guy is way, way better than me. Clearly a pro. But what kind? A hit man or a bounty hunter or even someone in law enforcement working undercover?

What am I missing? The question circulates like a mantra as I lie there staring out the windows beside my bed with their view of my porch and the unfaced bricks of the buildings across the alley.

And then I swing up to a sitting position so quickly that it seems as if some outside force propelled me. I know.

I can barely stand to wait the additional hour until TWO takes off with his red gym bag a little before noon. From my front window, I watch him amble down the walk in the courtyard and then disappear around the corner. I'm already holding another item from the PIBOT, my binoculars—a nice pair, Nikon Monarchs, 10×42, which offer an incredible field of view, even at a thousand yards.

I rush out to the porch. The mistake I made when I was trying to peek around his back shade is obvious now—I was facing the wrong direction. About three weeks ago the trees in the yards went from naked sticks to fully leafed in a matter of days. Yet even with the sight lines partially blocked by foliage, what remains visible from our back landing is Anglia and the Tech Park— and Northern Direct, the defense manufacturer mentioned in the *Wall Street Journal* TWO was studying at Ruben's. When I crouch with the binoculars, I can see Direct's facility straight on

and a maintenance guy in overalls working on the equipment on
the building's roof. The white shells beside him look like satellite
dishes but with a triangular arrangement of tubing mounted
over the center of the concave. They are microwave transmission
towers whose signals, from what I've read, are more secure than
cellular or landlines. Direct communicates this way with their
clientele in the military or the Department of Defense and the
messages going back and forth have to be highly classified.

That's what TWO is doing. The smoking is just a cover to
explain why he's outside at that hour. In the darkness, he's using
some device that's normally hidden in the trunk, a piece of equipment that allows him to intercept signals from Direct or monitor
something else that's going on inside the installation.

I have no idea who he's working for—the Russians or the
Chinese or just one of Direct's competitors. But I've finally
tumbled to his gig.

TWO is a fucking spy.

6. I'M LIKE A LOT OF WOMEN

Look. I'm like a lot of women with a little wear on them. I'm not interested in picking up some guy's jockey shorts again. I don't want to say there aren't any good men out there. But you know, Ricky is taken."

Rik gets quite a laugh from that. We are back in our cramped conference room with its harsh overhead lighting and no windows. The Chief has finally returned, but only after Rik called a number of times. We are less than two weeks from the hearing, which is when trial prep always gets super serious.

"I wish I was joking," the Chief says. "But at my age, the guys that are unattached? Losers. Most of them. Way more than most. They get nasty after a couple of pops. Or they're deadbeats. Or drunks. Or lazy. Or just pricks. These guys are the leftovers."

"No relationships?" Rik asks.

"Oh, sure," she says. "Now and then. And not every man turns out to be a jerk. But at this age, you know, there's not a lot of flexibility. You are who you are. I have a potty mouth? Yeah, I do. I can try for a few less f-bombs, and definitely mind my manners around your children, but you need to give up this shit about how your sainted mom acted around your father. So long-term? I've stopped believing in fairy tales. If he looks like a frog and croaks like a frog, don't expect a prince just because you kiss him.

"But that doesn't mean I have to take a vow of chastity. I like sex. Who doesn't? Well, that's a stupid question because from what I hear, there's a lot who lose interest, and not just women either. But I'm not one of them. So once or twice a month I get the itch and go sit on a barstool. If I come across a guy who has just a little idea of what he's doing and isn't going to bat me around, then I don't worry about who is taking advantage of who. There are a lot of men who are nice enough when you and them want the same thing."

The Chief lets her bluntness settle in for a second.

"These guys?" says Rik. He drops his index finger on the case file, referring to the three complainants. "Ever?" He has been willing to listen for a while, but sooner or later we have to know what the hell we are defending.

"Ever?" the Chief asks. "Long story or short?"

"Short to start."

"Short? Okay. One word answer: Yeah. That's short. Two of them, Cornish and DeGrassi. Third guy, Blanco? That's pure fantasy. I'll tell you right now Ritz got to him." She points at me, meaning my job is to figure out how.

"Okay," says Rik, trying hard to act unruffled now that we've got the facts. It's not like we didn't know this was coming.

The Chief, naturally, wants to defend herself.

"Escucha, okay. I'm the Chief of Police in this pueblito. That's not like a great way to have a personal life, okay? Think about it. Twenty-four seven, this thing"—she lifts her cell phone—"that's never off. If I sleep through the night, I'm ready to set off fireworks. And where do I go if I want to relax? Have an adult beverage? We got residency requirements. I have to live here in Highland Isle. Am I going to get behind the wheel when I'm half crocked? I don't think so. So my choice of establishments is limited to where I can walk." .

"You could bike," I say. Rik and the Chief both stare. That's the kind of shit I say. It makes perfect sense to me until it comes out of my mouth.

"There is rideshare," Rik finally offers.

"Uber and that? Sometimes I need to get. I can't stand around on a corner for ten minutes if two dudes are throwing punches. I go to the places I know. I'm not some kid who gets a thrill waiting behind a velvet rope for two hours. There's three or four spots I like. Me and a lot of other coppers. Because we all live in the center of town, since that's what we can afford.

"Not asking anybody to feel sorry for me, but I don't have a lot of choices. What should I do? I'm not walking around a bar with a name tag and shaking hands, waiting for some guy to ask if he can call me sometime. I'm not looking for a new adventure. Think I should go online, so every dude who's got a case pending in HI can shoot me a hot text? 'Mamacita. You look so good.' I know how I look. So if I go out for a drink, I talk to the guys I know. What I'm after, frankly, goes better when there's some familiarity, so I can relax and not worry about whether he's a serial killer. And on their side, those guys understand they don't need to buy me six rounds and make small talk. Everybody gets what they want. Six months later, I can't remember who was who."

Rik is a little impatient and gives her the side-eye.

"Are you saying you don't remember whether you were with these men?"

"No, I remember. But it was nothing like they're saying."

"Is the timing right, though, as far as you remember? DeGrassi in early 2019, Cornish about a year later?"

"You know, this isn't junior high. I don't write down who kissed me, but yeah, in those years? Answer is yes."

"And you never saw a problem bringing home guys who were under your command?"

"Problem? I don't know. Not if I'm drunk enough. And we're off the clock." She smiles as if Rik might think she was funny. He doesn't.

"Besides," she says. "Check the departmental regs. You see any rules against 'fraternization' as they call it? The FOP won't let you fire a cop for kicking the stuffing out of his wife or kids, or for having twelve citizen complaints in his jacket as a hitter, because each one is supposedly uncorroborated. So you think the union is gonna let a cop get disciplined cause of who he sleeps with? In this department, like most departments, there are no rules against personnel having a good time with one another when neither party is working."

"Even for the Chief?" Rik asks. "Aren't you management?"

"You mean it's okay for them and not for me? Call me narrow-minded, but rules are rules. Either it's right or it's wrong. I'm not saying I think P&F is gonna give me a medal. I mean, the commission can make up some lesser charge, I suppose. 'Conduct detrimental to morale and discipline.' If they want to shake a finger at me and give me thirty days, we can talk about that. But I'm not turning in my star. I followed the rules as I understood them. I didn't do anything wrong."

"Trading sex for promotions is a crime, Lucy," Rik says.

"And it damn well oughta be. But that never happened. Read their statements," the Chief says, "these three characters. Lying or not, not one of them claims I said or did anything to force them."

"They applied to be promoted," Rik says, "and you came on to them. That's what they say. That's not a good pattern."

"That isn't even close to true. But you need some context here. You know, you're a woman in charge, a little of that 'boss' stuff goes a long way. Cornish and Primo, these guys are my age. They were veteran cops when I got there, and you know, I was 'Sarge' on the job, but that never meant a lot, except I was the person to read their reports, pretty much like I was helping them with their homework in high school. With me, I walk into the tavern, I've always been 'Lucy.' We're on even ground. And you know cops. It's still thirty years ago. PC never happened. These guys were pinching my ass when it was half the size it is now, and they never stopped. And at a certain age, a woman's learned a few tricks. Maybe I'm not gonna model for the workout videos, but nobody ever went home saying it wasn't a good time. I didn't have to force nobody, and I didn't have to make the first move either."

"Two of these guys are married, Lucy."

"Not to me."

Rik frowns. "Well, you know Reverend Dalrymple better than I do," he says, referring to the minister who is chair of the Police and Fire Commission. "But the last I looked, adultery was still in the Ten Commandments."

"The Rev's a pretty realistic guy," she answers. "He knows the difference between the big sins and the little ones. And look, I'm not Jezebel. Yeah, I didn't ask anybody for his hall pass, but every married guy who shows up in your bed will tell you more than you ever wanna hear about the freaking troubles in his marriage. What's the legal thing? 'It speaks for itself?' These guys are out on the prowl every Friday night. You really believe it when the missus says, 'I didn't know a thing?' He's got a hard job, and once a week he's on his own. They've made their peace. We all have. Life, Rik, it's not quite ideal."

Rik goes on to question her closely about what she remembers occurring with DeGrassi and Cornish. As she claimed, her story is different than theirs on several key points, but this is what they mean by 'he said/she said.' It's up to me, of course, to find evidence to support the Chief's version of events, now that I actually know it, but I truly have no idea where to start. For a second I sit there feeling bad for both of us.

7. I RING TONYA

As soon as the Chief is gone, I ring Tonya. I was miserable enough when I finished up with her last time that I've been in no hurry to get in touch.

"I actually have that stuff you asked for," she says.

I tell her again she can slide it in an envelope with no return address.

"Easier to hand it over. Six at Mike's?" She doesn't give me time to answer.

When Pops went into assisted living, he gave me his car. There's nowhere to park it over at Aventura Center for Advanced Living, as the place is called, and he shouldn't have been driving anyway. Everybody in the family reduced their Xanax intake when he handed me the keys, and I took them pretty much for that reason. But it's not the ride I would have picked for myself. A girl with big-time tats and a nail in her nose gets some looks climbing out of a late-model Cadillac CTS. Tonya, who's walking up to the door at Mike's as I slide out from behind the wheel, is like everybody else and stops in her tracks.

"No way," she says. "You seeing a gangster?"

"It's mine," I answer. "Sandy gave it to me."

"He pay you to take it?" she asks. We head in together. "Who are you seeing anyway?" she asks as we come through the door, like there's nothing more to the question than how I think the Trappers will do this season.

"There's a guy in my building," I say, "but I don't know where that's going." I need to lie, just to keep her at a distance, and I have to say a man since she thought that was what I wanted, and I know it turns her off. But 'a guy in my building'? How the fuck did I think of that? Truly. The shit that comes out of my mouth.

To escape any follow-up, I go to the knotty pine bar to order our beers. A guy on my softball team, Slim Norris, is in front of me and we bump knuckles and joke. I always like being at Mike's, mostly because, for good and bad, I basically love cops. I love what they do and the truth they tell and the fact that there's never any hearts and flowers. The world they live in is tough and kind of ugly, and it requires some bravery to face that every day. Basically, I've tried to absorb their attitude and just get on with stuff and stop whining or wishing things were different.

When I get back to our high-top, Toy has just pulled a 9 × 12 envelope that was folded in half from the inside pocket of her jacket.

"There's your screenshots."

"Anything interesting?"

She shrugs. "They're both supporting Steven. That means they're not supporting Amity, which means they're against the Chief."

I look furtively at the papers inside, but there's pay dirt with just a glance. In DeGrassi's profile, for 'Employed by' he lists 'Vojczek Management.' Even better, Cornish's says the same thing.

"The Vojczek stuff?" Tonya asks, noticing my expression. "I thought you'd like that."

"I do."

"That's the good news."

"What's the bad?"

"Paulette Cornish won't talk to you."

"She forgave her ex?"

"Hardly. If Godzilla ate him alive, she'd give half her life savings for the video so she could watch it again and again."

"So why not help us make him look like an ass on the witness stand?"

"She doesn't like the Chief any better."

"Why's that?"

"She didn't say. It was just, 'Damn if I'll help *her*.'"

"You think maybe she believes what her ex is saying?"

"You kidding? As far as she's concerned, with him it's pictures or it didn't happen. How she sees it, the snake in the Garden of Eden could take lying lessons from Walter."

"So what's her problem?" I ask.

"I asked but she didn't explain. Lots of people don't like to get in the middle of somebody else's battles. Figure they can end up as collateral damage."

I shrug and fold the envelope in fours and shove it into my back pocket. There is an uncomfortable silence. The place is filling up and people are starting to shout over the music.

When I first met Tonya, there were a lot of awkward moments like this, but she actually talks now, so I don't know exactly how to read her. But something's brewing, probably whatever made her want to deliver these papers in person.

Finally, she comes out with a forced laugh and says, "I bet you never thought twice about me."

Oh fuck. I glance off to the walls, where there is a signed photo of Reagan, pictures from the funerals of three cops killed on duty, and framed insignia of each of the forty-two precincts in the Kindle County Unified Police Force. I know it would not be cool to just get up and leave.

"I told you I mentioned your name to the Chief," I tell her. "Said I knew you and always figured you'd be great on the job."

She gives me a bitter frown.

"I don't mean like that." She spends a second looking into her beer glass, where the light from one of the signs blinks on and off on the surface. Then she leans in, her voice a lot lower. "I thought about you," she says. "A lot."

Double fuck. I was afraid this was coming last time when she asked if I was happy. I never knew what was so great for Tonya in the couple months we were together—whether it had been the first time she rolled around completely naked with another woman or if it was just better sex than she'd had before. I didn't ask, because it wasn't long before I realized she was way more into me than I was into her, and I didn't want to take on that responsibility. I gave her hints that she should slow herself down, but it's part of who she is that she's always all-out determined. Within a couple weeks, late at night, after a beer or two, I was hearing the L-word a lot.

I am not sure I have ever been in love with anyone. I mean, I've met people who to start seemed cooler than a superhero. I've even done the live-together thing a few times, two women and one man, and on each occasion found it a great way to end a relationship. And yeah, I wonder now and then what's wrong with me. Sometimes when I think about love, I think, It will happen, but mostly I think it won't. And yeah, of course, sometimes I'm like everybody else and experience that longing so intense that it feels almost like it could lift you off the ground, the power of that dream of someone to want me and embrace me and accept me and all the rest of it. But then I sober up and touch down and realize it isn't going to happen. It's just not in me to put up with how annoying another person can be over the long run. Most people don't have the guts to face being alone, and long for love so they're not by themselves forever. But for me, being alone is often a relief. The height of the pandemic, when I didn't have to get face-to-face with anybody for a while, was a great time as far as I was concerned. And besides, that's how it is. We're alone. Which is why people find love disappointing. Because the part people want most will never come true.

But Tonya clearly yearned for all that stuff I never do: 'Define the relationship' and be exclusive. I started looking forward to the end of the academy so we could go our separate ways.

There was a kind of cute guy down the hall, Mike Fitzgerald, who'd spent five years in Afghanistan, and one day after classes, when we didn't have PT, we went out for a run and ended up back in his room, which, let's tell it like it is, was just a giant asshole move, I know it.

When Tonya found out—because I told her—she went off completely. And for her, the worst part seemed to be that it was a man.

'You're just a sightseer,' she screamed at me. I've heard similar stuff from a couple other lesbians when they figure out that I'm bi. Like I couldn't have been sincere about anything.

"I didn't handle things very well," I tell her now.

"You think?" she says. Her black eyes are starting to glisten.

"Yeah, I think I was a jerk, frankly. And I'm sorry."

I can see that apologizing isn't making it better. I lean across the table and touch her free hand.

"Toy, let me tell you the truth. You'd have gotten sick of me. Everyone does."

I mean it, I truly mean it, it hurts to say it, and she smiles just a little bit. But she can't help herself.

"I'm really different, you know. I've changed a lot."

"I can see that," I say. "I barely recognized you. I mean it. It's like 'I was lost and now I'm found.' It looks good on you." But her neediness couldn't be any clearer if it were a beacon. That never works for me. I hate feeling like I've disappointed someone. I had enough of that with my mother to last a lifetime. And Toy is a nester, whether she knows it or not. Ten years from now she's going to be married to some sweet woman, and they'll have a nice little apartment or bungalow where every tchotchke will be precious to them because they took forever to find it and decided on it together. And that is so not me.

"Toy," I say. "Let it be. You're good people. I was young and fucked up, and now I'm older and still fucked up. Truly, I mean it—consider yourself lucky."

I take a big gulp of my beer and clink my glass against hers. "Mega thanks," I say, but like last time I get to my feet quickly. I settle our tab with Dutch, the bartender, and don't look back as I head to the door. I know she'll be sitting there for a while, caught up in an unhappiness that for whatever reason still isn't old for her.

8. THE HEARING BEGINS

Chief Gomez's hearing before the Police and Fire Commission of the City of Highland Isle begins on May 9 in one of the municipal courtrooms where misdemeanor proceedings are also conducted. The prosecutor is the city attorney, Marc Hess, who got the job when Amity first assumed office. Rik, who's had cases with Marc for years, says Marc is a complete straight shooter who took the position because he never enjoyed private practice, especially hustling for clients. When Marc was appointed, Amity said all the standard things about giving him complete independence, but Marc, according to Rik, has pretty much held her to it. There's no question, for instance, that the mayor would have preferred that Marc not bring a complaint in the Chief's case—and certainly that he not go to hearing until after the election in November. But Marc said that with three sworn statements in hand, he had no choice but to proceed.

The Chief sits on the other side of Rik in her dress uniform, looking very much as she did when I first met her, including too much makeup for my taste. I asked her when she arrived if she was nervous, and she said, 'As fuck.' She's already made two trips

to the Ladies and has told me that she preferred facing a gun
on the street to this, where she has no control over anything.
Instead, she must remain mute and, as Rik has advised, show no
visible reaction to the proceedings.

Pops practiced mostly in the beautiful courtrooms of the old
federal courthouse, which have intricate woodwork and dramatic
frescoes in the plaster and pillars rising to three-story ceilings.
The municipal courtroom is what you get with justice on the
cheap. The place feels as confined as a sauna, so small that you
wonder if there's enough oxygen to keep the participants and
spectators from passing out. There's a nice blond wood bench,
elevated about a foot, with a projecting shelf, where the lawyers
stand, literally in the judge's face. Just a few steps back, in the
well of the courtroom, sit the two attorneys' tables, in matching
yellowish wood, no more than ten feet apart. A short wood
partition separates the spectators, but they will be so close to the
lawyers that Rik has instructed me to write notes, rather than
whisper to him, since there's a good chance the onlookers would
be able to overhear us.

Up on the bench now is not a judge but the three members
of the Police and Fire Commission, seated elbow to elbow.
The Reverend Cletus Dalrymple, the pastor of the AME Baptist
Church here in town, is in the center. The Rev has got a kind of
glow about him; he's a handsome older fellow with a gleaming
scalp between the wide white tufts over his ears. I've seen him do
his stuff at funerals and weddings, and he's one great talker who
can get pretty wound up as he goes on, although Rik says that
we should expect him to say very little here, where he tends to be
tight-lipped. Some of the white cops expected the worst from the
Rev when Amity appointed him to head the commission several
years ago, but it turned out that the Rev's brother is a police

chief out in Delaware, and there are also plenty of Black officers in his congregation. He is, like Marc, a down-the-middle kind of guy who understands that police officers have a hard job, that they deal with a lot of genuinely awful and dangerous people, and that, in response, they live by assumptions that have often led them to terrorize the poor community.

Although everybody looks to the Rev for guidance, there are two other members of the commission. The only one who really counts is a very thin white lady with a drawn face and drab gray hair, Mrs. Helen Langenhalter. Her arms appear as thin as pipe cleaners in the sleeves of her shirtwaist dress. She is a lawyer, still practicing, mostly doing tax work. She looks like she is scared of everything and could be blown away in a gust, but Rik says she's a kind of brainiac who knows all the relevant laws, including the Rules of Evidence. The third member, Josea Altabese, a big fat dude, was a cop himself back in the day and now operates a fire- and burglar-alarm company. Rik says Altabese sometimes feels obliged to speak up so he's not mistaken for a statue. He then says something so remarkably dumb that for a second no one in the room can speak or even breathe. He then shuts up and follows the lead of the other two.

The courtroom is full. The last of the COVID restrictions have been relaxed, but about a quarter of the folks here are wearing masks. The national reporters, who did a lot of ooh-la-la-ing when the charges first leaked, lost interest shortly after that and have disappeared. But there is still a line of local journalists in the front row, including reporters from all three Kindle County TV stations, the two newspapers and several websites. Roe Findlay is in the forward pew on the other side, his iPad mini on his lap. Roe is from the FBI's public corruption squad and led the investigations into a number of my aunt's and grandfather's clients.

He's a chubby red-faced guy who seems bothered that he's losing his hair, which he's always dabbing back into place. I liked a lot of the Bureau agents more than I expected to, when I delivered documents to them or came over to pick up subpoenas that Pops had agreed to accept. Most were extremely polite. Several were actually friendly. But not Roe. He's smug and couldn't quite keep from curling his lip whenever he saw me. I'm sure he thought I'd never get another job once Pops's firm disbanded, so I make it a point to go say hi before I sit down beside Rik at the respondent's table. Steven DeLoria, the mayor's election opponent, is in the back, looking completely camera ready—flawless suit, tie, even makeup. He'll go use his phone in the hallway as soon as the hearing starts, but he wants to be here to make a statement of outrage for the media when the hearing recesses.

Rik and I have been in overdrive the last couple days. I actually kind of love trial prep. It reminds me of getting ready for athletic competition—lots of practice on moves and plays, and then going home the day before and trying to forget what's ahead. That night, I would tell myself 'Don't think about it' in a kind of bleat that eventually put me to sleep until the morning, when my dad would come in to shake me awake with a loud, 'Game on!' My adrenal glands would fire up at once, so that my vision jumped and my bloodstream seemed to sizzle.

Just as the Rev grabs hold of the gavel to commence the hearing, my phone vibrates in my pocket. I slide it out enough to see the screen. I have a text from Tonya. 'The Easter bunny left you a present on the front seat of your car. Make sure you check it out. PS. Lock your doors! There's some joker who thinks it's funny to steal cars out of the City Hall lot.' I tuck the phone away as soon as the Rev starts speaking.

"All right," he says and recites the name of the case and its number for the record. These days, there aren't court reporters for this kind of administrative matter. Instead, a digital recorder is capturing the feed from all the microphones. If anybody ever needs a transcript—which we will if things go shitty for the Chief and she gets indicted—the audio recording can be fed into a computer, which will create one.

"The Commissioners have read the Complaint. The Respondent, Chief Lucia Gomez-Barrera"—the Rev pronounces the name precisely, rolling his r's—"has filed a general denial by way of an Answer. Does either party wish to make an opening statement? If not, I'll ask Mr. Hess to call his first witness."

The Rev barely takes a breath after asking about openings. All three of the commissioners serve as volunteers and have full-time day jobs. Like a lot of municipal boards, we are meeting at night. It's 6 p.m. and we won't go past 9:00. If need be, the hearings can also be held on weekends, but the Rev has no patience for the usual lawyerly shenanigans that slow down the proceedings, especially in golf season.

Marc, however, feels obliged to lay out for the record the agreements he has made with the US Attorney's Office. Marc's decision to proceed with the hearing led to a kind of legal food fight. Not only was the mayor aggravated, but so was the US Attorney, Moses Appleton, who I sorta/kinda know through Pops and my aunt. Moses showed up at City Hall to explain to Marc that holding a hearing could compromise the federal grand jury investigation, because the three pivotal witnesses would be exposed to cross-examination, where they might say a lot of stupid stuff. Marc held the same line with Moses that he had taken with the mayor. His only concession, recently made, was that he agreed not to force the Chief to testify, which would have granted her the equivalent of use immunity, a move that would have basically trashed any chance for the Feds to bring an indictment. Rik, of course, would love that and says that the Chief will testify whenever she's ordered to do so. If she isn't, Rik says she can't risk self-incrimination, and won't be able to present her defense until the grand jury investigation is over. The Reverend says all of this is premature, which irritates both Marc and Rik, who don't want the rug pulled out from under them later. Everybody repeats themselves at greater length. As a result, by the time the first witness is finally called, the lawyers and the commissioners are all pissed with one another.

That witness is Walter Cornish. Chronologically, Primo DeGrassi's testimony should come before, but Marc clearly thinks Cornish will do better on the stand. Like everywhere else, in court first impressions matter. Cornish is a shorter guy, with a Prince Valiant mane of gray hair. He wears a blue sport coat, which he could never button across his belly, jeans and—I notice as he rolls bowlegged up to the stand—tooled cowboy boots. That seems to say it all. A big-city guy who thinks he's cool as a cowpoke. He settles on the stand and gives somebody in the crowd a tight little smile: 'I've got this under control.' I look behind me to see who Walt is grinning at and half recognize a wasted-looking older guy seated a few rows back who's working over a piece of chewing gum. It takes me a second to place him. Moritz Vojczek. The man himself. He must have come straight from a business meeting, because he's in a suit and tie.

Cornish states his name and says he retired after twenty-five years of service on the HI force, achieving the rank of sergeant.

"When were you promoted to sergeant?" Marc asks. Hess is taller, Black, heavyset, with a thick mustache that could just as well be a smear of greasepaint. He's been super nice whenever I've come to his office to pick up or deliver documents.

"Say April 1, 2020."

"And were you promoted after agreeing to have sex with Chief Gomez?"

Rik objects that the question is leading, and after Mrs. Langenhalter whispers in his ear, the Rev says, "Let's take this part of the story step by step."

Rik has told me that Marc does not like trial work. He is smart and handles a few hearings when he has to, but he prefers to farm out most real litigation to private firms. However, spending $500 an hour for outside lawyers is not a great news bite in an election year, especially on a case that the mayor wants to lose. Given Marc's relative lack of experience, Rik expects him to make mistakes now and then, like the question he just asked.

"Do you know Lucia Gomez-Barrera?" asks Marc.

"Sure."

"Can you point her out for the record?"

"Stipulated," says Rik, meaning he won't go through the usual routine where Cornish lifts his hand and the Chief stands.

"How did you know Chief Gomez?"

"Superior officer. She was my sergeant at one point, not long after she came on, you know, and then she went up the chain."

"And what was the nature of your relationship?"

"Professional. On the job. That's it."

"And, turning to early 2020, had you applied for promotion?"

"Right. I applied, I tested. I was number one on the list."

"And did you have an encounter with the Chief in March of 2020?"

"I did."

"Do you recall the exact date?"

"March 6. The next Friday night was my son's birthday. And after that the bar was closed cause of COVID."

"Can you describe your encounter with Chief Gomez?"

"Sure. I was sitting around in a tavern called the Saloon, at Fourth and Madison, here in HI, kind of, you know, celebrating the end of the week, and the Chief comes up and asks if she could talk to me."

"Had you noticed when she came in?"

"Not really."

"Did you have a conversation with the Chief?"

"Sure."

"And was anyone else present?"

"There was a lot of guys sitting around. I know Primo heard her."

"Primo is who?"

"Primo DeGrassi."

"Was he an officer on the HI force?"

"Sergeant. Had about thirty days left before retirement. I was testing for the spot he'd leave."

Rik stands. "Commissioners, may I ask Mr. Hess to clarify that Primo DeGrassi, this corroborating witness, is also a complainant in this matter?"

Marc shrugs and says, "That's true."

"Convenient," says Rik.

Marc gives out a contemptuous little groan and asks to strike the comment, which Rik withdraws before the Rev gets a chance to rule.

"And did you have a conversation with the Chief?" Marc asks Cornish.

"Yeah. I don't know, we walked about ten feet away and she just come out with, 'I want you to take me home so we can party.'"

"And what was your reaction?"

"I mean, I was kind of shocked. That wasn't how I thought of her or anything. Not somebody who, you know, I considered in that vein."

"And what did you say to her?"

"Well, I mean, what could I say? I knew damn well that if she wanted to roadblock my promotion, she could. It's not like I'm a virgin or anything. But that wasn't how I was dreaming of spending my evening." There are a few snickers in the spectators' section, and Walter blinks and adds, "Just sayin."

"And how did you respond to the Chief?"

"I think I said okay and 'Let me finish my beer.' I wanted a minute to think."

"But did you eventually agree?"

"Yep."

"Why?"

"Like I said. I thought I'd have a pig's chance of getting promoted if I refused."

"When did you depart from the Saloon?"

"Maybe ten minutes later. After she told me we were going to party."

"And where did you go?"

"The Chief's house over on Summit."

"Who drove?"

"I did."

"Do you recall seeing anyone as you left?"

"I know the waitress, Kelsey Something, says she saw us, but I don't really remember that. That was a surprise to me."

"And did you in fact have a sexual encounter with the Chief at her house?"

"Yep. We had another drink and then you know—". The back of his hand zips off into space.

"And what happened after that?"

"I left. You know. It was all pretty strange."

"And did Chief Gomez say anything when you left?"

"I think she said something like, 'Thanks, Walt. It was a good time. I'll remember this.'"

"And were you in fact promoted?"

"I was."

"When did you get notice of that?"

"Couple weeks later."

"And did you ever discuss what had happened with the Chief with anybody?"

"Just Primo."

Marc looks over at Jennifer, a law student who's interning in the city attorney's office, and then says, "Nothing further."

The Rev, who's got prostate problems, says, "Let's take five minutes before cross."

I run out to the Cadillac and grab the envelope Tonya left there. There are about six pages inside. I read them over quickly and laugh out loud and dash back in, but the Rev and the other commissioners are already on the bench and Rik is on his feet in front of Cornish, ready to begin his cross-examination.

Rik is wearing a blue suit and white shirt, but it's finally warmed up, and given the crowd and the inadequate air-conditioning in the Municipal Building, he has already loosened his tie. It's an important moment for him, but everybody here is familiar with him, and he doesn't want to look like he's taking himself too seriously.

One thing Rik knows from experience is that it's hard to cross-examine a cop. They are used to testifying and, to put it bluntly, good at lying when they have to. Most cops would tell you in private that it's the law that forces them to cut corners. You bust a dude in Anglia, and a crowd of his gangbanger homies show up and get rowdy. So you cuff the guy and throw him in the cruiser and take off at once. Did you Mirandize him before depriving him of his liberty? Of course not. You weren't sticking around to wait for some m.f. in the crowd to start shooting. But the law, that ass, says all the dumb stuff that comes out of the defendant in the back seat—the false excuses or the remarks that show he knows all about a crime no one has mentioned—can't be used in court, because he wasn't advised of his rights. So yeah, you say you gave him Miranda.

That's just an example. Most cops are pretty sure they know the difference between the lies they have to tell to keep the lawyers happy—lies that, as one friend of mine from softball puts it, involve 'tightening up the case'—and the lies that really matter. Good cops don't make up confessions or put the defendant at the scene of a crime he didn't commit.

But even so, the demands of the job make them great liars on the stand. Their demeanor never wavers. They're placid as a pond in the summer sun and matter-of-fact, even if they're testifying that night is day.

"Now, I notice, Mr. Cornish, that Mr. Hess didn't ask how you're currently employed," Rik says to start.

"I'm a property manager."

"For who?"

"Vojczek Management."

"And how is Mr. DeGrassi employed?"

"Same. He came to work there when he retired in early 2020, and I started a year later."

"Do you consider Mr. DeGrassi a close friend?"

"He's a friend. I don't know about close."

"Well, you worked together on the HI police force for nearly twenty-five years, didn't you?"

"True."

"Were you ever partners?"

"Sure. Few times."

"Well, that period as partners comprised many years, didn't it?"

"I never counted it up."

"Were you partners while you worked in the Narcotics Bureau?"

"As I recall."

"And who was your lieutenant there?"

"The Ritz."

"Moritz Vojczek?"

Marc objects to the relevance of all of this, and Rik says he expects to tie things up when the Chief presents her case. We still haven't really had time to drill into the details with the Chief of her long-running feud with Vojczek.

"Well, until the relevance is demonstrated," says the Rev, "we don't need to hear any more about this."

"Very well," says Rik. "But I'd note for the record, Reverend Dalrymple, that Mr. Vojczek is present in the fourth row." This is a very slick move, since Rik didn't even bother to look over his shoulder before saying this.

"All right," says the Rev, who clearly hadn't noticed the Ritz and casts a long look in his direction. "I think you can move on."

Rik nods. "Now, Mr. Cornish, let's talk for a second about your promotion. Just to make it clear, it's the people seated to your left, the members of the Police and Fire Commission, who actually decide who gets promoted. Correct?"

"Her recommendation matters a lot. The Chief's." The commissioners know this is true, but Cornish didn't answer the question and Rik, to show he's in control, demands a response. Cornish says, "I guess." He answers the same way when Rik asks if the commission has occasionally rejected a Chief's recommendation.

"Now, in 2020, how long had you been seeking promotion to sergeant?"

"Well, there's an exam once a year, if there's an opening. And I took the test first in 2018, just kinda winging it. So a couple of years."

"And you decided to seek promotion because you were approaching retirement?"

Cornish makes a sour face. "What does that mean?"

"I'll tell you, Mr. Cornish. Your pension at retirement is based, in part, on your highest annual earnings, correct?"

"I don't know," says Cornish.

Rik goes through the pension formula and gets Cornish to concede that he'll be getting a good portion of the raise that came with his promotion every year for the rest of his life.

"And as a matter of fact, once you had one year at the rank of Sergeant, you decided to retire, just like DeGrassi before you?"

"Well, this opportunity had come up with Vojczek that was too good to pass up. Ritz really wanted us and made it worthwhile."

"So you and DeGrassi planned together to retire eventually and go to work for Vojczek after you'd been promoted?"

"Somethin like that, yeah."

There is a lot about this dual retirement planning that is helpful to the Chief. It shows the long-term coordination between Cornish and DeGrassi—and Vojczek for that matter—and that both men were confident they'd get promoted. For the moment, Rik just nods, rather than letting Walter know he's revealed something of value to the defense. He will wait until closing argument to tease out the implications of what Cornish just admitted.

"Now, in order to determine who gets promoted, there's a formula, right? Set by state law, correct?"

"Correct."

"Fifty percent is your standing on the exam. Forty percent is an appraisal of your on-the-job performance. And ten percent is your seniority in rank, correct?"

"That sounds right."

"And in the twentysome years of service, before you first took the exam in 2018, you hadn't wanted to be a sergeant, right?"

"I hadn't applied."

"Was that because you didn't think you'd get it?"

"No."

"You thought you were deserving?"

"Goddamn right." Cornish sort of flinches after he's spoken and looks over to the Rev. "Sorry," he says.

The Rev waves off the apology. He's heard a lot worse.

Cornish continues with his prior answer. "You know, I just didn't bother. I like the street. Okay?"

"Well, there were some problems over the years with your performance appraisals, weren't there?"

"Meaning what?"

"Meaning, for example, that there had been a number of citizen complaints? Especially about your conduct at the time of arrests?"

Marc objects that the citizen complaints are irrelevant, because they were no longer current when Cornish got promoted.

The Rev looks at Rik. "What's your point, Mr. Dudek?" Rik's real point, which he is leading up to, is that the way things worked around Highland Isle, a promotion for a senior officer on the verge of retirement was pretty much guaranteed, if they'd made a reasonable effort to clean up their act. But Rik also wants the Rev to hear that Cornish had a history of batting arrestees around, since the Rev knows what, in all likelihood, those defendants had in common.

Having rung that bell, Rik decides to withdraw the question, and the Rev responds with a narrow look. By reputation, he doesn't like it when the race card gets played with him.

"Now, the largest element of the promotion formula is the exam, right, Mr. Cornish?" Rik asks.

"Right."

"And you showed marked improvement there as well, did you not?"

"A little, yeah. You know, you can't improve that much on stupid." The room erupts, the volley of laughter echoing off the close walls. That's how it goes in court. Even a dumb little joke is a great break to the tension.

Rik smiles, too. It's Walter Cornish's first likable moment.

"Well, give yourself credit, Sergeant. Your score went from 78 the first time you sat the sergeant's exam in 2018 to 84 in 2020, right?"

"Right. I eventually figured out it wouldn't hurt to study."

There's laughter again, but not the gale he got the first time.

"And in 2020, how did you rank compared to other applicants, if you remember?"

"Number one, actually."

"And that, frankly, was because nobody else applied?" Rik gets the laugh this time, largely because Walter sounded so boastful. "And the last part of the promotion formula is your seniority in rank, which counts for ten percent. If the combination of performance and the written exam end up making you fairly equal with another candidate, seniority will do it, right?"

"Right."

"Well, would you say that there's an unwritten agreement on the HI force that if a senior officer is qualified, they are going to get the promotion?"

"I don't know." The commission knows, though. Everybody—
the FOP, the commission, the brass—likes a system where officers
can get promoted in order, if they've done a good job.

"When you first sought promotion, were you the most senior
person in rank?"

"No, Mooney had been on a little longer than me."

"And it was Mooney who got the promotion, right?"

"That's how I remember it."

"But in 2020, you were the most senior patrolman on the
promotion list?"

"I guess."

"Well, after Sergeant DeGrassi announced his retirement,
wasn't it pretty much agreed that you were going to move up?
Which is why no other patrol officers bothered to apply?"

"Agreed by who?"

"Well, that's what I wanted to ask you. Hadn't Chief Gomez
told you, several weeks before the time of this supposed incident
at the Saloon, that she expected to recommend you?"

Cornish pauses. His green eyes circle as he calculates, clearly
afraid that Lucy wrote down something about the conversation. In fact, the Chief says she'd already told the Rev that
she'd be recommending Cornish, right before the competitive
process had first opened up on New Year's 2020. The commission members in theory can't testify, and they're supposed to
base their decisions only on the evidence. But they have their
own memories, which, being realistic, no one expects them to
forget.

"Yeah, I think that might have happened."

The Rev, who has been watching Cornish carefully, appears
to nod.

"But she coulda changed her mind," volunteers Cornish.

"That's what I was afraid of." He doesn't quite smile, but you can see he thinks he scored.

"And leave the Highland Isle police force short a sergeant, even though your performance appraisals and test score had improved significantly, and you were the most senior patrol officer in the department—and the only one who applied?"

"She coulda," insists Walter.

The commissioners know the FOP would have put up a never-ending stink if the Chief denied Walter the spot in those circumstances. Because both Cornish and her realized she had no choice about moving him up, Walter would have laughed in her face if she'd really tried to use the promotion to strong-arm him into sex. That's another point Rik will save for argument.

He returns to our table to pick up the notes he made earlier, and I put my hand down on the pad and show him what I've scrawled there in large letters: 'Get an adjournment. I have something you HAVE TO see.'

Rik turns to the commissioners and says that I've just reminded him about all the material he's yet to cover, meaning that his cross is going to extend past the deadline of 9 p.m. For him, he says, this is a good place to stop for the night.

The Rev is unhappy, because it means they need to schedule another session this week, but he finally agrees to give Rik an hour, no more, on Wednesday night. With that, the Reverend Dalrymple bangs his gavel.

As soon as the commissioners are gone, and the reporters are racing for the door, Rik turns back to me and whispers, "What the fuck?"

9. WHERE IS TWO GOING?

'Where is TWO going for a couple hours every day with his little red gym bag? I've assumed he's a workout freak—but lately, I'm wondering if the bag is just a cover, like his middle-of-the-night cigarette. Is he really spending all that time on exercise? Maybe he's got surveillance equipment in the bag that he's changing out someplace near the Tech Park.'

Now and then I tell myself that TWO is none of my business. I could just hand my notes over to one of the FBI agents I met while I was working for my grandfather. But the Bureau gets complaints from every lunatic in the Tri-Cities area, reporting the arrival of extraterrestrials or zombies poisoning the Diet Coke in select refrigerators. I need something more solid on TWO before the FBI's own protocols would let them take me seriously.

And so I decide to start following TWO when he leaves the apartment in the middle of the day. They tell you in PI school, same as the academy, that you can't really tail a guy by yourself.

Either you stay too close and get made or you lay back and lose the subject. But I'm getting nowhere with only my 4-D imagination.

If TWO is actually working out, I've figured from the start where he is heading, since the only gym within walking distance is True Fitness on Hamilton Street downtown. During the dark months, November to February, I buy a monthly membership there and usually stop in on my way home from work. Once the weather is good enough, I quit and run outside a few times a week and switch to exercise bands and calisthenics at home instead of the free weights. My place smells a little like a sock afterwards, but I live on a pretty tight budget.

When I trail TWO for the first time, the day after Cornish began his testimony, my attitude is that losing him is way better than him noticing me. If he disappears, I can try again tomorrow, but I have no idea how I could explain why I'm on his heels without putting him on DEFCON 1. He'd get a restraining order, or punch me out, or worst of all, move.

I let him get a couple minutes ahead so that he's a speck a block away. He follows the route I take downtown to True Fitness, but laying back, I don't actually see him go in. Still, I'm pretty sure my hunch is good, although I'm also a little disappointed, since it means that he's not hovering in the bushes outside Northern Direct.

Instead, I do something I should have thought of a while ago and open a search engine on my phone. TWO leaves the building Monday to Friday within a couple minutes of noon. (On the weekends he cuts himself a break and doesn't leave until about one p.m.) Given the rigid schedule on weekdays, my bet is that he's taking a class at True. And when I go to that tab on their website, I see that he's either enrolled in Yoga for Seniors or a five-day-a-week class called Extreme Boot Camp. The instructor is some kind of CrossFit champion, and from the description, it sounds like the goal of the class is to bring you just short of cardiac arrest while you're on your lunch break.

True Fitness lies in those three or four blocks of downtown that make Highland Isle look stylish, with reconstructed facades on the storefronts and smart-looking signs over the doors or in the windows. The mayor used some of the federal pandemic money to make loans to keep merchants in business. Many of the shops have a Latin bent, since that community still prefers neighborhood stores where they can handle the merchandise and talk to the owner and maybe even bargain a little bit. There are also a couple fancy restaurants here that draw patrons from the entire metro area, including one, Miiciwa, which I can't really afford, that serves food inspired by Native recipes. ('Miiciwa' means 'Eat' in the language of the Miami tribes whose land this was before the white settlers drove so many out.) The Ritz, who I guess wants the downtown to thrive as much as the mayor does, expanded his management office a couple blocks away. I go in there now and then to pay my rent in person when I happen to be around.

I am standing half a block away from True Fitness, trying to figure out my next move, when a line of six people in running clothes emerges from the alley next to the gym. The instructor, a blonde woman who looks to be over forty and ridiculously defined, runs in place for a second, then turns and sprints down the block with the other five in the class in quick pursuit. I recognize TWO at the head of the pack, with a smooth stride that looks like he's not stressing.

I know, from the class description, exactly where they must be heading, which is over to the junior college, two blocks away. They'll do several sets of timed dashes up and down the stairs on the steel bleachers around the athletic fields, with a round of jumping jacks or butt kicks or spider steps in between. Then they'll sprint back to True for several rounds of punishing drills involving lifts and squats and push-ups with sandbags and kettlebells. I figure they'll be gone for maybe twenty minutes. As I walk home, I am coming up with a plan.

The following day—the Wednesday when the Chief's hearing is scheduled to resume that evening—I approach True Fitness around 12:15 from the other direction, knowing that the Boot Camp class will run straight past me. From behind a tree, I see TWO on the instructor's heels again. I watch until they are approaching the grounds of Greenwood JC.

When they reach the junior college, they continue straight ahead, rather than turning right toward the entrance. Instead, the whole group attacks the chain-link fence that marks the perimeter. It's your standard eight feet, but TWO goes over as if he were on springs. He's moving at full speed and finds a toehold in one of the diamond-shaped openings. As his momentum propels him upward, he grabs the top rail with both hands and vaults over in a single motion, sticking the landing on the lawn with plenty of flex in his knees. He runs in place to await the rest of them. Even the instructor is a few seconds behind him, and she and every-body else push the heel of their shoe into the fence on the other side to slow their descent.

With them gone, I head down the block to True with the backpack I bring to my workouts. My monthly membership here lapsed March 1, but I get a day pass at least once a week with their junk-mail flyer begging me to return. The girl with a big gold hoop nose ring who's at the counter watches as I fill the form in. She then looks back over her shoulder and calls out,

"Amal!" That is the manager, but who is in real terms the closer. They sell gym memberships like used cars here, every deal a stupid negotiation where you know they're trying to screw you.

Amal is a South Indian dude who kind of amuses me because he's one of those people who knows that I know he's playing me and goes for it anyway. He's slightly hunchbacked, but in his slick clothes and glossy hair, he comes on like he's Chris Pine. I can see him through the open door to his office, jiving with Rita, a tiny Black girl with a killer body who works as a trainer and who I, at one time, had my eye on. They are standing a little too close for it to be all business.

He starts out of the office with his game face on, primed to sell me a membership that will last for several generations after me, but he stops dead when he recognizes me.

"Clarice," he says. I've noticed before that he's really good with names.

"Amal."

Maybe Amal grew up with parents who told him that nobody really matters but your family, or maybe he just wants to prove that he's the coolest kid in school, hunched back and all. I figure fifty cents out of every extra dollar he can get me to cough up goes in his pocket and is, as far as he's concerned, a tribute to how smooth he is.

"Great to see you back, Clarice. What's up?"

"I was thinking about a class maybe. What do you have around now? I can get away from work for an hour."

"Now," he says. "Well, Allison does her boot camp, but that might send you back to the office limping. She was a drill instructor at Parris Island. No shit." I imagine there must be female DIs at Parris Island today, but I'm younger than Allison, and there sure weren't any there when I graduated from high school and considered becoming a Marine. At that point, except for nurses, women got nowhere near those kinds of roles. Knowing Amal, I'd take even money Allison wouldn't even turn around if I yelled 'Semper Fi.'

"I'm a little out of shape," I tell him, "but I bet I can handle it. Any chance I can observe for a few minutes?"

"No problem, but she just ran them out of the building. They'll be back in fifteen minutes if you want to hang around. Tell you what? Why don't you sign up, and if it's not your thing, we can do a refund?"

I can't help myself and roll my eyes.

"I think I'll take a look first, Amal. I'll go lift for a few minutes until they're back. I signed the day pass."

He shrugs.

"You know the drill," he says. I drop my driver's license in the plastic index-card box, complete with alphabetized file dividers, that sits on the front counter. Rita, Amal's little buddy, started on the counter, and I once handed her my concealed carry card as a photo ID, thinking it might spark her interest. Instead, she freaked and I had to turn my bag inside out to show her that I wasn't packing at the moment. Today's receptionist, the woman with the nose ring, hands me a towel as I go through the turnstile. I'm still not sure what the point is of holding on to my ID. It seems like a lot of work just to make sure they get their crummy towel back. Maybe they want to be sure they can identify the body if you collapse while working out.

True Fitness itself is pretty basic, with supergraphics on the painted concrete block walls and colorful tape wrapped around the exposed heating ducts. But the place is clean, with mad-intense lighting, and the equipment is pretty new. When I'm here

I'm always secretly comparing myself to everybody else. As long as I keep my back supported, I can press more weight than any woman I see in here.

There's a guy about my age but beefy who just finished doing bench presses with 140 pounds. I have always been able to press my body weight, but the instructor who was working out the lifter shouts at me when I slide onto the bench. I know I should warm up, but I can't resist showing off, and am straining for a third rep when the instructor-dude reaches me and eases the bar out of my hand. As I stand up, I pat him on the back and return to the counter.

"Just got a fucking call from work," I tell the receptionist. "Any chance I can score another day pass? I like barely used that one."

I know the system here. Anything that translates to money is going to be under Amal's control, and as I expected, she trots back to the office, where he and Rita are still flirting. I'll bet they've practiced some unusual yoga on the mats after closing time. While the receptionist is back there, I look into the plastic file to retrieve my ID, standard practice when the front counter attendant has stepped away. I palm my driver's license and then flip through the dividers like I can't find it. I only have to go from G to K to see what I came in for.

There's TWO. His ID is an Arizona Driver License that says his name is Joe Kwok, address 68 Bluebird Lane in Mesa.

At Mike's I've heard cop friends complain all the time about how good the phony IDs are now. The Chinese print them up by the thousands, blank stock that looks perfect, right down to the halftone background logo each state selects—for Arizona, it's the shape of mountains and trees with a green cactus outlined in front. The gold star of the Real ID program appears in the upper right corner, with a grayed-out thumbnail of his main photo just below. I run my finger on the edge. It doesn't feel quite right, like there's an added layer of lamination.

I concentrate hard to memorize what's here, and I'm still staring when I see Amal headed toward me. I flash my license to show him I've gotten what I was looking for, but he continues in my direction, worrying me for a second until he hands me a crisp new day pass.

"Hey," he says, "you know I can help you on the extra charge for the boot camp, if you renew your membership for a year."

What a pal he is.

"Cool," I answer. "I'll definitely think about it."

I head out and notice only then that I've still got their white towel around my neck, but I keep going. I have a dozen at home.

As soon as I am back, I light up my computer. As part of the PIBOT, Rik pays for the best of the background-check sites. If TWO is who I think he is, then even if this identity is phony, it will still be fail-safed so it doesn't blow up after a routine traffic stop or a few minutes' research on the net by somebody who wants to check him out. And that proves to be the case.

The background sites list a Joe Kwok at that address in Mesa. Joe is a consultant with a spotty prior employment history. He has no criminal record, no warrants outstanding. Like a normal person, he's got pages on Facebook and LinkedIn, where he lists himself as an alum of Arizona State.

I have a TracFone that I bought with an alias, refilling the minutes with phone cards I buy for cash. Even so, I mask the caller ID and dial the number that's turned up for Joe

Kwok. It goes to voice mail, where I get a chirpy greeting. "Hey, this is Joe, leave a number." I don't. Instead, I call back again to listen more carefully. The guy talking doesn't sound like TWO.

As I keep poking around various sites, I get some odd results. When I look for Joseph Kwok, not Joe, he has the same address on Bluebird in Mesa. This guy, however, is seventy-eight. It could be a father and son living together, I guess, but to double-check, I navigate to my fake Facebook account in the name of Clara Stern—my dead grandmother—and spray out messages to every-one named Kwok, saying, 'Looking for Joe of Mesa.' Then I go to Zillow. Turns out that 68 Bluebird Lane was listed for sale until February and now has been leased. And when I go to the Mari-copa County Assessor's Office, I see that the assessment notice in February was mailed to "Joseph Kwok, Estate Of." Then things get even stranger. The Arizona Office of Vital Records doesn't show a death certificate for Mr. Kwok, which makes no sense unless it was removed somehow. When I search Legacy.com for Joseph Kwok, I get 'No Results Found,' and the same thing on Ancestry. Even Google.

I'm about to head down to the Municipal Building for the resumption of the Chief's hearing when I receive an answer on Messenger from a woman, Dr. Marjorie Kwok in Vermilion, Ohio, who says her dad, Joseph Q., passed in January of COVID in Mesa, and how did I know him. She attaches a sweet photo of the old guy. No mention of her brother of the same name, which she'd have to do if he existed, to be sure which 'Joe' I was asking about.

'TWO—or the government that runs him—seems to have bought up the identity of poor dead Joseph Kwok, rented his

house, taken over his phone number and killed every obvious link to old Joe on the net, which requires some high-key hacking skills, like you'd find in military intelligence.'

I creep close to the wall I share with TWO and whisper, "Gotcha, gotcha, gotcha."

10. THE CROSS OF WALTER CORNISH

Let's talk specifically about what happened at the Saloon that night March 6, 2020, and your feeling that you had no choice but to go home with the Chief," says Rik, as soon as the Rev calls the continued hearing to order. "Was this the first Friday night you'd spent at the Saloon, Mr. Cornish?"

"Hardly."

"That was pretty much your habit at that time, right?"

"I don't know about habit."

"You were there often on Friday nights, right?"

"Sure. Me and a lot of guys. If I wasn't on weekend duty. We'd hang, you know, chitchat about the week and whatnot. The crap that happened. There's always crap that happened."

"The 'we' is other officers on the Highland Isle force?"

"Sure."

"Was Lucia Gomez-Barrera part of those groups?"

"Chief would come in sometimes. Later in the evening."

"Later in the evening meaning nine p.m. or later?"

He shrugs. Okay.

"And she would drink and gossip and laugh with all the officers, right?"

"Generally, yeah."

"And how long had you known the Chief?"

"Since she came on. Twenty years."

"Did you work with her on the street?"

"She sometimes backed us up in Narcotics."

"The answer is yes, you had worked together?"

"That's the answer."

"In fact, you knew each other well, didn't you?"

"I don't know what that means."

"Well, even when she became your superior, how did you address her?"

"I don't understand."

"Well, if you were just talking in the station or at the Saloon, did you call her 'Lucy'?"

"Sure. A lot of the older guys did. I'll give her that. She didn't get all puffed up or anything when she started moving up."

"And the talk, in the Saloon on Friday nights, it was, let's say, wide-ranging. Plenty of off-color talk, right?"

"Always."

"And the Chief was part of that kind of back-and-forth, right?"

"I guess."

"She didn't stand on ceremony. In the Saloon, she was on equal footing, right? Everybody called her 'Lucy,' didn't they?"

"Yeah, but she could think what she wanted to think. She didn't pull rank, but you know, she's still the Chief."

"But she showed up at the Saloon on Friday nights for years and never asked for any deferential treatment, did she? Going back to the days when she was your sergeant, right?"

Cornish seesaws his head around. He's not going to quarrel, though, and finally says okay.

"Now let me ask you about your memory of events. Do you

recall that it was you who approached Chief Gomez that night in the Saloon, that you spoke for about an hour, and that it was you who suggested you leave together?"

Cornish glares and sits up straight. "No, I definitely don't remember that."

"Well, this night when you left with the Chief, was that the first time you took a woman home from the Saloon?"

Kelsey, the waitress who was outside for a smoke and remembers seeing Cornish and Lucy get into his car together, knows Cornish well and says he would regularly go on the prowl as 11:00 approached. He'd start buying drinks for women and often departed with one. I have found two former force civilian employees who went home with Walter from the Saloon. Neither wants to testify, but they like the Chief more than Cornish and might in a pinch. But as it turns out, we won't get to go there. Marc stands to object.

Surprised and even a bit irked, Rik looks back over his shoulder and says, "What grounds?"

"Rape victim shield law," says Marc and explains that the law, now a rule of evidence, prevents asking the victim of a sex crime about prior sexual behavior. Rik recoils like he's been shot. He didn't see that coming. Mrs. Langenhalter and the Rev get into some animated whispering, but Rik withdraws the question and also gives Marc a little complimentary wink. Rik can be a good sport, because he's sure the commissioners know the score anyway.

"And did you drink when you were at the Saloon?"

"Course. It's a tavern. You pay your rent for your seat, so to speak."

"And what do you drink when you're at the Saloon?"

"Beer. Maybe one boilermaker to start. Beer after that."

"And in March 2020, do you recall what time you say you left with Chief Gomez?"

"Later."

"Ten p.m.?"

"Maybe earlier. I don't know."

"Is ten a good estimate?"

"Maybe. I don't really remember."

Kelsey, the waitress, who is supposed to testify next, is precise about the time, because Ike, her boss, knows she needs that smoke at 10:00 and doesn't mess with her break. I've interviewed Kelsey, a stringy-looking redhead with bad skin, a couple times. Marc had found her first. The owner of the Saloon, Ike Grbecki, told her to talk to Marc when he asked, since the city attorney essentially controls Ike's liquor license. But Kelsey doesn't like being in the middle. And Ike knows better than to make an enemy of the Chief. Kelsey was pretty straightforward with me about Cornish and will say on the stand that Cornish seemed to be squiring the Chief pretty happily. They were both laughing, and Cornish, playing the gentleman, opened the car door for her and even hung around to close it.

"You don't recall," says Rik to Cornish. "Yet you say you recall clearly that Chief Gomez approached you?"

"Yeah."

"Now, you started drinking about five p.m. when you arrived, with your first boilermaker? And how many beers do you think you had before you left around ten p.m.?"

"I dunno. Two. Three."

"You sat in a bar for approximately five hours and drank two beers? That's how you paid your rent?"

"Two or three, yeah."

"Do you know Kelsey Haelish?"

"Is that the waitress?"

"It is. And do you know that based on your drinking habits, she's going to estimate you had at least ten beers that night?"

"No way," Walter answers calmly. He knows that much alcohol in five hours would have put him way over the .08 alcohol limit in this state, meaning he was driving drunk.

"Does your memory get better or get worse after you've been drinking, Mr. Cornish?"

"I don't know if I've noticed."

"You haven't noticed that your memory of events that occurred while you were drinking is worse than while you were sober?"

"Could be, I don't know."

Both the Rev and Mrs. Langenhalter, even Josea, are all smiling discreetly. As a witness, Cornish is starting to leak oil.

Rik flips through the yellow pad he's holding.

"Now, you said on direct that your relationship with the Chief was strictly professional, is that right?"

"That's what I said."

"And that you were 'shocked' when the Chief approached you. That's a quote."

"I was shocked."

"And you were shocked because, again quoting, 'you didn't think of the Chief in that vein.' Right?"

"You take good notes," says Cornish, in a tone that suggests there is something sneaky about that.

"Now, do you recall ever saying in the squad room at the Highland Isle Police Station to a few officers, quote, 'The Chief is symphony class on the skin flute'?"

Several people in the room, who understand the remark, can't contain their sharp laughter.

Cornish, who knows from the way Rik put the question that we have a witness, gives it the back of his hand.

"So what?" he says. "Am I not supposed to kiss and tell?"

"You made that remark?"

He shakes his head. "I guess."

"Well, do you remember that you made that comment in 2017, a few years before this supposed encounter with the Chief?"

Cornish screws up his mouth while he considers his options.

"Well then, I guess I didn't say it."

"So now you're denying saying that? Which is it? Did you say it or not?"

"I don't really remember one way or the other."

"Well, do you know Sergeant Emmitt LaTreaux?"

Cornish snorts. "Oh, it's him."

"You don't like Sergeant LaTreaux?"

"We don't get on."

"You had an argument about something you said, and you two stopped speaking in 2018."

"What I said wasn't racist, but he thought so."

Marc stands to object about relevance. The Rev is frowning a little, thinking that Rik is trying to leverage race again, but Rik says, "I'm just putting a date on the conversation in the squad room." It was Cornish, not Rik, who said LaTreaux thinks Walter is a racist, and the Rev seems to recognize that.

"All right," says Reverend Dalrymple. "But let's stick with the squad room."

"Well, now that I've refreshed your recollection by mentioning Officer LaTreaux, do you deny saying in the squad room in 2017, 'I can tell you, the Chief is symphony class on the skin flute'?"

"Like I said. I don't remember that."

"Well, you couldn't have said it, could you, because you told us that as of March 2020, your relationship with the Chief had been strictly professional and you didn't think of her in that vein, meaning in a sexual way?"

Cornish just glares. "If I said it, I wasn't speaking firsthand. Must have been something I heard. I guess she got around. You know. Guys talk."

"And again. Just to reaffirm. Your relationship with the Chief up to that conversation at the Saloon had been strictly professional, and you'd never thought of the Chief in a sexual vein, and so you were shocked by her request. You're sticking with that?"

Marc objects that the questions were asked and answered, but Walter talks over him and says, "Because it's true."

"Now, Mr. Cornish, you're a single man, aren't you?"

"Yes."

"And you were single in 2020?"

"You've got that right."

"Had you been married previously?"

"Unfortunately."

"And your wife sued for divorce and claimed during the proceedings that you had been constantly unfaithful?"

Marc stands again. "Same objection. Mr. Cornish's behavior, alleged or true, is irrelevant under the rape shield law."

"There is no law," Rik answers, "that prevents showing that a witness has lied under oath about a material matter in the current proceeding."

Mrs. Langenhalter whispers in the Rev's ear.

"Then let's hear that proof," the Rev says.

"That's where I'm going," says Rik. He comes to the table for the package Tonya brought me, which clearly came from Paulette Cornish, Tonya's church buddy who didn't want to talk to me because she had no interest in helping the Chief.

"Do you recall learning during your divorce proceedings that your wife's attorney had hired a private investigator to follow you? And do you remember that her lawyer produced a number of affidavits from the investigator to you in discovery?"

Cornish scowls. "I thought that shit was confidential."

"Again, Mr. Cornish, no confidentiality order permits you to lie under oath."

Mrs. Langenhalter nods sagely.

"Now, do you recall, Mr. Cornish, that one of the affidavits from the private investigator stated specifically that he had followed you to the Saloon on Friday, May 16, 2014, that you had left in the company of a woman known to him as Lucia Gomez-Barrera, that you drove to the parking lot of a plant in Anglia and, to the investigator, appeared to be engaging in sexual intercourse in your automobile?"

Marc stands and says, "Isn't that affidavit hearsay?"

"We can call the investigator as a witness if you prefer, Mr. Hess."

The Rev intervenes. "Here's the question for Cornish. Did that happen? That thing in 2014? With the Chief?"

Now Cornish is in trouble, because he may be buying himself a perjury rap, having testified so emphatically that things between the Chief and him were purely professional until 2020. Quickly hip to his problem, Cornish looks at the Rev and says, "I'm not gonna answer that."

"I'm sorry, Reverend," says Rik, "but either Mr. Cornish sits for full cross-examination and answers my questions, or the commission can't consider his testimony. He doesn't get to come in here and answer all of Mr. Hess's questions but not mine."

The Reverend mulls while Mrs. Langenhalter whispers to him, gesturing with her free hand. She clearly agrees with Rik.

Having the momentum, Rik forges ahead to fill the silence.

"Can we agree, Mr. Cornish, that you didn't get promoted in May 2014 or anytime soon after this earlier meeting with the Chief?"

Cornish, confused about the legal ground he stands on, remains mute.

"Well," says Rik, "do I assume you also won't answer if I ask you about yet another prior personal meeting with the Chief?"

The Rev is staring at Cornish, his white eyebrows smelted together in an angry slash.

Walter is done, whether he knows it or not. The essential premise of his testimony has been shown to be a lie. He and the Chief were occasional fuck buddies. Nothing new in 2020. He wasn't forced. He wasn't shocked. And having been proven a liar under oath, there's no reason to believe him on any of the other details. When the Chief says on the stand that Walter came on to her in 2020, which is what she's told us from the start, her version will be essentially uncontested.

"The City withdraws the witness," Marc says.

"I'm done?" asks Cornish.

"Oh, you're done," says Rik.

As the room begins to clear, the Chief remains seated at the respondent's table. She has her hand over her mouth and is staring at the space the commissioners occupied, which is empty now. Rik touches her shoulder, right over the epaulets, and she reaches back to grip his hand for a second.

She was pretty defiant in the office about not apologizing for her sex life, but it's hitting her now how all of this sounds in public. Walter Cornish can initiate a fuckathon every Friday night in the Saloon. But the Chief's a woman, a personage in Highland Isle, and for a woman in a Catholic town, her behavior will still provoke a lot of nasty laughter. Rik will argue when he sums up that there are no explicit rules against 'fraternization' in Highland Isle. But the Chief's daughters and her neighbors are going to be reading about all of this, skin flute and everything else. She's won the round, but she isn't going home in victory.

11. IT TAKES ME TWO DAYS TO SEE TONYA

It takes me two days to see Tonya. Fact is I've enjoyed meeting up with Tonya a lot. I'm pretty amazed by how she's turned out, how strong and funny and cool she is. But after last time, it's way too clear what she's hoping. Like I said, I'm not going there with her again. And it doesn't do either of us any good to start picking at the scar.

But getting the investigator's affidavit from Paulette Cornish was a big deal—it changed the case and maybe the Chief's life, and Tonya deserves to hear me say so. And besides, I know we may need her help again.

I ask her to meet at Mike's and get there a little early. There is a woman at the bar, a very tall, blonde patrol officer in the Twenty-Second who I went home with from here one night after the second game of the softball season. (Because of the Chief's case, I've missed several games and practices, although, in a totally un-Pinky-like move, I actually explained in advance to Rory Leong, our captain.) This woman—Maura, I think—starts my way, but I give her a squinty little headshake, and she stops and instead lifts her Manhattan in salute, a classy gesture, and I smile back. Maybe another night.

There was a time in my life when I thought of sex as the most important thing I was going to do each day. I generally had no clue who I was going to find to hook up with that night, but the thought that that person was out there was exciting in itself, something to discover, knowing that the intense reality of the act would, like a glowing star, outshine anything else that would happen to me in the hours in between.

Although I don't like to admit it, my life is tamer now. The club scene is not so fun anymore. The men are all looking at the twenty-year-olds, and the lesbian places where I've gone for years sometimes make me feel like an old maid. This is a better venue, and most nights I arrive here after a game, I'll leave with someone, man or woman, maybe someone I've slept with before, more often someone new. I don't know if cops have more sex than other professions. Lawyers? Probably yes. NBA players? Probably no. At Mike's, there's always a squad of cop-girls, groupies looking their best, or what they think is their best—lots of scent and makeup, big hair, tight clothes—women who, to be plain, get wet at the sight of a badge and gun. And there is also the wartime WTF thing in the atmosphere at Mike's, turning this into a sexual free-fire zone. Many days on the job are as boring as a file clerk's, but most file clerks don't go to work knowing they will pass somebody on the street with a desperate wish to shoot them. And there's also cop privilege: I know the rules, I know the rules are important, I enforce the rules, so I don't need to follow the rules. Anyway, people here feel safer to me than some rando. Sex is just sex, doing one another a solid for a couple hours—then go home and don't look back. Catch and release, as they say.

When Helen died, Pops's rabbi, who presided at the funeral with a priest Helen liked, said very urgently, as part of her eulogy, 'We are not our bodies.' This was some big spiritual point that what was great about Helen was her spirit. And I thought Helen crushed it, she was almost as important to me as Pops, and I was truly shook when she died. But as I was sitting there at the funeral, I thought, Hell if that's true about me. I will always be awkward with people, and I'll eternally have a hard time maintaining focus on paperwork or reading. But for the most part, I've always been able to count on my body. I was a three-sport athlete in high school, a for-real Olympic hopeful on the board and even now I remain a standout pistol shot. And sex fits in with all of that, because in this realm, I deal with someone else with confidence and get back really positive responses.

Tonya arrives while I'm thinking about all this. She's carrying a draft beer for each of us. She puts the glasses down on the table and jumps up on the stool but doesn't remove her coat, sending the message she's not expecting this to become an evening, which is a relief.

"So I just need to say how totally awesome that was of you," I tell her.

She shrugs. "Don't thank me too much. I wasn't even sure at first if I was going to give the affidavit to you. Paulette—Cornish's ex—spent all this time going through the boxes in her attic because she wanted me to see what she had against the Chief. She was like, 'Show your friend *that* next time she wants to talk to me.' I warned her that everything is backwards in a trial sometimes, and it might even help you guys by showing Walt's a liar. But that was okay by her. Best of both worlds: Lucy's a tramp and Walt couldn't pick the truth out of a lineup."

"Well, Mrs. Cornish kind of got her wish. You can be as feminist as you like and say, 'I own my body and will do whatever I like with it,' but for a woman, you know how that goes down in public."

"Word," Tonya answers. I don't really need to explain this to somebody who was closeted into her early twenties. "Once I heard how it all played out at the hearing, I was pretty relieved, because I've kind of been waiting for the Chief's security system to bite her in the behind."

There's a beat while I try to remember what Tonya's talking about, which leads to that lost-in-space moment of panic because I'm not understanding something that everybody else does. But finally, I have to ask, "What security system?"

Tonya grabs my arm across the small table.

"Girl, don't you know there are cameras all around the Chief's house? The force put them in like four years ago. I was the liaison on that."

I've noticed the cameras whenever I come by the Chief's place to deliver papers Rik wants her to see, which, given the nature of the P&F proceedings, I can't usually drop off at the central police station.

"But the Chief said the video output is saved for thirty days," I answer. "Standard commercial system."

"No no no," says Tonya. "That was the original NVR. A few years back, some asshole was harassing her and sticking dog poop in her mailbox every couple months. The fact that we had such a hard time grabbing the guy kind of got the commander, George Leery, thinking dark thoughts and saying we were lucky it was just dog shit and not some crazy street gang that came to kidnap Lucy, because our security setup sucked. So we changed out all the equipment and I put a Thunderhead NVR in her den. Forty-eight terabytes. And it uploads every month to a cloud system with some really cool compression that only saves what you'd want to see, meaning images with full-frame motion. We can go back close to four years. Searching is a bitch, because most of it is people walking by when they take their pooch out, but a year later we nabbed Mr. Dogshit. He started in with, 'It's just a prank, I did it once.' We reviewed seven months and got him five more times. He caught ninety days in jail."

"Nice."

"Definitely. But the Chief was recused on the investigation because she was the victim. I guess she never got the details. Or paid attention. She's not exactly a techie. We all got our flaws.

"But I was worried," says Tonya, "with these guys saying she brought them home that it would all be on the system and would corroborate them and look pretty, you know, swampy."

With Cornish, it might have. But the Chief says DeGrassi's story is all wrong. And if she's telling the truth, there should be no sign of Blanco.

"Can you show me how to search the storage system?"

She makes a face and kind of draws her full shoulders in around herself.

"I dunno. That really puts me in the middle. And I mean technically, the department is paying for the storage and the equipment."

"Well, she's the Chief. Who else can give permission?"

Tonya touches her beer glass and says that she'll think about it. She's shaping her eyebrows these days, which she would have never even thought about in her lumbersexual days, and it makes it more noticeable when she shifts into that pensive look. By now I recognize it and realize things are about to go sideways.

"How's the dude in your building?" she asks.

"Interesting," I say. "But very mysterious."

"Is it a thing?" She is hunched over her glass now, almost like she's ducking.

"It's a weird thing," I say. "Rik keeps telling me to give it up."
I'm just making this up on the fly as fast as I can.

"Will you?"

"Not clear."

She nods several times and sinks back into radio silence for a while. I want to change the subject fast but, typically, find myself stuck for words.

"So, you know," she says, focusing exclusively on the table and running her finger in the circle of moisture that has gathered beneath her beer, "I was thinking the other day, just kind of wondering, I don't even know why, but if I had ever been like, 'Okay, you go be with boys if you have to,' if I could have ridden with that, you think it might have worked with us?"

It's all I can do to keep myself from groaning. I have been trying for several weeks now to kind of figure out what's going on with Tonya. And I am slowly understanding that I am a significant person to her.

Not that I ever had the same experience. My first time was at snowboard camp on Mount Hood in Oregon. I was fourteen, and my mom used a little bit from her trust fund to pay for the summer. It was like, Any price to get Pinky out of the house.

So I was feeling pretty vulnerable anyway, and I said yes to this guy from California named Milos who was seventeen and not a completely bad dude. He wasn't as smart as me, but he was really good-looking and seemed to have been with a lot of girls. But as soon as he rolled off, this hole opened inside of me, a canyon of regret. Not about the act, which wasn't much. Generally, I've never been very good about the future—it's just been a place I won't go—and at that age all I could see for myself was boarding. But even that young, I suddenly knew I'd be dragging this guy Milos around with me for the rest of my life.

Not only was I hearing everybody at school discussing their first time, but I'd listened to an entire radio call-in show a few months before on the same subject and was just blown away about how vivid it remained to all these people, eighty-year-olds with great-grandchildren and soldiers phoning from Afghanistan.

I'd said yes to Milos mostly because everyone at camp was saying I liked girls, and I knew I liked guys and wanted to prove it, even though I knew I liked girls, too, which was just wildly confusing. And so I got stuck with Milos, who I realized in the first seconds afterwards was really nobody I'd otherwise have chosen to remember. It wasn't like he was destined to win the Olympics—or even many local competitions for that matter. He was just a semi-okay person attached to a dick.

For me, really breaking through and getting into sex was a slow burn, a process—a girl, then a guy, back and forth, a little better each time, my pleasure almost like something I fought for. But for Tonya, I guess it was all at once, and I'm the one who flipped the switch. And I understand why that really matters to her. Inside all of us there is this secret self who lives in our yearnings, this me that burns to be in who and how we love, a slender thread of nerve sewing together head and heart and the parts below. That want, that thing, is as persistent as your heartbeat, no matter how much other people cluck or tsk, and it clamors for expression.

Letting it happen is like moving from a flat world into the third dimension. It means your life, finally, is real, not just something imprisoned in your head but an actual thing happening in the world. And if it's just one person who connected with you and brought you there and saw and valued that in you, he or she is always going to be special to you, which I understand, because that's who I was hoping Milos would be and who he definitely wasn't—someone I'd sorta/kinda love forever.

And okay, that's who I am to Tonya. But it's definitely annoying that she doesn't seem to care about the other side, namely what she is—or isn't—to me. She is stubborn. Even when she was the squinch-faced silent chick I first met, she was a stubborn soul who ran on only one gear—forward. And since I'm who I am, too, meaning the kind of person who basically isn't diplomatic or patient, I need to tell her how all this is going down with me.

"Girl, all this draking bout you and me? It wears me out, okay? Can't we hang without heading straight back to what went wrong at the dawn of time? I think you're truly awesome, but you know, we were never going to work out that way. We want different things. You weren't going to say okay to me seeing boys—any more than you'd say yes to me seeing another woman. That's not what's inside you. Okay, you're a lesbian, but you're a pretty traditional person.

"But that has never meant I don't think you're very cool. You are. You're this completely amazing person. And you've just like grown so much, it's like you're two feet taller and twice as smart and four times more confident. So I'm not like worried about whether you're going to find your one true love. You will. And I get it. You've passed thirty and it hasn't happened, and you start thinking back and wondering, Well, maybe she was here and I missed the boat. But you will find your woman, you will. But it's not me. I will never shape myself to just one person. That's just not what I want, even though everyone else does. It's weird, but you know, more and more I'm okay being weird.

"Now, you want to know what I *do* need? Not, frankly, that it seems like you will ever ask. What I need is a friend, a real friend, especially a female friend, someone I think is really cool and can be a pal, which, you know, because of my character defects or whatever, has been harder than all fuck for me to find."

She sits there staring, the black eyes glossy and her small mouth slightly parted. Her breathing is faster. In this light, maybe because the blood has left her face, I can see more of the rough spots on her complexion that are concealed these days with better makeup. I watch while she struggles to find words, which just aren't coming because she doesn't know which is greater, the hurt of what I said or its truth. She takes a big gulp of her beer and gets off her stool, and then another slug before she cinches her belt.

She nods twice, getting ready to speak.

"Call me when the Chief says we can come over to her house one night, and I'll show you how to search the cloud files. If I can scare up some time, I'll help you."

She smiles a little bit and grabs my arm again across the table, more gently this time, before she turns for the door.

12. WHERE DOES TWO HEAD AFTER HIS WORKOUT?

'Where is TWO heading after his workout? Boot camp is over at 1 and he doesn't get home until a little after 2. What is Joe Kwok (ha!) up to afterwards?'

Answering that question means following him again, not when he leaves the Archer but after he departs from True Fitness. Now that I'm spending hours each night going over what's stored on the Chief's security system, often with Tonya there to give me pointers, my time during the day has been limited. But the Chief has relatives in from out of town this week, which means we're not going to Lucy's house. Our next hearing date is still more than two weeks away, because the Rev is on vacation, and there's not a lot for me to do yet on the new cases Rik is bringing in. That leaves me free to take a stroll downtown around 1:15 every day. I carry a different hat and sunglasses and rain jacket each day so I can alter my look periodically and make my reappearances less noticeable. The forever winter of the Midwest, which was still showing signs of holding on a week ago, has finally been swept out of town by steady west winds, and we are having a string of great days that feel like they were sent by divine forces.

On my first try, I easily pick up TWO when he leaves the gym. As I guessed, he doesn't head home. Instead, both times I trail him he walks down Hamilton, along the line of brick storefronts with their gabled roofs, until he turns into a little café called Green Fruit. It used to be known as Rocky's, a straight-up diner, but when they reopened after the pandemic, they returned with a crunchier menu, serving stuff like tempeh and ancient grains as well as a very good old-fashioned burger. Man of habits, he goes there every time I follow him that week.

The only lesson I take from TWO's choice of restaurants is that we have the same taste in food, since Green Fruit is where I'd go for lunch, too, if I could afford to eat out daily. Each day I trail TWO and glance through the front window, he's at a small table alone.

On Wednesday, when I double back after putting on a hat, I see a bunch of middle-aged guys standing up directly behind TWO after their meal. The five of them exit the restaurant, passing right by me and crossing the street with a get-out-of-my-way attitude, like they were a fleet of pickup trucks. They are joking with one another and laughing too loud. Four of them are dressed similarly, wearing a black polo with a name I can't read over the left breast. Somehow it feels like they're still in high school and trying to look like each other. The fifth guy, who had his back to me when he got up, is wearing a sport coat, a heavy tweed fit for the winter, and I'd guess from the formless way it hangs on him that he probably never takes it off. He's got a wrung-out look and a funny duck-ass hairdo, even though he's balding, with his greasy hair straggling over the collar of his shirt. He's chewing over a toothpick and walks a step behind the rest, seemingly caught up in his own thoughts. It's the Ritz.

I'm startled to see him, and I stare longer than I should. He feels the weight of my eyes somehow and turns over his shoulder with a nasty squint, pretty much on the order of 'Fuck you looking at?' There's something brutal and scary in his expression, and I quickly head the other way, only daring to turn back a full minute later. The group has reached the Vojczek Management building further down the block, entering a side door beside the big picture windows. The Ritz is the last to head in, but before he does, he glances back, maybe even checking for me. He's peering in the wrong direction, since I didn't follow them, and I head home feeling like I've escaped.

'*TWO and the Ritz?!!! What gives?*' I can't fathom any connection, but when I tail TWO on Thursday and Friday, Vojczek's group is seated in Green Fruit for lunch when TWO arrives. It's the same the following Monday, and this time when I drift by, I stop and pretend to study the menu that is posted in a frame outside the front window. TWO, as always, is at a table by himself. He's thumbing his phone now and then, but he's next to the round table at the center of the restaurant where the Ritz's gang is seated, which also includes Walter Cornish today. TWO is no more than a couple feet from the Ritz himself, although they have their backs to one another. Sometimes TWO picks up his phone quickly, so it appears he's tapping a quick note.

Ritz's team aren't the type to speak in their inside voices. Even through the window I can hear it when they erupt in laughter. It dawns on me immediately that if you had a mind to spy on them, you could pick up quite a bit from TWO's position. I'm a little pissed when I realize that if I hadn't already embarrassed myself with my next-door neighbor I could be in there, too, seated close to them, maybe overhearing something worthwhile for the Chief's case—and getting Rik to pay for lunch.

TWO's routine remains the same. Sometimes I make several passes by the window, putting on or removing my hat or glasses or jacket before I saunter by again. One day, I lift my cell phone and pretend to use it as a mirror as I play with my hair, while I take a couple photos, which I scrutinize back home.

At first there doesn't seem to be much I hadn't already noticed. Whenever TWO goes in, he takes the closest table to Ritz and his posse and sits with his back to them, while he fiddles with his phone between bites of his sandwich. As I would expect by now, he orders the same thing every time, always whole wheat with avocado and the white wires of sprouts leaking out between the bread. One detail that strikes me, after passing by so many times, is that the Ritz is seldom speaking. He smiles a little when the group breaks out laughing, but he doesn't seem to say much.

The idea of TWO scoping out Vojczek is a little mind-bending, and eventually, when I look back at the shots I took, I realize that what I'm seeing may mean nothing. It's seat yourself at Green Fruit, no hostess, and any patron who wanted to enjoy lunch would choose a table nowhere near Ritz and his boys with all their loud guffawing. Coming in later in the lunch hour, TWO may not have any choice but to sit next to those guys, and in my photos, I see that the only open tables in the restaurant were, as I suspected, around the Ritz and his gang.

I'm still trying to make some sense of all of this, when, on the Thursday of my second week of following TWO from the gym, something big happens. Ritz and his guys get up from lunch earlier than usual. As soon as I see them stand, I retreat to the entryway of a florist across the street, rather than let the Ritz catch me lurking again. For one second, as they cross Hamilton, flouting the traffic, I fear they're headed in my direction, but then I recognize where they're aimed: two red F-150s with the Vojczek logo on the doors. I've seen the trucks before, but they're usually parked down the block in the lot behind Vojczek Management. They must have an appointment that requires a quick departure. Even so, the Ritz's eyes, cool and gray, flick up for a second and seem to pass over me, but apparently he's noticed nothing, because they all jump in the pickups and tear off in the same direction.

Less than a minute after the Vojczek team departs, TWO emerges from the restaurant. He's toting his red gym bag, which drags at his side in an unusual way, like he maybe stole a dumbbell from the club. He looks left for a second, in the direction that the Ritz and his guys drove off, and then boogies double time across the street. It seems like he's heading to the management office, but instead, when he reaches the corner, he heads down the cross street, Fenton. I'm about three-quarters of a block behind. I get to the corner as fast as I can, while trying not to hurry enough to attract attention. When I turn, there is no sign of TWO. I pick up my pace and head down the opposite side of Fenton, trying to scan the doorways and parked cars. I go about a hundred yards until I reach the alley behind the buildings on Hamilton. I've lost him.

Then, when I return toward the corner, completely bummed, I catch sight of TWO. He's at the rear of the Vojczek Management building, beside the two huge air-conditioning condensers positioned there. He's got on a blue jacket now, with some lettering I can't read at that distance. I creep a little closer and crouch down so I can watch him through the windows of a parked car. From the gym bag, he extracts a black box, about the size of a ream of paper. It's heavy enough that it takes two hands to lift it. He flips open one of the metal breaker boxes on the rear brick wall of the building and removes two coils of wire from inside. I can't see how exactly, but he clearly connects both wires to the black box, which he then sets down behind the condensers on their concrete pad. From where I am, the box is basically hidden, and I doubt anybody else would notice it in the shadows there.

TWO takes off, and I follow, still a hundred yards behind him. As he walks, he wrestles off the blue jacket and drops it back in his gym bag. I don't have my binocs—using them in broad daylight would attract too much attention—but I believe I saw the letters HVAC on the back. TWO was pretending to be a service tech, working on Vojczek's cooling system.

I tail him long enough to be sure he's headed back to the Archer, then I return to the Vojczek lot. I'm about a quarter of a block away when the Ritz and his team in their pickups race in. Given that the Ritz already clocked me on the street the other day, I'll probably be completely burned if he sees me in his parking lot. Maybe he'll tell me off or try to question me. I consider waiting down the street for them to go inside, but I don't have a disguise like TWO with his workman's coat. Worst case, if someone finds me back by the condensers, I could end up accused of installing the black box, which I have a hunch I don't want any link to. There's no choice right now but to head home.

Darkness cannot come fast enough. I literally pace around in the apartment, checking the sky every fifteen minutes as if for some reason tonight the sun might be going down earlier than 8:43, the time of sunset listed on my weather site. At 9:30, when it's full dark, I hike back to the Vojczek building.

I've brought a large brown paper bag, folded up in my pocket, and I shake it out as I head into the Ritz's lot. The recycling bins are next to the condensers, and if anybody sees me, I'll toss the brown bag in there, figuring to look like some green cheapskate who's using Vojczek's receptacles, rather than paying the municipal fee for my own. It's a good night to be doing this, since it's a new moon. There's strong lighting on the borders of the parking lot, but back here, under the building's eaves where I'm snooping, it's pretty dim.

I edge behind the condensers. I'm afraid to turn on the LED flashlight I brought and risk drawing attention. Yet I can see enough to know the black box is still there. I take several photos of it, using the night setting on my phone and a low-light app—part of the bag of tricks I installed a while ago. I check out the first couple shots to be sure I've captured the white label with its serial number on the facing end of the device, between the wires that run back up to the electrical box. I hunch down and gently try to maneuver the thing, but it's heavy as a concrete block. With two hands, I am able to lean it away from the condenser to get a shot of the brand name impressed into the metal on the front.

I look at the last photo once I've walked back to the corner. 'NoDirt' is what the machine is called. I was 99 percent sure before I walked over here, but now as I head back home, I'm just so f'g proud of myself that I have a hard time not giving myself a hug.

Friday afternoon, once Rik has come back from the usual morning of court calls and lunch with one of his courthouse pals—he's friends with everybody: the bailiffs, the guys who run the metal detector, a couple prosecutors and several judges—I knock and ask for a minute. I'm sure he thinks that it's about the video capture from the Chief's, since he knows that I've gotten back to 2019, where, if the Chief is telling the truth, there should be some great shit on DeGrassi.

Rik's face falls when I say instead, "So the weird guy next door?"

"Pink, come on."

"No, please look at this." I whip out my phone. "I've been following him."

"Jesus, Pinky. He's going to get a court order."

"No, wait." While I'm displaying last night's photos, I explain how I saw him install the black box.

"What is it," he asks, "this box?"

"It's called a NoDirt. It's an amplifier. It boosts whatever 1800/1900 GSM cell signals are coming from inside the building, so they can be intercepted up to a third of a mile away by a piece of equipment called a Stingray, which spoofs a cell tower. Once the Stingray is connected to a computer, you can isolate the cell phones inside the Vojczek building and pick up every phone number they call, every text they send, every e-mail. He can even use the Stingray as a location device, so he can see where the Ritz's cell phone, meaning Ritz, is at every moment."

By the time I got home last night, I had realized that the Stingray is what TWO's been storing in the ATA case. He's carrying it down now and then because it interferes when he needs to use his phone or Bluetooth devices.

Rik takes my phone to study the images.

"It's wired into the power there?"

"Exactly. You got a big-ass circuit for the AC. He tapped in before, because the wires were already in the breaker box. He must have gone over and done that when he was up in the middle of the night. I hear him crawling around a lot at two or three a.m."

"So why didn't he put this box in then, instead of broad daylight?"

"That seemed weird to me, too, but then I realized that he needs the phones on in the building to isolate their signals. He had to get over there while they were gone so he could see what IMEIs lit up when they came back."

Rik swipes through my photos again, mostly to give himself time to think.

"You're telling me this guy is conducting surveillance on Moritz Vojczek?"

"I sure can't see anybody else in that building worth spying on. And the Stingray next door to me—that's why I haven't been able to get a decent cell signal since he moved in."

"Okay, and he just happens to end up in the apartment next to you, somebody else who's trying to get a line on Vojczek? How weird is that?"

"Very weird. Everything about the guy is weird. But he's got to live somewhere within a few blocks of Vojczek's. And you wouldn't want to be right across the street in case the Ritz found that box. You'd want them to have to search a wider area, so you had time to boogie."

"And how much does this equipment cost, Pinky? The Stinger and the Dirt-free?"

"Stacks and stacks. A hundred fifty? Two hundred?"

"Oh fuck," says Rik. "Two hundred grand? This guy's not small-time."

"I been telling you."

"Is he a Fed?" Rik asks.

"Well, what do you think?"

Rik holds his chin while he thinks.

"If he's government, to put in that device, he'd need some kind of court authorization. Which requires Moses Appleton's office. And that makes no sense. That would mean the US Attorney's

Office wants Walter Cornish as a grand jury witness at the same time they're tapping his phone, which is bound to undermine his credibility. Unless this whole investigation of the Chief is a cover for an investigation of Vojczek. But for what crime?"

"The Chief thinks Ritz is still a drug dealer."

Rik looks like I feel, more confused as we trace through the possibilities.

"Okay. And what if your weird friend is not with the G?"

"That's possible. You know who makes that device, the NoDirt? The name's actually an abbreviation. It's Northern Direct."

"You think Direct is conducting surveillance on the Ritz?"

"Our back porch, mine and the neighbor's, gives you a straight-on sight line to Direct. I thought he was surveilling the facility. But now I'm wondering if Direct suspects the Ritz of doing something in the middle of the night to sabotage them or penetrate their installation."

"For what reason?"

"Well, Jesus, Boss, I'm just throwing stuff at the wall. Everybody says Vojczek still owns a ton of property in and round the Tech Park. Maybe the Ritz is trying to figure out if Direct is going to expand. They got this big new Defense contract. That way he'd know whether to buy more property or sell what he has."

"So they're conducting counter-surveillance?" Rik wrinkles his nose in doubt. "A Fortune 500 company can't get into illegal wiretapping, even if it's defensive." Then he lifts one of his thick fingers and sort of taps it on the air. "But if you mess around with a defense contractor, there's about a hundred federal criminal statutes involved. Which would mean your neighbor isn't DEA—he's DCSA." Defense Counterintelligence and Security Agency. "Maybe NSA. Those guys get their warrants from courts in DC."

That doesn't strike me as quite right.

"He's like a one-person operation. He never communicates with anybody. Maybe he's working for a foreign government. Or a different company?"

"That's conducting surveillance of Ritz *and* Northern Direct? Why?"

Mystified, we stare at one another. Then Rik's eyes drift up suddenly, as he's clearly gripped by another thought. When he finally focuses on me again, his look is stern, and he points me to the chair next to his desk.

The Chief's case has been hard on Rik, and his skin has got an undertone of gray. It's not just the pressure of the world watching but also the fact that he needs to keep the plates spinning in his practice. The publicity has worked out the way he hoped. He's been getting a lot of calls, meeting prospective clients and often getting retained. That's good, but it's stretched him even further, and he keeps vowing that as soon as the P&F hearing concludes, he'll hire an associate. I don't completely look forward to that. I'll be happy to see Rik get help, but another lawyer will push me down the totem pole. I won't be the first person he uses to bounce around ideas.

"Now, listen to me," Rik says and leans a little closer. "No one who can afford to spend $200,000 on surveillance equipment wants to get messed over by somebody playing Harriet the Spy. If he works for the government, then you need to know that obstructing a federal investigation is a felony, Pinky. And if your neighbor is conducting illegal surveillance, he can't get caught. That's pen time for him. Which means he needs to keep you quiet." His eyebrows narrow so he can stare at me even more intensely. "One way or the other, Pink, you are in a perilous situation. So whatever else, this much is clear: Leave. This. Man.

Alone." He takes a second for that to sink in, never releasing my eyes. "Do you hear me?"

"Yes," I say.

"Promise me you're going to knock it off and let this guy do whatever it is without you watching. Promise?"

"I promise," I say after a beat.

I don't mean it for a second.

13. MY NIGHTS AT THE CHIEF'S

My nights at the Chief's house make me like her even better, and I already thought she rocked. I see now why so many of her officers say she's great to work for. I come here straight from the office most nights, meaning I haven't had dinner, which bothers her way more than me. There is always a plate waiting on the desk where her computer is, a sandwich or some of the pasta she's whipped up for her own meal.

We think of powerful people as moguls in mansions, but the Chief, a genuine public servant all her adult life, has never had money. Her house is half the size of what I grew up seeing in the West Bank suburbs. Its tiny rooms are crowded with too much furniture, including glass display cases full of family mementos and knickknacks: a sculpture her older daughter did in seventh grade; a small stone head, centuries old, that was passed down on her mother's side of the family.

Nothing is out of place. The Chief is kind of a maniac housekeeper, something that as a pure guess feels like an immigrant habit, her mom's voice always warning her not to give the Anglos any excuse to look down on her. You can smell the air freshener and the Fabuloso when you walk in the front door. Whatever the reason, the Chief's the kind who unconsciously sweeps her hand across the desk to collect the dust when she comes in to visit me. I give her points for that, too, that she checks on me, so I don't feel like I'm toiling in a dungeon, since what I'm doing is, being honest, dull as fuck. I'm often there long after she's gone to sleep, but she stops by before turning in to thank me for all of my great work.

As for the captured video, it's been easier to move backward in time, because that allowed me to start with what's on the resident hard drive. Searching the cloud required a tutorial from Tonya, and I'm still not very skilled. I'm not surprised that in the newer recordings from earlier this year there's no sign of Blanco. But as Tonya suspected, there is stuff we'd rather that Marc Hess never see—which he won't, unless he's smart enough to ask to search the system once he finds out in court that it exists. It would definitely be a problem if Hess discovered the video of the Chief and Cornish I found on my second night here.

What you see on-screen from the camera mounted over the driveway is the two of them getting out of Cornish's Buick, each just a little slow moving due to alchohol as they head up the driveway toward the front door and what the system calls Camera 1. The Chief is in a shortish skirt—she still has nice legs—and her hair is big and fluffy, adding to the impression she went out looking for fun.

Just as she and Cornish are half out of sight, the Chief says very clearly, 'I don't know, Walt. Maybe this isn't such a good idea.'

'Aw, come on, Lucy,' Cornish answers. And you can see his hand take a firm grip on her shoulder. 'This'll be the best hour you've had all week.'

The tape clearly shows that the Chief wasn't demanding sex

from Cornish. On the other hand, there's a reason that she suddenly had second thoughts about going inside. Marc would contend that she said 'this isn't such a good idea' because it dawned on her that Cornish was up for promotion. From that angle, what's portrayed is not extortion, but it might be taken as bribery, Cornish offering a good time to make sure there's no hitch with him stepping up. Rik is afraid that if Marc sees this footage, he'll ask to reinstate Cornish's testimony.

Rik explained all of this to the Chief without asking her to watch the recording, but I'm not surprised tonight when she walks in and asks me to play the clip. She stands behind me while I sit in her desk chair, her hand lightly on my shoulder at first. When I look back to see how she's taking it, the Chief has the flat expression I'd expect from a veteran cop who's witnessed a million people fucking up. Except this time it's her.

Finally, she can't stifle a groan. "Señor Jesus," she says. "What a tool I am." She sits down beside her desk in a small chair. "Walt Cornish hadn't gotten near me on a Friday night for at least three years. And I damn well knew why. I was too old and fat these days for a big stud like him. But all the sudden he comes on and I think nothing of it, except, Well, maybe I'm not so bad after all."

I'm watching her quizzically. There's a part of this I'm missing.

"Don't you get it, Pinky? Walt was going to work for the Ritz. The Ritz put him up to this. Ritz had this whole sex-for-promotions thing planned out, even a couple years back. COVID delayed him, but Ritz loves to scheme, and he stuck to what he'd dreamed up."

"You think?" I ask.

"I *know*. The Ritz lives to outsmart everybody else."

I absorb that for a second.

"You know," I say, "we never really got the deets on what Ritz has against you."

She's still wallowing a little in her disappointment with herself, and she shimmies her shoulders to get out of that, a little like a dog drying off.

"Shit," she says, "where do I begin?"

"Didn't you say you rode with Ritz when you started in Kindle County?"

"Okay," she says, "yeah, that's the start." She shifts around in the chair and turns to the side so she has enough room to cross her legs at the ankle. "Ritz has always been kind of a big deal. He was an all-city basketball player, could shoot the ball apparently, which is how he first became 'The Ritz.' But on the KCUPD"— the Kindle County Unified Police Department—"he was a virtual prince because his father, Sig—Siegfried—was the mob's guy on that side of the river. Sig was watch commander in District Four, who would make the case go away whenever some meatball the Outfit cared about got cracked."

"And Sig pulled strings to get his son on the Force?"

"Didn't have to. Ritz was number one on the academy entrance exam. He's the brightest cop I ever worked with, if you're talking book smarts. He went to law school and business school at night while he was on the job and never broke a sweat. Supposedly he's done the course work for two different PhDs and even learned several languages. But Ritz—" She looks straight at me. "Un hombre especial," she says, tossing her thick black hair in amazement. "Most cops don't spend a lot of time wondering why people go wrong. It's like wondering why there are trees in the forest. People can be shitty. Period. The folks you arrest, they got bad impulse control or shattered egos. A lot of them are people who were kicked around until they learned to kick somebody else. But you know, a bad seed, somebody just flat-out born bad who lives to be wicked? You don't see a lot of that. Unless you know the Ritz. You and me, we're the dumbasses who follow the rules. He's Ritz—he's from a race of one that's way above us.

"So jumping in the Wayback Machine, I was assigned to Ritz as my first training officer when I was a rook. Back then there were plenty of guys on the job who hated getting teamed with women, let alone a Latina. Standard crap—we just couldn't cut it, supposedly. A lot of them tried to drive me out. If I requested backup, other cops would talk right over my transmission. I didn't get the Ritz as my trainer by accident.

"Second night, we're riding together, it's slow. Ritz takes a drive over to Kewahnee, nowhere near our beat, and ends up on McGowan, you know the block under the overpass from 843, where the working girls are out in their crazy outfits. He pulls into an alley and gets out and whistles to one of them, a girl in short shorts, stacked heels, and a fake white mink stole in the dead of summer. And before I can even ask what gives, he's got his pants around his ankles, and this girl is on her knees in the alley on his side of the vehicle. Of course, he looks back at me at one point, with this huge obnoxious grin. But I'd be damned if I'd let him get me out of that cruiser. I just did some reports until he busted his nut. And then as soon as he'd buckled his belt again, he says to the girl in mink, 'It wasn't good enough, Vondra. I'm running you in.' And throws the poor woman in the back seat. The whole deal, it was just an 'I dare you.' But really, can I beef because he arrested somebody? Besides, you grew up how I grew up, you don't go tattling anyway.

"But every night it's something else with him. About a month in, we get called in on a bust in one of the Italian social clubs. I'm new and I can't figure why so many units are responding. But

over in Kindle in those days, gambling raids always went down
the same way, whether it was Black guys throwing craps on their
knees in an alley or rich white guys in the country clubs playing
gin rummy for ten dollars a point. Just so long as there was a lot
of cash on the table. Whoever led the raid would inventory maybe
a hundred dollars. The rest would get divided among the cops
who showed up. And the guys we were supposed to arrest, they
never got booked, so they wouldn't bitch about what happened
to their money.

"That night, back in the car, Ritz hands me my share. Doesn't
explain. Just hands me a roll of bills. About two hundred dollars.
And believe me, I could use it. But afterwards I'm really upset.
This isn't why I joined. I'd just started seeing Danny, and he said
to me, 'Next time, don't touch a dime, just tell him to divide it
with the other guys. If you take that money a few more times,
he'll end your career. One night, Internal Affairs will be waiting
outside. The bills Ritz gave you will be marked, and everybody
else's pockets will be empty.'

"So I never accepted another cent. Ritz hated that. Because now
the tables were turned, and he couldn't be one hundred percent
sure what I'd say if Internal Affairs came knocking. All the sudden,
I'm reassigned—to the North End, naturally, which was another
kind of education. But it was better than riding with Ritz.

"Okay, so fast-forward eight years. I've just moved over to
Highland Isle as a detective sergeant, and damn me, guess who's
here? Sig, Ritz's dad, got caught running a burglary ring out of
the watch commander's office, fingering marks and radioing the
burglars whenever the real cops were on the way. Sig caught eight
years, Fed time, and it's huge headlines, so nobody wants his son
working over there. Instead Ritz hires on in HI, where his dad's
buddies still run things.

"When I got here, Ritz was already the chief of the Narcotics Bureau. And from what I hear over time, he's got the gambling-raid thing going on steroids. When they bust a dope house, Ritz doesn't just keep most of the cash. Now he's also taking half the drugs. With mandatory minimums and sentencing guidelines, what are the defendants going to say? 'No, I actually had more heroin?' Don't think so. And then, how I hear, Ritz sells the drugs he stole back to a few big-time dealers he's got something going with.

"Everybody on the force heard the stories, but I'm sure Stanley, the old Chief, was getting his share. Then Amity wins the election. The day she announces that I'll be the next Chief, even before I get sworn in, I call Ritz to my office and I tell him, 'You're done. Either git, or I'll give the FBI or DEA the names and dates on twenty drug busts you made where things smell funny.' So I get his resignation. And my whole force knows we're going to be doing things the right way from now on. But the Ritz's been out to get even ever since. And you know what his biggest beef is, what he rants about after he's had a couple of beverages? He was fifteen months short of his pension. Can you imagine? Hundreds of millions to his name, but he's still burned that I kept him from getting a little green check every month."

"And that's when he went into real estate?" I ask.

"That's another story," she says and looks at her watch. It's getting late, but I want to hear this and she's enjoying the telling. "Every cop is always looking for a side hustle, you know, pay a few more bills. While the Ritz was on the job, he bought a couple of apartment buildings. Since he's always got an angle, I figured it was a way to launder dirty cash—you know, book it as rent.

"But when Ritz got axed, and Amity started all the renewal stuff in town, he realized he could take that idea big-time. The FBI had pretty much smashed up the Outfit, but there were still a lot of them into dirty business all around Kindle County—protection rackets, bust-out schemes, frauds with Zelle and Venmo—which generate lots of cash they have to keep on the sidelines because they're scared of the IRS and money laundering. So Ritz starts putting together real estate partnerships, buying up property all over Highland Isle. These days I hear the money goes in and out in Bitcoin. But even back then, it was typical Ritz, proving he was smarter than everybody else and could make sure nobody could tie anything back to his investors. It was all Cayman bank accounts and Panamanian corporations, and partnerships inside partnerships, like a Russian doll, swapping properties back and forth. The boys who invested don't care about big profits—just give them back their money baptized. And Ritz's still basically a dope peddler. Which is the second reason he wants to get rid of me."

"How is a real estate guy a dope peddler?" I ask.

"You know anything about how the fast-food chains work? Danny's brother bought a bunch of Taco Tiempos. He wanted Danny to go in with him, but my ex, bless him, he loves the street. But anyway, Taco Tiempo or most of the other ones, the corporations own the real estate where the restaurant is and rent it to the franchisees, who buy all their supplies from headquarters and fork over seventeen percent of the gross.

"And that is what Ritz does for the big drug dealers. We've busted three major fentanyl operations in the last couple of years, I mean twenty people working in an apartment, and each time it's in a building Ritz owns. 'But hey,' he says, 'I can't keep track of what my tenants are up to. I manage half the rental property in town.' He knows I got my eye on him.

"So that's why he wants me out." She points to the screen

where I froze the image, which shows half of her, with Cornish outside the picture except for his hammy hand on her shoulder. "I know all that. And I still fell into Ritz's trap, because I was so freaking eager to think a slob like Walter was hot for me again. Jesus," she says. "Jesus."

She leaves the den without another word.

14. PRIMO TAKES THE STAND

On June 6, Primo DeGrassi takes the stand. As the Chief has put it, with Primo, what you see is what you get—a big, warm lunk. That's pretty much the way people talk about my dad, and so maybe that's why, when Primo walks in a minute or so late, I instinctively take a liking to him—until I remember why I shouldn't. Primo has kept himself in shape. He's got this wavy black hair and big shoulders and a nice face, definitely handsome for an old guy. Not hard to understand why the Chief would want to take him home.

On the stand, Primo displays none of Cornish's arrogance. He's like an eager child. He listens and nods respectfully and repeats the answers he rehearsed with Marc. He looks, honestly, like one of those people who's too dumb to lie. He isn't. He's too dumb to lie well.

Primo's story is that in early 2019, he decided to apply for promotion to sergeant. He was looking forward to getting his twenty-five and retiring, and he makes no bones that he wanted the salary bump that would increase his pension. He hadn't applied before, he says, because he was never great at tests.

Primo's job performance, in contrast to Cornish's, was always okay. He did whatever he was asked to do and generally well enough. The only citizen beefs in his jacket came, not surprisingly, when he was partnered with Walter. As far as his job reviews went, the one consistent criticism was that he wasn't always 'alert,' pretty clear code for the fact that the guy isn't what you'd call a Thought Leader.

Anyway, Primo applied, and ended up number one on the list, since he was also the most senior guy. Everything was looking good for him, he testifies, when he showed up at the Saloon one night in February and, just as happened with Cornish the following year, the Chief asked him to go home and party. He did it, and in fact the Chief required him to return several more times. He was a married man, he says, but he knew the increased pension would help his family.

With that little bit of amusing crap, Marc tenders DeGrassi for cross.

Rik goes straight at him.

"Now, according to you, Mr. DeGrassi, you began this series of sexual interludes with the Chief in late February of 2019, is that right?"

"Right."

"Isn't that in fact, Mr. DeGrassi, when your physical relationship with the Chief ended?"

"Not how I remember it."

"Well, Mr. DeGrassi, I take it on your many visits to the Chief's house, you noticed the security cameras there?"

"I seen 'em. But you know those systems. Maybe you get thirty days of tape."

"So you were not aware that an enhanced video storage system had been installed at the Chief's, which holds at least four years of surveillance footage, were you?"

Primo is accustomed to thinking slow. He holds still while he tries to figure out if this is actually as bad as it sounds.

Rik doesn't wait for him. "I'd like to show Mr. DeGrassi some video, Reverend, if I may have a couple of minutes to set up the equipment."

Marc is on his feet. "Members of the commission. This is a complete ambush. We received no notice of potential video evidence."

Rik shakes his head. "Commissioners, this is cross-examination. We are not obliged to assume that Mr. DeGrassi will lie under oath. And evidence for cross is not subject to discovery. It never has been."

Mrs. Langenhalter whispers in the Rev's ear and he grants Rik his recess.

Marc is hot on Rik's heels.

"This is bullshit," he says. "You and I have never played this way with one another."

"I got a client, Marc," Rik says wearily and walks away. No matter how Rik would deal with the recordings routinely, he's already explained his problem to me: the more time he gives Marc to think, the more likely Hess will ask to see any footage of the Chief and Cornish. Since catching Marc off guard is essential, Rik is willing to look like the typical courtroom snake.

Once Dorcas—a law student who works around Rik's office at times—and I have wheeled all the video equipment into the courtroom, Rik begins. There's a 40-inch monitor set up between DeGrassi on the stand and the three commissioners. The spectators are straining forward along the benches to improve their lines of sight. Tonight, like the second night of Cornish's testimony, there's no sign of Vojczek in the audience. Getting picked out of the crowd the first time was clearly enough to keep him home.

"Now, you told us, Mr. DeGrassi, that your encounters with the Chief took place in February 2019, right after you had decided to apply for promotion. May I show you just a few excerpts from the recordings, beginning, say, in January 2019, that might refresh your recollection?"

I work the computer, whose images pop up on the monitor. The first clip I found of the Chief and DeGrassi entering her house is actually from late December, but it took place during work hours, so Rik has formed his question carefully.

As each recording plays, Rik asks, "And do you recognize yourself, Mr. DeGrassi? Is that a fair and accurate image of how you and the Chief looked in January and February of 2019?"

Primo can't quarrel about the dates, because they were automatically stamped onto the recordings. After about six snippets, the Reverend interrupts and says, "We get it, Mr. Dudek."

"Now, what was happening, Mr. DeGrassi, was that you and the Chief had started dating, isn't that correct?"

"Dating?"

"Yes, making arrangements to see one another. You had dinner out, you went to the movies. And you visited the Chief's house. Right?"

Primo doesn't answer. He is unhappily considering his options.

"And the reason the Chief agreed to go out with you is that you told her that you and Mrs. DeGrassi were going to get divorced. True?"

"You know," says Primo. "Marriages. It was a rough patch."

"You told the Chief that you were getting divorced and that you expected to move out as soon as your youngest daughter graduated high school in June. True?"

"I don't know."

"And what happened, Mr. DeGrassi, is that once you were

dating the Chief, you decided on your *own* to apply for promotion. Correct?"

"No, she thought I should do it."

"Is that so? Isn't it the fact that she didn't even know you were applying until after you had taken the promotional exam?"

"I don't think so."

"You don't think so," Rik says. "Well, Mr. DeGrassi, you told us that you had a bad history on exams, didn't you? Wasn't your 84 much better than you'd historically done on other tests?"

"I guess."

"Didn't the Chief ask you outright whether someone took the test for you?"

"No, I don't think so."

As it happens, that whole scene where the Chief found out about Primo applying and where she questioned him about his score—that all went down on the Chief's doorstep. Rik nods and I cue up the clip, in which the Chief says, 'How the fuck could you do this without talking to me?'

"Does that refresh your recollection that the Chief hadn't known you were going to apply for promotion?"

"I don't know what she knew. Maybe I told her and she forgot."

"Shall we replay that clip, Mr. DeGrassi, so you can point out where you reminded the Chief that you had previously told her you were going to apply?"

The Rev, who always hears the clock ticking, interrupts and says, "We saw the video, Mr. Dudek. It speaks for itself."

"Agreed, Reverend," says Rik. "And in the interest of time, I'll also ask the commission to take notice of the fact that the 84 Mr. DeGrassi received is exactly the same score Mr. Cornish received a year later."

Marc objects, but nobody up there bothers ruling until

Mrs. Langenhalter, who doesn't ordinarily seem to like to speak in public, says, "The score is already in the record, too."

"Mr. Cornish is your close friend, isn't he, Mr. DeGrassi?"

"Walt? Yeah. We're buddies."

"You'd worked together for years?"

"Right."

"And you still work together for Vojczek, don't you?"

Marc, who's been trying to keep an unruffled demeanor and focus solely on taking notes, now objects that the commission has already ruled that questions about Vojczek are irrelevant.

"I didn't say 'irrelevant,'" says the Reverend, who seems to be recognizing that there might be something after all in the Vojczek connection. "But I think for now we can move on."

Rik bows just a little to accept the ruling, before facing Primo again.

"Now, aside from you applying for promotion, did something else happen in February of 2019 that also served to interrupt your relationship with the Chief?"

"I don't know."

"Well, didn't the Chief bump into Mrs. DeGrassi in the grocery store? Do you remember hearing about that?"

"Hearsay," says Marc.

Marc is right, but after Mrs. Langenhalter whispers to the Rev, he says, "I assume the Chief will testify about this later?"

"If that's necessary, of course," says Rik.

"We'll hear it now then," says the Rev and motions Rik to continue, figuring we're saving time overall, rather than forcing the defense to recall Primo later for this scrap of testimony.

"And Mrs. DeGrassi and the Chief had words in the grocery, didn't they? And didn't the Chief tell you later that Mrs. DeGrassi had said she had no intention of divorcing you and warned Chief

Gomez to stay the hell away from you? Did you in fact hear that from both women?"

In the last few days, I've made several visits to the City Market to see if any of the current employees recall what I discovered was a pretty infamous incident. None of them wanted to talk about customers, but one suggested that I speak to a former stock clerk, Angela Marcos, who is now a full-time student at State. Angela was willing to get on the phone, largely because it was such a wild story, a couple middle-aged ladies playing bumper cars in the grocery aisle. Angela had been filling the shelves near where the two women ran into each other—literally, because Mrs. DeGrassi had rammed her steel shopping cart into the Chief's. The Chief responded by doing pretty much the same thing, followed by a lot of yelling as the two women faced off with less than a foot between them.

"And so after you'd decided to apply for promotion, and after the Chief and your wife had words at City Market—isn't that when the following occurred?"

The next recording is from the Chief's doorbell camera. Primo is hammering with the brass knocker and screaming.

'Lucy,' he is yelling, 'Lucy! It ain't like that. Come on, let me in. I can explain this whole thing. It's not how you think.'

"Did she let you in, Mr. DeGrassi?"

"No," he says after again weighing how to answer.

"In fact, she refused to see you any longer, didn't she?"

"I guess."

"Would you say she was very angry with you?"

"I guess."

"And even though she was angry with you, and felt lied to and cheated by you, she did not stand in the way of your promotion, did she?"

"With strings attached."

"Right, she made an agreement with you, that if you would give her your signed paperwork for resignation, postdated for a year ahead, that she wouldn't block you from becoming a sergeant. You'd get the bump to your pension and leave the force after twelve months, when you finished your twenty-fifth year in service, right? And that's when you'd told her you expected to leave anyway? That was the deal, even though she remained personally furious with you?"

DeGrassi looks at me at the computer, trying to figure out what else might be recorded. There is no more, but Primo doesn't know enough to chance it.

"You could say that's what's happened," he says.

Rik looks at Marc and says, "Redirect?"

Marc passes on that. The session is adjourned until next week.

Rik goes over to make up with Marc, who's still beside himself with rage, trying to gather his papers on the desk and not getting very far with it.

"Why would you waste an evening of all our lives that we're never going to get back, just so you can look like Perry Mason?"

Rik does a little bowing and scraping. His obligation is to discredit the City's case in the most convincing way, he says, but maybe he was stroking his own ego.

"I'd have withdrawn his damn testimony if I'd seen that," Marc says. "You know me too well."

"Well, are you going to dismiss your case?"

Marc shakes his head. He doesn't know.

"I still have Blanco," he says.

"Strange you mention him, because I have a little preview," says Rik. "Blanco says Lucy took him home and did all kinds of nasty things to him. And there's not a single frame from any of the cameras where Blanco appears. He was never at that house any time close to when he says. So unless he dematerialized before going inside, his testimony is bullshit, too."

"I'll talk to him," says Marc and heads out, using his credentials to open the door in the back of the courtroom that leads into the City Hall Building.

The Chief, who's kept a rock face this whole time, is smiling now.

"Is it over?" she asks.

"I never take an early victory lap," says Rik. "There's plenty of time once you've actually won."

"Come on, Ricky," she says. "I want to sleep through the night for the first time in three months. Tell me it looks good."

"It looks good," he says.

Once she's gone, Rik looks at me. "Five bucks says Marc calls tomorrow to tell me he's canning the case. Maybe he'll wait a day because he's so pissed."

15. I DON'T HAVE THE GREATEST LUCK

I don't have the greatest luck. Sometimes I think I kind of bring this on myself because I'm not always in, whatever you call it, the here and now. Like the first time I got busted. I was sixteen and had broken my back the February before and got way into painkillers. Man, I loved that numb feeling, as if there was a lead casing around my heart that kept out all the upsetting crap that normally pierced me like X-rays. Anyway, there was a woman I had started seeing, Ophelia, a grad student in classics at the U, and I was over at her first-floor apartment in Center City, and I was standing in front of the open living room window with a blunt. And a cop walks by. I was too bent to notice. Until I heard his nightstick on the sill.

'Come outside,' he said. The officer was just doing what he had to, Pops explained when he took me home from the station. If the cop was a hard-ass, he'd have kicked in Ophelia's front door and tossed the place. But that's the point. Ophelia got lucky, and I didn't. I mean, who gets arrested by a cop who's just walking down the block to get a sub?

Within six months, I had been picked up two more times. On

the last occasion, after Pops again had arranged my release at about four a.m., he turned to speak to me even before we left the police station parking lot.

'Pinky,' my grandfather told me, 'I have noticed something throughout my years in this business.' He meant being a criminal defense lawyer. 'There are people who never seem to get caught. And people who always do. That second group, Pinky, become my steady clients. And you are one of them. I cannot explain this. It has nothing to do with intelligence. Call it luck, if you like. Or karma. Or fate. But you have to respect whatever force is operating.'

How Pops put this, telling me to accept the fact that the universe would cut me no breaks—I felt that. Which means that I should have listened to Rik when he warned me about leaving TWO alone.

The day after DeGrassi's testimony, since Rik is hoping Hess will call and shut the whole proceeding down, the boss gives me the day off. I sleep in, but around one, I decide to take a walk. I'm thinking I might pick up some lunch, it's a great day, but I know already what I'm going to do, even though I promise myself that I just want to be sure TWO's not up to any new tricks with the Ritz and that the NoDirt remains behind the condensers. It will, I tell myself, be the last time.

I wander downtown and wait up the block from True Fitness. Same as always, he comes out with his red gym bag and heads toward Green Fruit. He disappears around the corner. Making sure I don't get near enough to attract his attention, I eventually drift up to the café to take a quick peek through the window. I can't make him out at any of the tables, and on my second pass, I linger a second longer but still don't see him.

Until I turn around. I can't imagine how he got so close. He must have been hidden in the shade of the doorway to the shop next door. But he is no more than a foot from me. I'm not short, five eight and a half, but at well over six feet, he looms above me, especially since he's broader shouldered than he appears from a distance with that lithe frame.

"Looking for someone?" he asks. It's the utter coldness of his expression that is frightening. He waits a second for an answer, which I can't muster, then leans a few inches closer and whispers, "Why are you following me? It's been a month at least."

I don't know what to say. He's scarier than I ever expected, even on a busy street in broad daylight. But I'm tongue-tied mostly because I've plunged into this cave of disappointment in myself. Story of my life: I never ever know when to stop.

"You know," I say.

"No, I do not know," he says.

I can't ask him who he's spying for. Rik already told me how dangerous that would be. So with only a second to think, I go where my brain takes me, remembering my lame-assed bumbling in the hallway a few weeks ago when I asked him about coffee, and the way he misunderstood me.

"Sometimes I'm feeling someone, you know."

" 'Feeling?' "

"You know." I'm doing my best to act really embarrassed, which is not an act at all. "You know, somebody's kind of hot. You think, you know, we could click. I'm kind of into you, okay?" The only way I could be more obvious is to flash him, but he still seems slow to register what I'm saying.

"I am not looking for a girlfriend," he finally answers.

It's a confusing moment. I should be relieved that he seems to buy my act, and that maybe he's not going to turn me over to some Chinese special ops team that will kidnap me and fold me into a crate, where they will keep me until I tell them everything I know. But I can always surprise myself. And in the first instant I feel annoyed and maybe even disappointed by how fast he said no. After all this, the dude is just like, 'Swipe left'? If it wouldn't undercut my pose, I'd just tell him to fuck himself.

"Well, I don't need a boyfriend either, man. I'm just saying, you know, hang out. See what happens. Whatever. You know, it was a prank, man, following you? You're hard as all fuck to get to know. What do you *do*, man? You just walk around. I don't get it."

The blades have withdrawn from his eyes. Instead, he seems to be processing just how weird and unexpected I am. Suddenly he's the one caught off guard, which leaves me an opportunity to escape.

"Okay," I say. "Sorry not sorry. I get it. One-way street. I'll leave you alone."

I slide off with a quick wave, not looking back.

About eight that night, I'm on Facebook. For the most part, I think it's an incredible snooze. A billion people I don't care about doing stuff that makes next to no difference to me. The common wisdom, whether it's what people say or what blasts out of the Internet, never really seems to be describing my life or me. Reading all those posts just makes me feel weirder in the end.

Which doesn't keep me from wasting about one night a week. One laugh is all these people from high school, who would have done the Carlton Dance across the entire cafeteria to avoid having to say hi, now want to friend me, which is basically an offer to sign up for their fan club. I take it, but mostly to see how ridiculous they all are. Wow, here's news: During the height of the pandemic you just about went crazy. Aren't you special? And this one is definitely worth worldwide attention: While classes were virtual you led your daughter's second grade class in sewing the pieces of a quilt that were stitched together when in-person classes resumed.

I would say the main thing I've learned from Facebook is something I knew already: No kids. Not me. No grimy hand-prints on my sleeve. What in God's name would I do with a kid as fucked up as me?

Anyway, that's how I'm occupied when there is a knock on my front door. Leaving aside Arturo, the janitor, the only people who do that are the Jehovah's Witnesses, who slip past the buzzer into the building when one of my neighbors is leaving. Peeking through the fish-eye, I expect a couple guys in suits, smiling already and holding a handful of pamphlets. But it's TWO.

I immediately feel panic, and it grows while I try to figure what's up. Best guess is that he's thought through our encounter on the street and, with time to add things up, doesn't buy my bullshit. Now Mr. Superspy wants to find out how much I know. And what if I know too much—as I do? Maybe it's what Rik warned me about, and TWO is here to choke me.

But when I open the door, his affect is a lot different than it was on the street. He's in a pair of jeans and his hands are in his pockets, and he's slumped just a little, as tall people often do to seem less imposing.

"Okay if I come in?" He has kind of a thinking smile, like he's amusing himself with this request.

I want to say no. But how can I be into the dude one minute and then slam the door the next?

I look at him across the threshold.

"You know, man, that was really embarrassing when I thought about it. I'm sure I totally freaked you out. Sometimes I get inside my head and can't get out. But you don't need to worry. Just forget the whole thing, dude. I'll leave you alone. I promise."

His tongue rolls around inside his mouth. He doesn't say anything at first but points at my sofa.

"Mind?" he asks and edges past me.

The TV is on, some stupid romance show I wasn't really watching while I was on the computer. Gomer gives TWO the usual warm welcome and bares his teeth before scampering away. If your housekeeping standard is a FEMA site, which is my baseline, then he's caught me on a good night. There is an open can of tuna I ate for dinner on the counter, which I'm sure is stinking up the place, and some dirty clothes on the sofa arm—including, back to that whole luck thing, a bra and thong, not far from where he chooses to sit down.

"You want something to drink?" I ask. "Beer? I've got some whiskey, I think."

"Juice?"

Juice. I should have figured him for super healthy given what I know about his habits. I have some OJ. It's past its pull date but it's still okay when I taste a little on my finger. As I'm pouring, I keep calculating what is going on. If he was here to murder me, would he be drinking orange juice?

Handing him the glass, I say, still standing, "So do you have a name?"

He gives me a look. "You know my name, right?"

He couldn't have seen me at the gym. They were still outside when I shuffled through the IDs.

"Clarence?" I ask. "I'm Clarice, by the way." I offer my hand, which he takes briefly with a surprisingly weak shake.

"I know."

"You do?"

"It's on the mailbox downstairs."

"And yours isn't."

"Better that way."

"You on the run, man?"

"Only if you count a crazy ex. Definitely do not want to see her again."

"Is that why you're here, to ghost your ex?"

"Pretty much. There were some stunts. Sugar in the gas tank. Pounding the doorbell at three a.m. It was either have her arrested or leave." He smiles. "Or murder her."

I take a beat on that. The way he said it was almost like he's mocking me.

"And where is she?"

"Pittsburgh."

"That's where you're from?"

"That's where I came from."

"And why Highland Isle?"

"I have a client."

"And how'd you end up in this building? It's not exactly a tourist destination." I want to see if he'll even hint about the sight lines to Direct. But he throws up a hand as if he has no idea.

"The client chose it. Furnished it, pays the rent. Free is free," he says. As if he'd live in his trunk downstairs if that was what the client told him to do. But even saying this little, he's basically admitted that this location suits what the client has him doing.

"And what's your business?"

He frowns. I knew Twenty Questions was going to end soon.

"What do you do?" he asks. I like his accent. He sounds pretty much like a Midwesterner except the o's stay too long in his mouth, like he's swallowing an egg. American, I'd guess, but maybe born elsewhere.

"Me?" I answer. "I'm a private investigator."

"Oh yes? What do you investigate?"

"I work for a lawyer in town. Mostly I look at records. Or talk to people. I mean, I was a paralegal for years, so I do some of that."

" 'Paralegal,' " he says. "I hear that, but I have no idea what it means."

"It means you do the shit the lawyer doesn't want to do. Keep track of documents. But in this job, mostly I'm out on the street. Interviewing people. Witnesses. You know, 'Did you see the accident? How fast was everybody going?' It's actually a good job for me. Cause normally with people—I mean, I don't have a clue. I can't even look anybody in the eye." I glance back at him, having said all this vacantly staring at a spot on the wall behind him.

"And are you investigating me?"

I laugh. "Only cause I can't figure out your story."

He shrugs. "Why does that matter?"

"Well, hell, man. You live next door. There's never a sound from the place, but you're creeping around outside at three a.m. You're weird."

"You follow around everybody you find weird?"

"I do a lot of crazy shit, frankly. But I already told you. I'll leave you alone." I raise a hand. "Word of honor."

"Actually," he says. He takes a sip from his orange juice.

"Actually what?"

"What did you say? 'Hang out.' "

"You came over to hang out?"

He makes a face again. He's clearly not a talker. In fact, some sort of shyness has overcome him, seeming to shrink him down, or at least drive him back into his own core. I can see the effort when he surfaces at last.

"To see if you were serious," he says softly.

About *fucking*. It feels like a door hit me in the face: That's what he means. He came over to get it on. I act surprised, which I am. But men are, you know, pretty basic. And I kind of have it going on, at least enough that most of them don't turn me down.

Now what? I think. Now what?

From the time I began to understand what sex was, like as a tween, I've gone through moments when I could imagine it with everyone who came into sight. I mean, everyone: the thick-calved gal jumping off the FedEx truck, the hostile Asian guy behind the bulletproof glass at the convenience store and even the old lady hobbling down the street beside her equally old Shih Tsu. Which has led me to follow my imagination to a lot of stupid places, like finding how it would be to get railed by my Uber driver or to sneak off at a party with somebody's girlfriend. But I've never had sex when I didn't want to. I never hooked up with somebody on a dare. There was a lot of that in high school. 'I dare you to do the guy no one sits with in the cafeteria.' No thanks. Sex, whatever else, is about my fantasy, not yours. And no one is ever going to tell me what I've got to do with my body. Period.

So even if I've done this to myself, I'm not sleeping with this guy to keep up with my own lies. I will say what everybody has the right to say: I changed my fucking mind.

But okay, TWO is hot to several powers, no denying that. And strange, which makes him intriguing. And yeah, I've spouted off that random shit to Tonya, which means something is boiling around in the back of my brain.

"Okay, cool," I say and sit down with him on the love seat. I give him a long look, but I can tell he has no clue what happens next. He probably never got into the random college hookup phase or went home often with someone he picked up in a bar, and so he doesn't realize that his line is, 'Okay, where's your bedroom?'

"Koob," he says then.

I get it slowly.

"Your name is Koob?" I know at once, don't ask how, that this is so. And that totally changes our reality, the fact that he's willing to make this tiny investment in the truth and come out from hiding. We are really here now, both of us. "I never met anybody named Koob."

"It's Hmong. It's actually pronounced"—he says something like 'Con,' while pushing the entire word through his nose— "but in America I've always let people just say it how it looks to them. 'Rhymes with boob,' I said as a kid." He adds a slightly embarrassed smile.

I stare at him. "I thought Hmong were like midgets. I mean not really, but super short."

"My dad is Chinese. From Liaoning, where they're real tall. I take after him."

He looks at me again. And then slowly lifts one hand and touches the blunted point of the nail in my nose.

"Do you ever take that out?"

"It's a look," I say. Then I slide closer to him, so I'm right up against his arm and leg. They're like walls. "You afraid I'm gonna hurt you? I won't." I lean close and, of all things, lick him. His nose and then a couple other spots. And put my hand in his lap.

It goes nicely after that.

Pops, who was a close observer of me during the three years or so I lived in his house, would express occasional exasperation about my personal life. 'Pinky, really,' he used to say, 'can you not think of another way to get to know someone, aside from sleeping with them?' After about the second or third time he asked that, I said, 'Pops, cut me a break. Doesn't the Bible say when one of those horny old guys gets it on with like his daughters that 'he knew her'? You tell me another way to learn so much about somebody else as quickly.' It starts of course with what they look like naked, which is, if you're me, something always circulating somewhere in my mind. Even better, you learn about that secret person inside them—what they like, where their best spots are, and what they yearn for, which for each person is always a little snowflaky and different. And like I say, once I'm in bed, I stop being baffled by other people. This part I know. And the other person is not just putting up with me or being polite or looking baffled as fuck, but is really happy to be with me, which, more than any particular act, makes me happy too.

With Koob, it's a really good physical fit. His skin is as smooth as it looks, and naturally, he's ripped. I like his pace, and I like his junk. It's got kind of like a mushroom on top that hits the right spot.

Afterwards, he rolls down beside me. We are eye to eye and he's smiling. He runs a hand along my side, from my shoulder down past my waist.

"Tell me about your ink," he says.

"It was kind of a work in progress for years," I say. "You know, I kept adding to it. But now there's not a lot of open acreage left."

"Except here." He touches my breasts.

"Too painful," I say. "I'm really sensitive." I point. "The nipple clamps were torture."

"Any of the tats you have second thoughts about?"

"You mean like having an old boyfriend's name? I mean, I know a woman, she had the word 'Indefensible' tattooed across her belly.

She got pregnant and you couldn't even figure out if they were letters. That wasn't too strategic. She looked good afterwards, but the word was still kind of droopy. But no. All this popping color is kind of out of fashion because supposedly some of it ends up in your liver. Most tattoos now are two-tone. But I still think my tats are awesome. I mean, like when I was younger I'd stare at my skin tone in a mirror and think, I didn't choose this. So why not make it look how I want? Which is what I did. No regrets."

He takes that in.

"And do you ever feel naked?" he asks. "Or is it always like you're wearing something?"

That is a pretty cool question, because I've never even thought of that.

"I don't know," I say. "Maybe that's why there's no ink on the parts of me that most people aren't going to see. So I still feel naked when I'm naked." I hitch a shoulder, like I don't really have a clue. "People do all this shit and never understand themselves. I mean, I always have. When I was younger, it was worse of course. Sometimes I'd do stuff, I'd say stuff, and it was like I was on the outside watching myself, like I'd look at my hands, my arms, and I was there thinking, Whoa, guys, where you going?"

He smiles, on the verge of laughter.

"What about you?" I ask. "You do stuff where you don't have a clue why?"

He shakes his head solemnly.

"Not very often," but then he breaks into that smile. "Maybe now," he says.

"And how's that goin for ya?"

"So far, so good," he says.

"Cool," I say. "And by the way. You asked about my ink. What's this?"

I touch the only tattoo on him, which is on his left breast, over his heart, two arrows crossed over a sword, all of them in gold.

"Service," he says.

"What branch?"

"Army."

He's being coy. But so am I. It's Special Forces. I've seen it before although I could never remember on who. I noticed it, even in the middle of things, and thought to myself, So he *is* American.

"Where'd you serve?"

"Iraq."

"How was that?"

"Hard. Started at Haditha. Lot of searching for HVT."

"High-value targets?"

"Exactly."

"Saddam?"

"I was assigned to the task force. We chased down a convoy as they were trying to escape to Syria. We knew it was a bunch of Ba'athists and ended up in a hellacious firefight with the Syrians. We were sure we had Saddam, but it turned out to be a bunch of his cousins."

"Did you kill anyone?"

He frowns and turns away a bit. "Why does everyone ask that question?"

"Cause we want to know, man. I mean, war, it's like the essential human condition, kill or be killed, and most of us never get there. It seems pretty epic to me. I would have enlisted after high school, but like I told you, I broke my back snowboarding and they said I wouldn't pass the physical. But I was ready for the shooting. At least I thought I was."

"Thought you were. That's how to put it. People shot at me, I shot back. It's just survival."

There's a round scar on his leg.

"That part of it?"

"It was. Usual stupid thing. When you least expect it."

"Was that the end of your tour?"

"They moved me into comms. I would have re-upped if I was still eligible for combat, but it took a long time to get back the use of my leg."

"Is that why you work out so much?"

His head rolls back a bit. "How do you know I work out so much?"

"Dude, you leave here with a gym bag every day."

He shakes his head. "What else have you seen, watching me?"

"I'm seeing what I wanted to see," I say, and touch him gently down there. But he's not ready yet and sits up, looking around.

"Do you want a cigarette?" I ask.

He looks at me suspiciously.

"I see you out on the porch."

I get a very faint smile and an equally calibrated headshake.

"Not sure how it fits in with your workout routine," I add.

"Me neither," he says. "I wonder every time."

"There you go," I say. "Making no sense to yourself. Just open the far window," I say.

I am playing him a little, since I've figured his smoking is purely a cover. Instead, I end up pretty startled when he pulls a pack of Luckies out of a trouser pocket and lights up beside my far window, which doesn't hold an air conditioner. It's one of the first nights where the warmth of the day has lingered, and in the wash of light from the one lamp that is on, I'm disappointed to see several mosquitoes out already, sensing opportunity and smacking themselves into the screen.

I stand up. It's the first time I've been on my feet without my clothes, and Koob turns to look me over without apology. There's a little too much of me here and there, especially waist to knees, but I seem to have his full attention.

"I'm going to get some whiskey," I say. "You want some?"

"Neh. I don't drink."

"Any story with that?"

"You mean did I have a problem?"

"I guess."

"For a while. When I got back."

"Twelve steps?"

"One step: I stopped drinking."

I laugh.

"Go get your whiskey," he says. "It won't bother me." I tell him we could get high instead, but he just shakes his head.

When I return with half an inch in a glass, I sit down on the bed. He's at the window, having a second smoke, and studies me again.

"So tell me what it's like. Being a private investigator. Do you like that better than paralegal?"

"It's an awesome gig, frankly. Like right now, Rik, my boss, he's representing the chief of police. These former officers—well, two are former officers—they're claiming she made these guys have sex with her to get promoted."

That wide smile appears briefly.

"Yeah, kind of saucy," I say. "It's been burning down the Internet. But she didn't do it. Not really."

"'Not really'? How do you do that not really?"

"It's a story. Everybody's got a story, right? She's good people, the Chief. It was just sex, you know? Like, are you trying to get anything else being here? It's big fun. That's all. Right?"

He takes a moment, considering things. The way he moaned,

he better not make out like it was just okay. But instead he says, "Really big fun." He crushes the cigarette on the window ledge, then raises the screen and gives the butt a good toss so that it will end up in the small yard three floors below. Then he comes back to bed.

"Did you have to take a test to become a private investigator?" he asks then.

I explain the whole rigmarole, the training I did and the state exam.

"And do you carry a gun?" he asks.

"Sometimes. Do you?"

"I haven't pulled a trigger since I left the service. I had enough."

"For me, it's basically part of the job. Firearms training is required to get licensed. I have a concealed carry permit." I extend my index finger straight at him: "So watch it."

He covers his heart with both hands.

"And you walk around like that?" he asks. "Armed?"

"You mean was I strapping when I followed you?"

"Were you?"

I wasn't, but I have a feeling for some reason that he wants to hear me say yes, so I do.

"And have you ever had to pull it on someone when you were working?" he asks.

"I've made sure somebody knew it was there once or twice. Like we represented a woman who thought her husband had run her over deliberately in their driveway when he was backing out. He was all like, 'Why would I do that, the mother of my children?' He was a firefighter, and the cops gave him the benefit of the doubt, but we thought he had a girlfriend, and I managed to find him with her, coming out of his buddy's apartment. Man, he was angry, like volcanic, cause, you know, suddenly he sees he's probably going to prison. We were in the parking lot of this complex, and he grabbed a tire iron out of his trunk and started toward me. I just stood my ground and lifted my jacket and put my hand like that." I draw my right hand up under my left shoulder where the holster was.

"Is that where you carry it?"

"Yeah. Another advantage of big boobs."

Koob, who's sprawled on the bed now, hands behind his head, relaxed and naked and looking damned good, gets a kick out of those answers.

I get on my knees to open the gun safe under the bed, and I bring out both my pieces, a Glock 19 and the one I actually prefer to carry, a two-shot Colt derringer that spits out .45 rounds. We lay together, and I let him look them over. And here's the thing: It is way sexy, handling these weapons. We are both in a heat after only a second. I get on top this time, and right before I'm about to settle on him, he asks, "Are you a good shot?"

"Never miss," I say.

Super super hot.

Afterwards, he doesn't wait long to start putting his clothes on. I'm pretty much the same. After I get what I came for, I like to be on my way. I don't want to pretend to feel things I don't. That's why I always prefer to go to the other person's place.

With Koob, I decide to stay in bed and not follow him to the door, which would seem silly or formal. From the threshold to my room, he looks back. I can tell he doesn't know what to say.

"Thanks," I say. "This was great."

"Definitely," he answers.

"You know, come by when you like."

"Sure," he responds and heads out.

But I know he'll be coming back.

16. SHOOTING DAD

"Shooting Dad." By mistake, I put tonight's date with my father on my work calendar, something I don't realize until I'm leaving and Rik teases me about it.

"Jeez," he says, "I thought you and John got along." We have a good laugh.

But Rik is right. My dad and I have always been okay with one another. These days Dad is often numb and out of it, but he always brightens up with me. He doesn't want to talk about his troubles and is just eager to hear about my life, what I'm working on, people I'm seeing, funny stuff I've liked on social media, the shows I've been streaming. Unlike my mom, he even remembers what I tell him.

My brother and sister still say that as kids Dad paid more attention to me because I was a jock, which is no more than half true. I got a lot of his time, but I always felt he was making up for what went on between my mom and me. Still, I always knew he wouldn't turn his back on me, even when there was an uproar at school because I had punched out another kid or sassed my teachers or refused to do any homework. My sibs say we both had the same enemy in Mom, but the truth is Dad usually told me to back off and get out of my mother's face and accept her rules, trying to convince me my life would just be easier that way.

I told him I was sleeping with women a long time before I admitted that to my mother. He's much more conservative than Mom politically. He even voted for Trump the first time and might have done it again if Johnny and Ella, my brother and sister, hadn't said they would fly out from Seattle and superglue his fingers together to keep him from marking the ballot. But when I came out to him, I knew he'd be like, 'Whatever.' I am sure I'm the only queer person he thinks he knows. But the fact is I know my dad loves me. It would just mean so much more if anybody, including me, respected a single fucking thing he says or does.

Pops just sort of clenches his jaw whenever Dad comes up in conversation. Something bad happened between them before I was born, and neither one will say what. My brother and sister have always sort of channeled Mom and largely disregarded my father. By the time they were five or six, they didn't bother asking him whether they could watch TV or visit a friend. When they were going out, they wouldn't even ask him for a ride if there was a chance Mom might be home soon.

As for me, I have always felt kind of sorry for my father. Going back to when I was a little kid, I could tell there was something sad about him. It's like he thought he was a winner and then found out he was a loser. Which pretty much says it like it is. He was this All Mid-Ten tight end, and one of the biggest deals ever on campus at Wisconsin State. He went to rookie camp with the NY Giants, where he learned there were guys even bigger and faster. He's been tobogganing downhill ever since.

Since my childhood, he's had a hard time with work. Before

I came on the scene, he had been doing pretty well. My great-aunt Silvia, Pops's sister, helped him get a job working for her first husband, Dixon, who was this big-time baller on the Kindle County Futures Exchange, but the company more or less collapsed when Dixon died of a heart attack. After that, Dad found several jobs through the Wisconsin State alumni network, until, as he says, people forgot who he was. He's tried a lot of different things along the way. Somebody from State once hired him to sell package tours—a very odd gig for a guy who doesn't really like to travel—and then he got his real estate license, where he was no competition for the barracuda ladies. He hasn't had a full-time job in God knows how long, and went on social security early and is just scraping by. I used to think my mom might still be sending him money, and then a year or so back I realized she had passed the baton. My brother, Johnny, who picks up the phone to call me once a month, was with this startup that sold something to Microsoft. The company got onto the NY Stock Exchange, and now that little fuck, my brother, who has just turned thirty, is actually talking about retiring. I asked him straight up last year if he was supporting Dad, and he kind of avoided an answer, saying he just sends Dad a check now and then. Still. That made me pretty sad.

In the last fifteen years, since Mom kicked him to the curb, my dad has just gone to hell and drinks way too much. He always seems to be waiting to find someone else to tell him what to do, which inevitably turns out to be some rancid woman he's picked up at a bar or yoga class. In very little time, he has developed a completely toxic relationship with her. Twice now he's lost all his furniture when he ran screaming from one of these nutballs' places. When he's by himself, I come over to check on him in his scruffy little apartment to make sure he's not getting all his calories from alcohol. He's put on some weight, but he still works out at home, and for an old guy, he looks pretty good— big with rugged features. That's about the best thing he's got going for him, although at his age, women don't seem to be too picky anyway.

Once every couple months, my dad and I go to the Alamo Shooting Range out in Greenwood County. He grew up in a family of hunters and has always been into handguns, which my mom of course despised. He is very Second Amendment and judges every politician by whether she or he will try to take away his guns. I have the cop attitude, meaning I love guns but I still wish that every moron with money in his pocket couldn't just score one.

I go shooting with my dad for a couple reasons. One, I don't really like meeting him in a bar. He doesn't need another reason to drink, plus he's always looking around to check out the female prospects, which, you know—he's my dad. And second, even pushing sixty-five, he remains a really good marksman. We are both excellent, frankly, and we have contests, talking trash and laughing at each other, making up rules like you don't score unless you hit the other person's bullet hole, with an extra five points for a through and through that barely ruffles the target.

Afterwards, we go to the same dive nearby, which is famous for its burgers. People have always told me that I eat like a trucker, lots of beef and fried food. Most of the women I hang out with are pretty crunchy—even a lot of the dudes, like Koob—but I am definitely craving this burger, although I do hold on the cheese and bacon, so my dad isn't tempted to order his that way. He's not much on willpower.

"So how are you doing with the police chief case?" he asks. He eats like a dog and can't stuff his food in fast enough.

"Okay, I guess. Rik pretty much neutron-bombed the first two witnesses. Seriously. There was nothing left of them but a couple sweaty handprints on the witness stand. We've been thinking the city attorney might even flush the case, but he says he can't, because people will think the mayor pressured him to do it. The last big witness is next week, but we have a lot of good stuff on him, too."

"And what about your weird neighbor? Did you ever figure out anything more about him?"

"Oh, that got even weirder."

"How's that?"

"I'm kind of seeing him."

Dad draws back. Like I said, he's not much for disapproval, and over the years he's heard it all, so it tickles me when he comes on like a dad with this wary look.

"How did that happen?" he asks.

"Well, you know, Dad. Birds and bees. Besides, I think I kinda wanted it to."

"Yeah," he says. "That crossed my mind. So I assume he's not a spy."

"Beats me."

Dad eyes me as he takes a sip of his diet drink.

"Well, does he have spy equipment in his apartment?"

"I'm almost sure he does, but I've never gotten through the door. He's only been in my place."

"Okay, but what's he say he does to make a living?"

"Not much. 'Computers,' whatever that means. He gets pretty salty when I try to go there. Like I saw him last night and he just finally came out with, 'How about we do not talk about work—not yours, not mine. No questions either way.'" I amuse myself because I've gotten Koob's inflection down almost perfectly. But Dad still looks confused.

"Do you talk at all?"

"Sure. But it's odd stuff. You know, life in general. He's got kids. He misses his kids."

"Kids?" Dad asks slowly. "He's married?"

"Divorced. Or getting divorced."

"And you still think he could be some kind of federal agent working undercover?"

"I really don't know." I've asked myself if an FBI agent on assignment would start sleeping with the next-door neighbor, and frankly, I think those people are probably like everybody else and forget the rules now and then when it comes to sex.

"Well, do you like him?"

"Definitely."

"Why?"

"Well, you know, he's kind of intriguing. Smart. Kind of wry. He just feels like a really good person. But not needy or controlling. There's plenty of space. I like his vibe."

Needless to say, my dad is not the person I'm going to take advice from. If you want to know what is wrong with relationships in a couple words, you can look at my parents. Most of my life they were both gritting their teeth, and then once I graduated from high school, my mom just had enough. It couldn't have been much of a surprise to him, since sometimes a week passed without them even speaking a word to one another. But it killed him anyway, especially since she hooked up with Miguel in about five minutes. Miguel, who Mom insists I refer to as 'my stepfather,' is this ultrarich Spanish guy who is getting close to eighty. They seem to have gotten into classical music together and live more than half the year in Scottsdale, where they go to a lot of outdoor concerts. My mom likes to say that by moving to Arizona, she split the distance between her children, but the truth is that while she makes frequent trips to Seattle, she returns to Kindle County only every few months, and mostly to see Pops and my aunt Marta. She and I both take it as progress that we can now get through a kind of stilted lunch together.

As for Dad and her, even though they didn't have a good thing going, it was better than the alternative, the way he looked at it, which he's more or less proved since with all these women he seems to have found in a septic tank. Overall, my mom and dad had 0 in common. For years, I could never figure out how they even got together back in high school. I was in my twenties and walking down the street one day when it hit me out of nowhere like a missile: Sex. He was huge and good-looking, and she was this china-doll beauty, and the heat must have been something else. Then add on top of that the fact that both families hated the relationship, which probably cemented them together.

A friend of mine who immigrated from Poland taught me a Polish saying that translates as 'Sometimes families only look good in pictures.' Knowing my mom, it was probably a big plus to her for a long time that my dad and her made a gorgeous couple. They were on like the cover of the Wisconsin State alumni magazine twice, and in the suburban section of the *Tribune*. On his side, of course, it was always clear that she would inherit buttloads of money from her mother. But mostly, I think he liked how much smarter than him she was.

Sometimes, over the years, my parents have talked to me about memories from when they were together. For example, my grandmother—Clara, the one I'm named for—sent them to Italy for their honeymoon as a wedding gift, and now and then one of them will tell me something they remember from that trip. And it just knocks me out that it's never the same thing. She goes on about the view from the terrace of their hotel, and he talks about great runs he took. She remembers how dressed up the women were on the Via Veneto and eating these amazing fried artichokes, while he—this is true—says he got really tired of not being able to get anything but Italian food. Maybe any two people would be like that, different impressions and memories, but it seems to say a lot that they were living such separate lives inside their heads from the start.

I hug him goodbye tonight and we head off, both of us more or less happy to have been together.

"Phone me about what happened when your hearing is over next week," he calls. When I slide into the Cadillac, I'm as close to crying as I ever come, because it just seems completely terrible that the most exciting thing in his life is me.

17. FRITO

Fabian Blanco was called Fito at home. His white schoolmates, being mean or ignorant or just kids, turned that into 'Frito,' and I guess it tells you a little about Blanco that he accepted it. Anyway, that's still what he is called around the Highland Isle Central Station. Frito is a little chubby and is probably headed for a shape like Rik's or Pops's in the years ahead, but on the stand, sitting forward in his chair with his hands folded on the blond rail, he has the polish of a TV game show host: calm, good-natured and a little glib. He's got beautiful glossy black hair, parted on the side, and the sweet round face of a child. After he was sworn, he smiled at his pretty little wife, who came in with him and is seated in the front row. Clearly, she's here to show that she totally accepts her husband's story that he was extorted by the Chief, and that all has been forgiven as a result.

Headed to court, Rik was tense. He's this close to the biggest win of his legal career and is desperate not to blow it. Yet the truth is, we have caught Blanco in a supersized lie, claiming that he went to the Chief's house with her one afternoon in November 2021 for some porn-movie sex, not long before he was promoted to lieutenant. I asked Dorcas to back me up and double-check the video from the Chief's, and neither one of us has found a single frame of Blanco during the entire fall so much as waving howdy from the sidewalk.

Despite that, maybe just to psych himself, Rik has been telling the Chief and me that Blanco will still be a tough witness. No question, he'll look better than the two lying lunkheads the Ritz sent here already. And I admit that none of us can really explain why a good cop would come in and perjure himself, as Frito is about to do. Despite a lot of hunting, I have not identified a connection between him and Vojczek—I can't find anybody who's even seen the two of them together. The Chief admits she's never had an angry word with Blanco. And he's totally God Squad, a superserious Catholic who takes no part in the raunchy back-and-forth that's routine in the station. In fact, she says that Blanco shuts that stuff out so completely that she was amazed he understood enough to make up all the kinky shit he's claimed went on between them. On top of all that, over the years the Chief's added dozens of positive comments to Blanco's performance reviews that make him sound like maybe the most dedicated cop since McGruff the Crime Dog.

I'm sure in many ways Blanco reminds the Chief of herself. Also from an immigrant family, he is a former altar boy and Eagle Scout, a straight-A student in high school who immediately after graduation enlisted in the Marines and did a tour in Afghanistan. When he returned, he worked the midnight shift in a FedEx sorting station, going to classes on the GI Bill during the days and finishing his BA at the U in three years. He is one of those guys who said his whole life that he wanted to be in law enforcement and applied in HI because Kindle County, where he grew up, was going through one of its periodic hiring freezes. On the job, he was an instant superstar, with the highest clearance rate in the department both as a patrolman and as a detective. In the meantime, he used his nights to finish a master's in police science. He has three kids, a solid marriage, and attends Mass every Sunday with his wife and their entire family—brother, sisters and all four parents. He's never been seen at the Saloon.

Rik is also concerned by the fact that Blanco's promotion to lieutenant late last year did not go by the book. He had become a sergeant only eighteen months before the Chief encouraged him to take the lieutenant's exam. She says that was in response to the mayor's office more or less demanding that she make the command staff more diverse. Lucia Gomez-Barrera was the only BIPOC member of the brass, along with four white men. When Commander Leery, who got the job when Lucy moved up to chief—when Leery retired, the other senior officers were each elevated a rank. That created an opening at lieutenant that Lucy wanted Frito to fill. To do that though, Blanco would have to jump the rank of master sergeant. The Chief regarded that as a technicality. The master sergeants got $500 more a year but had the exact same duties as the other sergeants. Still, nobody on the HIPD had ever made lieutenant without being a master sergeant first. Because of that, P&F was reluctant, and the Chief admits she had to work them for a while to get Blanco the appointment. They will all remember that without being reminded by testimony, which Marc will introduce anyway.

Lucy has said several times that when her days as Chief end—assuming she gets to leave the job voluntarily—the leading internal candidate to replace her will be Blanco. That is as close as Rik will come to developing a motive for Blanco to cook all this up.

In final argument, he'll claim that Blanco, knowing that DeGrassi and Cornish were going to do the Chief dirty, decided to pile on, bettering the chance of a vacancy at the top he'd be a natural to fill. But the Chief has warned us that Blanco won't come off as a schemer, so this could be a pretty hard sell.

Blanco's testimony goes exactly as expected to start, covering his background and his rise in the department. He admits that he was excited when the Chief asked him to apply for lieutenant. And it appeared that P&F was getting ready to accept the promotion when, shortly before Thanksgiving, Lucy called Frito into her office and told him she wanted him to come home with her and party one night that week. Stunned and utterly confused, he told her no thanks, hoping it was just some half-baked romantic overture, but she quickly set him straight. If that was his choice, she supposedly said, he would never get beyond the rank of sergeant and would be permanently assigned to the midnight to 8 a.m. shift, with a lot of weekends thrown in. The Chief told him to think it over.

When he did, he could see she had him completely boxed. If he refused, he'd become an absentee father while his career remained on permanent spin cycle. If he quit and tried to catch on in another department, the Chief would trash him when they called her for a reference.

For a day or two, Blanco considered whether he could turn over on the Chief, but he realized no one would believe him. She'd already told him, supposedly, that she'd claim he was the one who'd come on to her, saying that explained why she did a one-eighty on his promotion. Blanco says he agonized another day about breaking his vows to his wife but ultimately decided that his choice was between being a bad husband for a night or a bad father for years.

"Did you tell her yes, then?" Marc Hess asks. He looks more confident than I'd expect, given the clubbing his witnesses got in the prior sessions.

"I did."

"Where?"

"In her office in the station."

"And how did she respond?"

"She got this kind of superior smile and said she knew I'd come around. And then she told me to get down on my knees and—" His eyes sink to the carpeting. "She wanted me to give her oral pleasure," he says.

This is completely new. Rik gives me a look like, 'Can you believe this shit?' smiling faintly. It will be easy to gut Blanco on this point, since he mentioned nothing like this in his prior statement.

"Right there in her office?" Marc asks.

"Yes, sir."

"And did you?"

"I hoped if I did it, that would be the end of it."

But it wasn't. They went from her office to the Chief's home, where, in his state of torment, he couldn't get it up. After about an hour of trying to talk sense to his dick, she said she'd be the man and pegged him. (When Lucy read that part of the complaint in our office, she laughed out loud, saying that she wouldn't know how to mount a strap-on without watching several YouTube videos. Rik and her didn't find it funny when I offered to demonstrate.)

Blanco says he was so traumatized by these events, he decided nothing could be worse. He went to the Chief and told her that if she ever approached him again, he'd go straight to the mayor. For whatever reason, his promotion went through. Since then, his dealings with the Chief in the station are as if the sexual insanity had never happened.

After Marc tenders Blanco for cross, Rik asks for a five-minute break. He chats with the Chief for a minute, who is pretty bubbly. Blanco has sort of tightroped out over the abyss on a really shaky wire. But as soon as she departs for the Ladies, Rik turns a dark face toward me and shepherds me to the far corner of the court-room behind the bench and next to the wooden staffs that hold the US, State and Highland Isle flags.

"I don't understand this," he whispers. "Marc's not Johnnie Cochran but he knows better than to let this guy make something up at the last minute like that goofy story about oral sex."

"Well, what's Marc supposed to do if Blanco shows up talking crazy?"

"Marc can't tell him to lie, but he didn't need to ask the questions to bring that crap out. He elicited that deliberately." Rik takes a long pause, chewing on his lower lip while he thinks, biting it so hard I'm afraid he may draw blood. By now, we've entered Rik's sweating season, where the change in humidity keeps him dripping whether he's inside or out. As usual, the perspiration sits in glistening little half domes across his brow and on his scalp, and with his jacket open, I can see the dark circles under his armpits.

Looking at him, I have one of those occasional moments that make my heart stall out with panic, because it seems like I am growing up, whether I want to or not. I have two kind of revelations that are as clear as a trumpet blast. Number one is Rik's in the wrong line of work. A guy who stresses this much in court is going to blow out his fuses pretty soon. He needs to find something else to do—house closings or regulatory filings. Which means that the notoriety and the accompanying burst of

business that the Chief's case is bringing through the door may
end up killing him.

That brings on revelation number two: People's big dreams
for themselves often are erected on the total fantasy that they are
going to turn into someone else.

"There are two possibilities here," Rik tells me. "One is very
good and one is very bad."

"Okay. What's bad?"

"The bad one is that Marc knows something big that we don't.
But that would mean Marc shorted us in discovery, and I can't
imagine him doing that."

"So that leaves the good one, right?"

"I guess."

"And what's the good one?"

"The good one is that when Blanco decided to start telling a
new story, Marc said to himself, 'Okay, you want to spin lies like
the first two guys, knock yourself out. When you get cut up like a
cadaver on cross, nobody will be able to ask why, or accuse me of
political motivations when we dismiss the case.'"

"That sounds right to me."

Rik is clearly not convinced, but the Rev comes out of the
door directly behind the bench and we quickly push our way out
from between the flags—all of them with the stiff feel of rayon—
to return to our seats.

Rik goes for the kill as soon as the hearing resumes.

"Now, you told Mr. Hess on your direct examination about
the Chief taking you to her house to perform various sex acts, is
that right?"

"To her home, yes."

Rik approaches him with the same photo he used with DeGrassi.

"And when you went to the Chief's house at 1412 Summit,

shown here in Respondent's Exhibit 4, did you notice these security cameras?"

"I've heard about them recently. I've never seen them."

"Does it surprise you to learn, Lieutenant, that there are no images of you at any time in late 2021 coming or going from 1412 Summit?"

"No," he says. "But there's a reason for that."

"You had taken an invisibility potion?"

The laughter rockets off the walls of the small courtroom. I even see the Rev draw a hand to his face to mask his smirk. Marc stands up to object and Rik withdraws the question.

Blanco then says, "As I said, there's a reason for that."

I saw Pops at this point many times, badly jamming up a witness who then thought they'd come up with some smart-ass way to sidestep the problem. Pops just wouldn't play. He'd raise a hand and smile patiently and say, 'I'll let opposing counsel ask you for the reason. I imagine I shall have some questions after that.' It was like saying, 'No one needs to be in a hurry to hear your bullshit.' He basically dismissed the explanation as worthless before the witness offered it.

Rik is a good lawyer, but he's not the equal of Pops, who sort of took over the courtroom the way a conductor commands a concert hall. Blanco manages to get out, "This place in your pictures, that wasn't where she took me. I thought she lived in an apartment."

Rik comes to our table. I'm ready and hand him the sworn statement from Blanco that accompanied the complaint in the case.

Rik goes through the foundational questioning, then asks, "Didn't you use the word 'house' in this statement you gave under oath?"

"Well, house, yeah, meaning where she lived. I didn't mean an actual house house. She lived in an apartment. It was nice, too."

Up on the bench, Mrs. L is nudging a document toward the Reverend, which has got to be Blanco's sworn declaration.

"And where was this apartment?"

"On the east side somewhere."

"'Somewhere?' You've been a police officer in Highland Isle for fourteen years now. Are you telling us that there's so much as a block in this city you don't recognize?"

"Normally. But I was shook, Mr. Dudek. I mean, I was on my way to hell, as far as I was concerned. I probably couldn't have told you my name at that point. I can go out and look around if it would help."

Rik stares down Blanco, who's made this offer with a straight face.

"Maybe she borrowed somebody's place," Blanco volunteers, unruffled by Rik's stink eye. "Where do her daughters live?"

Rik moves to strike that remark, which is granted. But Frito's done his homework. The Chief's older daughter lives in town. It's obvious now. Blanco came to court ready to rumble.

"And aren't there security concerns about the Chief's house? Concerns that have been borne out from time to time that she could be the target of vandals or confronted by unhappy arrestees?"

"I suppose that's true."

"You 'suppose'? As a patrol officer, were you assigned in earlier years to the Central District that includes 1412 Summit?"

"Years ago, yeah."

"And you're telling this commission that even though you patrolled that area regularly, no one ever pointed out the Chief's house as a place to pay attention to?"

Blanco looks up and sighs. "Now that you say that, I think it's true. But I had no memory of it. That had to be maybe ten years before this thing happened with the Chief."

"And did you tell Mr. Hess about this apartment?"

"Yes."

Rik is getting very wary, and visibly taking time to think.

"When was that?"

"He called me right after the last hearing session and told me that there weren't any videos of me at 1412 Summit, and I explained right then that I'd gone with her to an apartment."

"But you didn't mention this on your direct?"

"Mr. Hess told me you were going to ask about it."

Marc at this point raises his head like a dog that's just heard his name and looks straight at Rik. There's just a vapor of a smile that's gone almost before I can see it. He might as well have said, 'Fuck you, Smarty Pants. How you likin trial by ambush now?'

Rik comes back to the defense table. He whispers to me, "Now what?" I don't get it, and when I look at him blankly, Rik murmurs, "Marc's getting even with us. There's probably more."

"You can't sit down, Boss. The Chief might as well resign."

He gives a quick nod. He's too shell-shocked to have gotten that far ahead in his thinking. He adjusts his suit coat as he turns to face Blanco again, like he's changing out of his dirtied uniform.

"Now, prior to going to the Chief's 'house,' you claim you and she engaged in certain sex acts in her office."

"Yes."

"Did you mention this interlude in the Chief's office in the written statement that you gave the commission in March of this year?"

"No, but there's a reason."

"Please answer my questions. Did you understand when you first talked to Mr. Hess and prepared this statement to the commission, did you understand that you were supposed to include all significant information?"

"Of course."

"And did you also understand that in the big picture the proceeding that would result from your statement would be aimed at determining Chief Gomez's fitness to serve as Chief?"

"I wasn't trying to get her fired, if that's what you mean."

"What I mean is that you understood that the Chief forcing you to have sex in her office would be highly significant in a proceeding to determine her fitness to serve? Yes?"

"Yeah, I thought about that. But I was too embarrassed to mention it."

"You weren't too embarrassed to mention being anally penetrated by a sex toy, but you were too embarrassed to talk about oral sex?"

"I was too embarrassed to show the picture," says Blanco.

Rik suddenly might as well be a dead man. He can't move. I don't even see any sign he's breathing.

At that point, Marc stands up with a manila folder in his hand and opens it to Rik, who stares for several seconds and then does something I don't expect. He screams.

"This is an outrage!" It's truly the loudest I've ever heard him in court. Even he's shocked by the way he's bellowed. He takes a breath, then asks to be heard at the sidebar. But the courtroom is so small, the commissioners decide to ask Blanco to wait outside while the two lawyers move up to the bench. Rik is going at high speed as soon as Blanco closes the door.

"Mr. Hess apparently wants to introduce some kind of bogus photographic evidence that is highly prejudicial and clearly should have been produced to the respondent as discovery the minute Mr. Hess received it."

"It's cross-examination," says Marc, almost sweetly. You can just see that he's been sharpening this knife for days, lying awake at night and smiling, as he thinks about using that line, the one he heard from Rik when we first showed the video of Primo and the Chief.

I steal a glance at Lucy to see how she's doing, and I can't read her response. She's sitting back with one finger over her lips, pondering. But her posture seems odd to me. I would have thought, given what she's said to us before, that she'd be on the edge of her chair, trying to keep herself from springing up to yell, 'Bullshit!'

"This is below you, Marc," Rik says to him. "It is one thing for an advocate to hold back evidence that *contradicts* an opposing witness's testimony, because the lawyer has no obligation to assume the witness will lie. But it's quite another for the prosecutor to withhold a photograph that he knows is going to *support* his witness and spring it as a surprise. Mr. Hess orchestrated things so I had to cross-examine Mr. Blanco about this incident in the Chief's office, which the lieutenant had never mentioned before. And by withholding the photograph until cross, Mr. Hess is trying to avoid the objections he knew I'd make if this photo had been produced earlier, as it should have been. He realized I would have asked to postpone this session so I had time to consult with my client, and more important, to fully investigate the origins of what looks to me to be some kind of Photoshop production."

Marc, with a snarky little smile, offers his folder with the photo to the Reverend.

He says, "Perhaps the commissioners—" but gets no further

because Rik lurches at Marc and uses two hands to slam Hess's arm down.

Rik bellows again.

"*No, no!* I *demand* that this surprise evidence not be published to the commission, which will place it in the public record, until I have had a complete opportunity to investigate it. If the commission allows this surprise evidence to be received during my cross, you will be rewarding a monumental discovery violation. This is contemptible behavior. And I'll tell the commission and I'll tell Mr. Hess—there is going to be a complaint to Bar Admissions and Discipline. My client's future is at stake, and you can see from the expression on Mr. Hess's face that he thinks he's involved in a fraternity prank. In fact, given the magnitude of this discovery violation, the commission should just bar this evidence right now. That's my motion: Bar the photo. And any reference to it or the imaginary incident that it purportedly reflects."

The mention of a complaint to Bar Admissions and Discipline has changed Marc's demeanor. He seems to have wilted a bit and become far more sober.

"Now just a minute. I won't object to a recess. I do object to barring the evidence. Especially if the commission has no opportunity to see it."

The Reverend predictably looks at his watch. "We have time for another hour of testimony," he says, largely to himself. Mrs. Langenhalter is holding the Rev's arm, and the Reverend, clearly piqued by how out of control the hearing has suddenly become, motions to the lawyers in front of him with the back of his hand. "Step back. Step back. Let us talk about this amongst ourselves."

Rik returns to the table. He still has the folder Marc gave him, and I try to take it.

"I don't think Lucy should have to look at this right now," he says, but I realize that what concerns him is whatever her reaction might reveal in a courtroom still full of spectators and reporters. Instead, Rik pretends to scratch his nose and, with his hand obscuring his face from anyone else, he mouths to me, "Bad, bad, bad."

18. THE COMMISSIONERS CONFER

To confer, the commissioners turn their chairs fully about so their backs are to the courtroom, each hunching down to bring their heads together. In the interval, Marc comes over to our table.

"Maybe I got carried away," he says. He's looking very tentative, his hands raised in front of himself for no clear reason. It's pretty obvious that he wants to know if Rik is actually going to beef on him to Bar Admissions and Discipline.

"Get out of here," Rik answers, but of course he can't stop there. "Marc, let me tell you something. You should have talked to a real prosecutor to figure out how to handle something like this when it comes up in the middle of trial." The 'real prosecutor' remark is one that Rik knows will sting, because Marc is sensitive about his relative lack of courtroom experience.

"Well, just a second," Marc says. "I know the rules."

"The hell you do. If you even bothered to glance at them, you wouldn't have done it like this. And by the way, forget *me* doing an investigation. Did it even cross your mind that *you* should do a forensic examination to determine the bona fides of this piece of shit?"

Marc's lips revolve through several unhappy motions and end up in a little pout.

"Blanco's very convincing about this," Hess says. "You'll see."

"Convincing to who? Marc, you've never understood what is going on here."

"Is this your fantasy about Moritz Vojczek? Who has nothing to do with anything?"

"Marc, riddle me this. Ritz's right-hand man and his left-hand man show up to tell a bunch of absolute lies about my client, and you think that's just a coincidence?"

"Half our officers have worked for Vojczek at some point."

"Allow me to share something you learn practicing criminal law: There are a lot of mean, rotten people in the world. In this city, there are all kinds of folks who want to get rid of Amity and Lucy, both of them, because they are standing in the way of something nasty those people want to do. I'll be damned if I know what. But I'm sure Vojczek is one of them. And somebody else, God knows who, got Blanco in a hammerlock. But look at this from a distance, Marc. Your case is circling the drain and, like a miracle, Blanco shows up suddenly talking about an incident you never heard about, with a picture you've never seen. And instead of realizing this is all too good to be true, you buy the bridge he's selling and say, 'Super, now I can get even with my buddy Rik for pulling a fast one on me with DeGrassi.' With no thought to your basic obligation to be fair to Lucy.

"Marc, maybe a while from now, a week or a year, I'll go back to considering you a friend. But I tell you this sincerely—this case has gotten way, way, way out of your league. These jerks are taking you for a ride and you think you're in an amusement park."

About halfway through this rant, Marc's patience appeared to be wearing thin. His mouth is fixed harshly.

"Listen to you," he says. "*I* don't get it? Remember William of Occam? The simplest explanation is usually true. I know you and Lucy were pals in high school, and I grant you that she's a nice person and a good police chief. But power corrupts. And she's turned her officers into her pool boys. And you don't like seeing it in living color."

Marc walks away then with a disdainful toss of his hand.

The members of the commission have turned back around, and the Reverend taps the microphone stalk in front of him. Rik has remained on his feet.

"Okay, so we've talked about this amongst ourselves. Mr. Dudek, we've heard your objections, and this photo won't be admitted in evidence or published to the members of the commission until you've had a chance to consult with your client and do the tests you think need to be performed. But we have a lot of folks here who have given up their evening on a Monday night, and I hate to waste the time they've given us. So what we'd like you to do is to resume your cross-examination—"

"Reverend," says Rik.

"I understand, after you've investigated, you may have many other questions for Lieutenant Blanco. Our ruling will be without prejudice to your right to suspend your cross. But let's make some use of the time we have. All right? Mr. Hess, please bring Lieutenant Blanco back in."

Blanco returns with the same solid air, appearing unaffected by the eruption that followed his testimony about the photo.

Facing Frito, Rik sweeps his suit coat back and puts his hand on his hip.

"All right, Lieutenant Blanco, tell us your story about how this photograph allegedly got taken."

Blanco passes a second absorbing Rik's tone of naked disrespect.

"Well, you know, once I was on my knees, before she, you know, made me get started, she shifted her desk chair so she could watch in the mirror on the back of her door. And while she was moving around, I kind of snuck my phone out of my back pocket and held it at my side. I used my thumb to swipe left to open the camera. Then I shifted my grip and held down the shutter button so it took like two hundred photos. I was just hoping it was aimed in the right direction. But you know, I got lucky. That one was the best. I printed it out and brought it to the Chief, and I told her that if she even hinted at more of this stuff, I'd go straight to the mayor with the picture. Then I put that photograph in the locked drawer I have at home for police files I work on there, and deleted all the images from my phone. I didn't want to take the chance that I'd be showing photos of my kids and swipe the wrong way and there's, you know, the Chief with my head— Well, you can see for yourself."

Rik stands there, seeming to think while he processes what Blanco just described. In the meantime, Frito says, "Can I explain why I didn't want to talk about this—the oral sex?"

"You mean give us the explanation that you and Mr. Hess cooked up in his office? I don't think so. You can wait for Mr. Hess's redirect."

The Reverend interrupts. "It's your cross-examination, Mr. Dudek, but if you can indulge us, I think the question of why Lieutenant Blanco never mentioned this— I think that's important. So I'd prefer that the commission hear that now."

Rik flaps a hand like the useless wing of a dodo. It's futile to object, and his gesture implies that the whole session has been a complete hosing.

I understand the boss's frustrations, but overall, I have the feeling that after the Rev's years of dealing with Lucy, he definitely likes her, and up to now has kind of been on our side. He is sometimes a giant pain, especially when he's trying to squeeze the most out of every minute. But generally, I've been impressed by what an orderly, sane guy the Reverend is, which I didn't expect given the way he winds himself up when he's preaching. But in this role, he has a kind of measured demeanor, with his shiny scalp and big cufflinks and his old suits, carefully pressed.

Blanco again folds his hands in front of him as he begins his explanation.

"Well, basically, I decided before I talked to Mr. Hess the very first time, that I wasn't going to mention this incident, because I knew that sooner or later, if I answered questions honestly, you know, about everything that happened, I'd get to the photograph. And I didn't want to have to show it here in court. This whole thing, you know, it's been a horror movie for Marisel, my wife. To have to listen, it's got to be really really hard. But to see pictures?" Blanco, like a lot of people around here, says 'pitchers.' "It's taken a long time to get over this. As a couple. If she saw the photo—and I knew she'd have to look, no one could not look— we were just going to go backwards for a long time.

"So the first reason was my wife. And that was the main reason. But I also thought about the Chief. Leaving this whole crazy thing aside, she's been an outstanding boss. And I mean, that's a pretty revealing picture. And you can see that she's forcing me, with the—"

Rik raises a hand. "No descriptions of the photo, please, Lieutenant Blanco, until the commission has decided it can be admitted in evidence."

Blanco bobs his head in agreement.

"Right. I'm sorry. I'm sure that having all of this come out in the open, it's got to be devastating for her. But that photo is bound to make it ten times worse. So that's why I didn't mention this. And that's the truth, okay?

"But once the stuff came up about the surveillance video at the Chief's house— Well, frankly, given what I heard about Cornish and DeGrassi's testimony, I knew I'd be grouped with them and regarded as a liar. But those guys, they're retired. I'm still serving. And if a court or a commission finds you've lied under oath, that's the end, you know, you can never get on a witness stand again. My career would be over. So that's why I was forced to bring in the photograph. To prove I'm telling the truth about the whole story."

As Marc said, Blanco is pretty convincing. But it's obvious from Rik's posture that there's one person here who's not buying a word. He's listened to Blanco's little soliloquy with a kind of sick smile, except the part about sparing the Chief, where Rik literally covered his eyes and gripped his forehead in complete disgust.

"Okay," says Rik. "Let's get it all out on the table. What other surprises did you and Mr. Hess plan for me on cross?"

Marc objects, and the Reverend quickly motions him back to his seat.

"The ring, I guess," says Blanco.

"The ring?"

"Well, I know you haven't spent a long time looking at that picture, Mr. Dudek, but you know, when you do, you'll see that one of my hands is on the Chief's breast—"

Both of Rik's hands shoot up, but the Reverend speaks first.

"Enough, Lieutenant," says the Rev. "We don't want any descriptions of the activities shown in that photograph."

"Okay," says Blanco. He nods obediently again, as if he didn't understand before. "But, well, whatever is going on, you can see I'm wearing a big gold class ring. Which I brought with me."

He reaches into his jacket pocket and holds it up. There's a round red stone at the center.

"It's a class ring from St. Viator's in 1974," he says. "It was my uncle's. He died in Vietnam, during the fall of Saigon in 1975. And, you know, we were close, and he left me that ring."

"Which you happened to be wearing that day with the Chief?"

"Exactly."

"And so, you were going to wait for me to say, 'You're not wearing that ring now,' at which time you'd pull it out of your pocket, right? That was the plan with Mr. Hess. Correct?"

"Well, we weren't sure you'd ask, to tell you the truth. If you didn't, Mr. Hess was going to bring it up when it was his chance to ask questions again."

"He was saving the ring for redirect?"

"Right."

Rik stares at Marc, who refuses to look up. In the meantime, Mrs. Blanco hurries from the courtroom. Her face is rigid. She must have known this was coming, but apparently, it's like her husband said—the idea of the photo and what it shows is too much. Blanco lifts his face to watch his wife's departure with obvious concern. But Rik has never taken his eyes off Frito, studying him with an intensity that makes it seem he is almost trying to look inside the man. Rik doesn't seem anxious anymore. He's just fucking mad.

"Okay," Rik says. "Put it on."

"Huh?" answers Blanco.

"Please put the ring on, sir."

Blanco lifts his right hand and slides it onto his pinky finger, holding the hand aloft for a moment.

Rik opens the folder with the picture in it and actually smiles.

"Nice try, Lieutenant. The ring is on your left hand in the picture, isn't it?"

"I guess."

"And on your ring finger, not the little finger, correct?"

Blanco doesn't answer. It's the first time he's been lost for words since his testimony started.

"Do I take it that you're right-handed?"

"Yes."

"So if you manipulated your cell phone to take these pictures, you would have done it with your right hand, correct?"

"Well, I did do it with my right hand."

"Which isn't actually in the photograph, correct? It's outside the frame?"

"Well, I don't know how else you think this photograph got taken, Mr. Dudek."

"What I think, since you mention it, Lieutenant, is that this photo was completely manufactured."

Marc stands to object, and the Reverend tells Rik to get on with his examination.

"Happy to," answers Rik, and walks right up to Blanco. "Okay, Lieutenant. Lift your hand so we all can see, and put the ring on your left ring finger."

Blanco slowly raises his hand in the air. I—and probably everybody else—immediately notice his wedding band on that finger. Rik sees the same thing.

"Do you wear that wedding ring every day, Lieutenant?"

"Usually," he says. "But, you know. I didn't want to wear it that day, you know, if I was going to be with the Chief."

"Okay, so please take off your wedding band and put on that ring you brought with you today to corroborate your testimony."

Blanco looks at his hand and laughs meekly.

"You know, I don't even think it will fit anymore. I've gained a lot of weight this year. Especially once all this hit the fan. I'm kind of a stress eater."

"No kidding," says Rik coldly. "Put it on, please, Lieutenant."

It's a huge effort for Blanco to get his wedding ring off. He finally sticks his finger in his mouth and pulls so hard that the gold band flies from his hand and ends up at Rik's feet. Rik picks it up and says, "I'll just hold this for you. Let's put on the class ring."

"It won't fit," says Blanco. "Like I said. You can see with my wedding band how much weight I've gained."

"What I want to see is that ring on your left ring finger."

Blanco, of course, can't get it over his knuckle.

"Is that where you customarily gain weight, Lieutenant? In your joints?"

There is quite a bit of laughter. Blanco doesn't answer.

"That ring has never fit on your hand, has it?" Rik asks.

"I had it on. You can see that," Blanco answers.

"What I see," says Rik, "is that the ring doesn't fit you."

Marc objects to Rik saying what he sees.

"We can all see," says the Reverend.

Rik circles back to our table, thinking about what he wants to ask next.

"All right, this photo you've brought to court. You deleted everything but this image from your cell phone?"

"No. I printed out that photo and showed it to the Chief. Then I deleted all the images from my phone and kept that one printed photograph under lock and key."

"And this"—Rik holds up the folder—"this is the photo that you showed the Chief?"

"That's what I showed her."

"So if we do ink testing on it, we'll find that the toner was manufactured last year? Since you say all this happened in November?"

Blanco pauses. Ink testing is used now and then in the kinds of white-collar cases Pops handled in federal court, where documents are central, but I'll bet Blanco knows next to nothing about it, including how often toner formulas are changed. Rik may not either, but in his aggressive mood, he's a convincing fake.

"Well, actually," says Blanco, with the same phony bashful smile, "when I decided to show the photo to Mr. Hess last week, I took pictures of it beforehand and printed out several copies. I can show you on my phone." Blanco reaches into his jacket pocket and removes his cell phone.

"We'll get to your phone," says Rik. "But where is the original photo that you showed the Chief?"

"I don't know," says Blanco. "I brought it with the copies to show Mr. Hess."

"Mr. Hess," says Rik, "can you give us the original?"

Marc has already straightened up, clearly caught unaware by Blanco. Now he opens his own file folder and peers into it. Finally, he says, "I wasn't aware that there was a difference between the prints that I received. I'll have to look more closely when I get back to the office."

"Can I ask the commission to order Mr. Hess to forthwith produce the original photograph that Mr. Blanco has testified about, so that we may perform ink tests on it?"

Marc looks back at Rik. "You don't need to order me to do anything. I understand my obligations."

"Now you do," says Rik.

"Okay, gentlemen," says the Reverend. "Enough squabbling. Please get the original to Mr. Dudek tomorrow morning, Mr. Hess."

"You know," says Blanco. "Maybe I kept the original. I'll have to look, too."

"Same order please as to Lieutenant Blanco," says Rik.

"If I can find it," he answers. "I printed a lot of copies of the photo before I got it right. And then, you know, I couldn't just leave something like that laying around. So I shredded the rest. And maybe I shredded the original, too, by accident. I mean, I'm not saying that's what happened, but it's possible. You know, theoretically."

"So you decided to produce this evidence because it was the only way to support your credibility and keep your career from being roadblocked—and then you threw out the original?"

"I didn't say that happened. Just that it's possible. I'll try to find it."

Frito now seems like a weak imitation of the person who originally took the stand. His hands are flying around as he explains himself, and he won't stop licking his lips.

"And if he can't, I'll be asking to strike Mr. Blanco's testimony," says Rik.

The Reverend just waves a hand. He doesn't need the theatrics in advance.

"Now, you had your cell phone in your hand a minute ago, Lieutenant," Rik says. "Would you mind unlocking it?"

Blanco is quick to do that. "The photograph is right here."

"That's the photo of the photo, right?"

"I guess, yes."

"Would you mind navigating to the About panel in your settings? What model is that phone?"

"A model VI." He pronounces it as people do, using the letter names, rather than the roman numerals: 'Vee Eye.'

"Pretty old, right?"

"Sure. We have three kids, and you know about a police officer's salary, Mr. Dudek. I can't be buying a new cell phone every year like some people."

He must have noticed Rik with his model XVA. Rik always wants the new new thing. As soon as the next version comes out, he dashes to the store to get it. After that, for days I can look into his office and see him staring at the device, baffled about how to operate all the dazzling new features.

"Okay, Lieutenant, lock your phone again, then please show us how you did that one-handed maneuver to take that picture." Rik repeats Frito's complicated description—swiping left to open the camera and then keeping a finger on the shutter button—asking Blanco to confirm his prior testimony, which he does.

"All right, Lieutenant, with the commissioner's permission, please stand up, put your phone in your back pocket and then take it out and with the device down at your side, open up the camera function."

Blanco looks toward Marc, clearly hoping for an objection, but Marc is looking at Blanco like a stranger.

"Reverend," says Rik, "would you direct the witness?"

The Reverend tells Blanco to do as Rik asked. Frito gets to his feet. He actually looks shorter, and there's perspiration on his forehead. Blanco lowers the phone to his side, meaning it's hidden by the witness stand. You can see Blanco's arm moving, then there's a distinct *thunk*. He's dropped the phone and has to stoop down to pick it up. He tries again to open the camera, with his eye cheating down there this time.

"Please hold up the phone, Lieutenant, and show it to the members of the commission. Do you agree that the camera function didn't open?"

The three commissioners are leaning over the bench. Rik extends a hand to Blanco.

"Let me see if I can help you, Lieutenant," Rik says and takes Frito's phone. "I'm a little bit of a gadget freak, as you might have noticed, and I believe your problem is that those features you claimed you used—swiping from the home screen to open the camera, and what's sometimes called the machine-gun or burst function, meaning repeated snaps by holding down the shutter button—those features were added *after* the V.I."

After another wordless moment, Blanco laughs and tosses a hand in the air.

"I forgot. I traded in my phone a few months ago."

"You originally had what, a model V.I.I.I?"

"I don't remember."

"But you traded in a more advanced phone for a less advanced phone, is that what you're saying?"

"This one was refurbished. I got a straight-up trade for no money. The bells and whistles don't really matter to me." He puts on his shy smile once again.

The Rev is sitting straight back in his seat. He gives Mrs. Langenhalter a sidewise look.

"And the data was transferred from your old phone to your new phone?" Rik asks.

"Right."

"Okay." Rik looks up to the bench. "I'd like permission to keep Lieutenant Blanco's cell phone in order to have an expert perform a forensic examination."

"No!" Still on his feet, Blanco tries to grab the phone back, and Rik half pirouettes to avoid that. Frito then turns to the commissioners, kind of whining. "I can't lose my phone for what, days, weeks? Let me at least get a cheap burner tomorrow."

Langenhalter whispers to the Reverend, and their heads virtually meet while each of them covers the microphones as they talk.

The Rev says, "Mr. Dudek, give the lieutenant back his phone. Lieutenant, you'll deliver it to Mr. Hess by the close of business tomorrow, and Mr. Hess, you'll get it immediately to Mr. Dudek. And I'm sure you understand this, Lieutenant, but we expect the phone to be in the exact same state tomorrow as it is right now. And I suspect the experts Mr. Dudek is going to employ will be able to detect any changes."

"Well," says Blanco, "I don't know how fast I can get another phone."

The Reverend, who has a better nose for bullshit than I'd expect from a minister, gives Frito a narrow look.

"You set the timetable yourself, Lieutenant. If there's any reason you can't comply with the commission's order, we expect to hear from Mr. Hess on an emergency basis."

Rik and Marc and Blanco are all on their feet now.

"Is this a good point to adjourn Mr. Blanco's cross, Mr. Dudek? We can resume once you've got the results back of the various tests you want to perform?"

"Sounds good," says Rik.

Blanco gets off the stand, clearly agitated. He sails straight to Marc, Frito speaking loud enough for us to hear him protesting about surrendering the phone. Marc, for his part, doesn't seem to want to face Blanco. He's three-quarters turned away from him, probably because he'd want to slap the guy if he had to look him in the eye. What has to be burning Marc is the way he scoffed when Rik called him gullible.

As the room clears with the usual hubbub, I sidle close to Rik.

"Boss, you really got up off the canvas. You did great. Everything after their little bench conference? You crushed it."

Rik smiles. "Yeah," he says. "Sometimes you get on that roll. And you say to yourself, 'How come I can't be this smart all the time?' As soon as he took that ring out of his pocket, I could see it was an act, there was something phony." But Rik doesn't take long patting his own back. "All right," he says, "let's do the hard part."

I give him a look. I don't understand.

"Lucy," he says.

19. RIK IS RIGHT

Rik is right. The photograph is bad. The Chief and Rik and I are back around the conference table in Rik's office, where we each have had a long look before Rik closes the folder again. There's not much of Blanco in the picture. He's seen from the back, from the level of his shoulders. His right arm, supposedly holding the phone, is not visible. His left hand, as he said in court before he got cut off, is groping her tit, and his head is buried in her crotch, deep enough that her thighs are covering his ears.

As for the Chief, the view is nowhere as limited. She's seated in a big black leather executive chair. Whatever she wore to work—pants or skirt—has been discarded, and her full thighs are squished unflatteringly because they're thrown over Blanco's shoulders. And she is smiling in a way I've never seen from her before, which is, frankly, nasty and pretty repulsive. She's loving all of this, including, it seems, the ugliest part, which is that her service weapon—a .32 Beretta that she carries in a shoulder holster—is in her left hand inches from Blanco's temple. That to me is the shocking part of the photograph: not the sex, which always looks pretty strange when it's somebody you know, but what it reveals in the Chief, a kind of twisted piece of her.

"There's no mirror in my office," she says finally. "There never has been. You can call Stanley if you want," she says, referring to the former Chief.

"And what does that mean?" Rik asks. "You used somebody else's office?" Rik has lost his usual good nature. You'd expect the same from any trial lawyer who got bushwhacked with something this critical that his client never mentioned. "Let's cut the crap, Lucy. Is that you?"

"You're the one who said this is Photoshopped."

"I said it because that's my job. To cast doubt. But you tell us. Is that picture real or not?"

"I don't know."

"Lucy, is that you? Does that look like you?"

"In a galaxy far far away and long long ago."

"How long?"

"Twenty pounds," she says. "And my hair hasn't been quite that short in years. Every woman in the station will testify my hair was longer last November."

"But that's you in the Highland Isle police station with some guy, right?"

"It's not Blanco. That's one thing I can tell you for sure."

"Granted, Blanco's a liar. He wasn't at your house, and you've never had an apartment in HI. The ring doesn't fit him. He's not going to find the original print of the photo either. So in the long run, we don't have to worry about the US Attorney believing him. That's the good news.

"But Lucy, whoever cooked this up, Steven DeLoria or the Ritz or whoever else, to them Blanco's just a Trojan horse. They knew that whether Blanco is telling the truth is almost beside the point for their purposes. Once this image goes public, it'll be a sensation. Which the commission won't be able to ignore. Whatever break P&F was going to cut you because there aren't written rules against fraternization, or because DeGrassi and Cornish are lying oafs—they can't do that with this. This didn't happen in the privacy of your house after hours, Lucy, with some fuck buddy you've been bopping since you were both pups. You're on the job here, in a chair and an office the citizens pay for."

"I'm not the first cop to have sex in the station. I'm not even the first Chief."

"But you'd fire the ass of any cop you caught doing this."

"Maybe."

"It's an election year, Lucy. The mayor will have to do something."

She studies Rik. "Are you telling me to resign?"

Rik thinks about that for a while.

"I'm telling you we need to defend this," he finally answers. "And to do that, we have to have the facts. If this isn't Blanco, then who is it?"

She shakes her head. "I don't remember, Rik."

"How can you not remember? Because it happened so often?"

The Chief, who's kept it together pretty well so far, doesn't care for the sarcasm.

"Who are you," she answers, "my mother?" You can't be a police officer for decades without being sharp and tough, but the Chief has that woman thing of trying not to let people see it. Revealed, it's like a knife coming out of a sheath. "I don't know who it is, and I don't remember if anything like this actually happened. I can't tell you one way or the other if this is even real. Okay?"

Rik glances at me to see if I believe her, which I don't. We're all quiet, which gives me a chance to kind of think out loud.

"Okay," I say. "But let's just stay on the road you've been on, Boss. Our position is that this is a Photoshop, you know, the picture is manufactured, like you said in court. I guarantee you that with Blanco admitting that this is a photocopy of a printed picture, every expert will say that there's no way to be sure whether the original digital image was altered."

The Chief watches me and then gives a weighty nod. But Rik isn't satisfied.

"A Photoshop from what? You have to start with a real photograph, don't you?"

I look to the Chief and ask, "Could somebody have hacked your phone and found a picture like this that they pasted into an office setting?"

Rik holds up a hand to keep her from answering.

"Then you'd need to produce that photo," he says. He's warning her off before she lies. "Different question. Is there a guy out there who's got a photo like this that *he* took? At your house? Or somewhere else?"

She gets a little whimsical smile and gestures at the folder.

"Apparently."

"That still looks like a Highland Isle tunic to me," Rik says about Blanco's shirt, which is in that Sick Teal shade the HI department wears so they're not confused with the Kindle County Force, with all its frequent problems.

"Changing the color of something is easy digitally," I say.

"But Lucy is obviously in uniform."

"Or was," says the Chief with a sad little smile. Even to me, the person who invented inappropriate, Lucy's nervous humor feels childish and annoying.

"You can't just stick her face on another image, can you?" Rik asks. "I mean, it would look like a cartoon."

"We need to find an expert who can explain how those programs work," I say.

The Chief groans, thinking about the expense.

"And if we say, 'Photoshop,'" Rik tells the two of us, "then Mr. Not-Blanco better not show up and say this took place at the station."

"Not happening," says Lucy.

"Because?"

"Because it's a fucking Photoshop," she says. "This isn't real." Now that I've said the experts won't disprove that, she's suddenly a lot more certain.

Rik says it's time to go home. We're all tired. We gather our stuff and walk out into the night. The summer humidity, thick as cotton, has arrived, so that outside you never feel like your skin is completely dry. Even so, I've always enjoyed that sensation, because it takes me back to when I was a kid, and the heavy air meant I was free—not in school, not messing up, not getting scolded.

It's past 11:00 and the city is starting to fall silent, with the usual isolated urban sounds jumping out. A jacked-up vehicle with a big baffler on the muffler guns down the avenue, and someone's shouts follow. There are lights of a truck going into the Tech Park across the street, delivering something to Northern Direct or another business.

Given the hour and the surroundings, Rik walks the Chief to her car. That's kind of dear, since Rik, the escort, is the only one of the three of us without a gun. The Chief recovered hers from the lockers in City Hall after the hearing, and my two-shot is a few feet away in the trunk of the CTS. But I know he wants to give Lucy a hug, just to show he's with her, no matter what. He does that and says something to her that I can't hear. Maybe he's apologizing for losing it a little.

Then he returns my way and rolls his eyes and mouths, "Clients," as he strolls to his Acura, parked a couple spaces over.

I'm about a minute out of the parking lot when Tonya calls. I imagine she wants an update on the hearing, but she already knows all about it.

"I hate to tell you," she says, "but that picture is all over the Internet."

20. KOOB COMES BACK

Koob usually appears at my door every other night. The second time he knocked, I found him on the threshold with a brown paper bag. He handed it over as I stepped aside to let him in. It was a bottle of bourbon, nice stuff.

"I thought you don't drink," I said.

"I don't." He suddenly seemed shy. "But I enjoyed the taste on you."

"Awesome." I pulled the cork and took a slug straight from the bottle.

After our tumble, he laid there silent for quite some time. He got up to smoke a cigarette at the window and then returned, lying beside me again, still with nothing to say.

"Is this strange for you?"

He took his time forming an answer.

"Yes," he said.

"Too strange?"

He waited another second.

"Casual sex has never really been my thing."

"God," I answered. "I hate that term. It's not worth having

sex if it's going to be casual. The intensity is what makes it great, the way for a few minutes it's all that's happening in the universe. Right?" He seemed to be considering that. "Besides, what about when you were in the service? No sex just to get off?"

"Yeah, of course. But I never enjoyed it that much. You know, it was a need. And if you were single, something you were expected to do."

"You seem to be enjoying yourself now."

He nodded several times before he said, "Completely."

"Well okay, then. What's the problem?"

"I grew up on the fringes of a very traditional society. I like to think I am fully American, but sometimes I find I have a false impression of myself."

"You think you're doing something wrong? Or that I am?"

He didn't answer.

"Hey, look. If you're enjoying it, then don't yuck your yum. Cute girl next door? Fucks like a football player? Kind of amusing, right, when it crosses your mind?"

He smiled. He was beginning to find me entertaining.

"Still," he said.

"Is it because I'm a woman?"

He didn't want to say it out loud.

"Man, you know that's strictly cray-cray, don't you? Guys can wander but girls stay home? Where is that from?"

"I said I'm traditional."

"Well, it's a messed-up tradition. One thing I learned when I accepted that I liked women, too, was that I was never going to be fully myself if I waited for someone to give me permission. We want what we want. It's part of who we are. I have a thing for the weird guy in the next apartment, then I'm going for it. I don't care about anybody else's judgments."

He didn't answer. I'm not sure I'd been clear before about being bi. But he didn't seem stuck on that, so much as wondering if he could ever view our thing the way I was recommending.

Usually, we go at it twice and lay in bed and talk in between. I get in a mood with him where I just gush the volcano of strange shit that sometimes boils over in my brain.

For instance. There's a full-length mirror in my room—it was actually my mom's mom's and her mother's before her, and another mom before that. It has a thick gilt frame of cloud forms, and some of the silver backing has begun to oxidize near the top, leaving a few dark blots. But I was happy to get it when Pops moved to assisted living. I'm not much for history or ancestor worship or whatever, but with my grandfather taking what we both knew was another step toward the graveyard, I guess I was beginning to see the point of treasuring the past. I thought it would be very cool to look at my reflection where generations of women in my family had done it before. Like all those things, when you try to make a big deal of them, it doesn't last. Now and then I think about my great-great-grandmother examining herself in a corset and a feathered hat. But you know, day by day, it's just a mirror, and tonight Koob bends me over the bed and does me from behind, standing while we both watch our reflections, which probably happened back in the day, too.

As I am lying next to him afterwards, I say, "You know, when I was a kid, it made me kind of crazy at times. The thought."

He just looks for a while before quietly saying, "What thought?"

This happens to me now and then, a fugue state where I forget for a second that someone I like doesn't necessarily know what I am thinking.

"This thought," I say. "You never set eyes on your own face. You can look in a mirror. But that's a mirror image. Reversed.

You can see the face of every single human being in the world, except your own. Strange, right?"

He laughs, a quick cackle, surprisingly high-pitched, which I've heard from him several times now.

"And what do you make of that?" he asks.

"I don't know. Like I said, it used to make me crazy."

"And does it make you crazy now?"

I think.

"Well, I accept that I can't change it. It's a condition of life. But it's still kind of a headbang to realize that we will never actually see ourselves directly or the way other people do. Right? That's like kind of spiritual or deep, right?" I wiggle magic fingers in the air.

He lays there a second. He seems deeply struck by all of this, but I suspect that's mostly wondering just how strange this chick really is.

"Don't get trippy," I say. "I'm just being Pinky."

"Who's Pinky?"

"I'm Pinky. Some people call me Pinky."

"Not Clarice?"

"My parents called me Pinky. Something about being thirty made me start to feel I'd grown out of it."

"How old are you?" he asks.

"How old do you think I am?"

"I thought you were around thirty, maybe even coming up on it."

"I'll take that," I tell him. "I'm thirty-three. How old are you?"

"Forty-six."

That was about what I figured.

"And is Clarice any different than Pinky?" he asks.

"She's older. Not that I always like it."

"What don't you like? You're too young for backaches and sore knees."

"Actually, my back hurts all the time, especially in wet weather. Because I broke it boarding. But no, I try not to freak, but when I look in a mirror I can see my shape is changing a little. All the sudden a third cup of coffee makes my heart jumpy. Which makes me feel cheated."

"Cheated?"

"Sure. The calendar says grown-up, but inside I know I'm not done being an adolescent. Plenty of people would tell you I still act that way. So what the fuck are these gray hairs I pull out? And, you know, I never had any burning desire to be an adult. I thought they were mostly jerks. I still do, frankly. But when you're a kid, you think, Well, when I grow up, at least I'll finally be who I'm supposed to be. I won't be this piece of clay that changes with each new experience. I'll have a job. I'll have my own house. Maybe I'll pair off with somebody so I'm not always alone. It's all going to be different.

"And you don't know what a trap that is, that kind of thinking. I mean, mostly life *is*, you know. It *is*. Whether you're three or thirty-three. You get up. You're breathing. You're thinking. I still don't have a clue who I'm supposed to be. I just accept the flow of things. There really isn't a future or a past. Those are concepts. But you're alive only in the present. The *is*."

He looms up on an elbow, smiling down at me. We watch each other for some time.

"You don't know anybody else like me, do you?" I ask him.

"Definitely not," he says.

Two nights later, the Friday after Blanco's testimony, while we're laying still for a while before he recovers the energy to leave, I ask him, "So is it okay that I'm so different? I mean, is it good or does it, you know, make you kind of wary?"

He thinks. "It's interesting," he says.

I think, too. "I'll take that. I'll take 'interesting.' It's sort of positive."

"Better than weird," he says.

"Well, you are."

His lips compress in a smile mysterious as smoke.

"Still?" he asks. "Why is that?"

"Same as ever. Because you're up to something. I never followed you around enough to figure out what. But I know you've got something strange going on. I knew it the minute I saw you. I'm like a witch that way."

He frowns a little but doesn't answer.

"Like, why don't we ever get together at your place?" I ask.

He draws back slightly.

"I would not feel the same there. It would be quite hard for me to relax."

"This is another world? One door away?"

He tips his head as if that might be true. I laugh because I want to believe it. But I don't, not completely.

"It's because you've got all kinds of secret shit over there," I say.

He just stares, ticking his head faintly so there's no way to tell what the gesture means.

"You're never going to tell me what you're up to, right?" I ask.

He sits up.

"Why do I have to keep saying this? Do not ask me about my work and I will not ask about yours."

"You can ask me whatever you want about my work."

"No, I cannot. This case with the police chief. Tell me what she's said to you about that photograph." Koob had actually come over Monday night when I got home. I was really glad to see him. I told him I'd had a tough evening, but it turned out that was why he'd knocked. The photo, with a bunch of fuzzy circles in strategic places, had already turned up in his news feed—him and half the people who live in Highland Isle.

"I can't do that," I say.

He raises his eyebrows emphatically. Point made.

"I'm going to figure it out," I tell him. "You know I will."

He shows his usual resting face, meant to be unreadable.

Earlier this week, on Tuesday, the morning after Blanco took the stand, Rik went on the offensive. Since dozens of websites had published the photo of the Chief by morning—a few without even blurring out the hot spots, so to speak—he called a press conference in the early afternoon. It was held in the parking lot outside our building. By the time of Blanco's testimony, coverage of the hearing had dribbled down to a few local courthouse reporters, but now that things had turned pornographic, there were dozens of journalists fighting for elbow space. It was the usual free-for-all, with the camera operators edging each other aside and shining their lights. Amid all the flashing and buzzing of the equipment, Rik put on a face as solemn as a monument.

"This photograph is a fake, pure and simple. And knowing that it is a fake, someone chose to blast it all over the Internet, to embarrass and degrade Chief Gomez, because they will never be able to show in court that the picture is authentic.

"Mr. Hess has given me his word that he has no idea who leaked the photo. By contrast, Lieutenant Blanco has said nothing so far. Either way, the commission ordered Mr. Hess and Mr. Blanco to produce the original printed photograph this morning. The City hasn't done it, and I don't expect them to. I repeat: It's a fake.

"Furthermore, I stick by what I said last night. It is a dis-
grace that the City would offer in evidence anything so salacious
and unfair to Chief Gomez without hiring forensic examiners to
verify it first. They didn't, because their case was Code Blue and
they were desperate to revive it. Whatever second thoughts they
have now can do nothing to repair the damage done to Lucia
Gomez-Barrera. I am calling on the City to issue an apology and
terminate this hearing immediately."

In the office, Rik called Marc every hour, demanding the
original photograph. Blanco, supposedly, was more certain it had
been accidentally shredded. Marc apologized every time Rik and
him spoke, and finally asked Rik if he wanted the City to bring
in outside counsel for the balance of the hearing. I was in Rik's
office at the time.

"The hell," Rik answered. "Now you want to give this heaping
turd to someone else? You did this, Marc, and you get to hold it
in your hands while it curls up steam." Before he hung up, he said,
"And I'll tell you what else I want. I want Blanco's goddamned
phone on my desk by five p.m., just like the Reverend ordered.
Or is he going to say now that he shredded that, too?"

Instead, a little after five, we received a motion filed by a
local lawyer, Selena Rios Schwartz, a former deputy PA in Kindle
County, who Rik thinks highly of. She asked the commission to
reconsider its order regarding Blanco's cell phone. She claimed
that it was an invasion of Blanco's privacy to require him to turn
over the device, which was full of personal photos and messages
from friends and family, and some confidential police business.
Furthermore, she argued, Blanco had already testified that the
original digital image was not on the phone.

The commission issued an order Wednesday morning, denying
the motion. Mrs. L said, "We have reviewed the testimony from

Monday's hearing again. Lieutenant Blanco in fact testified that all data from the phone where the picture had once appeared was transferred to the current phone. That is a reasonable basis on which Respondent can demand to examine the device. The City cannot expect to offer evidence so critical without affording Chief Gomez a full opportunity to challenge it. Mr. Blanco's compliance with the commission's order is essential before we can afford any weight to his testimony."

Marc then joined Blanco in filing an emergency appeal to the Superior Court of Greenwood County, a move expected to buy Blanco a few days. But overall, Rik thought we were again on the verge of having the case against the Chief dismissed.

"What's Blanco's deal with the phone?" I asked. "He acted like the Reverend had shoved a stick of dynamite up his rectum as soon as Frito heard the order Monday night."

"My bet," said Rik, "is that what he wants to hide are his communications with the Ritz or Steven, or whoever put him up to all this."

"Can he just refuse to obey a court order?"

"Not if he wants to keep working as a cop. His only way out, under the law, is to take five."

"What crime would he say he was worried about?"

"First, he doesn't have to say. And second, we couldn't dispute it, if he hints that the phone will provide evidence of perjury."

"But then the Chief wins, right?"

"Sure," he told me, "she's odds-on to win the hearing anyway. But that still doesn't guarantee that Lucy keeps her job. That was the point of leaking the picture."

The claim that the photo was a forgery more or less protected the mayor from having to take an immediate position on the Chief's further employment, but that did not prevent several citizen groups, most of them clearly aligned with Steven DeLoria, from demanding Lucy resign. Then on Wednesday night, two jointly owned newspapers, the Kindle County *Tribune* and the Highland Isle *Beacon*, published the same editorial about the Chief. The papers said it was unfair to expect the Chief to prove a negative—that it wasn't actually her in the photo—but then turned around and claimed that unfortunately, unless she could do that, she couldn't function effectively in the job as chief of police, where, unlike a private citizen, she was required to remain above suspicion.

When I arrived at work on Thursday morning, the Chief was sitting in the hall outside Rik's office, waiting for him to get back from court. Up until now, she had held up well. She'd had some down moments, but in general, seeing these clowns lie live from the witness stand had enraged her and given her an air of continuing strength. The photo was the first thing to really get to her. Even with all her skill with makeup, you could see she'd lost color. She was wearing her glasses instead of her contacts, because her eyes were so irritated from lack of sleep, and she was not the usual beacon of positive energy. The dimples were on leave.

The editorials the night before had left her in a spin. She was finding it so hard to wait for Rik that she wanted to talk to me instead, even though I had just stopped by briefly to say hi while she was sitting there.

"Having half-naked sex shots on the Internet," she said, "that's like the old nightmare of running through the streets without your clothes on. My daughters have hung tough through this whole thing, but I can tell they're really embarrassed now. I can say 'fake' all I want, but everybody just assumes that's me."

"I get it," I said, and told her about something kind of comparable with me several years ago. Back then I went through a phase, which overlapped with when I started at Stern & Stern, where I regularly posted selfies of me and partners in the act on Snapchat (generally speaking, and by no accident, I thought I was lookin pretty killer in the pictures). My grandfather finally begged me to stop, because people were getting no work done in the office while they hovered over the screenshots they'd captured on their phones. I saw eventually that no matter how in-your-face I felt like being, I was providing the wrong kind of entertainment to a lot of people who were like gawkers going by a car wreck, high on my misfortune and stupidity and their relief that it wasn't them.

But I was nobody important, I'd chosen to put the pictures out there, and the lurid little snickers were mostly behind my back. Blanco's photo, by contrast, was literally front-page news, and she had to face the fact that the image would be chasing her around the Internet forever, whenever people searched her name.

"The whole thing with the picture is totally shitty," I told the Chief, standing beside her. "And yeah, your kids are embarrassed. But it happened. It's a few news cycles. By the weekend, everybody who wants to look will have looked. Monday it will all be boring."

She shook her head, not buying my optimism.

"I think the papers may be right." She meant about resigning.

"The papers are full of shit," I said. "Think about it. Somebody makes up a ton of absolute crap about a police chief, or anybody else in office, and that means that person has to quit unless they can show every single detail is pure manure. Whatever happened to innocent until proven guilty?"

She didn't respond to that. I wasn't sure Rik would be as positive, because a couple times when we were alone in the office, including right after his press conference, he seemed to have a lot of doubts. He thinks we may be close to the moment when the mayor jettisons the Chief. Plus, even *he's* lost a little confidence in her. We both know there's more to the story about that picture than she's told us. By claiming it's fake, Rik has put his own credibility on the line, meaning the truth that our client won't share may end up canceling out a lot of what he hoped to gain by taking the case.

But right then, the Chief was asking for my opinion, not Rik's.

"Look," I said, "I'm not the lawyer. But all Blanco's crap about the photograph and his phone means his testimony is worthless. So you're going to win the hearing, and the takeaway after a couple weeks will be that you got a massive railing. Rik may even figure out a way to sue the City and make them pay for this."

She was staring up at me, those big black eyes of hers swimming with pain and uncertainty. The whole exchange left me with a strange feeling, because our physical positions made it seem like she was the child and I was the grown-up, and my instinct is still to squirm whenever I'm in that role. But I held her eye, trying to look like I thought I was right, which I pretty much did.

21. STANDSTILL

Once the Superior Court orders Blanco to turn over his phone, he files another motion in the appellate court. Rik says this will accomplish nothing except buying Blanco a little time, but because we have no idea if the P&F hearing will continue, we pretty much go into standstill on the Chief's case. I get a chance to do a bunch of interviews on Rik's new matters, and also to take Gomer on long walks. I even manage to play both softball games for two consecutive weeks, which I haven't done since April.

But with time on my hands, I find myself dwelling on Koob, not in a gushy junior-high-school way but trying to put the guy together in my head. It's kind of ironic, because he has been occupying space in my imagination for months now. But he has gone from a one-dimensional mystery man to a three-dimensional person, known and intensely real in some ways, but with a life that's a complete blank, except when he's in my apartment.

"So what else are we going to talk about during the recovery period?" I ask one night, after he shuts down another attempt to get him to tell me about his work.

"What would you like to talk about?" Koob asks.

After a second, I answer. "Tell me about how you grew up. You know, living around the Hmong."

"Ah," he says. "I'm not sure I know how to talk about that."

But over his next couple visits, that is more or less the subject, when we're having conversations. I have already been looking at pictures online, and I bring my laptop to bed and show him the photographs. He hunches down next to my shoulder to see the screen, so I'm conscious of his size and the heat of his body, as I thumb through the images of the Hmong in their ritual dress.

"The traditional clothing looks to me like some of the native people in Peru," I say. I backpacked through Peru and Brazil one of the times I dropped out of college. He seems struck by my observation.

"Actually, I had a good friend in the service," he says, "another Ranger, who was Lakota, and a lot of what I was raised with and he was raised with—it was very similar. He told me a story about his grandmother coming to see him the night she died in the body of a wolf. And I had heard Hmong tells stories like that a thousand times. A lot of the myths and legends sound alike, too."

"What kind of myths? Tell me one."

He stares at the ceiling a second.

"Okay, this is a good one. This is how the Hmong explain why some people are left-handed: There was an enormous eagle who was eating all the people—all except the king's daughter, who had been sealed in a drum to hide. Far away, a great warrior heard about this and came to the village, where he could see no one alive. Eventually he tapped on the king's drum, and the princess spoke. And together they worked up a trap for the great eagle.

"At the first light, the princess broke free of the drum. The eagle swooped in and the warrior shot him through the heart with an arrow, and the eagle fell to the ground dead. The warrior opened the belly of the eagle and it was full of human bones. He worked all day and all night to put the bones together so that the people could return to life. But as he grew weary, he sometimes mixed up one side for the other. So that is why some people are left-handed and some are right-handed."

"Wow. That's a whole lot of story to explain something basic."

"Yeah. That's the Hmong way. Everything is connected. You do not ask a Hmong person how to get to the store, if you prefer not to know how the world was created first."

"Was it a strange upbringing?"

"It was not strange because my mom was Hmong but because it felt like we were not really anything. We lived in Minneapolis near my mother's parents. But they never accepted my father. There are whole Hmong clans descended from intermarriage between the Han Chinese and the Hmong. But those men always entered Hmong society. And my dad had no interest. He could not understand them, frankly. And I never blamed him. There are things about the Hmong that seem to have no parallels in any other culture."

"Like?"

"Like the Hmong Green and the Hmong White, for instance."

"Green and white?"

"Clans with different languages, different clothing, many different traditions. My mom's family are Hmong White, and most of them cannot even talk to the Hmong Green. But they do not live in separate villages. Hmong Green and Hmong White dwell among one another in Asia. And Minneapolis."

"And what about your mom? Was she on the outside like your dad?"

"Half and half. The other Hmong women were suspicious of

her because she could read and write, and speak English well. And was Christian, like my dad—they were actually Catholic, which was important to both of them."

"So did you do the whole Catholic trip? Schools and everything?"

"Until junior high. I hated it. But about my mother, even though a lot of Hmong were wary of her, she never wanted to break away from Hmong life completely."

"Like how?"

"Well, say she became seriously ill. She might go to a western doctor, but she could never believe she was going to get well unless she was also attended by a Hmong shaman."

"And how was that for your father, if they wouldn't accept him?"

"My parents were generally okay with that. But they had a strange deal."

I assume he means that his parents had a strange deal the way every marriage has its unique arrangements, but the next time we talk about it, a couple nights later, I learn that his parents got off to a very odd start. His mother was an interpreter in Laos, having been educated in a convent school run by American nuns from the Dominican order. She, and a couple of her classmates, were recruited by the US forces during the Vietnam War, to facilitate communication between the American soldiers and the Hmong who were helping them.

"Forty thousand Hmong fought for the US in Laos. Even though they were illiterate, they had a talent for operating electrical equipment and were skilled at calling in bombing raids." Koob's mother translated for a US captain. They fell for each other and got engaged. And then he was killed as the North Vietnamese were storming through the area.

"The Army moved her to South Vietnam for her own

protection, but she knew the Pathet Lao or the Vietcong would kill her as soon as the US left." Her fiancé, the dead guy, was Koob's uncle, his father's brother. And as the war was winding down, Koob's father, who'd also served in Vietnam, flew to Saigon and married Koob's mom so he could bring her back to the US. They'd barely known each other for an hour when the ceremony was performed by a priest Koob's father found.

"It sounds like something in the Bible, right?" Koob asks. "Marrying your brother's wife when he dies. I'm not sure what either of them expected. But it worked out. My mother says she felt like she'd known him a hundred years when they stepped off the plane in the US."

"They were happy?"

"I cannot say happy. Not that they were unhappy. But they were both too old-school to think about happy. Not like my kids, who demand happiness as a right. But they respected each other. They treated one another with respect. So if she needed to be sure there were Hmong shamans around, he understood that we could not leave Minneapolis. There are not many Hmong shamans anywhere else."

I ask him a couple nights later how he ended up in Pittsburgh, and he explains that he went to grad school there after the service.

"And that's where you met your wife?"

He nods.

"Is she Hmong?"

"No, she's white."

"Hmong White?" I laugh and he pokes me in the side.

"No, white. Like you. Caucasian. Which meant neither of my parents liked her. Of course, I was not about to let them tell me what to do, so I married her." He ticks his head in disapproval of himself. "I had the idea in the back of my mind, because of the way my parents got together, that any two people could make a good marriage." He wobbles his head again, for much longer this time.

His marriage, his family, is like a shadow always glued to him. Tonight it feels safe to ask him if he has pictures of his kids. He gets his phone and thumbs through, careful not to let me see the other images, until he turns the device around.

Both take after him, tall and good-looking.

"Your daughter's beautiful."

"She thinks so." He laughs. "She's going to college next year. She cannot wait and neither can I."

The story he told about how his parents met has sparked something strange in me tonight. The idea that things between people could be that haphazard, that you marry somebody because your brother was supposed to, has brought on the creepy déjà vu–type notion that our destiny, Koob's and mine, might be similar. How entirely random and amusing would it be if I ended up with Koob because I was stalking him? Could we be equally respectful despite all our differences?

But I know that isn't going to happen. For one thing, there's an obvious obstacle.

"You're not really divorced, are you?" I ask him, while he's still holding up the picture of his kids.

"No," he says finally, "but I'm not in Pittsburgh."

"But are you still thinking it over? Or just waiting for the lawyers to do their thing? I mean, have you ever taken off like this before?"

"I guess. A couple times."

"Which means you came back."

He smiles fleetingly, just because of how quickly I picked that up.

"She's not right. Seriously not right."

"You keep saying that. What is there to think over then?"

He lays there like a mummy for a second, utterly still, with his hands folded over his heart.

"I knew she was troubled. When we got married? That is what bothers me. I mean, maybe I lied to myself a little. But I knew something was wrong. I guess I thought I could fix her."

"But you couldn't."

"Of course not."

"Did you have sex like this with your wife?"

His head snaps around and he stares. It's a Pinky moment where I just say what seems logical to me with no clue how it will strike the other person. I attempt to explain.

"I'm just trying to understand. You know that saying: 'Batshit crazy makes my dick hard.' Maybe it was great between you that way, and you thought you could ignore the rest."

My reasoning appears to pacify him. He nods a few times and then stops to reflect.

"The truth is I do not remember. It is hard to believe there was nothing good, but it's all been overwhelmed by how crazy she is. After I married her, when I began to see how disturbed she was, I felt like she had tricked me by acting more stable than she is. But over time, I realized that in those early days she was just holding on. And then she lost her grip. For years now, she has had no control over herself. She's either quietly bitter or raging. And it changes as quickly as flipping a switch. I look away from her, like just to see what is on the TV, and when I turn back a monster is across the room. Once she gets worked up, she can seem almost homicidal. She veers around the house screaming, literally foaming at the mouth."

"What is she screaming about? You?"

"Me. Her parents. Our kids. People she knew twenty years ago. She makes threats. She's going to kill herself. Hurt our children. There have been decades of this. So I cannot remember what existed before."

I wonder if Koob is kind of dressing up his wife's problems. I've noticed that whenever couples stop getting along, they start saying the other person is crazy, exaggerating any odd behavior. Maybe it's what he needs to say, or believe, so he's comfortable lying here with me. And I'm okay letting that be the tale we're telling between us, since even shared lies can knit people together. But I'm not forgetting what he just admitted, that he's always gone back in the end. Deep down, I won't let myself believe that the story will be any different this time.

"And are your kids okay with you splitting?"

"Not a bit. My son always says, 'I'm not the one who told you to marry her.' They do not want to get stuck taking care of her, and they will have to."

"Divorce is tough, though. My parents split up when I was seventeen, and it set me back for years." I smile. "You don't want your kids to end up like me."

"They won't."

I'm a little hurt by his confidence, as if not many people could turn out this strange.

"Teenagers?" I say. "Don't be so sure."

"No, they grew up with a crazy woman. After that, normal seems really special. To both of them. Sometimes, frankly, I am frightened by how conventional they are. All they want is a house in the suburbs and enough money to go to the mall whenever they like." He rolls to his side to face me. "So what about you?" he says. "You're such a good investigator, you ask all the questions. But what about your family?"

"Me? It was just what your kids think they want. My parents were pretty conventional. Prom queen marries football star. Nice suburbs. Good schools. I mean, my mom was never real happy with him. But that was nothing compared to how she felt about me." I stop there and realize I'm going to tell him something as personal as what he has confided to me the last few nights, which is basically what he is asking for.

"Okay." I sit up. "You won't hear many people say this: My mother never loved me. Not the way she loved my brother and my sister. I mean, she thought she was being nice to me, and she was, like the way a lot of people are nice to their dogs. But that intense you're-me-and-I'm-you thing people have with their parents, that my dad has with me, that big central connection I can tell you have with your parents and with your kids? Nope. It just wasn't there. It was like the way absolute zero is the complete absence of heat. And, you know, I knew it from the time that I was little, and it really messed me up."

This is about the most courageous thing I can say about myself, and I haven't said it to many people—for obvious reasons, because they'll think, Wow, a kid even a mother couldn't love, better summon the fucking exorcist. Koob is listening with his familiar intent look and little visible expression beyond that.

"My parents forced me to go to all kinds of therapy," I say. "I'll bet you've never done anything like that?"

"No. That is how I live in between. I do not believe in the Hmong shamans. Or the American ones."

"Well, you know. A lot of it is just bullshit. Therapy is about the therapist. Period. They're always working out their own crap through you, and most of them have no clue they're doing it. But anyway, I saw one person, a kind of elderly German lady, she sounded like Dr. Ruth, and she said to me one day, 'I belief your mot'er never bonded wit' you.'" I'm pretty good at imitating accents. "Ze loss of her own mot'er was so traumatic for her zat she could not be a mot'er to you. She was still ze child in her own mind, still suffering ze child's loss.'

"I was so pissed off at this woman," I say. "I mean. She said it like, you know, 'Oh, today is Tuesday.' Like it was a meaningless detail. And it felt like the worst thing anyone had ever said to me. I would have said it myself, of course, my mother never loved me, but this lady was supposed to be an expert, and she was saying, 'Oh yeah, by the way, you're right.' I wanted to get up and throw her and her Eames chair through the window.

"But when I thought it over, I gave her credit. Because it's the truth. And because she was telling me that it was not my fault. Even though I lived my whole life feeling like it was. Maybe it isn't even my mom's."

I realize that Koob is holding my hand. And when I look over to him, he's fallen into a sober expression that I take as both amazement and respect. I actually lean down and kiss him, which doesn't happen much if we're not in action. He kind of hugs me for a second. And I find that I'm happier than I expect to be. My head is on his chest and we're almost nose to nose.

"I'm tellin you, dude, you don't know anybody else like me."

22. I AM WAITING FOR KOOB WHEN TONYA CALLS

I am just back from softball, kind of waiting for Koob, when Tonya calls about ten thirty on Thursday night, and I almost don't pick up the phone. On Tuesday, after that talk about his wife and my mother, Koob and I just burned ourselves up when we got it on again, every second spent with that kind of last-breath intensity. It was another velvety Midwestern evening, typical July, and even with the AC on overdrive, we were two slithery panting creatures when we finished. Koob fell asleep almost immediately. I watched him until I was sure he wasn't simply dozing, and then I drifted off, too, sleeping until I felt him jolt awake. It was close to three and he was reaching toward the foot of my bed for his clothes.

'No one says you have to leave, you know,' I told him.

He thought about that and laid down for another half hour, but by then he was wide awake and decided to go. At my bedroom door, he said, 'So maybe I'll see you tomorrow.'

When he didn't show Wednesday night, I was a little, okay, disappointed, much as I know better, but then I heard his front door slam sometime between two and three a.m., followed by footsteps next door and then the plumbing, and I realized he'd been out working, whatever it is he does.

That's why I expect him tonight. But I'm not going to let myself get into that, circling the field for anybody, and so I take Tonya's call.

"Toy, tsup?"

"Hey," she says. I can hear a police radio squawk behind her. "Hey, listen. I need you to meet me someplace. It's about the Chief and it's really important, but I kind of want to tell you this in person, all right?"

Does not sound good, but I don't ask more. I copy the address, which takes me to a buff-colored brick five-story tenement in Anglia, a sketchy part of town on the east side. There is a lot of gang activity around here and my first thought is that maybe some of the bangers are threatening the Chief, although it makes no sense that Tonya would need to call me, rather than reporting that internally. Two cruisers with the Mars lights spinning are double-parked in front of the building, and a boxy younger cop bars the way when I go to the front door. She demands ID.

"Fourth floor," she says after radioing up to Tonya. The building is in bad enough condition to make me appreciate Arturo and the Archer, which looks to have been built at the same time. The wood trim along the stairway and the railing haven't been varnished in forever, leaving splintery spots. Nobody's bothered to replace the light in a couple fixtures over the stairway, and the oriental-style carpet, close to a hundred years old, I bet, is worn through to the backing on the front half of each tread. There are a lot of smells here, none good: sour cooking scents, an odor of mold and something else displeasing. The door to one of the fourth-floor apartments, 4D, is open. The door jamb is splintered around the brass cup for the dead bolt, and I can smell something super foul as I get close.

It's a studio, one big room, so it doesn't take long to see the problem or to feel my body rinsed with intense alarm. Fabian Blanco looks like he got hung over a wooden chair like a pair of soiled jeans. His head is thrown back at an angle severe enough to inspire a wince, and his tongue's protruding in what EMTs I know call 'Giving the Q sign.' His legs are positioned crazily, his feet pointing toward each other, and his bluish color says it all. He's dead.

There's no dignity in dying, they say. The poor guy puked all over his shirt and trousers, and maybe even shit his pants. That's the intense odor I could smell across the room.

When I was in the academy, I did some ridealongs and saw dead people twice: One a gang member who was gutshot and bled out on the pavement within a five-foot circle of his own blood. The second was some poor old man in an SRO who'd bought the farm sitting on the can in the shared john. Tonight, same as the first times, I find that there is something about the sight that is both shocking and not shocking at all. I think, Yeah, that's where this is all headed, that absolute stillness.

So it's not so much death as who it is that sets the world shaking.

"Oh, fuck me," I say when I take a few more steps inside.

"I hear that," Tonya answers. I'm just seeing her now, in the galley kitchen, on the other side of a breakfast bar. She's writing stuff on her mini tablet. It's pretty clear that she got the call and rushed over. She's wearing khaki shorts and a very old black Rolling Stones T-shirt with a tongue hanging out of what I guess is supposed to be Mick's mouth. I see a female evidence tech, in uniform, dusting surfaces right near her.

Tonya meets me in the center of the room.

"Thanks for getting here so fast. The old guy next door was smelling something really funky. No one answered when he knocked. You know, it's the kind of neighborhood where a lot of strange shit is always happening, so he phoned the property manager, but when he didn't show up, he called us. The guy on patrol found the door locked, so he forced it with a crowbar. Obviously, he recognized Frito. As soon as the officer reached me, I was like, 'Don't notify anybody else yet. Especially the Chief.'"

"'Especially the Chief?'"

"Especially."

It's another of those moments when the air in the room seems too thick for me to get her meaning. I'm about to ask, 'Why not call the Chief?' when the point arrives like some heavy spacecraft thudding to a landing on my planet. Leaving aside a lot of the dudes Blanco's cracked over the years, who talk a lot of trash but almost never do anything about it—leaving those guys aside, the list of people who wanted Frito dead is probably not very long. And the Chief is right at the top.

Tonya goes on before I can ask anything else.

"I need you to go see the Chief right now and tell her to stay the hell away from here and not to ask questions, because I can't answer them. I have to call this in to the commander soon, but I wanted you to get to her first."

That's why she didn't want to say anything on the phone. So I could give the Chief a firsthand report that would leave no question about her supervising the investigation.

"And my recommendation to her, by the way," adds Tonya, "is that she bring in the Feebies."

"Why the Feds?"

"Well. A: Blanco was a witness in their investigation, so they're going to claim jurisdiction anyway, that's how they are, they always want anything juicy. B: Our department shouldn't be investigating alone, so that if this turns out to be a homicide, a defense lawyer for the killer can't say we rushed to judgment because we were so unhinged about the death of one of our own officers. And C: If Lucy brings the FBI in immediately, she'll look like she's not hiding anything."

I nod. "Good thinkin, Detective. And we're saying homicide for sure?"

"There's the dude who may be able to tell us." She points to a tall slender guy who has plastic gloves on and is gently lowering one leg of Blanco's khakis. This dude, the pathologist, is definitely something else. He is wearing a white short-sleeve shirt and a black bow tie, but if he's Nation of Islam, it's a new sect, because he's got a full black beard and big-time dreds, the kind that take years to grow. He's teased them out and sprayed them so they are wound around his head in a form resembling a treble clef. Last, he has got on a pair of white Beats headphones and is literally bouncing his chin to the music as he looks over the body.

"What the fuck?" I say to Tonya.

"Yeah, I know," she says. "But he's good. He's the top pathology resident at the U. Super super sharp."

In addition to the hip pathologist, I've noticed a second evidence tech, a gut-heavy guy in uniform, who's moving slowly around the room with what looks like a glorified flashlight called a forensic light source. It beams out ultraviolet and can show a lot of stuff, especially bodily fluids, like the sweat leavings that make up latent fingerprints. The female tech has continued dusting and taking lifts in the kitchen. I'm sure they photographed the entire scene already. These days in Highland Isle, the techs just use their cell phones.

The pathologist, still moving in rhythm, bops over to Tonya while I'm standing with her. He lowers his headphones to his neck.

"So. Anything?" she asks.

"Nothing much, at least not that I can see without disturbing the body. Only thing of note is what look like ligature marks, faint bruising, on his wrists and calves."

"Pre- or post-mortem?" I ask, and Tonya's head swivels so sharply I'm afraid she might have hurt herself. I lift a hand to show I understand her message—'Shut the fuck up, you're not even here.'

The pathologist thinks nothing of me speaking and answers, "Definitely pre."

"You think he was tied to that chair?" Tonya asks.

"That would fit the marks."

"Time of death?" asks Tonya.

"Looking at color and the degree of rigor mortis, I would say around twenty-four hours. We can tell you for sure when we see what's going on with his digestion."

Now that I am past the point where all my attention is on Blanco, I am beginning to take in what a weird space this apartment is. It's a little like the surface of the moon. There is nothing here, not so much as a calendar on the wall, and no furniture except the simple slat-back wooden chair Blanco croaked in, and another one that is positioned at a little white table, no more than thirty inches square, which holds a desktop computer with a huge monitor. Other than that, nada. No sofa. No bed. It's very clean, not so much as a dust ball in a corner, which makes it feel even more austere.

Dr. Hip, who Tonya calls "Potter," is answering her question about the cause of death.

"Nothing obvious now," he says. "No lacerations, no trauma to the head, no blood so far as I see. Right now, I'm feeling a heart attack. But we have to get him downtown."

"So not a homicide?" she asks.

He wags his head back and forth. "Possibly not. Just guessing."

"Suicide?"

"There's nothing here. I patted down his pockets for pills, and the medicine cabinet in the bathroom is empty. The stove's not on or anything like that."

He puts his headphones back on and picks up his black doctor's bag on his way out. I want to ask what tunes he's listening to, but I decide that's a little too Pinky.

"Anything else for me?" I ask Toy.

"Well, you're here," she says. "Look around for a sec and see if there's anything that strikes you. You always notice the strangest shit," she says.

"Thanks."

"You do. And obviously, don't touch anything or get in any-body's way."

"Obviously. Did you turn on the computer?"

"Nope. I'd be afraid to do it without some expert to watch. Assuming the Feds come in, that's the kind of thing where they're on their own level. My cell is picking up a wireless signal, and the router's in the closet. But I mean, talk about strange. Internet but no bed?"

"Maybe he was moving out?"

She shoots a finger at me.

"Good thinkin, Detective."

"Anything else like that?" I ask.

"He's got his wallet but not his phone. But I suspect he turned that over to the lawyer who filed the appeals for him. You know, for safekeeping while they're waiting for the court to rule."

I go to the kitchen first to look over the shoulders of the techs, who are now working together. They are like dogs with their noses to a trail, looking for the stuff normal people don't see. As for me, after a few minutes, I feel like I am both in my body and out of it. The fact that Frito, who's been the object of such intense attention in the weeks since his testimony, is dead now has me shook, the collapse of all the expectations built up even more upsetting in its way than the sight of him. But the detached manner that Tonya and the techs are working is instructive. Just do your job. At a time like this, that's what's required. Clear your head and work carefully.

There are a lot of prints on the counter, which is no surprise. The guy with the light has the refrigerator door open, and the only things inside are a couple diet drinks on the shelf and two bottles of water. It's an old model, like everything else here, and there's a crack in the plastic lining at the top. He pulls out his cell and takes some more photos.

I move across the room, over to where the closet door is ajar. There's enough light that I can see what is inside. Aside from the square router tower, there is a change of clothes pretty much identical to what Blanco has on—another pair of khakis and a gray polo shirt on a hanger. There are boxers and socks on top of a cheap set of white laminate drawers, which makes it pretty clear Blanco was spending some time here, God knows why.

In the bathroom, there's an oval of used soap on the sink and a soiled towel hanging limply on a bar on the shower door. I notice something else and call out for the evidence techs.

"Looks like somebody mashed a mosquito," I say, pointing to

the back of the bathroom door. There's a little smear of blood where it was crushed. "Does the blood look recent?" I ask him.

"Recent enough. A day maybe. We'll test it."

The forensic light, however, doesn't show much on the high-gloss paint. Prints are easier to find in the summer, when everybody sweats more, but a quick blow that doesn't linger on the surface still might not leave residue.

"This may be something," the tech grants me, before he goes to get the equipment he'll need to preserve the bug and lift the stain.

23. IN HIS COWBOY BOOTS AND BLUE JEANS

When I leave the bathroom and walk back out into the main space, Walter Cornish in his cowboy boots and blue jeans is strutting through the front door. That stops me in place.

Cornish also jolts and points at me. He asks Tonya, "What the fuck is she doing here?" I guess he noticed me in the courtroom. One thing about the nail: People usually do.

"Same thing as me," says Tonya. "Police business."

"And what the fuck are you doing here?" I say to Cornish.

"I said he could come up," says Tonya. "You're the property manager, right?" she asks Walter.

"True. Got a voice message to come over here from one of the tenants."

"That was like literally yesterday night," Tonya says.

"It's after hours, hon."

Talk about being off-key. Calling Tonya 'hon' is like poking her with an ice pick, and I watch her take a beat or two. Walter can see the same thing and wants to justify himself.

"Tenants here, they have what I call a high bitch ratio. I don't just come runnin when they call. I'd be here every day."

"Any chance you were here yesterday?" Tonya asks.

"None. Haven't been in the building all week."

"Any idea what *he*"—she nods to the corpse—"was doing here?"

"Some. I leased him the apartment maybe two years ago. Well, 'lease' puts it nicely. It's month to month in a building like this."

"And why does Fabian Blanco, churchgoing dad of three, need a studio apartment in Shitsville?"

"Well, he didn't tell me, but you ever hear of a stabbin cabin? I just assumed, you know."

This time it's a lightning flash: Here's what the Ritz had on Blanco. Blanco was keeping a place—and a person—on the side. Yet again, the same lesson: With sex, you should never be surprised.

"Did he come to you to find the apartment?" Toy asks.

"Kinda. I was still on the job. We were working together and I was probably talking about my side hustle with Vojczek and he said, you know, the usual baloney, 'A friend of mine needs a really cheap place.' I think I brought him over here the same day. He didn't want his name on anything. I let him slide on signing the rental agreement, because his 'friend' needed to keep this super-duper secret." Cornish shows his teeth like a hungry wolf and rolls his eyes. "He never even said out loud to me that he'd be the one using it. But I mean, Jesus, talk about don't bullshit a bullshitter. His 'friend' paid by money order every month."

"Did he mail that in, or did you come by to collect it?"

"I haven't set foot in here since he rented. No call to. The money order, with the address here typed in, showed up in my mail at the Vojczek office every month, and I was damn glad to get it that way. Collecting the rent here, man, I literally put on my Kevlar and bring backup."

I mouth to Toy to ask if the rent was up-to-date, and Walter answers that the most recent money order arrived earlier this week. Scratch the idea Frito was moving out.

"Was anybody else using this place?" Tonya asks. "Maybe the neighbors mentioned something?"

"The only thing the neighbors ever said," says Cornish, "is that they never saw *any*one go in and out. Now and then, they'd hear noise from in here, but nobody seemed to be coming up or down the stairs or even slamming the front door. The old man across the hall, Mr. Johnson, he asked if I rented to a ghost." Walter smirks. "I guess Frito and his lady were very discreet." Walter's eyes circle the room, and his predator's grin returns briefly. "Must be she brought her own yoga mat, huh?" he asks, referring to the fact that there's no bed. Once he's enjoyed himself for a second, he changes subject. "No canvass yet?" Cornish asks Tonya.

"First thing tomorrow." She means she'll have a couple other detectives or patrol officers talk to everybody in the building. Twelve forty-five a.m. is not the time to start knocking on doors.

Tonya has been making notes on her tablet as they speak, and pays attention to it for a second so she can catch up. While she's still poking at the thing, the tech who met me in the bathroom calls out to her. He's crouching in front of the chair where poor Blanco still sits. The tech has his light on a spot on the thick edge of the wooden seat, right between Blanco's legs.

"This lit up before," he says. I bend behind Tonya to see a dime-sized spot that's glowing blue. "But then the pathologist came in. I just took a couple of pictures and got out of his way. But I wanted to finish now. I moistened it just on the edge"— he holds up a clear squeeze tube of sterile water—"so I could get a speck on the transfer paper," he says, lifting the little absorbent square between the fingers of his glove. "I hit this with a drop of reagent just now."

"And?"

He shows her the paper where's there a spreading blot of very bright purple.

"Phosphatase present?" Tonya asks.

"Yes, ma'am," he says.

That's presumptive for semen.

"Blanco, you kinky little devil," I say. Tonya again shoots me a look that is purely lethal, but I don't have her attention for long. She takes a full step toward Walter Cornish, who's just opened the window over the fire escape at the back of the room.

"Jesus Christ, Walter!" One a.m. or not, she's raised her voice. "You forget everything you ever knew? This is a crime scene. Keep your goddamned hands to yourself."

"Fuck," he says, "it stinks in here." He's waving around a handkerchief. "I gotta rent this place again, you know." He shakes his head but closes the window and then runs his hand along the sill, like he's cleaning up the dust. The fact that he went ahead and touched something right after she asked him not to is clearly over the limit for Toy.

"Okay," Tonya says. "Time for our visitors to leave."

On my way out, I stop to take a closer look at the front windows for one second, then follow Tonya and Cornish out. Across the landing, there is a dark eye peering through a skinny crack beside the door.

Cornish is already on the first stair down.

"Walter, I need your cell," Tonya says. "Someone's gonna stop by to visit with you tomorrow. You too, Mr. Johnson," she says, shooting a finger toward the eyeball across the hall. The door slams immediately.

"No worries," Cornish answers. He hands up a business card from his back pocket, then makes a loud departure as he hops down the stairs in his boots.

Tonya has grabbed my arm to hold me here.

"Thinking?" she asks.

"Like anything? Even something off the hook?"

"Who'm I talking to?"

"I got a little feeling Frito's other interest wasn't girls."

"Because?"

"Something," I answer.

"Well, there you go."

"Impossible?" I ask.

"How would I know? He was pretty buttoned up. That could mean anything."

"Somebody tied him to a chair. And had him dribbling spunk. Sometimes those Catholic boys want to be punished." I remember, as soon as I've said it, that she's been going to church, but she doesn't seem to take it one way or the other.

"Lots of boys deserve to be punished," Tonya says, but she smiles a little. It's interesting how different she is, more like her regular self, just one step out the door and away from the body. "We'll know a lot more after Potter gets a better look at him."

I hop one stair down, then point at her as I recall what I wanted to tell her.

"Oh," I add. "And there's no screen on that window over the fire escape, which is different from the front windows. I noticed that when Cornish pulled it open. I bet you find the screen stored in one of the closets."

"Meaning what?"

"I don't know. But why leave off the screens in the summer?"

"Never got around to putting them back on?"

"Make sure the techs take a good look at that area, too."

I get a very appreciative nod. "Good thinkin, Detective."

I wave and head down.

"Thanks for letting me pull you away from your boyfriend," she calls out.

"I don't have a boyfriend," I say. I haven't thought of Koob since I got here, which I'm happy to realize, but then a bunch of confused feelings knot up again in the middle of my chest. "I was by myself, looking at Instagram and finding out that everybody else has a much cooler life than me."

She laughs.

"Peace out," I say.

"Peace," she answers. "Please go talk to the Chief."

"On my way."

I call Rik from the front seat of the Cadillac before I have even pulled away. It's another hot night, but I keep the windows up while the AC's kicking in, so the coppers who have showed up— there's six cars now—can't hear me. That many cops means a reporter will know all about this in a couple hours, no matter what Tonya's orders are. So if the Chief is going to be the person to bring in the Bureau, we've got to move.

Rik's phone rings for a while. It's past one. He doesn't sleep a lot, but he must have turned in. His voice is groggy when he finally says, "Pinky."

"Early night?"

"Asleep in my La-Z-Boy," he answers. "I was watching the Trappers get pummeled on the West Coast. I hate when I do this. My feet swell up and I can't get my shoes off."

"Well, Boss, I'm glad you're sitting down." I tell him what

there is to tell. About every ten seconds he says, "Aw, fuck."
When I'm done, he just says, "Fuck, fuck, fuck."

"Do you want me to go talk to the Chief myself?"

"I'll meet you at her house in forty-five minutes. Wait for me
in the driveway."

The Chief is in a housecoat and definitely looking the worse for
it without her makeup. It's like seeing a mollusk that's crawled out
of its shell somehow. Her pretty face is always painted so perfectly.
Now she's pale, with a decided heaviness to her jawline that the
cosmetics help obscure, and all the wrinkles around her eyes are
out from under cover. We're seeing the Chief as she is beneath it
all, and it's someone considerably less upbeat. It's like her smile
came off with the makeup. I realize that Lucy seldom sees those
dimples when she's looking in the mirror late at night, alone.

She puts on coffee, while Rik and I sit down in her kitchen,
which has one of those corner nooks, with benches on two sides
built around a table. You can see it must have been great when
there were four of them here.

She brings a pint of cream from the fridge, as she takes a seat
across the table with a weary weight.

"Okay," she says. "Two o'clock in the morning and both of
you here, so it isn't good news."

I suppose if you're a big-time bad guy like a murderer you've
got to be a decent actor, but if this woman had anything to do
with Blanco's death, then Meryl Streep should just pack it in and
send Lucy referrals. As I tell the Chief where I was and what I
saw, her mouth parts slowly and everything else seems to fall out
of her face, both blood and sense, while her black eyes deepen in
mystification.

It takes her a couple minutes to process, but the Chief immediately agrees to Tonya's request to remove herself from the

case. Lucy's less convinced about calling the Bureau, who treat everybody else in law enforcement like they're the dumb baby brother.

"It's the way they take over," she says. "It's their case and everybody else is the butler."

"I think Tonya's got control of the crime scene," I say. "She's already sent stuff to the lab—the pathologist is doing the post right now. So the Bureau will have to play nice with her if they want her to share information. They pretty much have to treat her like a partner. There's joint jurisdiction. You can't tell the locals to 'go fish' on a murder."

"And another thing," says Rik. "I'd much rather deal with Moses than the local PA. A lot of strange stuff can go down with an elected prosecutor in a year when people are headed to the polls. I don't know what kind of ties Steven has to Jonetta Dunphy," he says, referring to the Greenwood County prosecuting attorney, "but their dads were both in office at the same time. Steven is gonna do everything but straight up accuse you of murder, and God only knows what Jonetta would do to humor him. Moses is completely straight. Pinky even knows him a little."

I called Moses a couple months back to introduce Rik, right after our first meeting with the Chief, and I was downright thrilled when the mighty US Attorney called me back so quickly. He wanted to ask me about Pops, but he was very nice to me, too. Usually, if you're not another lawyer, you're an absolute waste of time.

It's near three when I get home. Since Koob is often roaming around at this hour, I graze my knuckles on his door. It's another night where I'd be happy for company. Even with that tiny little knock, the lock gives way and the door swings open. I stand on the threshold, trying to figure what to do next.

"Hey, Koob," I call. "It's Clarice." I take a step inside, and my butt kind of puckers with the feeling of taboo: I'm finally within the inner sanctum, where Koob keeps all his secrets. "Koob," I say again. The next time, I'm loud, and then I'm really loud, immediately regretting the last shout because of our neighbors. He must be out working again.

Koob's apartment, which I saw empty when I was scouting out places, has a much more upscale look than mine now, well furnished in contemporary industrial style. Koob said his client is paying the rent, so they must have leased this furniture, too. In the living room, there's a long angular black leather sofa with round leather bolsters at either end, and a huge TV, but no sign of headphones. I'm still debating whether I should walk in further, since I know he won't like it, but hey, what kind of superspy leaves the door open? I can say I was worried about him.

His kitchen is big enough for a sort of Danish Modern table, and in his bedroom, the queen-size bed with a square wooden headboard has been made, the geometric spread and matching pillows arranged evenly. It's no surprise he's tidy. But what I gather from the made bed is that he hasn't been to sleep yet. Overall, the air here is weirdly reminiscent of Blanco's apartment, that empty solemn feel like it's not really a home.

I don't begin to worry until I look back at the living room. There's a desk there that matches the kitchen table, but nothing on it, not even a computer. Koob has to have a tricked-out machine to monitor the kind of surveillance equipment I saw him install behind Vojczek's, which means he took his powerhouse laptop with him for tonight's spying. But I see no sign of the Stingray that I've always assumed was here to pick up the signal from the NoDirt.

I retrace my path through every room, opening each drawer,

in which I find nothing but a little paper dust. I'm beginning to get a very weird feeling. In Koob's bedroom, the closet is empty except for bare hangers, one or two of which have ended up on the floor. On my knees, I find a single black sock underneath the dresser. In the bathroom, there's a bluish squiggle of toothpaste in the sink and a used bar of soap in the shower, but nothing else. Walking into the kitchen, I recognize a scent I've been smelling since I walked in here, a disinfectant spray, meaning he was cleaning recently. Then I finally notice two keys on the breakfast bar.

I sit down at Koob's table. In my chest, a lot of different feelings are banging into each other, and my thoughts aren't any clearer, circling one way then the other. But one conclusion is solid.

Every fucking time, I think. It happens every time.

He's gone.

24. FOR ADVICE

Since junior high, there has only been one place I go for serious advice. My dad, much as I love him, comes out with shit that makes even me wonder if he is a member of another species, and my mom has never gotten beyond 'What did you do now?' I'm not sure I believe in the afterlife or mediums, but somewhere in my inner fibers I'm sure Pops will still be showing up long after he's gone, when I really need him.

So on Saturday morning, I go—as I have been going for an hour every Saturday since we all got our second shots—to Aventura Center for Advanced Living. If the owners had their way, you'd move into Aventura when you turned fifty-five and never walk out again. It is meant to be just like the Ritz—the real Ritz—but with walkers. The attendants all wear sport coats and they treat even me in my combat-style boots and nail like they think I'm actually Rihanna in a thin disguise.

Pops is in what they call the middle phase, which means Assisted Living. He has a nice little suite with all the plugs and outlets so that they can give him oxygen, for example, or run an IV drip, neither of which he currently needs, thank God. He has a cheerful attendant named Florence, who makes sure he takes all his meds twice a day. Pops moved in here at the start of 2020. In January, about two weeks after they closed the law firm, he took a terrible spill at home. He fainted, I guess—a problem with his heart meds, it turned out—and hit his head on one of the kitchen counters and ended up with a serious concussion. I came back from grocery shopping and freaked. He was lying on the tile, bloody to the shoulders from the head wound and frighteningly out of it. It was his second serious medical incident within a couple months, and he decided on his own that he needed nurses nearby 24/7.

I wait for him in the so-called Day Room, where there are big windows and fancy drapes and furniture in muted tones. I am in one of the few easy chairs provided for those of us who can still get out of them. Not long after Reception has called up to announce me, I see Pops stumble in on his cane, tossing up a hand in greeting. He looks older every time I come, sagging a little more and getting noticeably yellow. His cancer remains at bay, and his heart condition is under control, but now his liver and kidneys are in decline. Plus he has a harder time than ever getting around.

But he is so goddamned happy! He has had a great time here. He started his own YouTube channel, where once a week he sits down to give his summary of the latest legal news. He has somehow figured out how to integrate all kinds of visuals into his videos, like charts and photographs. Trump, who produced a legal confrontation every week, boosted his viewership, he claims, and he now has about 2,000 followers, which is mind-blowing. I couldn't get that many people to follow me if I was dropping money on the street.

Most of his mood, we all know, is due to Sondra, his cute

little girlfriend, who is right beside him with a hand on his elbow. Sondra moved in here with her former husband after his second stroke. He was almost twenty years older than Sondra—there's a story there that Pops either doesn't know or won't tell—but lasted five more years. By the time he passed, Sondra was happy to stay, since these days you need a golden ticket to get in. She's seventy-eight anyway, but in great shape. She's still pretty sporty and leaves at least once a week in the summer to play golf at her country club, with Pops as her chauffeur in the cart.

I was over here every day when Pops first moved in, and by the second week I noticed her lingering around him.

'I think she likes you,' I said.

'I think so, too,' he said. 'And I like her as well. But I am uncertain how to approach this.'

'Are you talking about getting married?'

'Lord no,' he said. 'But this is a small community, Pinky. I enjoy it here. If things do not go well with Sondra, it might become very uncomfortable for both of us. And I am hardly certain that I need this kind of thing as I creep up to ninety.'

I'm not the person people usually come to for relationship advice. But if there is any human being I truly get, it's my grandfather.

'Look, Pops,' I said. 'I always thought you had an awesome thing with Helen.'

'As did I.'

'So that means you're good at relationships. You can manage the give and take, you get a lot out of it. And you absolutely want to do it, because from what I can tell, it takes a fuck-ton of determination that I, frankly, have never had.'

He laughed. Pops always finds me amusing and endearing. 'All true.'

'Then go for it. It's your nature to pair up.'

I know he would have reached the same conclusion on his own, but given how happy he has been, I'm proud that I gave him that little nudge.

Now the three of us sit down around a table and have a brief chat. Sondra has fourteen grandchildren and two great-grandchildren, so there are always photos to look at and funny stories. Eventually I kind of cough and say I have some confidential legal business I need Pops's advice on.

"Of course, of course," she sings, and hugs me and then flies off, right after kissing Pops on the top of his bald head and reminding him that they have a bridge game at eleven. He turns to watch her go, like he can barely stand to have her out of sight.

Everybody in the family, me included, is grateful for Sondra, but we all roll our eyes when Pops describes her as just like Helen. Helen, Rik's mom, had this incredible thing: If you mattered to her, it felt like she could take an MRI of your heart and lovingly absorb you on your own terms. Sondra is cute as a button—her hairdresser maintains her curly blonde bob, and she's still fit looking—plus she's one of those smaller women who always get called perky, meaning bubbly and positive and warm. On the other hand, she's about half as smart or interesting as Helen and, leaving aside her looks, doesn't seem to have much else going for her. She grew up in the suburbs and never left, raising her family within a mile of her parents' house. She is very sweet but doesn't know much except the best places on the West Bank to eat and shop. Then again, being fair, she is really good at taking care of other people, which I guess is a superpower of its own.

Anyway, Pops is totally smitten. They were already talking about spending nights together when the pandemic closed in on this place and forced everybody into life behind locked doors.

After the two families consented, they became a pod of two. Pops says it was just like another honeymoon. I will never get it when it comes to couples, which I suppose is the lesson of the week. I keep thinking that at some point, I will ask for the spicy details of what exactly happens in that bed they share, given that Pops is looking straight down the barrel of ninety, but I never quite have the nerve. It works for them, whatever it is.

"And what exactly is this legal problem?" Pops asks warily as soon as Sondra is out of sight. I can tell he's afraid that I'm back to my old ways and have gotten busted or am about to. His face lifts noticeably when I start out by telling him I'm not in trouble.

"I just don't know what to do," I say. I have always shared pretty much everything with him, even though he has sometimes sat through the details of my personal life like I'm a doctor putting one of those Popsicle sticks right down his throat. He knows about the Chief's case—I have been keeping him posted weekly—and he heard about Blanco's death on the news. But what I haven't told even him, until now, is that Koob and I got a little involved, since before that I'd been rattling on to him like everybody else about my weird neighbor, the spy.

"Even so, I still have no real idea why he was in Highland Isle," I say. "He would never talk about work. And here's the hard part, okay? The night that Blanco was killed, Koob was supposed to come by and he didn't, and instead I heard him get back next door at about three. And then at some point the next day, probably while I was at work, he vanished, emptied the apartment and is just gone."

"No communication?"

"No." I can't pretend that doesn't irritate me. How much effort does it take to slide a note under my door? 'Bye, it was a blast.'

"And as I recall, your assumption was that he was some kind of surveillance expert?"

"I mean, I don't know what he is actually. He seems like such a sweet guy, contained and all that, but really genuine, so, you know, a hit man, it doesn't compute. But a hired killer is probably insanely good at compartmentalizing. And he was Special Forces, so it's not like he was trained to teach preschool. And then, I've thought at times, Who says he's alive? Maybe somebody came and whacked him and cleaned out his apartment while I was gone."

Pops buttons up his mouth to think all of this over.

"All right. And what's the precise question, Pinky?"

"I mean, do I have some kind of duty or something to the Chief to tell anybody about all this?"

"Is the Chief a serious suspect in this death?"

"Well, not serious, but they haven't ruled her out. It's just a strange situation. Rik keeps telling her that the city attorney has no choice but to dismiss the P&F complaint against her, since Blanco's dead and his testimony doesn't count because he can't be cross-examined. But for some reason, probably because it's so political, Marc hasn't done it yet. The mayor's opponent, Steven DeLoria, keeps insinuating that maybe that's why the Chief killed Blanco, to get the case dropped. We think Marc doesn't want to add fuel to that fire. In the meantime, Moses—"

"How *is* Moses?" Pops asks. "He actually came out here for lunch a couple of months ago."

"He's a good guy, you know. He issued a statement saying that at this point there are no persons of interest regarding Blanco's death, so that kind of kiboshed Steven's bullshit."

"Good."

"Right, but Moses could say that because they still don't know if it was actually a homicide. The autopsy didn't show anything, so the best guess right now is natural causes, probably cardiac arrest—maybe during rough sex. But there's no damage to the heart muscle and no blockages in the arteries. Apparently, on rare occasions, somebody can get so stressed that there's a spasm in the main coronary artery. Or maybe he got like a freak electrical shock from some appliance that shorted out, which given everything else, they're guessing might be a plug-in vibrator.

"But there are two injection sites on his upper arm they can't really account for. They're trying to find Blanco's doctor, to see if he got any shots recently. It's even possible that the marks are mosquito bites, because some people don't react much to skeeters. The police pathologist took a tissue sample, which they're sending to a bug specialist."

"An entomologist?"

"Right. I found this squashed mosquito in the bathroom, and the blood inside it was recent. Type A positive. Which isn't Blanco, by the way, meaning someone else was with him.

"All in all, though, the injection sites are probably needle marks, up high on the arm so they wouldn't show when Blanco put on a short-sleeve shirt in this weather. But it's at a funny angle to be jabbing yourself, so he was probably getting high with whoever he was messing with, and they were shooting up one another. But even though that makes sense, the preliminary tox screen showed nothing. It will be a few days before they get the final word on that. But the bottom line right now is a whole lot of who-the-fuck-knows."

Pops nods through all of this and takes a second to ask a couple more questions to be sure he has the details straight.

"Pinky, it sounds like you were at the crime scene—you say you found this mosquito. Why was that? You're very well informed, given the usual secrecy in a homicide investigation."

"The lead detective is actually a woman I met in the academy, Tonya Eo."

"I remember Tonya!" he says. Pops never seems to forget anything about me, and he confirms that vague memory I have that I brought Toy out to the West Bank with me when I visited him and Helen one weekend back then. I guess there may have been a second or two when I was more serious about her than I remember now. Anyway, Pops says he picked up at once on how smart she is. "I thought she would get over her shyness," he says. "She struck me, frankly, as being in culture shock."

"Completely. And you were right. She's just totally crushing it as a cop. She's so self-confident now it makes me jealous."

"And you're seeing her, too?" Like I say, he knows how my life works.

"No, we're just buds now. It took a while to work it out." I explain that Tonya wanted me at the crime scene to get word to the Chief. "She probably tells me more than she's supposed to, like about the autopsy. But she really respects the Chief and kind of wants her to know what's going on without informing her directly. And I came up with some good stuff when I was in the apartment, so I mean I'm sorta-kinda part of the investigation."

He nods like 'It's Pinky, so there are never straight lines.'

I say, "The apartment was definitely wiped down, like all the surfaces in the living room. Whoever Blanco was with was scared of something. Here and there there's ridge detail that isn't Frito's, but there's nowhere near enough to identify somebody from the print database. Maybe they could confirm if there was a definite suspect, but you can't work the other way."

He understands. "And your concern is that perhaps your friend could fill in some important details?"

"Well, who knows? I mean, the only real connection between

him and any of this is inside my head. I wouldn't have any reason to think he even knows Fabian Blanco's name if I hadn't talked to him about Blanco's testimony and that photograph. Maybe Koob bouncing suddenly is just a coincidence. Or maybe he was sick of me.

"But you know, on the other hand, I'm really down for the Chief, who's gotten incredibly messed over, and I want to do anything to help her. But if I talk about this dude, Koob, everybody's going to end up super pissed with me. You remember Rik made me promise that I was going to stay away from him—"

"Just so. I recall telling you that Rik had given you excellent advice." He raises his eyes to give me a little poke.

"Yeah, okay," I answer. "But like I say, nobody's gonna be okay about Koob. Tonya, she's trying to be cool, but she's just got this thing about men, especially me and men.

"So like I'm seriously confused. And I know I could throw a lot of shade at this dude and the way he ghosted me, but you know, we said free and easy, hit and run was fine. If he turns out to have no connection with the case, then he'll think I pulled him into this because I'm a vengeful bitch. And I hate that kiss-and-tell shit anyway. I mean, what people tell you in bed, that should be like what you say to your priest and lawyer, don't you think?"

He smiles a bit. "That is not a privilege recognized in court."

"But it should be. Right? I mean, it is if you're married."

"Well, let's not debate the law, Pinky. The question is how we solve your problem."

"Right," I say. "Like every now and then I think I should just hunt him down and press him to the wall for answers."

Pops shakes his head vigorously for the first time.

"That is the one thing you clearly should not do. Go confront someone who might be a hit man, Pinky? No. And whatever his activities in Highland Isle, it is obvious that he did not want to explain them or the reasons for his departure with you. Undoubtedly, he had to make a quick getaway. As Rik told you some time ago, even if all your friend was doing was illegal wiretapping, he cannot talk about that freely without risking legal jeopardy. And besides, dear Pinky, how would you find him?"

"Well, how many people named Koob do you think there are in Pittsburgh?"

"If that is truly his name."

"That's his name," I say. I am emphatic enough that it surprises even me, and Pops draws back.

"But there are many places in the world to run to besides Pittsburgh, surely?" he says.

"He really missed his kids," I answer. "He went to Pittsburgh."

"Just so," says Pops, which means he gets it. He raises his face to look straight at me then, a look I love because it means his big brain is working at high speed on my behalf. Finally, he says, "Pinky, I think we find ourselves in a familiar spot."

"What spot is that?"

"Well, I suspect you have come here largely to talk to yourself. I can provide an answer to your legal question, which is, very much as you have said—you have no concrete information beyond your own suspicions. Because of that, I see no duty to share your concerns with anyone—Rik or the Chief or Tonya. You can keep your peace. For the time being. It might be wiser to speak up now, because in the event that this fellow ends up in the middle of the investigation, everyone will have some sharp questions for you. But my guess is that there will still be time to volunteer details if something more solid materializes. For example, if they had found something in that seedy apartment, which suggested the use against Blanco of sophisticated electronic surveillance, well, then it would have been time to come forward."

"Understood."

"And I can certainly tell you what the most foolhardy course of action is, which is to conduct a private manhunt for someone who clearly does not want to be found."

"Okay."

"Yet we both know that as usual, you are going to do what you want. I would say you have come here only to find out if you are actually free to do so."

"Okay. And what is it that I'm going to do?" But he's right. I know.

He reaches for my hand.

"Please text me every hour to give me your exact location in Pittsburgh. And tell me now that you will understand if I contact the FBI when I don't hear from you."

25. SQUIRREL HILL NORTH

Becoming a PI may involve firearms training, learning what's legal and what's not and mastering all the smooth moves of the PIBOT, but in twenty-first-century America, even the super-sleuths Humphrey Bogart played would be pretty much shit out of luck without first-class Internet skills. As I often admit to Rik, I learn more there than I do on the street.

Like I told Pops, finding a guy named Koob in Pittsburgh is not a challenge. I leapfrogged from the Pennsylvania Public Information List—which is basically voters' records, containing must-have nuggets like name, sex, date of birth, party (Koob is an independent), residential address and mailing address—to the Allegheny County Recorder of Deeds and the Allegheny County database of property ownership and assessment, and then to several online services where you use all of that information to pick up stuff like cell phone numbers. Along the way, I acquired some mildly surprising info. Koob has gone by several names— Koob Xie, Koob Hsieh, Koob Shay and even Cooper Shay. Even more startling, crazy Mrs. Xie, who calls herself Melinda Shay, seems to be a well-established real estate lady.

I depart from Highland Isle in the Cadillac at about eight p.m. on Saturday, when I can just blast along the interstates, and by six a.m. Sunday I am parked down the block from the house Koob owns on Wightman Avenue. The neighborhood of Squirrel Hill North lies within the city of Pittsburgh and is frankly the kind of place where I could see a grown-up Pinky settling, in a different life. It's very hilly, with a lot of beautiful old houses—colorful frame Victorians and hulking Tudor-style places with heavy brown beams on the upper stories surrounding the windows and tracing angles on the white stucco facades.

As for Koob's house, which I guess is Mrs. Koob's these days, it's older, in an architectural style I can't name. Set a good twenty feet above the street, the place just screams out suburban substance, which comes as no surprise given what Koob said about his upbringing and never feeling like he belonged to any community. I'm sure the big-ass house gives him a sense of being rooted. It's redbrick, with the steep gables of a Victorian, a single triangle with a window on the high point of the third floor. On the ground, an enclosed screen porch wraps around the house. Within a large sloping lawn, two sets of concrete steps with iron railings help a visitor climb the hill to the front door.

Having gotten this far, I am not quite sure how I'll actually find Koob. My operating assumption, given everything he said about how loony Mrs. Xie is, is that he stopped by to see his kids but isn't putting his head on a pillow here. So I prepared something that will make Mrs. Xie point me in the right direction.

Around 8:15 a.m., after I stroll by and see some figures moving through the dimness of the first floor, I return to the CTS and grab a cardboard box—a one-foot cube—and a clipboard, both of which I brought from Highland Isle. I carry them with me up the two separate concrete staircases. The bell is on the outside of the porch, but the tooled oak door within, leading to the house proper, flies open, and a woman, who I recognize as Mrs. Koob from brokerage company headshots on the net, advances to the screening.

It seems way too early for the Sunday open houses, at least it would be around Kindle County, but Melinda is already dressed for success. She has on a tailored white linen suit, and her blonde hairdo might as well have been shellacked in place. Given the way Koob talked about her, I was expecting one of those characters in soiled rags who wander around like zombies in movies about nineteenth-century madhouses. This woman, credit where due, is totally put together and damn attractive, if that's your kind of thing. Her manner is cold and instinctively angry, but definitely not out of control.

"Ace Messenger," I say. "We have a delivery for Cube—" I squint at my clipboard. "Zee?"

"Here," she says as she pushes open the screen door. "I'll take it."

I lift the clipboard. "He's gotta sign."

"Hold on," she says and zooms back through the heavy front door, calling out, "Koob!"

Oh. I can feel my heart taking on some added weight. In general, even for a one-nighter, I stay away from married people, with occasional exceptions for supposedly straight women who have a secret thirst a dude could never fulfill. Gay or straight, though, somebody living with their spouse inevitably views their thing with me as something extra on the down low. I always end up with the feeling that there are three people in bed, which is not that much fun when one of them is someone you didn't invite. As in so many things, the cheating men, generally speaking, are worse than the women. I've been through enough of these guys

that I now recognize a type, like Primo DeGrassi, who says he's
going to leave, just as soon as blah blah blah, which might as well
be when the universe stops expanding. But I didn't see Koob as
one of them.

But here he is, emerging from the doorway into the house
that his wife went through thirty seconds before. He's in running
shorts and shoes with an old Carnegie Mellon T-shirt, and he's
about two strides from the screen door when he finally looks up
and stops cold. I've seen a lot of different moods on Koob, but
I've never watched his smooth face shrink with what is almost
certainly panic.

He comes the rest of the way to the door and whispers, "I'll
meet you down the block." He hitches his head slightly in the
direction where I'd parked.

"When?"

"Two minutes."

He turns away until I whisper, "Better take the box, man."

He wrenches the screen door open and grabs the parcel,
retreating inside.

I go about a hundred feet down the street and watch his house
from the other side. He emerges a couple minutes later, in the
same outfit with the addition of a fanny pack belted around his
waist. He looks directly at me for one second and then, in a flash,
is in a dead run in the other direction.

I say a bad word and fly after him. I am not in Boot Camp
shape, like he is, and I realize after the first few strides that I'll
never have the endurance to keep up with him. On the other
hand, even in military-style footwear, I might gain ground on
him in a dead sprint. I am really fast. Once I've halved the
distance between us, I yell his name. He looks over his shoulder
and kicks it up another gear. I keep pace only for another block.

After two more, I'm falling behind, and after another quarter mile, involving a hard slog uphill, I have completely lost sight of him when I reach the crest. Best guess is that he took a left into an alley that cuts in midblock. I jog up there but see no sign of him, although he could be crouched behind any of the garbage and recycling cans. I take a second to think. He must be figuring that I'll spend time searching for him, checking various possible hiding places.

Instead, I double back, jogging, and wait at the mouth of the alley that runs behind his house. I amble in a few paces and take up a position on the other side of a detached brick garage, so he won't be able to see me from the corner. I am pretty sure he's got his cell phone in that fanny pack, but if he wanted to talk, he wouldn't have taken off running, so I squelch the idea of giving him a call.

I wait there for quite some time. Initially, I'm glad to rest. It's a great summer day, and I'm sweating hard. Eventually, I pull my pants legs up to the knees and sit down on the walk to enjoy the sun. I check my phone and remember to contact Pops. 'Still alive in Pittsburgh,' I e-mail him, then drop a pin in a map app and text that to him, too, knowing that he probably won't find a single person in the Aventura Center for Advanced Living who can make heads or tails of it.

A little before 9:30, Koob saunters by, cooling down from his run, his tee completely sweated through. I wait until he's gone past me, then I step into the alley and call his name.

What happens next I don't expect. In a Special Forces move, he hits the pavement as he's reaching behind him to the fanny pack. He rolls once and ends up on his belly with both hands on a semiautomatic pistol that is pointed at me.

"Whoa," I say, and raise my hands halfheartedly. "Don't shoot, cowboy." I have the two-shot derringer in my shoulder holster, which is under the open blouse I'm wearing over a tank top, but he is freaked out enough that drawing on him might make him pull the trigger. He stares at me for a second, then gets to his feet slowly, still in firing position, his arms outstretched, one hand bracing the other.

"Go away," he says.

I'm too shocked by this whole thing not to be Pinky.

"I thought you didn't own a gun."

"I bought one," he answers.

"Why is that?"

"It enhances my credibility. I told you I don't need a girlfriend."

"Hey, man. That's not why I'm here. I'm working. I just need to talk for a minute."

"And what work is that?"

"Frito Blanco died the night before you left. Maybe murdered."

There's a small hitch before he says, "And who's Frito Blanco?"

He's got to be lying—we talked about Blanco for quite a while—but I go with it and say, "He was the last cop to testify against the Chief. The one who came up with that photograph."

"Sounds like you ought to talk to the Chief about what happened to him."

"Well, I'm here to talk to you. Are you telling me, old pals and all that shit, you don't know anything about Blanco's death?"

"What I'm actually telling you," he says, "for a second time, is to go away. Now." He reaches behind him to stow the weapon and then turns and heads down the alley toward home.

I check a restaurant app and walk downhill three blocks to Murray Avenue, where there's a Tudor-style strip of stores, including a café where I stand in line until I can get in for brunch and a chance to use the facilities. This is the second time someone has pointed a gun at me—the first time was when I was investigating for Rik on a divorce case—and I can now say for sure that whenever that happens, it's a crazy high adrenaline experience. I sit with a mixed sparkling water and lemonade, trying to calm down, so I can figure out what the hell is going on.

First off, using a handgun to get rid of some chick you want to forget is pretty extra. So either he thinks talking to me will expose something life-threatening, or he's totally tripped out about someone else.

Second, there is no way I'm just gonna fuck off. Maybe what's spooking him has nothing to do with Blanco. Maybe it has to do with the shit he turned up about Vojczek. But the Ritz is the man behind the curtain on the Chief's case. Overall, Koob's act in the alley makes me pretty sure he knows stuff I need to hear.

There's a nice park nearby, where I wander after eating. Eventually I take a seat on a bench to call his cell. Maybe the phone will be less threatening to him. I'm slightly amazed when his number turns out to be disconnected, since it came up on several sites.

More thinking. I return to the CTS. There's a space open right across the street from Koob's house, and I park the Cadillac there. I want him to know I'm not leaving.

About six p.m. a text arrives. It's very cute since it comes with no return number, meaning he masked it, which also makes it clear he's got another phone or SIM card. 'I WILL hurt you, if you come near my family again. Go away. I will never talk to you.' My best guess is that he's upstairs peeking out a window to see how I'm going to react, and I unfurl my middle finger and hold it out the car window for a minute.

* * *

After dark, I sneak out the passenger door so I can go back down to the shopping area to buy something for dinner. I've just settled back in the passenger seat to eat my Chinese when my cell buzzes. It's Tonya.

"Girl!" I say.

She starts right in. "Where are you? I came by your place last night to talk to you and stopped there again on my way to work this morning."

"I'm out of town," I say. "On a case."

"This case?"

"I'm not sure. It might connect. I don't know."

"Is this a lead you got from the Chief?"

"Not completely. Something I more noticed on my own."

"At Frito's?"

"Completely independent. Probably nothing to do with Blanco."

"Listen, boo. I'm not digging you dodging my questions. I've told you a lot of shit I maybe shouldn't have, and like the only excuse I have is that I'm trading information, okay? I'm telling you because you're telling me. Get it?"

"Okay."

"So what are you doing?"

"I'm trying to talk to a dude who has some stuff on the Ritz."

"Explain."

"I can't. And I'll never be able to. Any chance I get this guy to share, I'll have to guarantee it's on a double super-secret tip-top DL basis. He's totally scared. He already pulled a gun on me. There is no way he'll even breathe the same air as me if he thinks I'm going to repeat one word he's saying to the cops. And he's hip enough to ask."

"Well, whatever you get, I have to hear about it."

I think.

"What if it's like a CI situation, maybe?" I ask. "No names. Nothing to identify him."

"Well, I can't enroll him as a CI. I don't even know who he is."

"Okay. Then enroll me."

She takes a second to think that through, and as it turns out, we both like the idea. If I'm carried as a confidential informant on the Highland Isle PD records, she won't have to give up my name to the FBI. It also offers her a little cover on what she's told me, since it can be called part of a CI exchange. And I wouldn't have to give up anything that would endanger Koob, so long as I make the limitations clear now.

"So I have no obligation to tell you anything I've learned from our client," I say.

"Naturally. But I have to hear everything to do with what happened to Blanco. You can't pick and choose."

"Okay. Like I say, it's a dream this guy will even talk to me."

"Is this the dude you were seeing?"

"No," I say. Simple excuse: It's none of her business.

Toy can flip the switch to angry in a second, and I can hear her breathing into the phone and reeling herself back in.

"Why did you want to talk to me?" I ask.

"We interviewed Mrs. Blanco last night. Marisel."

"General background?"

"Sort of. We're still looking for Blanco's phone."

"The lawyer didn't have it?"

"Nope. Said Blanco wouldn't hand it over even to her. So we thought maybe he left it at home. But no on that. We wanted to sit down with Marisel anyway. She's positive he was offed."

"Why?"

"Well, you remember she walked out of the courtroom when Frito was on the stand?"

"Sure, but I thought the sex stuff about Blanco and the Chief was getting to her."

"Well, she says what bothered her was that Frito was fibbing a whole lot."

"About?"

"That ring for one thing. She's never seen it before. And the uncle for another."

"There was no uncle?"

"He did have an uncle. But the guy died in prison. And he didn't finish high school. And she was like, 'There's no way Fabian would lie under oath, unless someone was threatening him.'"

"Well okay. So maybe there was a lot Blanco wasn't sharing with Mrs. Blanco, right?"

"Apparently. But she's positive someone was forcing him to lie."

"The Ritz?"

"She has literally never heard Moritz Vojczek's name."

"Cornish?"

"She remembers Walter. Blanco liked him. Kind of a friend."

"Did she know anything about that apartment?"

"I didn't tell her. You know, she's got enough going on right now. But when I asked about Frito's habits, like what he did or where he went when he was chilling, she said all he did was work super hard and spend time with his kids."

"And any feedback from the Bureau on the computer in the apartment?"

"My Bureau guy says there's nothing on it. Apparently, Frito was using it to read a thumb drive or memory stick. Some form of external media. That's all they can say right now. The people in the spook section, the FCI guys"—foreign counterintelligence—

"they have some tricks, you know, shit they get from the code writers at Microsoft that would let them drill into the metadata left on the machine, but it's not for sure they'll do it, especially since we can't say it's a murder case. I mean, the Bureau, they have some rules, man. Rules and rules. Every second you've got to be paranoid you're going to step in shit. But they have amazing resources. I'll give them that. They actually have a bug guy at HQ who flew in to talk to me yesterday."

I'm hearing a funny note in her voice.

"Toy, what's this stuff about you and the Bureau? Are they trying to recruit you?"

"You know the patter. Always a place for a BIPOC woman. They could be playing me, making me think I can join their team so I give them everything they want."

I can tell right now she's thinking about this seriously. 'FBI' would definitely work for her parents. It would change the sound of 'queer' in a city minute.

"And what did the bug guy say?"

"He said the insect squashed on the bathroom door is a tiger mosquito."

"A *tiger* mosquito?"

"Tiger, right."

"You mean it's got like stripes?"

"Jesus, Pinky," she says. "Where do you come from? I wasn't asking what kind of fit it was rockin."

"Well, what did you ask?"

"I listened. Tiger mosquitoes are known to bite the same person several times. So maybe we get lucky and with DNA we identify somebody who was with Frito in the apartment. The bloodstain was definitely twenty-four to thirty-six hours old. And it's not the Chief's or Frito's, they're both O positive."

"Fabulous, right?"

"Maybe. The tiger mosquito typically travels about three hundred feet in one day, meaning the blood inside it could have been extracted from anyone in the apartment building. You know, like it bit somebody on the third floor and floated in through that open window looking for more."

"But the stain's A positive, you told me."

"Yeah, so are thirty-five percent of the people on earth. Also possible it's a mix."

"Okay."

A second passes.

"So like we're straight, right?" she asks. "Whatever you get, wherever you are, you'll tell me everything this dude knows about Blanco, whatever he saw or smelled."

"Deal," I say. I promise I'll call her tomorrow.

I'm sleeping in the passenger seat of the CTS, fully reclined and pretty comfy, dreaming that Koob has moved into the Aventura Center for Advanced Living, when the harsh feel of light on my lids and a strange knocking wake me. When I come to, there's an intense LCD beam burning out my eyeballs, and I cover my face and squirm around. The light is lowered but the rapping continues. It's a uniformed cop, young, Latino maybe. But he doesn't look ready for war.

"Miss," he says when I roll down the window.

"Officer?"

"We had a report of a woman asleep in a car. One of the neighbors called it in. Said it looks like you're young and violating curfew. Maybe a runaway."

"You're makin my day," I tell him and hesitate, just as I start to reach for my wallet. I had put it in the glove box so I wasn't sleeping on the lump, and I explain where it is and what I'm doing so he can say okay before I open the glove compartment. I press the button and lift my hands as the box drops open and he runs his light over the interior.

"Okay," he says.

I hand over my wallet—not so smart, but I'm still groggy.

He looks at my license and shines the flashlight back in my face, then helps himself to a look at the other cards in my wallet.

"PI?"

"Yes."

"You're not licensed here, so don't tell me you're working."

"Okay."

He hasn't gotten to the concealed carry permit, which could be real trouble if he figures out I'm strapped, since I have no permission in this state to be hiding a gun, which right now is under the driver's seat. But instead, he hands the wallet back.

"I think maybe you should move on, Miss Granum."

"Officer, I'm not trying to be a dick, but what am I doing wrong? I checked the signs. It's not a no-parking zone."

"Public vagrancy?" he asks.

"You mean a homeless person can sleep in a cardboard box on the street and I can't take a nap in a Cadillac?"

The guy seems to have a sense of humor, and his eyes narrow as he tries to decide whether to smile or go hard-ass.

"Miss Granum. I don't think you drove ten to twelve hours from Highland Isle for a vacation, at least not one where you sleep in your car. You're staked out on somebody. And we already agreed you're not licensed to work as a PI in this state. So make it easy and move on. There's a public parking lot down on Murray. Well lit. You'll be safer there."

This is where I can hear Pops's voice. Let Koob win this round.

Any answer but yes and the cop will get me out and frisk me and search the car and find the derringer.

"Okay," I say. I hop across the center console to the driver's seat and start the car, and pull out carefully.

But I'm back in front of Koob's by eight a.m. This time I see his daughter head out, maybe for a summer job. She's one of those girls, pretty and graceful, I used to hate because everything seemed so easy for them. There's probably a lot that bothers her, but she still moves like nothing can touch her. Then Melinda drives off in her BMW. Once they're gone, I walk up to the front door and ring the bell. I ring it about twenty times before I hear voices in the house—Koob yelling at his son, I think. I hear the dead bolt being opened and Koob emerges, still looking back over his shoulder and exchanging words with the boy. When he turns, he sees me and the derringer that I have in my hand at hip level.

I use one finger to indicate that he should come closer. He complies, walking about halfway to the screen door. I speak in a voice a little bit above a whisper.

"Your turn to listen," I say. "I drove ten fucking hours to talk to you, instead of just dropping a dime on you to the cops and the FBI, which was my other choice. But have it your way. I'm sure both agencies will have a lot of interest when I tell them you have been doing all kinds of super-weird stuff for a couple months and that I saw you install a NoDirt behind the Vojczek office. And that you totally vaporized within hours of Blanco's death. So you don't need to explain it to me. You can explain it to them."

He thinks, but when he answers, he doesn't say what I expect.

"She just went to pick up a prescription and will be back in five minutes. If she sees you, she will go nuclear."

"I don't care about your f'd-up domestic situation. I'm going back to the public lot on Murray Avenue. And if you're not sitting in the passenger seat in my car in the next fifteen minutes, I'm calling Tonya Eo, who's the detective sergeant in HI who's working Blanco's case, plus whoever she tells me to contact at the Bureau. You can run from them, or talk to them, or hire a lawyer, I don't care, but I'm done making you my problem. I'm your best choice by a million miles. But be stupid or whatever. I don't care."

His eyes move a little as he tries to take in what I said.

"How is that? How are you my best choice?"

"I'll explain it when you're sitting in my car. It'd take too much time now and like, God forbid I upset Melinda."

I shake my head, just to show how little I like what I'm finding out about him, then go back down the walk.

26. KOOB MATERIALIZES

Koob seems to materialize in my passenger seat. I had backed the Cadillac into a space in the open-air lot on Murray. The way he snuck in means he must have cut through the privet row behind me, and then slid along in a crouch beside the car. He pops the door and jumps in without ever standing to full height. I just stare. This guy is completely terrified of his wife. It's beyond disappointing.

He's in his running stuff again, so that must be his excuse for going out.

He briefly returns my look, in his mute show-nothing way, then stares out the windshield toward the canopy of trees in full leaf on the other side of the lot.

"I need to say this. I really like you, Clarice."

His declaration makes me absolutely furious.

"Oh, for fuck's sake," I say, and on impulse slug him in the shoulder. Hard.

"Jesus," he says.

"Forget junior high, goddamn it. Blanco is dead. Do you know about that or not?"

He is still rubbing his shoulder while he lays his black eyes on me. He says calmly, "You were going to explain why I'm better off talking to you than the police."

I describe my deal with Tonya. He thinks it over while I clean up a little in the car. I still have the crumpled bag from a fast-food place in my lap, and I suspect the Cadillac is thick with fried smells. I crack a window, but in response to his immediate look of alarm, slide it shut again.

"Anything I tell you," he says, "that cannot get back to the Ritz. If it does, he will know exactly where it came from."

Tonya has already promised that all information I get will go no further than her, and I tell him that.

"Okay," I say. "Is the Ritz the reason you bought a gun?"

"Basically."

"Did he threaten you?"

"Not yet."

"So why do you think he might?"

Koob, always slow to speak, takes even longer this time.

"I think the Ritz killed Blanco," he says.

Whoa! I roll that over for a minute.

"Did you see him do it?"

"I saw him getting ready to do it."

"While you were surveilling him? Had you followed him?"

Koob is the master of the subtle expression, almost as if his smooth face will allow no more. But just from the small movement of his lower lip, I know something is wrong. He pivots in his seat to face me fully.

"I work for Ritz. Worked. *The* Ritz," he adds, with that sealed smile.

"What the fuck? Doing what? What is your gig anyway?"

"You know what I do," he answers.

Furious, I slug him in the shoulder another time. He recoils and then points a finger at me. "Not again."

"Would I ask what you do if I knew the answer? What the fuck do you do?"

"Electronic surveillance."

"Phones?"

"Phones, computers. When I finished grad school, my Lakota buddy from Special Forces got in touch with me. He said there were a lot of people who needed the kind of services he and I could provide. It was more interesting than sitting in an office or a lab. With much better compensation."

"And who hires you?"

"We do some government work," he says, meaning to be vague. "Stuff they cannot do on their own. Frankly, many times I do not even know who we are working for. There's a target. I am told what's needed. Darnell, my friend—he gets the jobs. The less I know, the happier I am."

"And how did the Ritz find you two?"

"I really do not know. There have been more private clients in the last several years. Somebody leaves the government and tells someone about us. The private clients pay exorbitantly, because the risks are greater."

"And the Ritz hired you when?"

"I started around March 1, perhaps a little earlier."

"To do what?"

"As I said."

"Can you be more specific?"

"I could. But I am not going to be. I will tell you about what I witnessed that night in Blanco's apartment, whatever I observed. That's what your police friend wants to know, correct?"

"Correct."

"The rest of what I did or was doing for the Ritz is not pertinent."

"But you needed a sight line to the Tech Park, right? That's how you ended up next door to me?"

"To start," he says.

"Well, was there another reason you were there?"

Again, he turns back slowly to face me. This time, I think I can detect some kind of discomfort constricting his eyes and brow.

"You motherfucker!" I say. "You were spying on me?"

"You were spying on me, Clarice. You saw a great deal more than you ever admitted to me."

"Fuck you." I digest that for a second and then, with my anger rising, try again to slug him in the shoulder. He's quick and leans forward so that I barely graze him, while he pivots to grab my fist.

"No," he says. "I asked you to stop that. You are very strong. I am going to be bruised for a week. Any more, and I'm getting out of the car."

I just shake my head rather than apologize.

"Fuck, man," I say. "I liked you, Koob. I really did."

"I like you, too, Clarice. A great deal. You are a remarkable person."

This is why I've generally passed on relationships, because the end always sucks—it's-me-not-you, the standard sales pitch in reverse. I know I should ignore his compliment. But I think he means it, at least kind of. I still believe this guy. Which was probably always my downfall.

"And you were trying to pick up whatever I was learning on the Chief's case?" I ask.

"I was simply recording what appeared on your computer. As I said, I am given an assignment and I perform it. My surmise to start was that the Ritz wanted to keep track of you because you, too, had a line of sight to the Tech Park. Of course, over time, I could see what you were doing and understood that my initial assumption was completely wrong. But it was a while before I understood why Ritz cared about your activities."

"And how did you get into my computer?" I ask.

"I tapped into the cable connection for your Internet in the basement."

That's why he was trotting down there! Not to visit his damned storage cage. Ace investigator, my ass.

"And when you had lunch at Green Fruit, is that why you were always sitting behind the Ritz? To report to him? You were talking when you were back-to-back?"

"Yes. In Mandarin, by the way."

"*Man*darin?"

"He speaks well. The Ritz is very, very bright."

"Do you *like* him?"

" 'Like'? He's interesting. But no one likes him. Largely because he does not care to be liked. The Ritz is pleased to repel people. But that is a kind of freedom. It makes him very frightening."

I try for a second to remember why I'm so shocked.

"But I saw you plant the NoDirt behind his office."

"You were meant to. You were getting too close, Clarice. You were far more resourceful than the Ritz had anticipated when he put me in that apartment. But it would not be beneficial either to him or me if you figured out what I was doing. So we decided that the best solution was to make you think I was watching him."

"Instead of me?"

"Instead of you. And my other targets."

For a second, I wonder if I even have the heart for the next question. But I do. I will always claim my homeland in the harsh region of the truth.

"And you were fucking me to get information for Vojczek?"

"No!" he says sharply. He shakes his head several times, with as much outward emotion as I've seen today. "We assumed when you saw me plant that device that you would stop your spying, because you would conclude I was most likely a government agent or someone else who could make serious trouble for you if you got in my way. But you continued. Which was very undesirable. If you ever realized that I was at that restaurant to speak to Ritz, rather than keep an eye on him, you could go off in many unwelcome directions. So the simplest solution was to confront you and to be emphatic that there would be harsh consequences if you continued to trail me. That was the point of catching you on the street. I told Ritz only that I had delivered the message. But I kept to myself how you responded."

"And why was that?"

He offers that secretive smile. "It was a feeling. It was none of his business to start with. But after a few hours, I realized I had found your offer quite provocative. Quite." He glances my way for just an instant to observe my reaction. "Perhaps more so because I had no idea if you really meant it or were just making excuses. And then there was the fact that you had actually looked quite hurt out on the street. So it seemed like I owed you a visit, one way or the other.

"Yet I never should have knocked on your door without first informing my client. The minute I walked into your apartment, I felt I had entered a space where all the restrictions I normally accepted did not apply. I suppose I wanted to experience your kind of freedom on your terms. But having chosen not to tell Ritz, I was committed to that course. He learned nothing about our personal—" He hesitates. "Contacts," he says. His little smile seems a bit more ironic. He turns to me again, as he has at critical instants, fully revealing his face so I can witness his sincerity. He is utterly calm. He could be lying his ass off, but I'm not sure I see why. "I told you not to talk about work," he adds. "And we did not."

I know I'm upset—it's like somebody's run a rototiller over my heart—but dealing with that will take a lot of time. I just breathe until I'm confident I can put my reactions aside well enough to think.

"And could you follow my laptop wherever it was, or only when I was next door?" I ask.

"Only next door. I mean, when you reconnected, of course I could see what had been added. I was following your phone with the Stingray, but I learned very little from that. I knew you were working at the Chief's house, for example, but I had no visibility into what you were doing there. A four-terabyte drive is far too big for the capacities of my equipment." He stops then to lift a hand. I've noticed before that his fingers are slender and shorter than I'd expect for his height, and he cuts his nails back. "This is more than I have agreed to tell you, but I do not want to mislead you, Clarice, and it concerns your client. But you need to promise me that it will be held as information about your client that you are not obliged to pass on to the police."

"Tonya understands that I have to protect my client first. But if it's about the Chief, I need to tell Rik. Only he'd never hurt Lucy."

He nods. "I had been in the Chief's computer for quite some time, but that had nothing to do with keeping track of you. Hacking was one of the services we had agreed to provide Ritz from the start."

"You were in the Chief's computer? As part of learning about her case?"

"There was next to nothing to learn there. The Ritz was concerned, frankly, with just one item."

"On her computer?"

"Yes."

"What?"

"That picture."

"The photograph that Blanco took?"

"Right."

"That was on her computer?"

"Right."

"And how did it get there?"

"As I told you, I do not tend to ask questions. Ritz thought I might find it there and I did. That was all I knew." He nods to himself. "And I am the one who posted it on Reddit, the night Blanco testified. Ritz asked me to do that."

"You were the one who leaked it?" I rear back to study him, increasingly perturbed by the stoical way he's admitting to some really bad stuff. "You realize that was a completely shitty thing to do to her, don't you?"

He lifts a hand, not quite owning it, but not fighting either.

"I am in the business of invading people's privacy, Clarice, and seldom to their advantage. Nothing I do is 'nice.' That is one of many reasons it is so lucrative. Initially, to me your computer or the Chief's were typical targets. I have no interest in the larger context. Of course, the more I came to understand how intent the Ritz was on destroying Lucia Gomez, the more I wished that I had had nothing to do with any of it. But I could hardly step away then. And the Ritz is smart enough to have figured out how to post the photo anonymously on his own, if I did not."

I am pretty much levitating from this entire conversation. I close my eyes for a second, just so I can grab hold of myself. What else? I think. Oh. Small detail.

"And tell me about Blanco's murder." Despite what he said to start, there is a part of me preparing to hear Koob tell me in the same shameless way he's been speaking that killing Blanco was another of the not-nice things he did for Ritz. I am relieved when he repeats himself.

"I did not see a murder," Koob answers. "I already told you that. That's merely my surmise. Around eleven p.m. that night, just as I was about to visit you, I received a call from a blocked number. I had set up that phone for Ritz—it was untraceable, but he called me rarely. I was surprised to hear his voice at that hour. He said he needed to see me immediately and gave me a crazy set of instructions, an address and an apartment number which I was supposed to enter from the fire escape. I could not imagine why until I noticed as I was climbing up that on the lower floors, the fire escape ran behind a frosted window in the bath, meaning the neighbors would ordinarily not see me or anyone else coming or going that way. When I got there, the Ritz and Walter Cornish were arguing with Blanco."

"Was Blanco tied up?"

"Not then. Blanco was sitting in this wooden chair, and the Ritz and Cornish were on their feet. It looked like Blanco was a kid talking to the principal."

"Any idea how long they'd been there? Did you come in at the start of the meeting?"

"No one explained. From what I heard, I think the three of them had agreed to meet at that apartment after Blanco had apparently informed them that he was not going to turn over his telephone in response to the order from the commission and the courts. Blanco had hired a lawyer and the lawyer had told him to plead the Fifth Amendment. And the Ritz was adamant Frito should not do that. Vojczek was trying to convince Blanco that there were alternatives."

"And what were the alternatives?"

"Me, I suppose."

"Explain."

"The Ritz handed me Blanco's phone and told me there was stuff there in a hidden archive that Ritz wanted me to remove, and remove in a way that a good forensic examiner would not be able to detect."

"What kind of stuff? More images of him and the Chief?"

"I never opened them. There were definitely some JPEGs there. And a couple of apps, a VPN and Tor, which is a browser designed to leave no tracks. I knew that Blanco was cruising the dark web. Ritz kept asking why Blanco was stupid enough to put that shit on his phone, and was that not the reason he had this place?"

"'This place' meaning the apartment?"

"That was how I understood it."

"And what was Blanco doing in the apartment?"

Koob turns his head deliberately from side to side. "I cannot say. Something unsavory."

"Maybe Frito and his friend were looking at dirty pictures?"

Koob just shrugs.

"So what happened?" I ask.

"I told the three of them that it was simple enough to get rid of what was there. But I couldn't promise that a good forensic examiner would miss the deletion. It's much harder to mess around with the operating system on a phone—there are fewer moving parts, so to speak. A really qualified person might be able to detect that something had been removed and, perhaps, the prior activity, if they were good enough and knew where to look."

"Okay. And what did they say when you told the Ritz that?"

"The three of them started arguing. Mostly it was just Blanco and the Ritz. They were yelling but trying to keep their voices down at the same time, if you can imagine. Blanco said he was going to plead the Fifth, and the Ritz tried to reason with him. Vojczek said that the worst that could happen if Blanco turned over the phone was that some expert might offer an opinion that material had been removed and Blanco would adamantly deny it. It would be a standoff. Blanco actually laughed at him, which probably does not happen to Vojczek often, but Blanco said Ritz was telling him to jump out a window and expect a soft landing. With the Chief against Blanco now, she could use the expert's testimony as a basis to ask the commission to remove him from the force. Which they were likely to do."

"Were you saying anything?"

"No. Ritz clearly had not been prepared for my answer about the phone, and at one point, he more or less cross-examined me, trying to minimize the possibility of an expert recognizing the deletions. From the other side, from the dark web side, the applications Blanco was using would make it impossible to track his activity. But on his devices, unless he had taken precautions he seemed to know less about, there would always be signs of his search history. And that is what I said."

"How did the Ritz take that?"

"Angry. Frighteningly. He was furious with all of us. It comes straight to the surface with him. Very few humans can bring forth, unguarded, that kind of look of lethal rage. He starts working over his chewing gum and his eyes become as hard as a snake's. Did you ever see that look?"

"I haven't been closer to the man than fifty feet."

"Good. Keep it that way. But I was not about to let the Ritz intimidate me. The way I do business, I do not have group discussions. One of my essential terms is that I talk only with the principal. It's far safer for me that way. That's why we were speaking in Mandarin at the restaurant. I was not pleased doing show-and-tell in front of Cornish and Blanco."

"And what happened between Frito and the Ritz?"

"More agitation. Blanco said several times that Ritz had ruined his life, and the Ritz scoffed and told Blanco he ruined his own life. Blanco said—" Working to recall the words, Koob looks out above the trees and the power lines, while his filmy partial reflection hangs on the front window. "Blanco said either way, he was not taking a chance on going to prison. He had not hurt anybody. This was his own private thing, and it never involved anybody else. Ritz laughed at him and said, 'That's why it's a five-year mandatory minimum, because it doesn't hurt anybody.'"

"Meaning?"

"Again, I cannot say. Blanco said, 'My deal with Walt and you was that I'd do what you wanted so my private life could stay private. And I did it, and now you want me to take a chance that all of this will explode anyway, that I'll lose my job and lose my family and go to prison. And that's not happening. I'm taking five. My lawyer thinks the way this will play out is that after I assert my privilege against self-incrimination, my testimony will get stricken from the record, and that will be the end of the hearing. Finito. So we'll never get to the point of the commission formally ordering me to turn over the phone. But if they do, I'll have immunity.'"

"Then Ritz said, 'Listen, you pervert, you take five and Lucy gets away with it.'"

" 'Lucy gets away with it?' Is that a quote?"

"That is definitely what the Ritz said."

"Any idea what Lucy would be getting away with? Ritz and Cornish didn't really think she'd forced Frito to have sex, did they?"

"I have no idea what they believed or did not believe."

"Okay, and what happened then between Vojczek and Blanco?"

"Blanco said something like, 'Look, I'm done with you guys.' And he stood up to leave, and Ritz just shoved him right back down in the chair and said, 'Not yet,' and then nodded to Cornish, who had this black satchel. He took out some zip ties and they fastened Blanco to the chair by his wrists and ankles."

"Was there a fight?"

"Not really. As I said, the Ritz is scary in those moods. Blanco kept telling them that tying him up was ridiculous and unnecessary."

"So if Cornish had zip ties, they must have been thinking from the start that they might need to keep Blanco there."

"Probably. Blanco was saying things like, 'I don't know what you think you're going to do to me, beat me or whatever, but I'll never be able to do what you want.' And the Ritz said, 'By the time I'm done with you, you're going to be begging to make me happy.' "

"That's when I left—after that threat, because Ritz was clearly prepared for something ugly. As I went out the window, the Ritz was yelling at me not to go, but I had been dragged into a situation I wanted no part of, and which went far beyond my agreement with Ritz. He seemed to be committing another felony in my presence every few minutes—suborning perjury, intimidating a witness, assaulting Blanco. I was much too exposed, with a virtually infinite range of bad outcomes for me. I went back to the Archer and started clearing out. The car was packed and I was gone by five a.m. I could not say goodbye to you, because I knew you would never stop asking questions."

"You had a car?"

"It was in the lot behind Vojczek's office. I had no need for it while I was there. Keeping the smallest footprint, avoiding inter-actions, remaining anonymous whenever possible—that's always my preference when I am working."

"And when you cut out, what were you thinking was going to happen to Blanco?"

"I had no insight into their exact intentions. But I never thought that Blanco's life was in danger. The Ritz is much too smart to kill a cop."

"It doesn't sound like the Ritz had much leverage over Blanco," I say. "Frito was going to follow his lawyer's advice, and no matter how pissed Ritz was, it's hard to understand what the Ritz would gain by killing him."

"Agreed. Except for the look on the Ritz's face. I would say that this is a person who does not react well to being told that he's powerless." Koob nods once as he thinks about that. "After I got back here to Pittsburgh, I read the *Beacon* online every day, because I was curious about whether Blanco ever turned over the phone. I was shocked when I saw the headline that he was dead."

"Any idea how they killed him?"

"None. But Walter had that little satchel with him. As you already said, they seemed to have come prepared for various scenarios."

I take a quick lap in my brain.

"So it's still possible that Blanco was so terrified of the Ritz and Cornish that he had heart failure? I mean, it's still not a murder for sure."

Koob has clearly not considered that. His hands and shoulders rise: Anything's possible.

"For my own sake," he said, "I have to assume they killed him. Because if they did, then eliminating me would make sense for them. I am a witness, but one with no known connection to the case or the Ritz. Which is why I am carrying a weapon."

"I'm not going to say I feel sorry for you, Koob. You link up with a jackal, don't be surprised when he decides you're the next meal."

He smiles faintly.

"And what about what you were doing for Ritz originally," I ask, "whatever it was that brought you to Highland Isle? There was something besides spying on me, right?"

He just offers a slow, solemn shake of his head.

"That is not up for discussion," he says.

"Why?" I ask.

"Why won't you tell me about what the Chief has said to you?"

I make a face. "I don't think I ever heard of the spy-client privilege."

"What I do professionally, Clarice, comes with a lot of risks that I try to minimize. Darnell always has a cover, including supporting witnesses and documents, innocent ways to explain why I have my equipment or what I am doing with it. I am as careful as I can be. And I never talk about what I do. It is safest for me."

"Okay. But I'm just thinking your way. You're gonna be looking over your shoulder for the Ritz, or Cornish, or someone they might send, for a long time. So best for you is if somebody figures out how to bring Vojczek down."

"Best for me is if Darnell can pacify Ritz. He hasn't been able to reach him yet. But he will remind Ritz that he violated our understanding when he brought me into that apartment. However, Darnell will make it very clear that going to law enforcement is never an option. It would put an end to our business and could quite easily lead to incarceration for both of us.

"And that is the truth, Clarice. Giving the police hints about what Ritz may be doing is not in my best interests. And besides," says Koob, "your friend would never protect me with regard to that."

"Because?"

"I am confident she will not."

"If the Ritz killed Blanco, I think she'd be down for any way to get him."

Koob takes one second and then turns his head again several times.

"You didn't kill anybody, right?" I ask. I've been wanting to ask that out loud for a while now.

"Of course not." He actually sounds insulted. "And as to this other matter, the things I came to town to help with, I know so little that the only person I can get in trouble is myself. The Ritz is very careful. He's been doing business in cryptocurrency since long before most people heard the term. And he does not put his fingerprints on anything illegal. The fact that he was in that apartment was fully out of character. I imagine they felt a face-to-face was the only way to change Blanco's mind and keep up the pressure to get Lucy out of her job."

"Do you know why he wanted that so badly?"

Again, the slow shake.

"Ritz isn't planning on killing the Chief, is he?"

"I would have bet a large sum that he would not have killed Blanco, so I will not make predictions. He hates her, I can certainly say that. I truly have no idea why."

Neither of us speaks for a second.

"So you needed sight lines," I finally say. "What were you watching?"

His head keeps turning back and forth steadily, even though he is smiling slightly at my persistence.

"Okay," I say. "What if I swear I won't tell this part to Tonya. What if it's just between me and you? If I can connect what you tell me to anything on my own, I'll give Tonya that lead, but she won't hear about anything to do with you."

"I would be taking quite a chance, Clarice."

"I'm the woman who drove ten hours not to burn you. Come on, man. If you could take down Ritz without leaving any trail back to yourself, that would be perfect, right?"

He touches his lips with a slender finger, reflecting on what I've suggested, but offers no further response.

"What if you just say what *you* were doing?" I ask. "Nothing about Ritz. But just what I could have noticed spying on you, if I were a little better at it."

He smiles. "You did exceptionally well."

I have my usual squirming reaction to a compliment, but don't want to get distracted.

"I know you were watching something, right?"

"As you say, you already know that."

"And it was at the Tech Park, right?"

"Go on," he says.

"But where? Northern Direct?"

"You could have seen me looking in that general direction."

"But maybe not Direct specifically?"

"Not Direct," he says.

"The front gates?"

"Perhaps."

"But why does Ritz need to import a surveillance expert just to keep an eye on the front gates?"

Again that tiny smile, then he takes a minute to ponder.

"Here is what you could find out on your own, with some reading. There are very complex anti-surveillance systems around Northern Direct. Which basically means the entire section of the Tech Park where Direct is located. Highly classified communications take place between DoD and Direct, requiring extensive precautions against interception. They use signal jamming machinery near the site. If you get within one hundred yards of Northern Direct, your cell phone won't work. There are powerful cameras watching anyone who comes close, and if you were to, say, take a photograph, you will find DSS hunting for you. They are set up there to foil any kind of surveillance, even the most sophisticated means employed by government actors. So if you ever wanted to conduct counter-surveillance of that section of the Tech Park, you would need some expertise."

I think. "And you'd have to watch from a distance. Right? Their lens finders would pick up anything close."

"That's a logical deduction."

"But you weren't out back every day. Just like two to three a.m. a couple times a week. True?"

"Very early Tuesday and Friday."

"And like I eventually noticed that you'd moved down a few steps so I couldn't see what equipment you were using. But say I was a little more curious and crept closer. What would I have seen?"

"I do not believe you could have been more curious."

"Okay, but what equipment would I have seen?"

"You might have seen me occasionally looking through a pair of specially made thermal imaging binoculars. On one side there was a photodiode that could detect infrared or ultraviolet emissions. The other lens was standard thermal, heat-sensing."

I go through the PIBOT catalog in my head.

"But that's way more than typical night-vision goggles. Were you watching for someone using night-vision equipment? Because you could definitely detect that with those binoculars."

He smiles again. "As you say."

"So you were watching for somebody who was surveilling the place from a distance. Competitors or government actors?"

"I do not know, not for sure. Nor was I told what was taking place at the Tech Park. I can only offer conjecture based on other equipment I was using regularly."

"Which was?"

"You could not have seen that. I did not use it outside."

He means the guessing game is over. But I'm not ready to quit.

"Were you breaking the law by using this other equipment?" I ask.

"Arguably not. But not a good argument."

"So the binocs, they're legal. I know that. So illegal means you were probably overhearing something."

There's his little smile. I'm clearly amusing him by the way I'm piecing stuff together.

"But it wasn't stuff you could pick up with the Stingray," I say. "Because you already said that Direct blocks cell traffic. So you were probably listening to radio broadcasts. Like with a police scanner? But that's legal."

"Again, by reading, Clarice, you might learn that the FBI, for example, has been finding ways to protect its high-range radio frequencies for quite some time by using a digital signal. They are very hard to penetrate."

"So you had a digital scanner in there?"

"I might have. Backed up by some excellent software."

"So that's why the Ritz needed you? In case the Feds were watching him?"

"We are done with this subject, Clarice. And I am counting on you not to pass along the little I have said."

I cross a finger over my heart. "Never," I say.

But I understand now why he said Tonya wouldn't protect him. Nobody gets a quick pass for thwarting law enforcement.

"And were they actually watching—the Feds?"

"I never saw any sign of that in more than four months. Frankly, once the Chief's case was over, the Ritz was probably going to give me his thanks and send me on my way and deliver a few more bitcoins to our intermediary. But as I say, we are done discussing my activities."

"Okay." I flip through the files in my brain as we sit silently. The street is getting more crowded, traffic growling along and many pedestrians strolling the block. Public transportation must be nearby, because a lot of folks carrying briefcases are in line in front of a bakery. The customers who emerge are carrying white paper bags and often cups of coffee or tea.

"Can I go back to the night with Blanco?" I ask. "I have one off-the-wall question. Do you remember any of them getting a mosquito bite?"

Koob emits a light surprised laugh.

"As a matter of fact, Cornish was complaining about the mosquitoes." He lets his eyes rise again as he recalls. "At one point, he used the bathroom and banged the wall and screamed he'd gotten the little mother."

I can't really think of anything else. Two women in the parking lot are shouting goodbyes. One approaches the SUV beside us, and Koob slumps and turns his face away from her, but she never gives us a look.

"And you like never even hinted to Ritz anything about, you know, us?"

He faces me again. "Never. As I said, he would be irate about the possibility of conflicting loyalties. And besides, Ritz is not a man to trust with your secrets. He would leverage anything he knows I care about. I told him nothing about my personal life, for that reason."

I'm not 100 percent positive what Koob meant with his remark concerning the things he cares about, but it sounded like he was including me, and in response my heart has gone all squirrelly and schoolgirlish. But I'm too bashful to push, like he might take it away if I do.

"Well, I have to say, man, to me your personal life looks pretty fucked."

"Unlike anyone else's."

"You talk about your wife almost like she's a rabid dog, and then you run back here to the same house and just basically cower from her."

"Clarice, it is a delicate situation. I take one day at a time, for my son's sake. Thirteen months from now, he will leave the house." He visibly sighs, then faces the windshield again, cutting off the subject. "Anything else about Blanco?"

"Not that I can think of."

I realize that Koob has been blunt about his work, sort of for the same reason I wear the nail, so there are no illusions. And yeah, I realize it's theoretically possible that he's making shit up about the Ritz and Cornish as a way to blame them for a murder he actually committed or had a hand in. People can fool you, I guess, and let's face it, Koob fooled me already, spying on me from the apartment next door. And yeah, my radar for other people fails often, but really, could it be that messed up? I know there's a lot more to a person than you find out in bed, but you still find out quite a bit. Koob Xie does what he does because the world is a rough place, but at his core, to me he'll always feel like a tender guy, and definitely not a murderer.

He's taken hold of the door handle. He faces me full-on for a second and, being Pinky, I suddenly lean over to hug him, and without hesitation, he hugs me back. It lasts a moment, then he slides from the car and takes off at a run.

27. THIS HAS TO BE THE DUDE

Ihis has to be the dude you were seeing," Tonya says.

"Toy, if you—or anybody else you work with—tries to find this person, I promise there will be an actual murder to investigate."

"Just saying."

"Stop saying. We had a deal and I've kept up my end. I've told you what he says happened in Blanco's crash pad while he was there. But you can't just go confront Cornish or the Ritz with that."

"Of course not. What happens in God-knows-where stays in God-knows-where. I don't burn CIs."

It's about nine p.m., and I've been home from Pittsburgh for an hour. Toy stopped for carnitas at Ruben's, and we're eating off the coffee table in front of my couch, drinking beer. We take a beat to let the air settle between us. Toy's in her summer civvies— shorts and T-shirt and no bra. Looking at her relaxing on my raggedy sofa, I somehow flash on Koob sitting there. I guess it will be a while before I let go of that.

"So, you have to work Walter Cornish, right?" I ask her. I spent a little time while I was driving back trying to figure out how Tonya can safely exploit Koob's information. "You've got an angle on Walter, right, because he told us he hadn't been in that apartment for two years?"

Tonya has brought the mini pad she uses to make notes and she touches it here and there for a while.

"Definitely," she answers then. "He said he hadn't been in the apartment since he rented to Frito. And he wasn't in the building the day before. Walter made both those statements not long after he came in. And repeated them to the patrolman who spoke to him the next day."

"And remember he opened the window over the fire escape and was waving around this handkerchief, supposedly to clear the air. I say he was cleaning up, making sure he'd wiped all the prints after everyone came in and out."

She nods repeatedly. She likes it.

"If you find a way to confirm Walter was there the night Blanco died, a way that doesn't involve mentioning the CI, you can come down on Cornish pretty hard."

"Two problems," she says. "Number one, I lost my magic wand on the way over, so I don't have any evidence, except for your guy's word, that Walter was present. And second, even if I had that proof, I'm not sure Walter will just crumble."

"You said the techs picked up some ridge details in a number of places. Maybe that window?"

She looks again at the mini.

"Yes. A couple spots on the outside of the window."

"So Walter's prints are on file with the department, right? Maybe they can do a comparison and say the ridge detail around the window and other spots around the apartment are a match."

"That won't do it," she says. "Walter will claim any prints from him were left the night Blanco was discovered, not the night before, when he died." We all would testify Tonya was screaming at him about touching stuff—although that's suspicious in itself, given his experience.

"What about the mosquito? Have you checked Walter's blood type? It's probably still in his personnel file, right?"

She likes that idea and promises to work on it.

"But look," she says, "it's gonna be a hard flip, getting Walter to roll over on the Ritz. I don't know if proving that he lied to us will do it. He'll make up some fairy tale to justify fibbing."

"Like what?"

"Maybe he'll say he was protecting Frito. I don't know. But a dude like Walt, bullshit flows through him like blood."

"Don't forget he also committed perjury at the P&F hearing."

She groans. "You can just hear him. 'So I forgot that I bonked the Chief before the flood. A guy like me has a lot to remember. That ain't perjury.'"

Tonya, we both know, can be pretty contrary, but she's not trying to be difficult. She's making good points.

"And don't forget, Pink," she adds. "We can't even prove it was murder yet. Even your boyfriend has no direct evidence of that."

I want to tell her to stow the 'boyfriend' crap, which is basically old stuff between us. But I let it go because whatever I say might provide some link to Koob's identity.

"You can see the problem, right?" she says. "The only thing that will turn Walter Cornish is a murder rap. Perjury? Obstruction of justice? Those kinds of beefs can't put him inside long enough to make it worthwhile to dime out someone as dangerous as the Ritz. The story around HI has always been that when he was a young cop, Ritz did hits for the mob. You know, he'd pull over the target on a dark street like it was a traffic stop and pop the poor bastard as soon as he'd lowered his window to show his license. Walter's heard those tales for sure."

I understand. We're not close on Walter. She says yes to a second beer while we're thinking.

"So any news on your end?" I ask, when I hand over the bottle. "Tox screen?"

"Nothing much showed up. Frito was taking Xanax, I guess. His doctor says stress of the job."

"But he wasn't strung out on something, so Ritz might have a lever on him?"

"Heroin. Meth. Fentanyl. The tox screen covers all the standard addictive substances."

I think. "But you found his doctor? Any recent injections?"

"Ten-year tetanus shot, but that was two months ago."

"New COVID booster? Cops, where they go, they should be careful."

"No record of Frito getting another jab in the state health department's database. And Marisel knew nothing about him taking any shots. And why two injection sites?"

"Maybe the first syringe jammed? That's probably happened." She makes a face.

"What about our friend the tiger mosquito?" I ask.

"There's no sign of the mosquito toxin in the skin sample, but I guess it dissipates quickly. Still, the expert really doesn't believe a mosquito left those marks."

"Maybe Walter and Ritz shot Frito up with something after the CI left?" I say.

"Like what? Truth serum? That's a date-rape drug, so it also would show up on a regular tox screen and in the blood chemistry." She takes a second, then says, "We've got a lot of blind alleys."

"At least you have suspects now."

"If your informant wasn't the one who killed him." She gives me a pretty hard look.

"Not this guy," I answer. "And besides, if he was blame-shifting, he'd put Walter and Ritz in on the murder directly, wouldn't he?"

She considers that and seems to nod. Then she sits back, sort of gathering herself.

"There's one other thing," Tonya says. "You and Rik need to have a heart-to-heart with the Chief. About that picture."

Because of what I promised Koob, I haven't told her that the photo of Blanco and the Chief was on Lucy's computer. But now I wonder if she's learned the same information on her own. It turns out to be something else.

"That ring," Tonya says. "The one Blanco brought to court?"

"St. Viator's 1974?"

"Exactly. The school is closed, but they actually have an archive at the Board of Ed, including the yearbooks. I sent Mimi Yurz over there."

"And you got a surprise?"

"For sure."

"Blanco's uncle actually went there before he dropped out of school?"

"No chance. But there was a name that stood out."

"Hit me."

"Moritz Vojczek. 'Class clown,' by the way. Remember that one next time somebody asks you if you think people change."

Driving back to Highland Isle from Pittsburgh, I had called Rik from the highway. He was going to be in the office late, preparing for a suppression hearing on a new case in federal court, and we agreed he'd stop by my place on his way home. He has Gomer the Turd with him, since I had to unload the dog on short notice, and Rik and I agreed, when I first took Gomer in, that Rik would keep him for a couple days in a pinch, so long as Rik's daughter isn't home from college or coming back soon. Gomer seems to like Rik more than me, but only a little. Gomer's big talent is making all humans feel rejected.

Rik arrives while Tonya is still there. Gomer runs all over the place, wagging his tail and sniffing everywhere to find out what's different, then goes to his bed in the corner and takes a bite on each of his toys to reestablish himself.

Rik and Tonya are somewhat awkward around each other. Their relationship, which was minimal before, was basically adversarial, and now there's that strange feeling of SheKnowsThatIKnow-ThatSheSaid. Rik asks for water—he doesn't drink much—and I get him a bottle from the fridge, and he and Tonya clink beverages when she's on the way to the door. Once she's gone, he spreads out on the sofa, occupying most of it. He's beat.

"Successful trip to Pittsburgh?" he asks.

I drop a stitch on that one. All I'd told him was that I had a good lead and that I would explain more when I got back.

"Sandy called me this morning to see if I'd heard from you today," Rik says. I still had been turning big circles inside myself after talking to Koob, and I drove numb for several hours. I had forgotten to call Pops until I was getting close to the Tri-Cities.

"Pretty successful," I say.

Rik takes in what I've already told Tonya with a flat calm. It's the defense lawyer thing. You're never surprised by the bad shit people do. Like Tonya, he wants to guess the source.

"I promised him he'd be treated like a CI," I say. "Tonya agreed to that in advance."

"This has to be your weird neighbor. Only how does he get into a room with Ritz and Blanco if he's conducting surveillance on Ritz?"

"Not relevant. Not now. But there's another piece I didn't tell Tonya yet."

When he hears that the Blanco photo came off the Chief's computer, Rik looks like I slapped him. When I add what Tonya just told me about the ring, he gives up a deep-body groan.

"Clients?" I ask.

He tries to smile, but remains silent. Gomer has wandered back to us and Rik is scratching the dog's ears while he thinks.

"Man," he says finally and chugs the water. Then he does some deep breathing. "Okay," he says at last. "We better talk to Lucy right now. I'm going to be tied up all day tomorrow, and things might move fast." He looks at me bleakly. "There's a lot we don't know."

28. TIME HAS LAID A THICK HAND ON HER

When we arrive, Lucy is in her sweats. She still has some makeup remaining, but just like when we came over after they found Blanco, you can see that time has laid a thick hand on her recently. My heart pinches at the sight of her across the threshold, because I suspect what's coming now might be her worst moment yet.

As she holds open the door, she says, "God, I really thought we were done meeting like this."

She has a nice screen porch out back. The air is heavy but there's a cooler breeze, and we sit in the weak light as a loose ceiling fan knocks rhythmically, whooshing overhead. She brings a glass of water for each of us, then takes a chair across from Rik and me at the table, which is made of some kind of smooth plastic.

Rik starts by saying, "Pinky has a source."

After I describe the conversation between Ritz and Cornish and Frito, she mutters, "Motherfuckers." She's said all along that Blanco was Ritz's marionette, but the confirmation is still infuriating.

I look to Rik, hoping he'll handle the harder stuff with her, but he simply circles his hand in my direction. In a tone as flat as I can make it, I tell the Chief we now have information that the picture with Blanco was on her computer, a long time before Frito showed up with it in court. And that Ritz apparently graduated from St. Viator's in 1974, meaning he probably owns one of those rings.

Rik takes over then. He wipes his face with a hanky from his pocket, then keeps it in his hand.

"So, Lucy," he says. "Being sort of philosophical, I've always accepted that a client has the right to keep secrets from her lawyer. But you know, flat-out misleading her legal team—well, to put it nicely, it's counterproductive. Sooner or later, the client blunders into quicksand, often with no way for the lawyer to pull her out.

"Which means we're at kind of a critical moment now," he says. "This CI information confirms that the P&F case against you is a fraud and that you had nothing to do with whatever happened to Blanco. I'm sure Tonya is going to be working hard this week to corroborate Pinky's source."

Lucy interrupts, turning to me.

"What exactly does Tonya know about the picture?"

"Only Saint V's," I answer.

Across the table, the Chief covers her mouth with her hand, thinking.

"But," Rik says, "that's actually our problem. As soon as P&F dismisses, maybe even before, Moses will announce that the grand jury has closed its investigation of you. And assuming the CI bears out, the locals will state publicly that you're no longer a person of interest in connection with Blanco's death."

"That's great!" Lucy says. "Isn't it?"

"Well," says Rik, "sometimes good news is bad news. Because the Bureau and Tonya are going to want to interview you. And they'll ask all about that photograph, every detail—who what and where. And lying, Lucy, that's not an option. Your only way out is if you can take five. And since you're no longer a subject on extortion or Blanco's homicide, asserting your privilege requires being able to say in good faith that you're at risk of being prosecuted for another crime, maybe one they don't know about yet."

"Okay," Lucy says. She doesn't look up at Rik, instead watching as she drags her finger around aimlessly on the table. "And if maybe I could do that, what are the chances it leaks, you know, that I invoked my constitutional rights?"

"Pretty good, I'm afraid," says Rik. "Moses and Tonya are principled enough to keep it to themselves, but they aren't the only investigators who will know you did that, and if an officer with some loyalty to Ritz hears about it, so will their favorite reporter. Which raises a separate problem. How will you answer the journalists, who are going to demand to know whether you engaged in sex acts in the station?"

She peeks up at us for an instant with a grim smile.

"So the mayor has to give me the boot. And the Ritz gets what he wanted all along."

The fan above keeps chopping the air and clicking faintly, while none of us speak.

"What's the solution?" Lucy asks.

"I don't know," says Rik, "because I don't know what really happened."

The Chief absorbs that but continues skating her finger along on the table, kind of doodling. I try to make out what she's drawing, but there's no telling.

"How about if you ask me questions," she says finally, eyes still downward. "I mean, that might be easier. For me."

"Well, let's start with the basics. Is that photo real or has it been Photoshopped?"

She takes her time before saying, "Real enough. It's cropped."

"To cut out what?"

"Me holding my cell phone in my left hand for one thing."

"You took the picture?"

"Yep."

"And the guy is who?"

"Not Frito. I told you the truth about that."

Rik has been allowing a full measure before asking each follow-up question. Now he is clearly weighing his options: Be open-ended or cut to the chase. He looks almost as pained as she does.

"It's the Ritz, right?"

The Chief stops her doodling and takes a heavy breath. But she still won't look at Rik.

She says, "Right."

"And when was it taken?"

"About twelve years ago. Sometime in the month before I was sworn in as Chief."

"And that office had a mirror on the back of the door?" I ask.

"It did," she says. A little dragging note of shame is in her voice. She definitely intended to mislead us. We all pause for a breath, until Rik speaks again.

"And about the picture—I take it you and the Ritz had some-thing going?"

She groans, making a sound like a frog. "Please. I've never been that hard up."

"Okay," says Rik.

Her eyes finally rise to Rik and me, shifting back and forth between us, although in the dimness I can't see what they hold. She utters a huge sigh.

"Man, I *so* don't want to tell this story," she says, then adds that it's time for a real drink. I go with her to the kitchen while she pours some whiskey and soda in a highball glass. She hands me a beer from the fridge. Rik asked for another glass of ice water. He still has a half-hour drive when we finish. And I'm sure he wants to be clearheaded to think all this through. In the kitchen, the Chief doesn't say anything besides, "Miller okay?"

We take the same places at the table. The Chief folds her hands, like she's on the witness stand. She's looking toward us resolutely.

"You know," she says, "how you tell yourself when you're young, 'If I ever get the chance...' Meaning, if I can get even for something really wrong, I'm going to do it. Like when I was a kid, there was a bar in Kewahnee, I don't know where the owner thought he was, but he had a sign in the window, 'No Beaners,' just plain like that. I can tell you, the day I became a police officer in Kindle I hotfooted it over there, but by then it was a video store. But that dude, if he was still there, he was not going to have a good day. I mean, maybe I'm a shit to carry grudges, but you know, why get sworn if it doesn't matter to you about setting wrong things right?"

Rik nods, just to show he's with her.

"So you know I've told you stories about riding with the Ritz when I was a rook. And about his little games with the hookers. I sat through that grotesque little performance several times and it always ended with one of these young women in the back of the cruiser, weeping or raging. And those girls, you know they're tough, they were used to a lot of bad shit happening to them and they'd just laugh if you talked to them about justice, but this was still too much, it being the po-lice, emptying his pipe for free and him running them in anyway. And I thought, if I ever get the chance to treat this motherfucker the way he treated those women—" She stops and takes a good healthy slug from her drink.

"So okay, I get appointed Chief in Highland. And one reason the mayor hired me, frankly, was because I wasn't in Vojczek's orbit, and there was no way to get control of that department without getting rid of him. It wasn't just that he was a criminal, stealing drugs from the dealers, or inventorying only half the money if he busted a deal going down. All the cops in Narcotics, they'd become addicts in a way, cause they were hooked on the extra money, and even the guys who cycled through that section, who'd taken just a little, they had to protect the Ritz to protect themselves. There was no bigger message I could send than to ax the jerk and say, 'We are going to start fresh.'

"I whistled him in within a day or two after getting appointed. I'm still not Chief for two weeks, and I tell him straight up, he's got two choices. Resign. Or I'll go to DEA and the FBI with every rumor and story I've heard about him stealing drugs during busts. That's a great US Attorney's Office investigation. Ritz's logic all along is, No copper will turn on me, and nobody believes a drug dealer. But the way the Feds do this, they build a case piece by piece. They'll run down to the prisons and start interviewing dealers, and they'll get a dozen of them telling basically the same story. A lot harder to call twelve guys liars. And several defense lawyers will say they heard the same thing at the time of the bust. A cop will roll on him next. So what I'm telling Ritz about the Feds, that's a genuine threat.

"But what does he say? I mean, cops. 'I can't resign now,' he says. 'I've got fifteen months to my pension.' The jagoff has probably stolen a quarter of a million in cash that he's got stashed in his crawlspace, but that's his thing, he can't lose his pension. And that's when I get a flash of genius. Here we are: If I ever get the chance.

"'Well, Moritz,' I say, 'if you want fifteen more months before you go, then I guess you better get down on your knees and make it worth my while.' We went through, 'You're kidding, you don't mean it,' but I told him I was stone serious. 'Down on your knees and loosen up your tongue, I want it going a hundred rpms.' I took off my pants. I was sure he would quit on the spot. But he thought it over, and then he sinks to the floor.

"Well, as soon as he got down there, I reached for my cell phone. Then I thought of the gun, that would be a nice touch. And before he really got started, I say, 'Moritz, look over your shoulder,' so he's nose to nose with the gun barrel, and while he's got this look of terror, I get four or five pictures. The last one, he'd faced my crotch again, ready to get down to business. That's the one he gave Blanco, but in the rest, you can see who it is.

"So that was all I wanted from the jump—the picture. I mean, I know the Ritz too well. People seeing this image, that would be beyond humiliating, on his knees in front of a woman, with a gun to his head and giving her what she wants. But I wasn't really going to let the creep touch me. Especially since even with thirty seconds, the twisted fuck was completely getting off on this. Yes, it's total humiliation for him—and he's panting. The other reason he cropped the photo on that side and enlarged it a little is because he'd already stuck his right hand down his trousers.

"'No,' I say. 'I can see on second thought, Ritz, you're never going to be any good at this. I'm just gonna let the Feds get you out of my hair.' Well, it's a good thing I was holding a pistol. Cause he's enraged. Degraded, and now he's got blue balls too.

"'What happens to the pictures?' he says. 'You gotta get rid of them.'"

"'Neh, I don't think so,' I say. 'I'm just gonna hold on to

them. And if you ever mess with me or this department, I'll make sure everybody you'd hate to see them does.'"

"Wouldn't that have embarrassed the shit out of you, too?" I ask.

"Well, first, it was a threat—I doubted he'd ever want to find out if I meant it. But I can promise you, if I ever arranged for somebody to see those photos, my face would be blotted or cut out entirely. No one would be able to say it was me.

"And it worked. Until now. With DeGrassi and Cornish and Blanco, I knew it had to be Ritz getting even, because he'd figured out a way to make sure I wouldn't dare drag out that picture, not when these guys are saying they got forced. The Ritz, he's smart, I always knew that. But I never saw him as a techie. I had the pictures in a password-protected file. I was pretty shocked when Blanco was passing around that photocopy in the hearing. Any idea how he did it?" the Chief asks me.

"Ritz paid someone to take a stroll through your computer," I answer.

"How long ago? Recent?"

"Recent."

She reaches out then to touch my hand.

"You know, when I saw Blanco with the photo, I hate to say it, Pinky, but my first thought was you."

"*Me?*" I'm angry at once and in a primal way. It's always me, it's always my fault, especially when it's not.

"You were back in my study for a week, right next to the computer. But it was just for the first second I had that notion. Then I couldn't make sense of it."

"I hope not."

"I was thinking scared, Pinky."

"Okay." Some of the poison is still circulating through me. The Chief looks back to Rik. "So what do I tell the Feds or

Tonya in our little sit-down? This story, it wouldn't have sounded so good twelve years ago, but these days? They'll fire me in a heartbeat, right?"

Rik doesn't take long to think. "They kind of have to. And you have no real criminal exposure. It was extortion, maybe sexual assault, but it's way past the statute of limitations. So no Fifth Amendment. And yeah, there's no way in today's world anybody's going to give you a gold star for this one, Lucy."

She nods with a sad weight. "Well, okay, at least I'd be getting fired for something I actually did. And I gotta tell you: Stupid or not, it felt *good*. It was like the story with the lion when he got that thorn out of his paw. Almost worth anything. But I guess I'll be finding out now whether that's true."

After a moment in which all of us are taking in the scope of her current dilemma, I ask a question.

"What if we could show what a complete piece of dirt Ritz is, why the Chief had to get rid of him? Does that help?"

Rik floats his hand like a drifting leaf—mezza mezza.

"And how would I even do that, Pinky?" the Chief asks. "I've had an eye on the guy for a dozen years."

"My CI had this hunch that the Ritz is up to something over in the Tech Park. Does that make sense to you, Chief?"

"Vojczek was one of the initial developers. And everybody says he bought a lot of land waiting for Phase Two. But it would all be through offshore trusts and middlemen."

"But does it make sense, that he's got something dirty going on there?" I ask.

"Anywhere and everywhere."

"Any guesses what he'd be doing?"

"With Ritz I always think drugs first, but in the Tech Park?"

Rik has heard enough.

"It's late," he says. He's got that hearing tomorrow and we could all do with time to think.

The Chief walks us to the door. She gives me a hug.

"Sorry," she says. We both know she's talking about doubting me. "It was just a stupid thought I had for one second. There was no point in saying it now," she says, "but I wanted you guys to understand. It's why I felt at first that I couldn't play straight with you. Then, you know, once I was on that road..." She moves a shoulder.

"It was a logical thought," I say. "But I'm all for you, Chief."

"I know that. That was what I told myself."

Rik and I walk back to our cars, both parked in the Chief's driveway.

"Clients?" I ask as we're parting.

"Clients," he says.

29. AFTER I LEAVE THE CHIEF'S

After I leave the Chief's, I head home, but not to sleep, just to grab a few items from the PIBOT: first off, my night-vision binoculars, bought from army surplus; second, a cheesy fake mustache that I purchased years ago in a toy store; and finally, a set of old license plates that I took out of the garbage when one of Pops's neighbors on the West Bank got a Tesla. (The grifters in the State Capitol require more expensive tags for electric vehicles, supposedly to get even for the lost gas tax.) I have the plates on magnetic holders like auto dealers use when you take a new car for a test drive. I slap them on the Cadillac, and then cover my hair in a baseball cap and stick on the mustache and drive over to Harrison, the street opposite the Tech Park. Remembering what Koob told me, I've put my phone in airplane mode. The point of the mustache and the phony plates is so that even with the high-powered cameras outside Northern Direct, nobody will be able to figure out who was watching when they look at the CCTV feed in the a.m. But I can only do this for a few nights before they keep someone on duty to come out and question me.

Everybody says the Ritz is a clever guy, and this is a pretty good example. Assuming he's up to no good here, he's basically got Northern Direct playing the part of guard dog, with all their fancy anti-surveillance systems thwarting anybody who might want to keep an eye on him. Being a former cop, and undoubtedly understanding some things about the way federal law enforcement works, he realizes that agencies like DEA would keep a wide berth around the Tech Park, rather than tangle with the Defense Counterintelligence and Security Agency, who generally squelch other investigations on their turf in the name of national security. But Ritz still wanted Koob on the lookout. Either Vojczek is paranoid or he's into something so big and outrageous that DCSA would let the crime-fighting agencies operate here.

While I'm sitting on the place, I look over my texts that arrived before I went on radio silence. There's a message from earlier in the night from a woman I've hooked up with now and then, who's inviting me over tomorrow night. She lives out in the suburbs with a guy who's made zillions in home electronics, and she says he'll be traveling on business. I've been there a couple times. There are a lot of photos of him and NBA and NFL players on the shelves, and he's got a real lounge-lizard look, clothes too tight for the body he has now and dye that makes his hair laughably black. He's got to be at least twenty years older than her. I don't think my visits are secret, because she's asked a couple times if I'd consider coming over when he's there, but he leaves me cold, and I've made excuses. But with just China alone—maybe a made-up name—I decide, yeah, I'll be there.

A lot of people, when a relationship, or an attachment, whatever you want to call it, ends, they need a breather. But I've always preferred to jump right back in. Having a fun time with somebody else always makes me realize I haven't lost as much as

I think. China says she has 'two beans,' meaning two capsules of Molly, which kind of guarantees it will be crazy monkey sex for a few hours, and that's a good thing right now.

I'm listening to some Dua Lipa to keep myself awake, since I didn't get a solid night in that parking lot in Pittsburgh, but I drift off anyway, for maybe an hour, leaving me uncertain as to whether I missed the whole show. But I get lucky. About 2:45 a.m. a panel van approaches the front entrance of the Tech Park, which is wide open at this hour. Northern Direct, about fifty yards to the left, has mechanized iron gates and a guard visible in a little hut, but the truck doesn't head that way. Instead, it goes right and circles all the way around Direct's huge installation. While the van is moving, I drive about two hundred yards north down Harrison to keep the truck in view. It finally parks beside another building, a low structure of formed concrete. A long-haired dude in a T-shirt, cargo shorts and flip-flops jumps out, opens the rear doors of the vehicle and picks up a wooden fruit crate—full, from the way he maneuvers it. Moving slowly under the load, he carries the box toward the back door of the company, whatever it is, on the north side of the building. He appears to hand over the crate to somebody—I can't really see through the open steel door—and waits there, while the person inside apparently empties the crate. Then the driver returns with the box to the truck. It all looks so matter-of-fact, he might be dropping off groceries, except for the hour. The delivery guy closes up his van and zooms off. Koob proved to me yet again that a one-person tail rarely works, so I kill any thought of following him.

Instead, I stay put until the first light begins coloring the horizon, then head home to sleep. I consider calling Koob to find out if he was actually getting paid big bucks to be sure nothing went wrong with a two-minute delivery out of a panel truck, but I check that notion, too. I know that Koob and I are done-done, for all purposes.

Tonya comes over as soon as she gets off duty Tuesday night about six p.m. I've just finished a little online research about the Tech Park. As near as I can figure, the plant behind Northern Direct is called Vox VetMeds, which is in the business of making specialty medications for animals. It turns out, not too surprisingly, that most veterinary pharmaceuticals are manufactured by divisions of the same companies that serve humans. Vox, according to its website, focuses on niche products that big pharma doesn't want to deal with, like antibiotics that happen to work only on horses, or products for zoo animals whose size makes the usual human meds ineffective, creatures like giraffes and rhinos and elephants. About the only tie to the Ritz is that Vojczek led the phase of development in the Tech Park that brought VVM in, but he didn't even show up for the press conference when Vox's new location was announced. There's video online of the mayor speaking. She clearly expected to be treated like the second coming of Dr. Dolittle, best friends with the animals, and instead ended up defending herself on environmental concerns the reporters raised about the disposal of any dangerous chemicals that Vox might use. At the end of the video, Amity looks like she'd be perfectly happy if they just tore the First Amendment out of the Constitution.

I give Tonya a beer. She's in her plainclothes detective stuff, including an unstructured jacket that makes her look a little boxy, which is probably what she wants for work. As soon as she's seated, she says she has big news.

"Your stuff about a secret section on Frito's phone was a great lead," she says. "The Bureau guys had already said that Frito's work computer was like the apartment computer. Frequent insertion of external media."

"Memory stick, thumb drive?"

"That was the Bureau guy's guess. We turned Frito's office upside down again. Then I asked Marisel if I could come back to take another look at that locked drawer Blanco had at home for police stuff. I was searching for like a secret compartment. But with a flashlight, I saw on the steel slides—you know, the mechanism that holds the drawer and lets it open and close—in the back, there was like a magnetic hide-a-key thing. Inside there were two USB drives."

"And?"

"I had to wait for the Bureau computer guys at the Center City office to bust through the password protection, but they did."

"And?"

Tonya edges forward on the sofa so she has my eye.

"Kiddie porn."

That's a load. "Frito? Kiddie porn?"

"Kiddie porn," she repeats. "It fits together with what your source told you about the Ritz referring to a five-year mandatory minimum and Blanco talking about his private life and keeping it private. And the Ritz calling him a pervert. That's why Frito didn't want to turn over his phone, I guess. Because those were the dark web sites he'd been visiting."

"Kiddie porn?" Frito sure fooled a lot of people with all his crap about clean living, but I guess that's who he desperately wished he could be.

"That's on the deep deep DL. Nobody wants Marisel or the kids to have to hear about that."

"So that's what he was doing in the apartment? You think he was messing with children there?" The one emotion that dominated my childhood was this intense feeling of powerlessness. Because of that, I've always thought that anybody who touches a kid for the wrong reasons belongs in a running sewer underneath the basement in the lowest level of hell.

"Well, you can't tell for sure," says Tonya, "but there's no evidence of that, nothing the child abuse unit has picked up. From what Frito was saying to the Ritz, and what they found on the face of that chair, my guess is what he did there was watch that stuff and pull his crank."

"And that's what the Ritz had on Frito, that he was watching kiddie porn?"

"Best guess. I don't know how they figured it out, but Frito would have been their bitch if they had. Even for simple possession of that shit, you usually catch a lot more time than five years—closer to eight."

Years ago, Pops defended a seventy-year-old corporate executive who got caught visiting a kiddie porn site that was an FBI front. He was a solid-seeming guy, head of the board for the Kindle County food bank. Given the weird array of sexual fantasies that have inhabited my brain most of my life, and since all Pops's client did was look, I was ready at first to stick up for this guy's right to his unfulfilled desires. Then I saw some of that stuff, which, honest and truly, brought up my lunch. You pay for that shit, then you're making it happen, and any time it happens, there's a kid who will probably never recover. So make room in the sewer.

But it's a really sad crime. Pops's client went off to prison—seven years, in his case—still swearing to his wife and kids he had no idea how that crap got on his computer. He probably felt they would find him less repulsive if he could have told them instead that he tortured animals. And from what I saw of

Frito, I can imagine the wheel of torment he was riding. Every time Blanco got off in the apartment, he told himself he would never do it again and begged God for forgiveness. But sooner or later he was back, trying to banish the images from his brain that he knew were going to send him straight to hell, while his dick was like an iron bar. They say most often the people who are hung up on those fantasies were preyed upon themselves by some sick bum when they were kids. So there's that, too. Sad all around.

I finally ask Tonya if there have been other, less dramatic developments. A fingerprint examiner compared Walter's cards in the municipal files with the fragmentary prints found in Blanco's apartment. "She says," Toy tells me, "we have about a quarter-inch of what is probably from Walter's palm on the outside of the back window, about a foot up from the bottom. But there aren't enough points of comparison for her to testify to a positive ID. Just 'might be.' And Walt will say it happened when he opened the window the night we found Blanco."

"How do you touch the outside of the window a foot from the bottom, when you open it from inside?" I ask. "Walt left that when he was coming in."

Tonya agrees, but the main point is that without a solid, positive ID on the palm print, we still don't have a good angle to work Walter.

"How we doing on my mosquito?" I ask.

"Better. Walter's A positive. But like I told you, so is about one in three humans. We need DNA before we have any chance of scaring him."

"If you ask him to provide it, what's he do?"

"He probably hires a lawyer and tries to fight it. The worst part is we've got diddly chance to roll him if we go down that road.

Vojczek will probably be paying for Walter's lawyer and tuning in on every development."

"Okay. So do you have a plan? Without burning my guy," I remind her.

"Right," she says, "max respect for your boyfriend."

"You know this boyfriend joke stopped being funny a while ago. You're like picking at a scab."

"Sorry," says Tonya. "I didn't know he'd drawn blood."

"He didn't. But you might. So give me your plan with Walter."

There's a brief silence while Toy and I retreat to our corners. I guess we're always going to bicker like exes now and then, aiming for the tender spots.

"Well," she says, "I think I'll invite him to the station for a cup of coffee. Tell him I need his advice."

"From Walter? Advice?"

"Yeah, I'll drop the mosquito thing on him, just slide in the A-positive part, and how the tiger mosquito doesn't go very far and can bite a bunch of people, and tell him we're trying to figure out if we can actually get DNA from everybody in the building. Like can he think of a way to get a cheek swab from each tenant? The great part is he'll really really want to help, because he's gonna be hoping the mosquito bit somebody else. He'll put on his thinking cap real tight."

"Okay, but I don't understand what you get out of this?"

"Oh," says Tonya. She smiles full-on, which you don't get a lot of from Toy, who's self-conscious about her crooked yellow teeth. "What I get is the DNA off the rim of the coffee cup."

On Friday, I am hoping to sleep in, when Tonya calls to ask me to come to the station for an 8:30 meeting, half an hour from now. I had spent another night sitting on the Tech Park, just to be sure

I didn't z my way through the arrival of like a huge tanker truck or something else more conspicuous than a little panel van. But no: same time, same station. Fruit crate through the back door. Then I saw what I'd missed the first time. From the way he held the crate on his hip as he reopened the truck, I realized it wasn't empty. He doesn't just make a delivery—it's also a pickup. That was part of what the Ritz wasn't telling Koob. Maybe the surveillance Ritz was most concerned about would start when the truck left the Tech Park and the driver headed for his next stop.

"Tsup," I croak into the phone, while I try to return to the here and now.

"Walter's coming in for another meetup," she says. "I just told him we've made a little progress on the mosquito thing, and I need to talk to him about our next moves."

Walter also visited the station Wednesday morning, and Tonya used the patter we had discussed about the tiger mosquito and how to get DNA from Walter's tenants. In response, he was more visibly shook than she expected, and maybe because of the talk about DNA seemed to realize that Tonya might actually be trying to get his. He took his cup to the sink in the break room and washed it out, right in front of her, even while she told him several times that she'd take care of it and finally tried to take it away from him.

And then the goof, like bad guys always do—or the ones that get caught, as Pops would say—messed up. Tonya's office looks right out on the parking lot, and she watched as Walter, in his cowboy boots and page boy, sauntered back to his car. But he was undone enough by what he'd heard inside that he made a quick turn and headed for the little clutch of officers and civilian employees that's on the far end of the lot in every season—a rotating cast, but all there for a cigarette break. Walter still knew everybody and bummed a stick and stood around listening to the gossip while he sucked the ciggie down to the filter, then flicked it in the bushes. Tonya was out there with an evidence tech within two minutes of when Walter peeled out of the lot in his antique GTO. They found the butt safely lodged between the branches of the privet. She took it straight to the Bureau, who got the thing to the lab at Marine Base Quantico by the following morning. With a quality reference sample—which the cigarette butt, uncontaminated by anyone else's DNA, was—they could do automated DNA, meaning that in about two hours, the core loci in a specimen are analyzed and catalogued in CODIS, the national DNA database. By nightfall Thursday, they reported a 100 percent hit on the comparison between the mosquito blood and the saliva from the cigarette, meaning only one white man in two billion shared the same combination of alleles (which is more white men than there are on earth, by the way).

My role this morning, as Toy has explained it, is to sit there and shut up until she asks me for something. We are in another detective's cubicle with the half-height partitions of rimpled plastic— it's not quite an interrogation room, but more formal than having coffee in the break space. Walter looks worse for wear since I saw him at Blanco's, heavier and with a bleary look around the eyes, which does my heart good, but he's got more than enough arrogance to have plenty on hand for this occasion.

He stops dead when he catches sight of me, just like the night they found Frito's body.

"Well, well," he says, "look who's here again. The nasty nail. You two seem to be joined at the hip," he says, "although maybe I missed the point of connection by about six inches." The one problem with crawling through the bushes for the cigarette butt, Tonya told me, is that Walter still has pals around the Central

Station. Tonya asked for this meeting, well aware that Walter might now realize he's between the crosshairs. When he agreed to come in, she thought there was a chance he was still in the dark, but his open hostility is not a good sign. Given that, it's a little hard to figure why he's here.

"Sit down, Walter," says Toy, when he asks about me. "She's an occurrence witness. Just like you."

"Yeah, okay." He plops down. "No more coffee?" he asks with a sick smile. "I knew you were working me," he says.

"Walter, since we seem to be letting our hair down, let me tell you something you should have realized a while ago: You're not as smart as you think you are. The Ritz doesn't need anybody else to be the brains of the team—and you're not. To him, you're the same kind of toadstool as Primo."

Tonya is good at this, going for the vulnerable gaps between the armor, and Walter actually changes color.

"We're only going to need a sec, Walter. I just wanted you to know we solved our DNA problem with the mosquito."

"Oh yeah?"

"The DNA? It's yours. Now, the way I have this in my notes, you told us you hadn't been in that apartment since you rented it to Frito. And that you hadn't even been in the building for several days."

"I think you got that wrong," Walter says.

"Well now, you'll see why Ms. Granum is here. What's your memory, Pink?"

"The same. Not in the apartment since you showed it to Frito. And about the building, I think what happened, Walter, is that Detective Eo asked if there was any chance that you'd been around yesterday—meaning the day before they found Frito's body—and you said none, and that you hadn't been in the building all week." I'm good at this stuff, the word for word. I have a hard time processing in the present, but I can bring the past back in detail.

"Yeah, well," says Walter, "that's what I said and all, but it's not true. After I was over here to see you Wednesday, Ritz reminded me. Some jamoche who got evicted the week before, an asswipe named Turnberry, came in the office fussing about wanting his security deposit back. And on what turned out to be the day Frito bought the farm, that day, I came over to the building with another guy, just so Mr. Turnberry could remind himself of the holes he'd kicked in the walls and the number he'd done on the plumbing. Back at the office, we've got the records of Ritz sending me out. So I guess that's when that mosquito bit me. When I was downstairs with Turnberry." He smiles thinly. Now we know why he showed today. He heard about the cigarette butt on Wednesday, and the Ritz helped him cook up this weak-ass alibi.

"The guy who came with you," I say, "who's going to back your story, any chance that was Primo?"

Walter gives me a little tight f-you grin, and says, "Funny you should mention it."

"Funny," I say.

"And Turnberry, any idea where we find him?" Tonya asks.

"You'll have to check under every viaduct in the Tri-Cities metro area."

Toy nods.

"Walter," she says. "You have until the close of business today to save your life. You come back here, with or without a lawyer, and say you're ready to spill, no holding back, and tell us what happened in Frito's apartment the night he died, where we all goddamn well know you were—"

"Neh, I don't know that," says Walter.

"Well, the fingerprints say otherwise, Walter. They also put you in the apartment the night before. But we can skip that for the time being. You come back, say you're ready to roll, and I'll take you over to see the US Attorney personally, who might even cut you a deal for immunity."

"Immunity," says Walter, "means you don't got enough to prosecute. Otherwise you'd be offering reduced time."

"Immunity," says Tonya, "means you can walk out of this today, and only today. You know how the Feds work, Walter. They've got tons of resources and they're going to focus a lot of them on little old you. Your ass will be on an ice floe a month from now. But I promise, Walter, when we put you in on Frito's murder, you'll do state time, not federal. No country club life for you, Walt. You go to Rudyard where the big boys take a number for the chance to turn your rectum into a wide ditch."

Walter listens to her with the same simpering smile and holds up two fingers. He touches the first with his other hand.

"Number one, you got no proof Frito was murdered," he says, folding down his index finger. "And number two, you're never gonna get any proof I was involved, cause I wasn't. Next time, call Mel Tooley Jr. He'll be my lawyer."

Walter leaves his middle finger extended for several seconds before he gets up to leave.

30. DEAD END

With Walter flipping us off, Tonya and the Bureau are pretty much at a dead end concerning Frito's death. As Cornish said, we still don't even have proof that Blanco was murdered.

Instead, I spend the rest of the day Friday trying to figure out what the Ritz's interest is in Vox VetMeds. I'm behind on assignments from Rik, but I'll catch up over the weekend.

I call the outside law firm where Rik sends real estate closings for our clients. I ask one of their paralegals, who I've worked with before, for some help. But him and I don't get very far. All the property in the Tech Park was originally transferred to the city before being sold to the current owners like VVM, as Vox VetMeds is known. The identity of the seller or sellers to the city is behind the blank wall of a land trust, which you can't get around without a subpoena. Why Ritz was even referred to as the developer of the second round, after Northern Direct took what they wanted, is not completely clear.

As for VVM, there's not much I can figure out about the firm either. It was incorporated in Delaware, but the shares are not traded on any exchange, and none of the big pharma mutual funds list any ownership in the company. On the incorporation papers, the president/secretary listed an address in Baltimore, and when I search the web, I learn that he's a former VP with one of the big pharmaceutical companies, who worked in their pet medication division.

I call him at VVM from my TracFone. I say I'm a reporter working on a piece about veterinary pharmaceuticals for a business publication, and he says, very nicely, that they never talk to the press.

"Why so secretive?" I ask.

"This is a regulated industry, as you know. We'd rather communicate with the FDA and the FDA only."

"But you're not trying to hide your shareholders, are you?" I ask.

He laughs and says, "We're privately held," and adds, "Goodbye."

Having gotten nowhere, I decide to go out and take a quick look at the place in the daylight. It sits on what I'm sure is regarded as the worst site in the Tech Park. It's in the rear corner, with the highway roaring directly overhead. To get to VVM, you have to drive all the way around the park, an extra half mile. Northern Direct has such a huge security perimeter that VVM barely has a parking lot. There's a twenty-foot chain link topped with razor wire between the two companies, and a smaller fence on the highway boundary, which doesn't need much protection since it backs up to a steep overgrown embankment leading down from US 843.

On the other hand, it's a great site if you don't want anybody to see what you're doing. The rest of the Tech Park stretches several blocks to the north. Direct's installation obscures VVM's entrance on the western side of the building. And the southern boundary of VVM's site is next to the off-ramp from 843—there is more weedy undergrowth and scrub bushes underneath.

There is no place to park if I don't want to be seen, so I leave the Cadillac at Rik's office and hike several blocks out of the way, until I can approach on the south side from beneath the off-ramp. I cut through the weeds, finally reaching a point where I can duck in beneath the steel undergirding, and then whack my way forward. It's an incredibly junked-up area, full of the crap people throw out their windows as they're flying off the highway, especially beer and soda cans and the wax cups from the Big Gulps that everyone who litters seems to get. There are old cartons of all sizes, and the kind of shit people have nowhere else to dispose of—rusted pieces of rebar, a used air conditioner and a mattress that somebody must have snuck in here after dark. The local dogs have clearly found the place, and it smells of poop, and the ground is a mixture of gravel and mud. I keep an eye out for rats as I camp out on the other side of a heavy bush, so I'm at least partly obscured from the cameras behind Northern Direct. I quickly find that the mosquito abatement people don't bother with treatments under here—it's like the bugs have sent out an APB saying, 'Free lunch.'

I've got my hat and mustache again, and have lost my nail, just in case the Direct surveillance cameras pick me up behind the greenery. It's pretty dim here under the off-ramp, and I doubt that even equipment as sophisticated as what Direct uses can both focus in today's strong sunshine and simultaneously record clear images in the shadows. If I'm wrong about that, some Fed will be yelling at me shortly, but in the meantime, I have positioned myself on the same line as Northern's eastern fence, an angle from which I can see the front doors of VVM and the red logo on the building.

A couple cars come and go, but there is not much activity until we approach closing time. With the summer weekend ahead, people start bouncing around 4:15, dribbling out over the next hour, and I photograph all of them with my EOS and a telescopic lens, so I can blow up the faces later. Near five, the night security guard arrives in his blue uniform, and for some reason he catches my attention, maybe just because I figure he's the one on duty when the panel truck arrives in the middle of the night. Conveniently, he stops to say hello to several of the departing employees in the parking area, and I machine-gun maybe thirty images of him before he disappears. He's a good-sized white guy with a belly, and he reads as retired law enforcement or something like that, maybe an ex-firefighter. From the start, I have this feeling that I've seen him before, and after he enters the building, I flip through the pictures I've taken of him on the camera's digital screen.

It's five minutes later, while I'm watching the last people depart from the front doors of VVM, when the circuits in my brain finally connect. Now I remember! I've seen the security guard out of uniform, ambling across Hamilton in the center of Highland Isle, facing the noontime traffic with the indifference of a moose. He was part of the beefy, too-loud lunch group seated behind Koob. *That's* who he is. He's a member of Ritz's squad.

"Him?" Tonya says, when she comes to visit me at Rik's office on Monday morning. "That's Secondo DeGrassi. Primo's brother. They call him Sid."

Whenever I've had time over the weekend, I've tried all kinds of Internet searches, with no luck putting a name to the security guard's face. I'm reluctant to ask for Tonya's help, but when she called to say she was on her way over to talk about something important, I decided that I have no choice, even though I know she'll demand to know why I was taking his picture.

"Why do you have an eye on him?" is what she says.

"Is he a former copper?" I ask.

"Tried to get on. But he's"—she roughens her voice and drops it two octaves—"'not so good with the reading and writing shit.' Primo is the bright child in that family."

"No way."

"Way. I think Sid got sworn in some burg upstate, but he didn't last long. But second time, Pink: What's the deal with him?"

"Can't say." She's sitting in a wooden chair next to my desk, and she gets that hard angry face, which is part of the core Tonya.

"Bullshit. This more Secrets of the Boyfriend? I told you I had to hear everything."

"I told you I'd share everything he said about what happened in Blanco's apartment. That's what you asked for, and that's what I've done. And if I connect Sid to Blanco, I'll tell you why I was sitting on him. But I don't have that yet."

Her nostrils flare. "Don't play me, Pinky. I love your ass and all that shit, but if I decide you're shining me on, you'll have a federal grand jury subpoena faster than you can say those words."

That threat has always been in the background, but she's never said it out loud.

"Toy, you're my friend, okay? My good good friend. One of the few I have. You don't need to shake a stick at me, or whatever you think you're doing, because I don't cheat my friends. Period. But let's be honest. I'm in a tight position here. One dude is dead and this person, my source, he's afraid that Vojczek will try to kill him, too. And based on everything I know and you know, he's not thinking crazy. So cut me a break, because I made this guy promises, too, and they begin with saying that I—and you—will try to keep him alive."

She unclenches her jaw and breathes.

"Okay," she says, "but I'm the police, you're not the police, and I'm the one who has to decide what's reasonable."

"I can't tell you anything more about Sid right now."

She ticks her head a little.

"You said you had something urgent to talk about, right?" I remind her.

"Right," she says eventually. "And it kind of relates."

"To Sid?"

"To what we were just arguing about."

"Okay."

Tonya shifts her shoulders to get herself back to her subject.

"I went to church yesterday and Paulette Cornish literally stepped on several people so she could sit down next to me before the service started. And she's all like, 'Where were you last week? I needed to talk to you.' And I told her, I had a very late night that Saturday."

"Like a hooking-up late night?"

"I'm seeing somebody," says Tonya. She tries to keep a straight face, but there's a smile leaking through. I reach out and give her a little rap on the shoulder.

"Good thinking, Detective."

"She's young," Tonya says. "In college. Rising junior."

"Okay, so old enough."

"And definitely mature." She stops, seemingly distracted by her feelings about this woman. "I never knew I liked young."

"That's because that's what we *were*."

She laughs. That hadn't quite dawned on her apparently.

"Okay, back to Paulette," I say.

"Right. She was like super stressed, and I said, 'Why didn't you call me?' and she was like, 'I can't call the station, people know my voice. This is the safest place for us to talk. Only you can't tell anybody that I told you about this.' I'm like, 'Wai-wai-wai-wai wait.' She had all kinds of conditions, something about her kids, and I have no clue what she wants to tell me, except I ask, 'Is this about Walter?' And she says, 'Definitely.'

"And there is no way I can enroll this woman as a CI. The commander won't like another CI, because I've already enrolled you. And the Bureau will throw a fit, thinking I'm hiding information from them.

"Plus," she says, "Walter still has friends around the station, like we saw when he showed up on Friday. If Walt learns she was dishing on him, he'd find somebody in a ski mask to break her arms and make sure her jaw was wired shut. Literally."

"Literally," I repeat. "Okay, so what's the answer?"

"She talks to you."

"The woman who didn't want to talk to me two months ago?"

"Well, first of all, I told her that it would be for her protection. And second of all, you guys kind of passed the test."

"Explain."

"You never revealed where you got the PI's reports you sprung on Walter on cross. Cornish always believed that Paulette had never seen that stuff. To prevent Walt from going postal on her for having him followed, Paulette's lawyer told Walter's attorney that he'd hired the PI and wanted to keep the affidavits counsel to counsel, so he could spare Paulette."

I'm not following. "Well, how did Walt think we dug up the reports?"

"According to what their son told Paulette, Walter stiffed his own divorce lawyer on most of his fee, so Walter figured this attorney was a pal of Rik's and got even by handing off the file to you guys, under the table."

Cops think lawyers are scumbags and will always act like scumbags. I think that's what they mean by 'prisoner of your own misconceptions.'

"Okay. So I talk to Paulette."

"And then you talk to me. But you won't give me her name or any identifiers; she's just another source of yours. She's behind the CI wall."

This, to say the least, is rather artificial, but it will keep Tonya from having to cough up Paulette's name to the FBI, who might be less concerned about protecting her from Walter. It will all probably come to nothing anyway, given the crazy suspicions Tonya says Paulette always has about her ex.

About six p.m. that night, I am standing near the entrance of City Market with a shopping cart in which I've placed a few cans of dog food, when a tiny lady with short hair and a nose that's completely red at the tip gently nudges her own cart next to mine.

"You recognized me?" I ask quietly, and she laughs out loud. One advantage of having a nail through your nose. We walk side by side down the aisles. This is the same place where the Chief and Wanda DeGrassi played the supermarket version of demolition derby.

When Paulette turns back from her first stop, a shelf with eighteen different varieties of Cheerios, she says to me, casually, "Here, you can borrow this bag. Just give it back when you can." She plops a reusable red cloth bag in my basket. I can see the edge of another bag made of green plastic inside, but for obvious reasons, I act oblivious.

Paulette is about five feet tall, and if you were being unkind, you'd say she's mousy, but she has really good energy—bright eyes and a generous smile. She's in a shirtwaist dress of pastel plaids and ballet slippers. I always start out with a favorable impression of short women who don't go for six-inch heels.

"So my son, Rudy," she says, "my baby, he's a senior in high school. And he still spends Wednesday nights with his dad, and every other weekend. And Walter's an okay dad. Even I'll admit that.

"So our agreement is Walter brings Rudy back Thursday mornings in time for me to drive him to school on my way to work. And Rudy, he's a kid—"

"Wait," I say. "What day are we talking about?"

As Tonya thought, Paulette's referring to the Thursday Blanco's body was discovered—the morning after Dr. Potter figures Frito died.

Paulette goes on with her story. "We drive half a block and Rudy says he forgot his calculus book. There's time, so I circle back and—this is weird—Walter's still there. He's got the lid to my garbage can open. Rudy runs back inside for the book, and I say, 'Walt, whatcha doin?' 'Just had some trash in the car. You ain't gonna charge me, are you?' Ha ha ha. He yucks it up. He thinks he can lie to everybody, but I lived with this guy too long. I just stare him down until he leaves. I can see from the way he's looking back and forth to the garbage can that he's thinking of taking whatever he dropped in there with him, but it's Walt, and that would mean he was giving in to me.

"He drives off, and as soon as he's gone, I get out of my car and look in the trash and there's that green plastic bag that's in your cart now. I was just throwing it in the trunk when Rudy came back, and I'm like, 'Doesn't your dad have garbage service at that building?' And Rudy is like—" She grabs my arm and stops her cart. "Nobody hears about any of this, right?"

"You and I will discuss whatever I'm going to say to Tonya. And I'll only say what you decide. Just like I told you on the phone."

"Okay, okay." She nods and moves ahead. "Rudy says his dad has been kind of running deviant code, as he puts it, since the night before. Rudy was in his room studying late Wednesday night when Walt put his head in and said he had to go out for work. Which happens. He's a building manager and, you know, nothing breaks at the right time. But Rudy says his dad's got like a doctor's bag with him, which is odd, cause this guy, he doesn't even like doctors. And then Rudy says his dad doesn't come back until after Rudy's alarm goes off for school. And Walt's grouchy as hell at breakfast. You know, 'Eat your fucking Pop-Tart, I didn't get any sleep.'"

"Did Rudy say Walter had that bag that ended up in your trash with him when they left for your place?"

"Rudy had no idea what I was talking about when I asked about trash pickup at Walter's. But can you believe this? The bastard is throwing his syringes in my trash? I don't know what he's shooting, but can you imagine that? He wants to get rid of it, and he remembers my garbage gets collected first thing Thursday a.m. So I don't know if it's a police matter or not, but if he's some kind of drug addict now, I don't want him within fifty miles of my kids. Some of those guys in Narcotics, the Ritz especially, they liked that stuff. Walter always claimed he'd never go near it. But Ritz is a bad influence, right?"

The timing fits, if I'm doing the math correctly.

"I don't want to look now, obviously," I say, "but what's in that bag exactly?"

"You'll see. A couple used syringes and a pair of those rubber-ized plastic gloves. I don't know anything about this stuff, but maybe the gloves can be stretched out so he could use them to tie off? Isn't that what they call it when they try to get their veins to pop out?"

That doesn't sound like a good guess to me, but what I say is, "I assume it's okay if I get this to Tonya?"

"And no one knows it came from me, I mean not on paper."

"Exactly. We'll let them analyze it, and then Tonya will get back to me and I'll get to you."

I part from her then, since the less time we spend together in public the better. If anybody asks, we met through Tonya and were just saying hello. But before I wave goodbye, she says, "You should come with Tonya one week to St. Stephen's. You might like it more than you think."

She's a nice person, she means this kindly, and it's important to her, so I just say, "You can never tell."

I get in the Cadillac and look in the bag, and the air goes out of my tires. What she called 'syringes' look like EpiPens, each a white cylinder with the needle inside inserted via a green plunger on the other end. There's a brand name printed on the pens, and I turn them carefully through the bag until I can read it. After I google, it's clear that Paulette has unraveled Walter Cornish's deep, dark secret—he has become an insulin-dependent diabetic.

Dead end again.

31. THE FBI INTERROGATION OF WALTER CORNISH

The FBI interrogation of Walter Cornish takes place on August 1 in the Bureau offices down at Federal Square in DuSable on Monday afternoon, one week after my meeting with Paulette. The Chief and Rik and I get to see the video that night.

Moses Appleton informed Rik about four p.m. today that both he and Jonetta Dunphy, the local prosecutor, have determined that the Chief is no longer a person of interest in connection with Blanco's death. Therefore, Moses suggested Lucy watch the video to determine on her own what further role she should have in the Blanco investigation, although he hinted pretty clearly that she should have none. I was invited because I'm the one who produced the insulin pens and, given Walter's responses, might have further info to get or give via my informant (Paulette). Rik is here, too, mostly out of FOMO (fear of missing out), but he also has a legitimate reason to be present, since the Chief may need legal advice before deciding whether she should resume supervision of her department's share of the investigation.

This viewing takes place in a conference room in the FBI field office in Greenwood County, which is a little storefront that could be the site of an insurance agency. Rik didn't want us showing up together in Center City, where reporters might take it to mean that the Chief was under further suspicion. With us are the heads of the investigation for the two law-enforcement agencies that have been cooperating with pretty good success, Tonya from the Highland Isle PD and Don Ingram from the Bureau. Don is an uber-quiet Black dude who I met before on one of Pops's cases. He's super competent and looks like a former jock, like many Bureau agents, but he's a little like Koob in that he seems to rehearse anything he says several times in his head before letting go of the words. Tonya likes him a lot and says he's on the FBI fast track. He will become the ASAC—Assistant Special Agent in Charge—in the FBI field office in Philadelphia next year.

Before Don runs the tape, Tonya gives us the backstory. Walter was accosted by Don and a female agent, Linda Farro, as he was collecting rents at several of Vojczek's east side buildings, not that far from where Blanco's corpse was discovered. The Feebies showed Walter their credentials in their black leather wallets and frisked him immediately, taking the pistol they knew he would be carrying. He was wearing Kevlar, too, which he'd told us was his practice when extracting rent payments in that part of town.

Tonya watched the initial stop from a car across the street, where she and two other FBI agents were waiting as backup. If there is never another great moment in her life in law enforcement, Tonya says, it has all been worth it to see the look on Walter's face when the agents showed him their creds. Apparently, his head jolted back slightly, all the bullshit and attitude falling from his expression as he raised his hands halfway up, like he was going to surrender. Tonya adds that she will always believe Walter was hearing her earlier warnings to him screaming in his head.

The agents requested Walter to come downtown. Walter asked

if he had any choice, and Don, in his usual way of saying as little as possible, replied that right now they were making a request. He never stated that if Walter said no, he would be arrested, because that would have triggered Miranda warnings, but Walter seemed to take heart from hearing this was voluntary, pepping up a little and putting on his oily smile, ready to try to bullshit his way out of this.

The tape begins as Walter enters a conference room with Don. It's a little bigger than ours at Rik's office but far from stylish, with low gray tweedy-type swivel chairs and a table, shiny with the cheap gleam of its laminate top. Three other people soon follow Walter in, starting with Moses Appleton, the United States Attorney, who Walter would recognize from TV. Moses has brought one of his favorite assistants, Dan Feld, a tall slim intense guy with a mass of shiny black hair, more dramatic than Frito's. He was Moses's trial partner on Pops's and my aunt's last trial. Moses is kind of a square, both in terms of his manner and his build. As my Aunt Marta, his close friend, says, Moses comes from a background, growing up in the Grace Street Projects, that has left him unable to fathom paying more than $149 for a suit. He's got a rough complexion that makes him look like he's never fully shaved, and an old-fashioned mustache above his lip that he probably keeps because he's afraid his wife and kids wouldn't recognize him without it. My aunt says he has a better sense of humor in private than you would guess, but in this kind of setting he's all business, never riled but also not wasting much energy on charm—he's the chief federal prosecutor in a metro area of three million people, so fuck charm anyway. As soon as Walter sees him, he knows that his balls are in a vise, since the United States Attorney wouldn't be here just because he's heard that Cornish is an amusing guy to hang with.

Don starts the conversation, telling Walter that this meeting is being videotaped and that any statements Walter makes can be used against him. If he likes, Walter may simply listen.

Walter, being Walter, adds, "Yeah, that's what we said. I'm just gonna listen."

The last person to come in is Tonya, who has the injection pens, rubber gloves and green plastic bag in three thick transparent envelopes, sealed off with wide orange FBI tape that says EVIDENCE in big black letters every couple inches—pretty intimidating in itself.

As we're watching on the TV monitor in the side room of the field office, Toy says to the Chief and me, "We knew it would throw him completely when he saw me." Well aware of how much she hates certain kinds of guys, I realize she probably got quite a thrill out of strolling through the door.

On-screen, as soon as she's put the evidence packets down, she says, "Walter, you know, you're not supposed to put medical waste in the trash. There are some sanitation workers who would like to have a word with you."

Walter has been staring at the injection pens since she placed them on the table. Without looking up, he finally says, "I knew that bitch would give me up. She's been waiting her whole life for this. Her kids will never talk to her again."

"Walter!" says Tonya sharply. "A couple things. One, I don't know who you're referring to, but I assume you mean a woman. So you should know that it was a CI, someone who's ex–law enforcement, who handed this stuff over to us."

"Yeah, if that twat had nothing to do with this, then how come I'm sitting here?" Walter says. He means, how would they know the automatic syringes and gloves have any connection to him?

"We'll get to that," says Tonya. "But the second thing I

wanted to say is that if you think your ex gave us this stuff, then threatening a federal witness in the presence of the US Attorney, an assistant US Attorney and two FBI agents—well, that would be so low-level stupid that I wouldn't even believe it about you. But since you're wrong about her, you may get away with that one."

Walter absorbs all that.

"I think I want a lawyer," he says at last.

Moses speaks up then.

"Mr. Cornish, you're certainly entitled to a lawyer at any time. But since we all know that the lawyer you mentioned to Detective Eo, Melvin Tooley Jr., is bound hand and foot to Moritz Vojczek, you might want to wait a bit. Because once Mr. Vojczek is on alert about all of this, then your bargaining power is going to be steeply reduced."

"I'm not turning on Ritz," says Walter. "I didn't do anything anyway, and even if I did, I'd never dime out the Ritz."

"Well," says Moses, "I'm not certain you fully appreciate your situation. Why don't you let Detective Eo tell you a bit more." Moses nods to Tonya.

"Walter," she says, "let's get straight on something to start. You know, just asking around the station, no one ever heard anything about you being diabetic. Are you a diabetic?"

"No," he says. "And that shit's not mine, if that's what you're thinking." He points at the pens.

"Each of these pens, Walter, was wiped with alcohol to remove any fingerprints. But the insides of the needle and the dosing cylinder, the ampoule, you couldn't get to them, and they are positive for the presence of a drug called carfentanil. Did you ever hear of that?"

"Nope," says Walter.

"Well, it's like fentanyl on steroids. It's a hundred times the strength of fentanyl and ten thousand times more potent than morphine. And you might be interested to know that Dr. Potter reanalyzed Lieutenant Blanco's blood and urine and his hair samples, and there is a heavy presence in all those specimens of this drug, carfentanil. That's what killed him. An overdose of carfentanil."

"That's bullshit, too," says Walter. "How I hear it, the tox screen on Frito turned up nothin."

"The standard tox screen, Walter, doesn't include carfentanil. Which the Ritz probably knows. Fentanyl, yes. But not this compound. That's why we had no idea for so long how Blanco died."

"I never heard of that shit. Those pens, whatever you call them, they don't have nothing to do with me. You already told me, they been wiped. So there are no fingerprints."

"Well, that's peculiar, Walter, because when we received the injection pens and the gloves, they were together in a green plastic shopping bag with a drawstring. And I guess you were careful to carry the bag by the string, but you touched it at some point, because that bag has several of your prints on it. I would bet you didn't wipe it carefully when you dropped the syringe and gloves inside or disposed of everything together. Even a hard guy like you gets a little panicky when you kill somebody."

Walter shakes his head like he's still not buying it.

"Someone's setting me up and grabbed a bag I used to put me in this. Those pens, whatever they have in them, they ain't mine and have nothin to do with me."

"No, I'm sure you wiped them down. And when you did it, you were wearing these gloves, because the trace amounts of an isopropyl alcohol solution on the injection pens and the gloves are chemically identical: same bittering agents, same amount of water, identical concentration—sixty-eight percent—of actual alcohol.

"And you know, Walter, you're kind of an old-fashioned cop. Your last decade on the job, you were pretty much on cruise control and didn't bother learning a lot of new stuff. It wouldn't have even crossed your mind that it was a hot summer night when you killed Frito." She stares at Walter, while she waits for him to make the connection, which he doesn't.

"You sweat in the summer, Walter. Especially in heavy rubber gloves. And when you perspire, you leave behind your DNA."

"That's more crap," says Walter. "There's no DNA in sweat. Don't they say that?"

"You can't believe everything you read on the Internet. Yes, there is no DNA in the liquid that comes out of our pores. But when you sweat, you slough nucleated skin cells that contain your DNA. And your DNA, Walter, is all over the inside of the gloves. So we now have a lot of evidence against you, Walter. It's your DNA in the mosquito that was crushed the night Blanco was killed, proving you were there. Not to mention a partial palm print on the outside of the window you guys probably used to get in and out of the apartment. We also ID'd your DNA in the gloves used to wipe down that syringe. And the bore of these needles that were in that plastic bag with your fingerprints fit with the injection sites on Frito's upper arm. Those automatic syringes, Walter, were used to kill Blanco. And on top of all that, we have your lies about when you were last in the apartment and in that building.

"Now, Walter, it's not my job to decide what's proof beyond a reasonable doubt. That's Mr. Appleton's responsibility. But I think if you ask him, he'll tell you he's got a great case against you for the murder of a federal witness." When she explained why I was going to get to see the tape, Toy said that if Walter actually goes to trial, I'm going to need to lean on Paulette to testify. But Tonya's confident she will ultimately agree. If Paulette was off the ground with rage about the notion of a drug addict around her kids, then she's going to be in actual orbit when she hears Walt is a murderer.

"And you know, Walter," Tonya says, "I have an odd sense of humor, but I think that's pretty funny. The reason Blanco was a potential federal witness was because the US Attorney was still investigating this phony 'sextortion scheme' that you and Primo and the Ritz had invented about Chief Gomez. That's like cheap irony, right? You're going down on federal murder because *your* lies created federal jurisdiction in the first place. Pretty rich, right?"

I guess they told Tonya to drive the knife in as deep as she could and then to twist it hard. And it's clear she's having a great time playing bad cop, hanging Walter figuratively from a meat hook.

"And here's another amusing thing, Walter," says Tonya. "I'm pretty sure I remember you were one of the guys around the station who bitched the loudest when the legislature abolished capital punishment in our state. I kinda agreed with you about that, frankly. But guess what, Walter? The federal system, that's your dreamland. The US courts still have the death penalty. And even though they don't sentence a lot of folks to die on the federal side, one of the crimes for which there have been executions in the last few years is murdering a federal witness. And then you throw on top of that the fact that the man you killed was a cop? Sounds like a capital offense to me. A lethal injection for a lethal injection? That's old-fashioned justice, right?" She is trying hard not to smile as she stares Walter down.

The camera is facing Walter. Listening to Tonya, he seems to be wavering between indignation, which straightens him up, and instants of absolute panic in which he shrinks.

Moses speaks up then.

"This is what we can do for you, Mr. Cornish. Ten days ago, I told Detective Eo that I would authorize a grant of immunity for you in exchange for your absolute and complete cooperation. We knew you'd lied about being in the apartment where Blanco died. But we still hadn't established that Lieutenant Blanco had been murdered. We thought your honest answers would prove he was, and that you could help us apprehend the other person or persons responsible for that crime. And I believe she warned you then, as I'd asked her to do, that a deal for immunity would be off the table if you walked out of the room—as you did—and that there would be no second chance, once we gathered more evidence against you. And that is precisely what has happened. You decided to roll the dice, you rolled badly and, frankly, that choice has cost you your freedom.

"You are going to the penitentiary, Mr. Cornish. The conversation we are having now is simply about how long. It's up to you today to decide if you will be imprisoned for the rest of your life—no matter how that life comes to an end—or for a shorter period that will allow you to enjoy your later years as a free person. What I'm offering today is a ten-year sentence for the first-degree murder of Fabian Blanco in exchange for your complete cooperation about that crime and every other crime you are aware of, federal or state. Nothing held back. No one protected. We expect to hear everything you know about Moritz Vojczek, and beyond that, the officers you served with when you were still on the force in Highland Isle." Calm and relentless,

Moses waits a second for what he says to sink in, as he keeps his deep-set eyes on Walter.

"I have to say, Mr. Cornish, that I understand that this is a very hard moment. I've been to many meetings like this in my thirty or so years as a federal prosecutor, and I have seen many, many people at the point you've reached now. I understand how hard it is to walk into a room thinking of yourself as a free person—and then being told that you are going to lose your liberty for a substantial period of time. If it makes it easier for you, something similar to what you are experiencing happens every day to thousands of people when they are told that they have a serious form of cancer or other dread diseases. In your case, the treatment, as it were, will last longer than, say, chemotherapy does normally. On the other hand, the cure is guaranteed. Ten years from now—a little bit less, assuming you behave well in confinement—you can resume your life."

Moses stops again.

"Ten years?" Walter finally asks.

"We're talking about murder, Mr. Cornish. Of a police officer. What do you think Lieutenant Blanco's wife and parents and children will say about ten years? They'll feel it's not much more than a slap on the wrist. Ten years is a very good deal, Mr. Cornish. And I promise you, just as you've already experienced, my offer won't be good tomorrow if you walk away today. Tomorrow it will be fifteen."

"And I can't have a lawyer?"

"No, no." Moses shakes his head vigorously. "No, you can consult with any lawyer you like. But the lawyer who has been representing you in connection with the Police and Fire hearings, Melvin Tooley Jr.—the lawyer we have been dealing with, or trying to deal with, to secure your grand jury testimony—he has been paid by Mr. Vojczek. Am I right? In fact, he represents Mr. Vojczek in several other matters, doesn't he?"

"Melvin? Yeah."

"Well, if you choose a lawyer who's obligated or willing to tell Mr. Vojczek that you've become a government witness, you are destroying the value of your cooperation, and so we would have to withdraw our offer. Because that, frankly, is a lawyer who is not actually representing you so much as Vojczek. If you want, we can probably get a member of the Federal Defenders Office over here to consult with you right now. Or you can call anyone else who is actually independent and available ASAP. But a lawyer who Vojczek pays is a nonstarter, because they can't get a retainer from Mr. Vojczek without explaining that you have grave legal problems. Vojczek will understand the implications at once."

Walter mushes up his face like he ate something awful.

"So I get a lawyer who will suck me dry and then wave goodbye when I head off to the slammer?"

"Mr. Cornish, I understand that you only have hard choices. But that is the situation you created for yourself."

"And completely cooperate? That means wear a wire on Ritz?"

"It may."

He shakes his head. "I couldn't do that. I couldn't pull it off, for one thing. The Ritz has all kinds of detection systems running in his office, and everywhere else for all I know. You can't even bring your cell phone when you go in to see him at work. And that's the only place he talks any kind of business.

"And that would be a death sentence anyway. You could hide me in the darkest hole and Ritz would find somebody to snuff me there. He probably will anyway, if I turn."

"Mr. Cornish, we wouldn't do anything to undermine our investigation. And if we agree that you're not actually capable of carrying out any particular operation, then we won't ask you to do it. But complete cooperation means exactly that. You do what we ask you to do to bring people to justice, and you make a full commitment to it. Once your role becomes public, we'll provide protection for you, twenty-four seven, wherever you are."

I think about the cowboy swagger Walter brought with him to the witness stand during the P&F hearing and which is generally his standard mode. It failed him momentarily earlier when he was first listening to Tonya, and now it's completely evaporated. Cornish has slowly sunk in his chair, so that he is beginning to look like he's melting. He is making all kinds of reflexive movements with his jaw, rolling it around, almost like he wants to be sure it still works. A full minute passes in silence.

"And Walter," says Tonya, in a much nicer tone, "we understand your worries about the Ritz. But do you think he'll just give you a pat on the back when he finds out that we have these syringes? He knows exactly where the pressure is going to be applied. There's already one witness murdered. If it's two, does it get much worse for him?"

Tonya is completely right. And you can see that recognition spreading across Walter's face. He can say no to Moses and get indicted, and maybe face capital murder, and the Ritz will know as soon as that happens that his only chance to avoid charges himself is by guaranteeing Walter's silence. And there's only one way to be certain Walter will not speak. Walter, to his credit, does not say anything as naïve as 'The Ritz would never do something like that.' His eyes have been racing around, but now they go still as a burden settles on him. It's like Moses said. Walter walked in a normal person, but now he knows, like the nightmare you can't get out of, that something really bad is going to happen to him. His only choice is how bad.

"Are you ready to proceed?" Moses asks finally.

Walter's Adam's apple bobs before he speaks.

"And this is all on tape, right, about the ten years. You can't back out?"

"Not if you cooperate completely."

Walter nods and stares at his hand and takes a deep breath, a man about to dive into freezing water. But he still can't quite do it. He asks for five minutes by himself.

32. YOU HAVE IT WRONG

You have it wrong," Walter says, when the recording resumes. Tonya says they left Walter alone in the conference room, while the rest of them gathered in the corridor around Moses, complimenting him and Tonya, who'd done an epic good cop/bad cop on Walter. Moses remained utterly solemn. Linda Farro said, 'Bet he talks,' but Moses gave her a sharp look. He never bets on anything, for religious reasons.

After five minutes, Ingram went in to tell Walter it was decision time, and then from the doorway motioned everybody into the room, where they took the same seats. Walter immediately started speaking in a dry voice.

"It wasn't murder. It was an accident, Frito dying. Ritz just wanted him to stick to the story, like he agreed to do from the start. With the Ritz, you make a deal, you gotta keep your end."

"And the story was that the Chief forced Blanco to have sex?" Dan Feld asks on-screen. Now that there is no need to persuade Walter through a mix of intimidation and humiliation, it's Feld who conducts most of the questioning.

"That's what Frito was gonna have to stay with."

"And why wasn't Blanco willing to do that?"

Walter repeats exactly what Koob said, about Frito having decided to assert his constitutional rights, rather than turn over his phone. That incensed Ritz because he said Lucy would walk away from the whole thing and still be Chief.

"And why didn't Vojczek want Lucy to be the Chief?" Feld says.

"You'd have to ask him. But for us, it would be even worse if Frito got immunity. If he told everything—and he probably would because he was such a fucking Boy Scout and that scared of going to jail—then Primo and me and maybe the Ritz, we're looking at perjury.

"So we'd told Frito we needed to meet. Ritz brought in an electronics guru he had on retainer, a guy named Joe from Arizona, to delete all the disgusting shit on Frito's phone. But Joe, he was definitely not happy to be there, and he got kind of pissy and was basically like, 'Hell if I know' when Ritz asked him whether a forensics guy would be able to see what had been erased."

Don Ingram interrupts to ask a few questions about Joe, but Walter has no information about Koob, including what he was doing for Vojczek.

"After that," Walter says, "Frito was not changing his mind. Ritz was pretty sure we'd be able to scare Frito back in line or even pay him off. But Ritz, he's always got a plan, and our just-in-case was to inject Frito with that shit—the super fentanyl, that's what Ritz called it—and keep him stoned nonstop for like maybe thirty-six hours, however long it took to make him into an addict. I guess the stuff is that strong. And Ritz, you know, if he tells you you're an addict, you'd believe it anyway. Ritz figured that once Frito went into withdrawal, he'd be begging to get back in on Ritz's sing-along. And we'd have Frito on a string after that."

"Who got the carfentanil?" Feld asks.

"Ritz brought it."

"In the injection pens?"

"Yeah."

"Where did Ritz get these pens?" Ingram asks. "Is he diabetic?"

"Hardly. Well, at least not so I know. The only thing the scrawny bastard eats are sweets, so it doesn't seem like it. He told me beforehand the carfy stuff is so powerful that it's dangerous even to handle, so he would have it prepackaged in those pens. Plus, that made it a lot safer to carry around. No cop is looking for illegal drugs in a diabetic pen."

"Any idea where he got the carfentanil in the first place?" Don asks.

"Where? Not exactly. But Ritz is a fucking junkie. He's got plenty of connections."

"And how was it that Lieutenant Blanco got injected?" Feld asks.

"After Joe left and we'd tied Frito up, the Ritz offered him money—you know, 'Like how much will it take?' But Frito wasn't budging. The deal from his side was that there would be no chance of his, you know, interests getting exposed. And turning over his phone, you know, that put him at risk. He kept telling Ritz, 'I've done what you asked, I've repeated every word from your script. I kept my end.'

"So Ritz made like he was thinking and walked behind Blanco, and then like a cobra striking, almost quicker than you can see, he gave Frito the first jab right through his shirt in the upper arm. Frito didn't even get a full sentence out of his mouth before he nodded off. That seemed fine. But then about two hours later, Ritz injected him again, and that was it. Frito was dead in like thirty seconds. He vomited all over himself and then he was gone. I mean, Ritz was shocked. He kept feeling Frito's pulse, and then we laid the chair back so Frito was on the floor, and I pushed on his chest and the Ritz tried to breathe for him, puke and all. He read me out about not having an EpiPen, or Nava-whoosy, the opioid antidote crap, like I even had a clue. The Ritz is the one who thought he knew all about that stuff, the right dosage—twelve micrograms, I think he said—and whatnot. Ritz said afterwards somebody gave him the wrong information on how long that shit would stay in Frito's bloodstream. Or maybe the second pen was just loaded wrong and had too much. But killing Frito, that was a stupid accident."

There is another heavy silence, both on-screen, among the people in the room witnessing Cornish's interrogation, and here in Greenwood County, watching later. We're all thinking about poor Blanco and the all-out stupidity of how he passed.

"You know enough about the law," says Dan Feld, "to realize, Mr. Cornish, that what you took part in is still murder. You can't inject someone with a drug that dangerous and say, 'Not my fault,' when he dies. You subjected Lieutenant Blanco to the risk of grave bodily harm and intended to do that."

Walter's face knots up in confusion. "Are you changing the deal?"

"Hardly," says Moses. "We're explaining why you're getting a very good one."

"And why do you think Ritz is a user?" Ingram asks.

"That's what everybody thinks. Him using, that goes back to our time on Narcotics. Sometimes on a bust he'd pinch off something and say, 'A little takeout.' I've never seen him shoot up or anything, but now and then he closes the door to his office and says, 'Time to get happy.' So yeah, my opinion, he's an addict. I guess you'd say addict. Although he never has to worry about where the next dose is coming from."

"Why is that?" Ingram asks.

"You mean where does he get the shit from? I have no idea. You heard the saying about how the left hand don't know what the right hand is doing? That's how Ritz organizes stuff. I collect rent, I hire the janitors and the repairmen. Now and then somebody needs some persuasion on one thing or another, hiring our company, for example, Primo and I have done that. But with Ritz, there ain't no channel surfing. You stay strictly tuned in to what he told you to watch. So I don't know about him and the dope."

"Is the Ritz a dealer?" Tonya asks.

"You can't prove that by me."

"Do people say he's a dealer?" says Ingram.

"Listen, people talk so much wild shit about Ritz that if you believed it all, you'd think he could start his own religion. He's smart, super-duper smart. And hard. And really careful. If he's on that stuff, he's got a lock-certain supply. So maybe he deals to be sure it's around. But I bet there's a stone wall between him and wherever it comes from. You'll never catch him dealing hand-to-hand with anybody."

Moses and Feld and the agents are all scribbling notes.

"If Vojczek is that careful, why was he there with Blanco?" Moses asks.

"I had got nowhere with Blanco, talking, threatening, whatever—nothing. His mind was made up. Ritz was out of his skull that this whole long plan with Lucy was about to unspool. And he knew he was the one guy who'd really scare the shit out of Frito. I was surprised he was willing, but that's how much he hates Lucy."

"Had Blanco met Ritz before?" Moses asks.

"Never."

"So who recruited him to this scheme in the first place?" asks Moses.

"Me. I mean, I did what Ritz said. Somebody—this Joe character, I think—drilled into Frito's computer while he was using it and did quite a tap dance on Frito—even used the camera in Frito's computer to take pictures of him in front of the machine diddling himself. And a dozen screenshots of what he was watching."

I'm startled by this information, and immediately honked off that Koob held out on me and never said he had hacked Blanco. But then I remember our deal. He promised to tell me only about what happened the night Blanco was murdered. The full details on the jobs he'd been hired to do for Ritz were off the table. He made exceptions for what mattered to me directly—spying on me and penetrating the Chief's computer—but only on the condition that I would not pass that on to Tonya, and I still haven't. I'm still not sure if he felt obliged to keep Ritz's secrets, or if his actual motive was to hold back any information that might make it easier for the FBI to identify him. But when I replay what Koob said when I asked what Frito was looking at on his computer, he said something like, 'I can't say,' meaning one thing and me understanding another.

"Ritz told me to go over and show all those pictures to Frito. When we did, I really thought we were gonna have to dial 911. He didn't quite faint, but we actually had to find him a paper bag to breathe in. Once he could listen, we told him he had an alternative, just an hour on the witness stand and nobody would ever know."

"When was this?" asks Moses.

"Early March?"

Moses looks to Feld to give him back the floor.

"Let's return to the night of Blanco's death," Dan says. "What did you do once you realized Blanco had passed?"

"Whatever we could. We cut off the zip ties on his arms and legs, and I actually went to an all-night pharmacy to get some alcohol and those gloves so we could wipe the place down for prints. By the time we were done, the Ritz had kind of talked himself into thinking this wasn't all bad that Frito had croaked. You were right—he knew they don't screen for that drug on the autopsy, and he thought most pathologists wouldn't see the needle marks where they were. And we were done worrying about what Frito might say if he got immunity. No way I was seeing anything good about Frito dying—I was just all messed up about this—but Ritz, he was like, 'Shit happens, Walt, make sure nobody ever sees this stuff.' He took the SIM card out of Frito's cell and told me to get rid of the phone and the used injection pens."

"What happened to the phone and the card?" asks Ingram.

"Ritz told me he was going to melt the SIM with a lighter. The phone, Ritz said to throw it in the river. You know, because the water would kill the thing. I did it soon as I left. But we both knew the damn syringes would float. Ritz's idea was for me to find some public restroom where they have those red plastic boxes on the wall—what do they call them, 'sharps containers'?" After she got the autopsy results and learned about the injection sites on Frito's shoulder, Tonya identified every sharps container within a mile of Blanco's apartment, but the disposal pickups had all taken place by then and the contents had been incinerated. Once I got the bag from Paulette, we all realized that even if Tonya had thought of the containers sooner, it would have turned up nothing. Instead, Walter explains why he ignored Ritz's direction.

"Am I gonna stand in some men's room," Walter says, "where anybody can walk in any second and see me with the shit in my hands that killed Blanco? No chance. I had to get home to my kid, so I just took that stuff with me."

"And where did you dispose of it?" Tonya asks.

Walter smirks at her. He's definitely not buying her act about Paulette.

"I dropped my kid off at my ex's the next morning, and the bins were out front, it was garbage day. I still had the bag with the needles and the gloves in my trunk. I thought it was pretty funny, putting that shit in her can. It wouldn't go wrong, but if one in a million it did, guess who's getting hotboxed?" He's not in a laughing mood, but he still manages a smile. If you ever want an advertisement against getting married, it's Walter and Paulette, bound in shared hatred.

Ingram asks, "And Blanco's phone went in the river, as planned?"

"Exactly," says Cornish. "Threw it out the car window as I was going over the Bolcarro Bridge."

Moses has heard enough. He announces that everyone should take a break and the agents will get Walter a sandwich or something. Moses and Feld are leaving, but they will see Walter again. Later today, agents Ingram and Ferro will ask him more questions. The tape ends.

The Chief is still staring at the monitor.

"Ritz," she says, like it's the worst word in the English language.

Rik asks Tonya to step out so we can discuss the point Moses wanted the Chief to consider, whether she should resume command of the investigation. The answer is clearly no. The Ritz's and Walter's role in framing her—trying to end her career, maybe even put her in prison—means she has too clear a motive to get even with them. She'll need to stay far away. Tonya will continue to report to the commander, the HI department's number two.

"You think the Bureau is going to run Walter in wired on Ritz?" the Chief asks Tonya when she comes back.

"They aren't sure he's got the stones to get away with it," Tonya says. "And the Ritz is probably too smart to say anything incriminating anyway, no matter what Walter tells him. You don't really want the Ritz against Walter in a think-fast contest."

The Chief nods emphatically.

"The Ritz will see through Walter from a block away," she says. "Ritz will babble a bunch of exculpatory shit, no matter what kind of pretext the Bureau cooks up for Walt."

Rik, however, believes that the Bureau will have no choice but to try something in that vein. A case built only on accomplice testimony is not strong. Ritz will trot out the standard defense, discrediting Walter by claiming Cornish killed Blanco on his own and is just offering up a big name like Ritz's to shift the blame and reduce his time. No matter how trite or typical, that story might work. As they say, for the jury it is always opening night. The G needs corroboration for Walter.

"And by the way," says the Chief, "what the hell is carfentanil, and how'd it get into my city?"

"It's starting to turn up here and there," Tonya says, "because there's a shortage of illegal fentanyl. The Chinese got shamed into cutting off the manufacturing of the precursor chemicals. Apparently, the dealers have started cutting what they get with small doses of carfentanil. It's a tranquilizer, but not for humans."

It hits me quick.

"Let me guess," I say. "It's intended for large animals like rhinos and elephants?"

Tonya gives me a weirded-out look.

"That sounds like you're not just guessing." she says.

33. THE CHIEF DECIDES

Rik, as usual, walks Lucy to her Toyota. Once they stroll off, I motion Tonya to the Cadillac, where we sit together in the cushy front seats. Tonya shakes her head about this car every time she's in it.

I say, "I think your Bureau buddies should check with the DEA to see if any companies in Highland Isle have informed DEA that they're going to manufacture carfentanil."

"Okay," she says.

"My hunch is DEA will tell you that there is one place, a company called Vox VetMeds, VVM, in the Tech Park."

"Ah," says Tonya.

I tell her that someone should sit on VVM starting tonight after midnight, using no radio or cell phones and watching out for the various anti-surveillance systems at Direct. After what's leaked from Highland Isle to Cornish and the Ritz, I tell her it would be better if it was her or the FBI on the stakeout.

"About three a.m., you're gonna see a panel truck make a delivery and take something away," I tell Toy.

"Bust the driver?"

"Not yet. Because that would put Mr. Vojczek on high alert. Maybe tail the truck with somebody you know won't fuck it up. If they follow the truck and get enough for probable cause, your Bureau friends could place a covert GPS tracking device on the vehicle. Find out where he's going, who he sees."

"Good thinking, Detective."

"So what's leaving the factory in the truck is, wild guess, carfentanil," I say.

"Okay."

"And if you sit on the place about 4:45 p.m., you'll see the night security guard arrive. He's still on duty when the panel truck shows up."

"Secondo?"

"Secondo. No chance Vojczek didn't put him in there, but I bet there's a layer or two between Ritz and whoever got the order at the company to hire Sid."

"But we think Ritz owns the place?"

"Maybe not on paper. Moses's team will have grand jury subpoenas, so they'll probably do a lot better than me in proving that. But given what's going out the back door, I bet Ritz is careful to keep his distance. Maybe Ritz is controlling the board somehow. Or he has somebody fronting for him as the main shareholder. But he told Walter all about carfentanil before he showed up with it in Blanco's apartment. And there's only one place in town it comes from."

"DEA makes companies like that keep a close count on all the chemicals used to manufacture that stuff," Tonya tells me.

I think for a second.

"Okay," I say, "so now we know what the panel truck is delivering—replacements for what's used to produce the carfentanil."

Tonya tilts her head at me like a curious dog.

"How much of this did you come back to town with, and how much did you figure out on your own?"

"The second. I've had this feeling for a while that Ritz's thing with the Chief has to do with the Tech Park. Only I thought it was about Northern Direct. That's why I started watching."

From her wary eyes, I can see she knows I'm bullshitting and why.

"But Joe from Arizona," she says. "That's your guy?"

I don't answer her.

"Only you couldn't have gotten back and forth from Arizona that fast. Did you meet him someplace in between? Kansas City? Colorado?"

I give her a death stare and reach across to open the passenger door without another word.

On Thursday, Rik asks the Chief to come in to the office. Rik is already preparing to move into a bigger office upstairs, and the conference room feels even more cramped now that I know that. He's interviewed a woman about my age who has two kids and is interested in working part time as his associate. Rik is finally getting what he wants. I just hope it doesn't kill him.

"Well," says the Chief, who looks far better rested, when she rolls in, "it can't be terrible if I'm not in my nightie." She is in fact in uniform.

Rik points her to a chair and gets her coffee.

"There's a complication," says Rik.

"Okay."

"You know I've been waiting for Marc to dismiss the P&F complaint since Blanco died, and he keeps dragging his feet. He finally fessed up this morning. The Reverend and Mrs. Langen-halter don't want to close the case yet. They have no question that the first two witnesses are liars and that Blanco's testimony needs to be stricken because there was no cross. But, the Reverend says, it seems to have been conceded by the defense that you were sleeping with officers under your command. He thinks you need to answer questions about that before the case is dismissed."

"Ah." The rosy look she had a second ago has vanished.

"Those weren't the charges," I say. Rik gives me a kind of startled smile, like, 'Look at you, getting all technical.'

"True," says Rik. "But they can amend their complaint when-ever they like, if we force them to."

"And if I just say I'd rather not," the Chief asks.

"They can order you to testify, and probably will. I've already explained to Marc that the FOP contract has no rules about 'fraternization' between officers. He knows that. But you can guess his answer—you're management."

"Are they going to fire me after all this?"

"The Rev hasn't told Marc what they're thinking. But Marc suspects they'll want some admission of questionable judgment and behavior. Maybe they'll reprimand you with a brief suspen-sion, so the rules are clear going forward. But they'll acknowledge the ambiguity as a reason not to remove you."

Her face is squinched up in consternation. That outcome was what the Chief said she would accept to start, but it doesn't sound as good after being on the rack for three months. She's ready for this to end. It's like COVID. It never goes away.

"But won't the commissioners ask her about that picture?" I say.

From the way he bobs his head, I can tell Rik didn't want to go there yet.

"There may be a way to finesse that," Rik says. "Moses won't want any mention of the Ritz in public. Maybe the commission will accept that the photograph was taken before you became Chief and is beyond the scope of the complaint."

Lucy shakes her head sadly.

"Steven will go whoop-ass as soon as I concede the picture is real. Rik, you're the one who told me the night Blanco testified that the mayor can't just say okay about sex in an office the public pays for."

Rik doesn't answer. He's thinking. But she's right. Logic says she should resign now, if testifying will doom her anyway.

"Actually," I say, "I've been thinking about something."

"Uh-oh," says Rik, but he's smiling.

"What if we can flip the script?"

"Okay," says Rik. He's wary but interested.

"What if the big news about the Chief has nothing to do with this? Or is much much larger than all this?"

"And what might that be?" the Chief asks.

"How I got this idea, Chief, was listening to you thinking out loud about Walter, and you saying that sending him in on the Ritz didn't seem like it had much chance of success. And I started thinking, Well, what if the person who makes the move on Ritz is nobody he'd ever expect and who has no connection to Blanco's murder? Somebody he hates enough that he couldn't resist the chance to speak to her?"

"*Yo?*" The Chief touches the buttons on her service blouse. But her mouth turns down thoughtfully.

"What would Lucy have to talk to Vojczek about?" Rik asks. "She can't call and say, 'Let's chat about offing Blanco.'"

"We'll think of something," the Chief says. "I just need to get him talking."

Rik stares at her. "A couple of nights ago we were hearing

how the Ritz murdered Blanco. That's who you want to sit down with, Lucy?"

"The Bureau will cover her," I say.

"The Ritz will want to meet in a bank vault," says Rik. "Someplace where surveillance is impossible. And the first thing he'll do is search you for a wire."

For a moment, the Chief's look is unreadable. Only her eyes move while she considers things.

"I like it," the Chief says.

"I don't," says Rik.

"Ricky, I'm a cop. It's my job. The Ritz is a blight—on this town, and humanity, frankly. If Moses buys in on this idea, I want to do it. P&F or not." She smiles a little. "And it sounds like fun."

34. WALTER LOVES SPILLING

According to what Tonya hears, Walter loves spilling tea about the Ritz behind his back. To keep his cover, Walter is still going to work every day at Vojczek Management, and then detouring from his nightly trip to the tavern to meet for an hour or two with Ingram and other agents at another off-site, in the North End.

Even to those who have known him for decades, the Ritz, according to Walter, is 'fuckin strange.' While he was on the job in Kindle County, he met Jewell Green, a civilian employee, legendary beautiful and just divorced from a doctor who ran around on her. Jewell's mom was white and her father was Black, and because of the dad, Ritz's mother wouldn't even be in the same room with Jewell. Ritz married Jewell anyway and supposedly never spoke again to his mother, who he described as 'mean as a stick.' According to Walter, Jewell was the Ritz's true better half—warm and gracious as a diplomat, unlike Ritz, who is almost always sullen and uncommunicative, with that sinister vibe. Just before the Ritz left the Kindle County Unified Police Force, Jewell and he split. Walter says there are many stories about why, and no one knows the truth. Some heard the Ritz brought home an STD. Several say it was because Jewell wanted children. A few people claim they saw Jewell with bruises. And many others, adding two and two, think Jewell DQ'd Vojczek because he'd started using. Walter still has no idea what actually broke them up. Jewell subsequently had one child, a son born during her brief relationship with an officer named Harris. The kid is solid and reportedly can't stand the Ritz.

Despite their breakup, the Ritz and Jewell never divorced and remain in close touch. He hasn't lived with her for roughly two decades, but he still has dinner at Jewell's every Sunday night in a big McMansion on the West Bank that he supposedly bought for her after they separated. Walter says they speak by phone every day.

For a while the Ritz had a Chinese girlfriend who had started out as his language tutor, but as his drug habit has become more regular, he seems to have lost interest in women. Years ago, Ritz used to say he knew how to tame the dragon by chipping— reducing his doses over the course of a week—but Walter hasn't heard him make that claim in years. Instead, Ritz seems to live the junkie's dream of infinite supply. He tends to spend his nights alone in the penthouse of a Trump-branded high-rise on the other side of the river, which Ritz owns and runs. According to the Chinese girlfriend, who was bitter when Ritz dropped her, he reads about whatever esoteric subject he's currently studying— recently Walter says there are books around the apartment about the architecture of Pompeii—while listening to jazz, until he fixes for the last time that day and drifts into a nod.

Because it's all need-to-know around the Ritz, Walter can't say what Sid DeGrassi is up to. Even Primo is in the dark. Sid is totally close-mouthed about what he does at the plant. Walter's guess is that Sid's main job is to act dumb and see nothing, responsibilities for which he possesses great natural aptitude.

Tonya, however, has gotten more insight about what's happening when Sid is on duty. After a week of rotating in and out of FBI surveillances, she has seen Sid let an after-hours cleaning crew into the VVM building every night about eight p.m. The company, Vojczek Sanitary, is another subsidiary that does the end-of-lease or storm cleanups in the Vojczek buildings around Highland Isle and Kindle County. Yet there is also a regular janitorial crew that works during the days at VVM. The cleaners who show up at Vox VetMeds put in a full shift there and, according to the agents who have tailed them, never clean any other building. When the Bureau finally ID'd one of the guys, he turned out, no surprise, to have a master's in chemistry.

Aside from Sid DeGrassi and the cleaners, there is no other visible connection between Vox VetMeds and the Ritz, with one further exception. In VVM's annual report in Delaware, they list the names of their three board members. One, Yolanda Green—also VVM's general counsel—is a lawyer in her thirties who practices in a small firm in Kindle County. Based on photos on her Facebook feed and info from Ancestry.com, both of which the Bureau keeps an eye on, she is believed to be related to Jewell, Ritz's ex, on her father's side and is probably Jewell's niece. When I share this with Rik, he laughs in a snorty disbelieving way.

"The Ritz seems as clever as they say. He's got privilege insulating everything. Yolanda can't be forced to disclose her communications with Jewell—or Vojczek—because of the attorney-client privilege, and Jewell will never have to testify about the Ritz, because she can still claim marital privilege. Our friends in the US Attorney's Office have got their work cut out for them."

Moses and Feld, however, seem to have a plan, although

they don't share much of it when Rik and I bring the Chief to
meet with them and Ingram. Pops has always described Moses as
methodical, and from the bits and pieces I hear, Moses's attitude
seems to be that Vojczek is into so much bad shit that they will
eventually get him for something. Feld at one point remarked
that the Ritz is the guy they dreamed up the RICO statute for—
a one-person crime wave.

Toy has also been in touch with DEA about Vox VetMeds.
Carfentanil is legally available in the US these days only as a
compounding drug, meaning a made-to-order prescription for
a single customer. About eight months ago, Vox was granted a
registration as a controlled substance manufacturer in order to
compound a generic form of carfentanil for the Kindle County
Zoo. The zoo has made two compounding requests, both of
which VVM reported to DEA. What is important is that the
registration gives VVM a reason to acquire the chemicals needed
to formulate the stuff and to keep them on hand.

From the start, all the Feds seriously *love* my idea of running
the Chief in on the Ritz. Even if it doesn't work, it won't blow
Walter, and Lucy is, of course, the last person in the world
Vojczek expects to hear from. By now, with a non-subject letter
Rik got her from Moses, which protects the Chief if she tells
everything, the Feds have learned the whole story about her and
the Ritz and the picture. And Feld, who has the kind of conniv-
ing imagination that makes you glad he chose law enforcement
instead of crime, has come up with a scenario that everyone
thinks has a good chance to get the Ritz talking.

To lay the groundwork, at Feld's instruction, Rik asks Marc
Hess to inform the press that the commission has required
testimony from the Chief. Marc took the request as part of our

press strategy to get ahead of the story. After the articles go up saying she will testify next week, the Chief phones Ritz's cell—a number she got from Walter—when surveillance puts him in his office in downtown Highland Isle. She makes the call from the Greenwood field office, with six of us listening.

"It's Lucy, Ritz."

Long silence, before Vojczek says, "Where the fuck did you get this number?"

"I'm the police, remember? The phone companies bark and sit when we call. You and I have to talk."

"Fuck we do," he answers.

"We need to have a word, Ritz. And I don't want to do it on the phone." That was Ingram's idea, to come on as if the Chief is wary of surveillance.

"We have zero to talk about, you and me."

"I have to testify next week, Ritz."

"So it goes."

"Well, you're going to be hearing your name now and then. I want to give you a little preview. For both our sakes. You just tell me where and when we get together."

He hangs up with no goodbye.

There is silence over the weekend, and then on Monday, midday, Ritz tells Walter that he needs him in his car Tuesday morning. He doesn't say why, but when Walter asks around the office, he hears that Ritz is getting ready for some kind of meeting tomorrow. It's just a guess that the Ritz is about to set up something with the Chief, but the Bureau calls a late-night conference on Monday at an off-site to get the Chief ready, just in case. Naturally, both Rik and I are invited to attend.

35. AS SOON AS I ENTER MY APARTMENT

As soon as I enter my apartment, I sense something. It's about six p.m. Monday, and I've returned to walk Gomer the Turd and to eat before we meet with the Bureau technicians. But I know I'm not alone. Gomer is in the far corner of the living area with his little eyes racing. He usually retreats there when I have visitors, as if he needs space to plan his future actions. And even if it's below the threshold of actual hearing, I sense somebody else's breath.

"Toy?" I ask.

"Don't shoot," I hear him say. Strangely, I haven't yet reached under my arm for my gun. Koob steps out of my bedroom. He is thinking about smiling but isn't positive how that will be received.

"Wow," I say, absorbing the total-body shock.

"Sorry," he says. "I tried to call you."

"'No Caller ID'?"

"That's my name," he says with the same suggestion of a smile.

I was with Rik and a client and couldn't answer when my phone lit up about 3:30 p.m. I assumed it was the FBI with details about tonight's meeting, which I then received from Tonya by text.

"I was kinda thinking I'd never see you again," I say. "What's going on?"

Life is not a rom-com, at least not mine. I suppose there's a chunk of me that would get a thrill if he said he'd left his wife and was here because he needs to hang with me every day and thinks I'm great and is all in for me. And there's another, maybe bigger part of me that would never believe that or would be totally freaked about any commitment. But there's nothing in me that really expects him to say that.

"I understand there's a meeting tomorrow," he says. "Involving your client."

I'm alarmed at first, then realize who he's been talking to. Neither Walter or Lucy is sure yet about a meeting. I take a beat to remind myself Koob and I are back to being on opposite sides.

"Then you know something I don't," I say. "Where did you hear that?"

"The Ritz called me."

"Okay."

"He wants me to provide counter-surveillance. He thinks it may be a setup."

"Really?" I hitch a shoulder, noncommittal. "Then why would he go?"

"Well, he has faith that his comms guy will outwit law enforcement, I guess." He comes closer to a smile than usual, as he compliments himself. "And I think he's concerned about what your client will say about him on the witness stand."

"Last time I saw you, you were afraid Ritz might kill you."

"I have not completely disregarded that thought. But it turned out when Darnell called the payment intermediary that Ritz had fallen way behind in what he owed us, which helped explain why I just took off. And the Ritz does appear to accept that cooperating with law enforcement would be lethal for our business. Not to mention our freedom. It's also been weeks and nothing bad has happened to Ritz or the matters that concern him. So I think he feels reassured."

"Still. Why not tell him, 'Nice knowing you'? Why take the chance?"

"As I said. Ritz owes us a great deal of money. He's been playing some excuse about a sharp rise in the price of bitcoins. But the transaction will supposedly take place the instant he sees me tomorrow. It's the kind of power play you would expect from Ritz: You quit when I say you quit. And obviously, showing up again will probably lessen any suspicion he has that I turned on him."

"Is this the money he owes you for spying on me?"

Koob knots up his lips to keep from smiling again.

"For many services. It is a lot of money, but if this *is* an undercover operation, probably run by the FBI, given their earlier involvement, then I would rather not be there—at least not without some preconditions. Obviously, I have no interest in being held for questioning."

"We don't talk about our clients. Remember?"

"I understand."

"So what I know or don't know, I have nothing to say."

"Understood. But I have spent some time thinking this through. If I show up tomorrow and it is a sting of some kind, then I like to think I will figure that out. Whatever means the FBI employs to intercept the communications, radio or recorder or even a laser tap—do you know what that is?"

I nod. It's a dream addition to the PIBOT. The mechanism uses a laser to turn the vibrations of speech against a hard surface, usually a window, into sound, applying the same principles involved in a microphone.

"Well, whatever devices are in use," he says, "I suspect I will detect them. Certainly, if I were the FBI, I would not like to take that chance. So I want to propose a win-win. For me. And your client. And the FBI."

I tumble my hand forward, indicating he should explain.

"If I recognize something, I will keep it to myself," he says. "I will go through the motions, searching, using the appropriate machinery, but if I uncover anything—" He extends a thin finger over his lips. "And all I get in exchange is a day pass. I come and I go. No one detains me. No one comes looking for me afterwards."

"And if I say I can't help?"

"I head home now."

"Explaining what to the Ritz?"

"Too risky, I suppose."

Which would be like posting a 'STOP' sign. If the surveillance guru has decided meeting Lucy is too perilous for *him* to show up, Ritz won't proceed either.

Koob has reasoned this through carefully. Bottom line, the Bureau needs to accept his terms. It's the only way the Ritz will see Lucy.

"And just say it turns out to be law enforcement?" I ask. "Won't Ritz think you were part of it, if he gets rolled up?"

"He may. But my name will never appear on any government witness list. And I can say the feds must have developed some advanced technology that fooled my machinery. The federal agencies go to great lengths not to disclose their newest surveillance techniques, even at trials, and the courts usually permit them to keep their secrets. I'll have some deniability. And frankly, if Ritz is under arrest, he will have less time to bother with me. Darnell and I both think this is the best course for us." Koob looks at me in that unflinching way he employs when he's getting to some uncomfortable truth. It's a cool deal for him. They get their money. They never turn on Ritz visibly. And they silently assist in apprehending somebody they now know to be a true sinister shit and a killer.

I tell him I need to make a call or two.

"Go walk for an hour," I say. "And hey, do you mind taking Gomer with you?"

I phone Rik first. Then Tonya. She calls back in about forty-five minutes.

"The FBI *hates* being dictated to," she says. "Some of them just wanted to say, 'Fuck him,' but the cooler heads realize they have no choice. Still, Joe, or whatever his name really is, has to understand that he can't play games. If they think he's tipped off Ritz, this deal evaporates and your guy ends up in cuffs. So he better be super convincing when he tells Ritz it's cool to go ahead. And they were emphatic that you can't confirm to Joe that it's a law-enforcement operation. They don't want to take the chance that he'll let something slip to Ritz beforehand, even by accident."

When Koob returns, he's brought carnitas from Ruben's. I laugh and we sit down at my table.

"Just play it out tomorrow," I tell him. "One way or the other, you'll be able to go on your way."

"Thank you," he says.

He talks to me about his daughter while we're eating. He sees no signs she's growing up. It's sex, drugs and rock 'n' roll. And shopping.

"That's not a good feeling," he says, "to look at your own child and think, You're shallow."

"And young," I say. "She's young. People change. Right?"

"Sometimes."

"The way you describe your wife, your daughter's got a lot she's getting over. So maybe that's why she needs to stay on the surface."

He looks up like he's never considered that.

At ten to nine, I fold the food wrapper and get ready to go. I have told him only that I have a meeting with Rik.

"Where you staying?" I ask.

He shrugs. "Ritz would pay for a hotel."

"You can stay here. But," I say, having considered it, "no hooking up. It wouldn't be fun for me. I mean, it would be fun. But not afterwards."

He nods several times. "I have been thinking the same thing."

I think he means it. He looks kind of relieved.

"So, you know, help yourself to the sofa," I tell him.

"Okay," he says. "If I'm not here, I will talk to you before I go."

We hang there by the door.

"Oh, just, fuck," I say and hug him quickly before I leave.

36. THE SESSION WITH THE BUREAU TECHS

The session with the Bureau techs takes place at the off-site in the North End where Ingram has been seeing Walter—a down-on-its-heels office building where the door to the Bureau's second-floor space identifies the enterprise inside as 'National Industries.' It's been a little creepy finding out that the federal government has all these random little hideouts around town. Inside the small office, it's the same inexpensive stuff, a conference room with portable metal walls and an oval table with a shiny plastic surface.

Don Ingram and Tonya are here, along with Rik and Lucy and me. The star of the show is a thick-set woman named Mulligan, who has big hands and a short do that looks like permanent hat hair. She has arrived from DC to brief the Chief on the equipment the Bureau will be using tomorrow. According to what Tonya told me, Mulligan had wanted the deal with Koob to include specifying the counter-surveillance equipment he'd employ. But that was scotched by higher-ups who said it would confirm this was a law-enforcement operation. I was pretty sure Koob wouldn't have been willing to go that far anyway.

Mulligan has that annoying habit of identifying everyone only by the role they play in the operation, as if they have no conse-quential human existence beyond that. The Ritz is 'the target.'

"Our understanding," Mulligan says to Lucy, "is that the target has employed a well-trained surveillance expert, so we have to assume the target's defenses will involve the latest and the greatest—devices to detect anything we might use to watch or hear: cameras, laser taps, radio transmissions, bugs in the room, GPS transponders. And whatever the target actually says out loud is going to be covered by an ambient noise machine that produces blank sound in the same frequency ranges as human speech. The goal of that is to make sure that even if you have a recording device—and you will, two in fact," Mulligan says, lifting a finger toward Lucy, "or a radio, ditto, what is captured will be completely unintelligible. We have a few tricks of our own to counteract that."

"Our source"—that is how she refers to Walter—"says that he's bodyguarded two of the target's meetings with an outsider in the past. Each time the target had personnel on hand to do the initial search of that person. We assume tomorrow that will be the CS guy." Counter-surveillance. Aka Koob.

"After that," Mulligan continues, "in the past, the target used his own vehicle for the conversation. That gives him a controlled setting that he can sweep in advance for bugs or GPS devices. Expect the same tomorrow. The target will drive, so no one else hears what he's saying. By moving, with his own people on all sides of the vehicle and watching for any tail, he thinks he can defeat most surveillance. After he's confident he's not being followed, he has previously parked under a viaduct, a road underpass—the source says both times it was the same site in the North End in Kindle County, not far from here—to defeat any

SCOTT TUROW

aerial surveillance, drones, et cetera, and to block the radio signal from any broadcasting device he's missed.

"We think he's very likely to park there again. Whoever has advised the target about the site is right—that's a tough location to surveil. But we have ways around that.

"The main problem for us is the noise machine. As I said, you will be equipped with two digital recorders." Mulligan reaches in an envelope and places both on the conference table. Each device is amazing. One is a physical car key, a perfect match for what the Chief uses to start her ten-year-old Toyota, and the second appears to be a magnetized entry card, the kind that opens the electronic lock on a door. She'll carry the card, along with a couple similar pieces of plastic—ATM and credit card—in a stick-on envelope attached to the back of her phone.

"We used the phone recording of you and the target last week to develop a signal envelope for each of your voices. The microphones in each recording device are directional—and noise canceling. They will enhance everything within the signal envelope and add a digital marker. If you keep one of these recorders close to you, we'll have no trouble extracting your voice afterwards by computer.

"But we need your help to make sure we get the target's side of the conversation. The closer you can place the second recorder to the target—"

"You mean Ritz," the Chief says. Mulligan is like an actor who can't break role, and her Bureau-speak is irritating, especially to a local like the Chief, who hears it as part of the FBI's We're-So-Special horseshit.

Mulligan more or less growls but nods, and the Chief says, "Just checking. Okay, second device as close as possible to the Ritz. What else?"

"Keep your voice up, as much as you can."

"I will, but Moritz is a low talker."

"Well, we have some ideas about dealing with that. We're going to ask you to go to the meeting wearing these." She slides a pair of behind-the-ear hearing aids out of the envelope.

Lucy pulls her mouth around dubiously.

"Won't Ritz find it strange that I'm suddenly wearing these?"

"Who says it's sudden?" asks Mulligan. "Your hair is long enough that you could have been wearing them for months with no one noticing. You just need to be ready to explain that you damaged your hearing somehow when you were younger, and recently it's gotten worse. Did you like rock concerts?"

"Not much," says the Chief, "and nothing headbanging. But I was detailed to the gun range as an instructor when I was still in Kindle County."

"Perfect," says Mulligan. "So the ear protection they gave you turned out to be defective. Right?"

"Typical low-grade Kindle County crap," answers Lucy.

"The other point with the hearing aids is that the surveillance expert probably won't let you keep them on. He'll take any electronic device you're carrying away from you, or he'll remove the batteries, probably both, if he's as good as we believe. Supposedly, the CS guy won't be alerting the target to our equipment, so he may let you hold on to the aids with the batteries pulled, which is great, because the high-frequency radio we've installed in the right hearing aid has a secondary power source. If CS keeps them, don't worry. The radio will probably get blocked under that bridge anyway, and our principal means of keeping track of you will be a laser microphone that we'll begin using as soon as you get in the target's vehicle."

"Is it worth bothering with those if they're going to get

confiscated?" the Chief says, nudging one of the hearing aids with a polished nail.

"Yes," says Mulligan, "because if they take away your hearing aids, you'll have a reason to demand that the target speak up—which will help us overcome the sound machine. So make a fuss, however CS decides to disable them."

"Ah." The Chief grins.

"Also," Mulligan says, "pay attention to the sound machine the target uses. It will have to be in plain view, because he won't want to muffle it in any way. If we can identify it, we can reproduce its signal range afterwards, which will help us remove the interference digitally from what we've recorded.

"As I said, our principal means of overhearing the conversation as it's taking place will be a laser microphone." Mulligan asks the Chief to sign a consent form, so that use of the laser mike doesn't violate the federal wiretapping law, then takes a second to explain how the tap works. They're betting Ritz will park where he has before, and have already positioned a laser on a lamppost. There will also be one in an FBI tail car in case Vojczek surprises them and stops somewhere else. Apparently, the Bureau's machines emit some additional beam that hides the laser from the devices that can ordinarily detect them.

"Remember," Mulligan says, "the first purpose of these listening devices is your safety. If you scream louder than his sound machine, we'll hear you. Your safe word will be 'Nazi.' And if he makes a second sweep for bugs, you say 'spaghetti.'"

"'Nazi' and 'spaghetti,'" the Chief repeats. I'm glad to hear this part. The Chief has been impressively unconcerned for her physical safety, but in the academy, I was taught that anybody who is within nine feet of you can kill you with a knife before you can draw your weapon. So she'll be in the danger zone, sitting in a car with Vojczek, especially unarmed. But no matter what Ritz does, she should have time to scream.

"For his initial sweep of you, the CS guy is probably going to use an electromagnetic field detector, which will alert him to any active electronic device—like your hearing aids or cell phone. Assuming the target or his people are close enough to see the indicator lights go off, the CS guy will have to play that straight. Once he's used the field detector, he has to turn it off, because it will just keep up that high-pitched alarm in response to the sound machine running. He might test the vibrations on the car's windshield, too, but we don't expect the target to go riding around with dampers on the glass that would interfere with the laser tap. That's a known trick for dope peddlers, which means it's an invitation for a police stop."

"Yeah," says the Chief. "Heaven forbid Ritz looked like a dope peddler."

Mulligan responds with a tight smile.

"In order to get through the electronic field detector, every-thing we're equipping you with can be turned on and off. The hearing aid radio is controlled by the battery door. When that's open, the radio will go off. But the recorders I just showed you, the key and the card, will require you to activate them manually after the search." Mulligan shows the Chief the buttons on the center of the car key and the logo on the key card. The switches are heat as well as pressure sensitive, so it won't require a lot of manipulation for the Chief to turn each recorder on again with a casual motion.

Mulligan asks the Chief to practice with the buttons. She does it twice but waves her hand at more maneuvers. When Lucy started as a patrol officer in Kindle County, Narcotics tapped her frequently to work undercover. She wasn't known to the dealers as a narc and her Spanish was perfect. She rolled up half a dozen of those dudes. 'I was pretty good,' she's told me, meaning she freaking killed it. She said it was like running sprints on a high wire, but she loved the whole deal—the acting, the danger, the improvisational reactions. She's confident she still has the same chops.

On the way out, Don Ingram stops me.

"Your guy made a great deal here. He's smart enough not to try to have it both ways, right?"

"He keeps his word," I answer.

Once I'm in the Cadillac, I'm sort of amazed by what I said, my faith in Koob as this upright individual, given all the plays we ran on one another. Can you be an honest spy? But I meant it.

I'm happy to think he's at my place, waiting for me, but of course he's not. There's a note on my table—maybe the first time I've seen his handwriting, which is very neat, almost like calligraphy.

'Better I leave,' it says. I consider the grammar for a second, unsure if it's shorthand or a leftover from the way his mom spoke English. Better you stay, I think, and then immediately decide it's not, he's right. It's easy to feel a little swindled because Koob is still enmeshed with his wife, whether he knows it or not, but it's the wrong time on both sides.

I know they say that people change for love, and I've seen it. I went to high school with a woman named Randi Berkowitz, who fell for this Pakistani guy. I ran into her at the mall, and she had on this hijab that draped down over her shoulders, and a floor-length skirt with four little kids clinging to the hem. And she definitely seemed happy. Living by these rules, which she'd probably never even heard of when she was in high school, felt right to her—a way to express her true self, the person she'd chosen to be.

But deep inside, I know I'm still not ready for just one person and may never get there. The most I can take away from the whole thing with Koob is that maybe the idea is getting a little more tempting.

After looking at the note another second, I fold it up and place it carefully in my top desk drawer. I'm sure I'll take it out and hold it for a minute now and then.

37. THE MEET

A little before eight a.m. on Tuesday morning, Tonya calls me and says, "It's on." Ritz's assistant at work has phoned the Chief's cell and told her that Mr. Vojczek wants to meet with Lucy in thirty minutes at the tables outside a coffee shop on Madison, about a block from the Vojczek Management office.

Rik and I will not be allowed to observe anything on the street, since we could interfere unwittingly, but given what's at stake for the Chief, Toy has gotten us seats at the Greenwood County off-site, which will be the communications center for the operation today. With half an hour to get there, I dash out the door without remembering to pee, and I spend the entire drive waiting out every light with my foot tapping.

I beat Rik by a few minutes, and what I walk in on looks like a low-rent version of Mission Control. There are four huge computer monitors set up on a long folding table, and two men and two women with headsets are seated on stackable plastic outdoor chairs in front of the screens. Dan Feld is in a metal folding chair, rocking back and forth against the wall. He tosses me a tiny wave.

Toy comes to greet me and to explain what we're watching.

"Ritz has Walter and a couple of his other guys shadowing the Chief to be sure she isn't being followed," Toy says. "Which is kind of a hoot, because we're way ahead of them." She points to one of the monitors where I can see an overhead view of the Chief's Camry on its way from the station, just pulling onto Madison.

"A drone?" I ask.

It turns out the FBI has a long-standing arrangement in Highland Isle and Kindle County to share the feed from the cities' 4K CCTV surveillance cameras that hang over many intersections. The legend is that the cameras are so powerful that in good light you can read the date on a dime lying on the street.

The Chief parks right across from Coffee Kingdom. "Here goes," she says to herself when she grabs the door latch. She knows she has an audience. The output from the tiny radio in her right ear is exceptionally clear so far, broadcast in here on a couple speakers on standards at either end of the table.

On-screen, the Chief walks into Coffee Kingdom and comes out with a latte. She's left the jacket of her uniform, with its rows of buttons, and her star, back in her car. Ingram recommended that, figuring Ritz would be concerned that the uni would draw attention to the unexpected sight of the two of them together. Instead, she's wearing the straight blue skirt that has no markings, which she says she prefers to pants in the August heat, and the teal tunic, without decoration at the shoulders, that she puts on for dress occasions, when there's no chance that she'll remove her jacket. She looks pretty much like a civilian.

A minute later Ritz passes by on foot, with his greasy duck-assed do and his big-heeled cowboy boots. A pair of jeans hang loosely over his bony behind, and he's got on his standard tweed sport coat. Although I should have realized it a while ago, it finally dawns on me that Ritz wears that coat to hide a gun.

Passing the Chief, he does not look back, but Koob, as is his way, seems to appear from nowhere. I don't realize for a second that it's him. He's disguised so that the FBI or whoever doesn't learn what he really looks like. He's got on a full fake beard, big shades, a baseball cap and a broad phony nose. But his air is relaxed. He's in a pair of khakis and a long-sleeve shirt and is wheeling a good-sized rolling briefcase behind him. Very business casual. Just another guy going to work. He walks straight up to Lucy.

"Chief, would you mind joining me down the block?" He points her to Ritz's big black SUV, a Lincoln Navigator, parked a few spaces ahead of them. The CCTV cameras are better in low light than I thought, and the two techs working across the room enlarge and brighten the image of the Chief and Koob as they climb into the back seat together. In the meantime, Tonya catches my eye. She's shaking a limp hand in front of her chest and mouths the word, "Da-a-a-ng," obviously referring to Koob, disguise and all. I flip her off. Rik, who's been in the seat beside me for a few minutes, is laughing.

"Turn towards me, please, Chief," Koob says and frisks Lucy deftly. He motions for her to remove her cell phone and her keys, which she's carrying in the two pockets of her blouse, and he appears to place them on the back seat of the car between them. At that point, Koob reaches into the big briefcase and takes out a machine I've seen in magazines. It's about a foot square and a few inches tall and is called 'The Hunter,' a black box with lights. It deploys several different kinds of countermeasures, including electromagnetic field detection and lens finding. Koob looks right out the back of the SUV, so I know the machine has picked up the 4K cameras, but he'll tell the Ritz that's normal.

Next he finds the Chief's hearing aids and asks her to remove them, extracting the batteries as soon as they are in his palm. He looks down at them for a second, long enough to make me think he's on to something. She picks the left one out of his hand—the one without the radio—to put in front of the machine. She opens and closes the tiny battery door a couple times, and there is no audible response from the Hunter. She's demonstrating that it's solely a hearing device, with no power without the battery. Koob smiles so faintly that probably only I notice. He's heard a great deal about the Chief, and I take it that he's impressed by her utter nonchalance in attempting to foil the machine and cluing him about which hearing aid to test.

He picks up her cell phone next, handing her back the case as he removes the device from it. Using a couple jeweler's tools, he extracts the SIM card from the side and then cracks the back off the phone and jimmies out the battery. Finally, he picks up her car key and the fob that's attached, whose yellow buttons open her trunk and lock the Camry's doors. He uses the same tools to remove the watch battery from the fob. He holds the physical key in his hand a second—he's sensed something there, too, I suspect—but he lays it down.

Koob then turns off the Hunter and puts it aside, staring down at the car seat. Through the back window, we can't see Koob or the Chief below the waist, but I know what he's set on the rear bench—the hearing aids, the Chief's car key, the open fob, and the various pieces of her phone. He probably would have bet from the start that this was a law-enforcement operation, but now he seems to be calculating. In the end, he picks up her car key and hands it back to her but holds on to the cell phone and the hearing aids. After another second's hesitation he closes the battery doors on the aids so that the radio comes back live.

"I need those," the Chief says. "I'll be deaf without them. And

I'm not letting my cell phone out of my sight. There's too much confidential stuff on there."

Koob studies her. He has to figure that she knows about his deal, but he's trying to decode her communication.

"I think Mr. Vojczek will keep all these until after your meeting. Okay?"

"Well, make sure he's careful with the hearing aids," she says. "They cost five grand. And keep this with the phone, I don't want to lose my credit cards." She snaps the case, with the cardholder attached, onto the body of the cell phone. She makes it look like a tough fit, but I know she's activating the recorder in the entry card.

"Nice to meet you, Chief," Koob says, as he slides toward the car door.

"You too," she says. "But please do us both a favor and stay the fuck out of my city in the future."

He raises a hand to his temple in mock salute.

The man and woman operating the camera hanging over the intersection on Madison pull it back so that we can see Koob heading toward Ritz. The radio in his hand makes little clicks as it knocks against the other hearing aid.

"She's clean," he tells Ritz. He's speaking English, rather than Mandarin. I guess Ritz and he have agreed that when they're out on the street, English will attract less attention from passersby than a white guy rattling on in Chinese. The Bureau is prepared with some AI translation software, and a woman on the other side of the table must be in charge of that, because she sulks as soon as she hears the English.

"Lenses?" Ritz asks.

"Nothing but the CCTV over the intersection."

"Laser?"

"The machine picked up nothing."

The Ritz nods and thinks. "So you think I'm okay?"

"That is what the equipment indicates."

"Good."

"Are you all right from here?" Koob asks.

"If you did your fucking job."

Koob extracts his own phone from his back pocket and scrolls through it for a second. At first, I can't believe he's reading his texts right there, then I realize what he's looking for. Apparently, Darnell has confirmed that the money Ritz owed them has been paid.

"I'll be going now," Koob says.

"Maybe I'll call you again."

"I apologize, but you should know that we will not accept repeat customers when there have been payment issues."

Ritz shrugs. "It was a misunderstanding, but suit yourself."

"Just a policy," says Koob. He turns and turns back, as if he had forgotten something.

"I told your guest in your back seat that you would be holding on to these until the end of the meeting." He hands over the hearing aids and the cell phone—with the activated recorder still in the credit card sleeve on the back.

"You checked all this?"

"The batteries are out of everything. They're dead. She's afraid you may misplace her hearing aids, but to be safe, I would not give them back until you're finished." Ritz nods, clearly satisfied with Koob's cautiousness. The Ritz drops the small collection of items into the inside pocket of his jacket right over his heart. An agent in front of the last monitor on the right stands straight up, shaking his fists over his head in a pantomime of cheering wildly.

Tonya murmurs to me, "Your guy is good." The only better location for capturing Ritz's voice on the recorder would be if

Koob somehow got Vojczek to wear the key card as a necklace right over his voice box. As for the output from the radio in the right hearing aid, it might eventually be limited, depending on where Ritz parks, but the techs would rather have the microphone closer to him. The Chief will be available later to review her end of the conversation.

Before departing, Koob manipulates something in his briefcase. A waterfall of white noise begins at once. Koob gestures to the briefcase, but we can't really make out the precise instruction. Ritz ends up strolling toward the Lincoln, rolling the briefcase behind him. Without a backward look, Koob strides off purposefully, passing out of the top of the picture on the nearest monitor.

Another of the agents in the room with us, who's wearing headphones, tells Toy, "Channel 4," and when she moves a switch on the radio, the broadcast from the laser tap trained on the Lincoln comes in over the speakers. We can hear the Chief humming faintly. I think it's "Don't Stop Believin'."

The noise of the sound machine intrudes as Ritz slides in on the driver's side. He places the briefcase on the passenger seat, reaching into it. We can't see what's he's doing, but it's immediately plain that he's brought out the small white-noise box since its timbre intensifies, turning what's overheard from the laser microphone into an undifferentiated fountain of hissing sound. But the Chief's voice remains audible, as she speaks at volume.

"Jesus Christ, Ritz, turn that fucking thing off. Your gadget man took my hearing aids. I won't understand a word you say."

"You won't hear me say a thing, Lucy. I'm listening to you." With the radio right over Ritz's heart, his voice is now far clearer than the Chief's.

On cue, she immediately answers, "What's that?"

For a second, Ritz slaps at his jacket pocket, apparently willing to give her back the aids, then seems to reconsider in light of Koob's advice. Instead he reaches down and somewhat reduces the level of the white noise, prompting another fist wave from the same agent, who I now realize must be the sound guy.

"When you get hearing aids?" Ritz asks.

"It's about a month," she says, and explains about the shooting range and how she finally gave in to her daughters, who'd been telling her for years that she needed them. It's why she grew her hair out, she adds.

"Yeah," says Ritz. "I'm headed that way, too."

He motions her to the front seat, but she says, "No, this is what I call a comfortable distance."

"I thought you can't hear me."

"Just keep your freaking voice up, Ritz, and I'll hear you fine. I know goddamned well you're packing, so sitting behind you feels just a little safer."

"You're still an amazing pain in the ass," he says.

"I don't like being here any more than you do. Let's just get this done with. I don't have that much to say."

The Ritz lifts a finger to hush her. "Just hold your water for a while," he says and starts driving. He follows a typical path to detect a tail, turning right and left at random, sometimes suddenly. He barrels down a couple alleys and executes quick U-turns in the middle of the street. The laser microphone fades in and out as they're driving, mostly out, but we can still hear what little is being said through the radio in Ritz's pocket, especially since the Chief is speaking loudly. She laughs repeatedly and says several times, "There's no one following us, Ritz."

"Shut up, Lucy," he answers after the third or fourth maneuver with the car. "We'll talk when I want to talk. You're the one who asked for this meet."

Following ten minutes of evasive driving, Ritz heads over the Bolcarro Bridge into the North End of Kewahnee, and the car disappears from the screen for a while. Rik grabs my arm, afraid the Bureau has lost eyes on the car, but after no more than a minute the Bureau techs pick up the feed from the CCTV cameras in Kindle County. Ironically, the North End is the city's highest crime district, so the closed-circuit cameras have a view of virtually every block.

Toy is listening intently to her headphones, and I tap her shoulder and point to my own ear to ask what she's hearing.

"The follow cars," she mouths. Despite the good vision from the cameras, three or four FBI vehicles are still trailing Ritz, with Don Ingram in charge. They are far enough behind Ritz's detail to be sure they won't get made, but still in the vicinity so they can race in if the Chief suddenly needs help.

Eventually, just as Walter predicted, Ritz arrives at the underpass he's used previously. It's in Pulaski Park, several square blocks of green space with two little lagoons and bike paths. The park is named for a Polish hero of our Revolutionary War. By night, it's supposedly neutral territory for the gangs, but that agreement somehow hasn't prevented seven young men from being shot here in the last year.

The third and fourth computer monitors light up with the feed from the Bureau's own cameras, which were positioned here earlier to shoot through the front and rear windows of Ritz's car. Now both angles are up on the monitors. I tap Rik's shoulder to be sure he's noticed. He's been unusually quiet and intent. I know he's concerned for Lucy, but as a guy who's obsessed with consumer electronics, the technology on display here has him under a spell.

Positioned below the underpass, Ritz's vehicle sits beneath the iron girding of the roadway and the steel surface of the bridge above. The radio signal is more broken up now, but the laser microphones still produce sound clear enough to understand, despite the constant interference of the sound machine, which sends out an oscillating rush of noise like someone breathing loudly in your ear. After some hand gestures from Tonya, the tech arranges it so that the laser mike is coming from one speaker, and the radio in Ritz's pocket from the other.

"Do I have permission to speak now?" is the first thing the Chief says on-screen after Ritz has come to a halt.

He lifts a hand. "Okay, go," he says.

"P&F is going to require me to testify."

"You said that. It didn't make a lot of sense to me. You know, I've been following this case, because I have such great affection for you after our years working together, and I thought you were a big grand jury target. Last I heard, Moses Appleton was kicking and screaming about them ordering you to testify, because if you get immunity, that would put him out of business."

"The federal investigations are done, apparently. No thanks to you."

"Why you blaming me?"

"Go fuck yourself, Ritz. I'm not even going to pretend to pretend. Anyway, the FBI has concluded that the three assholes you sent to whiz on me were all liars. So I'm no longer a subject or target of an extortion investigation."

"Liars? Walt and Primo just had little memory lapses. Happens to everybody. And what about poor Blanco? Why do they think what he said wasn't true?"

"For one thing, his wife, Marisel, told them that Frito never had an uncle who died during the fall of Saigon or went to St. Viator's. I think Frito had some other issues, too, but nobody's explained them to us. I'm not asking questions, though, if they say I'm out from under."

"Okay. But from what I read online, I thought you had another issue."

"Which is?"

"Rumor is, all of Blanco's fibbin made you so angry that some say you had the poor boy capped."

"There've been some developments there, too."

"Such as?"

"No business of yours, Ritz. I didn't come here to discuss the Blanco homicide investigation with you."

"Is that what it is now? A homicide investigation?"

"What's the deal, Ritz? Why so interested in Blanco?"

"Some guys follow sports. I like police investigations. Never got it out of my blood."

"Hah," she answers, but returns to her subject and says they need to talk about her testimony.

"And why should I give a crap about what you say under oath?" he asks.

"The photo."

"The photograph of you forcing poor Blanco at gunpoint to pleasure you? It was shocking," says the Ritz. "I was truly shocked. It was pure justice that he took that picture."

"Ritz, I'm not gonna act like we're characters inside some video game you invented. You and I both know Blanco didn't take that photo. And you and I both know you had somebody hack my computer to get it."

"I don't know anything like that," he says.

"Ritz, I still have three more pictures. Your guy zapped the ones in my photo library, but I still have the old phone with the originals. You weren't any better looking in those pictures than you are now—but it's definitely you. And I won't be deep-sixing any evidence, because frankly, I've already shown them to Rik, and he doesn't work that way. I've avoided giving him an explanation so far. But pretty soon, I have to tell him and then the commission why Moritz Vojczek has his head between my legs and my service weapon on his temple."

For the first time, Ritz seems to take a second to reflect. The Chief goes on.

"My guess, Ritz, is that's not a look you like any better today than you did then."

"Okay," he says. "What are you thinkin?"

"I'm thinking I'll say, 'Ritz and me had a little fling. Both single people. No big deal. And that photo was just a joke between us. We took a lot of weird pictures, if you want to know. But when I was appointed Chief, I knew it could get sticky for a lot of reasons. So I cut off the relationship. And Vojczek was so pissed with me he quit the force. Then when this thing started, Ritz got a laugh by giving Blanco the photograph and telling Frito he could say it was him.'"

Ritz tilts his head while he stares at her for a second.

"Aren't you the fuckin little nun who used to ride around in my cruiser, saying you'd never lie under oath?"

"I guess I grew up, Ritz. I don't have a lot of choices at the moment."

"Imagine that." He tosses up his face as he sneers. "And you want me to say I took the picture?"

"Right."

"No chance. I got zero to do with Blanco. I barely knew the guy."

"Okay, how about something closer to the truth. I'll say I took the picture and my computer was hacked a few months ago. I can prove that. Just not who. But the photograph got to Blanco from someone who wanted to bolster the case against me and figured, given how much you hate me, you wouldn't set the record straight."

"If that's what you wanna say," he says.

"What I'm asking, Ritz, is if you can back that story?"

"Sounds to me like I would be doing you a big fucking favor. You smell like roses this way, when you're really just a stinking bucket of shit. Maybe I'll tell the real truth. How you violated my fuckin civil rights and all that."

"By threatening to tell the FBI you were robbing drug dealers?"

"No idea what you're talking about. You never said shit to the FBI, did you? You a sworn officer of the law and all? Either you were derelict in your duties or that's just a bunch of bullshit."

"I got you off the force, Ritz. Which meant no more strong-arming the dealers. So that was pretty good law enforcement as far as I'm concerned, especially since I didn't have any firsthand evidence. You want to tell the real story, I can go down that road. I bet the FBI wouldn't regard you stealing narcotics as too old to look at. With RICO, they can prosecute you for crap that happened before your grandparents left the old country. I just kinda thought you'd rather I didn't say that. That's why we're fucking sitting here. To figure out something that works for both of us."

"You'd never tell the real story. They prosecute me, then they can prosecute you for sexual assault or something."

"No RICO there, Ritz. And besides, I got a non-subject letter. Rik already told them it's you in the picture."

"I think you're talkin shit. You admit blackmailing me with

that picture and the only thing Amity will be able to do for you is maybe help with a job as a barista at the place you got your latte. Cause you sure as shit aren't gonna be her chief of police."

"Which is why I need you to say that the picture was just you and me having fun."

He doesn't speak for a second, then says, "I'm still not liking this deal from my side. What do I get?"

"You mean besides me not mentioning that you were stealing narcotics? That sounds like plenty. But what else do you want, Ritz? You've beaten me up pretty good. I admit it. And being honest, I don't really have it left in me to go another three rounds in this cage match. But what you've been doing to me—this is about more than revenge. You got a goal here, besides making me miserable. You could call off Steven tomorrow, if you wanted to, and make me a nonissue in the mayor's race."

"I don't control Steven, Lucy. Sorry."

"Right. You want to know what my goal is? If I hold on to this job for three more years, I get to thirty. That's a great pension. Ninety percent of my current salary, plus an annual cost-of-living bump for the rest of my life. For a guy with money like you, that's not much bigger than an ant's behind. But you know, I'd really be okay. So tell me, Ritz. If I run up the white flag, what is it you need? We're sitting here, nobody listening. Whatta you want to leave me be for three more years?"

"Sure, I lost my pension, but you get yours. Not happening."

"You landed on your feet, Ritz."

"It was mine. I worked for it. I'm still more pissed about that than the goddamned picture."

"And you've gotten even the last few months. And some. So you tell me, what else do you need to let bygones be bygones?"

Ritz is looking over his shoulder at the Chief in the back

seat. The mean snarl has never left his face, even while he's pondering now.

"You know, Lucy, what a lot of people have against you is you're a shit police chief."

"And why is that?"

"Well, Stanley, he was a great police chief."

"*Stan*ley? And how do you figure that?"

"As I hear it, he was not a curious person."

"I see. And what do I have to ignore? It's something in Highland Isle, obviously."

"I wouldn't know anything about that. I was just saying Stanley knew how to do his job. Stay in his lane. He knew what was his business and what wasn't."

"Well, how am I gonna know what lane to stay in?"

"I don't know, Lucy. I really don't. But if somebody ever calls you to say, 'Stay away,' then I'd stay away, if I were you. I mean, that's my advice. It's nothin to me either way. But Steven and all them? They might appreciate it."

"Okay. But how am I gonna be sure this stay-away person speaks for you?"

"You're a smart lady, Lucy. You'll be able to figure out what you need to know. And what you don't."

"And you leave me be for three more years for that, right?"

"I don't know. It's not up to me. I'm just a bystander. I got nothing to do with any of this."

"Okay, Ritz. Fine. What's your guess? If I can shut my eyes a couple of times when somebody tells me to, do I get three more years?"

"We'd have to see."

"See what?"

"Well, you're on the ropes now, Lucy. Word is Amity is wishing she cut you loose months ago. So if somebody was going to bail you out of this, they'd have to be certain that you know where the lines are painted on the road."

"Okay. Fine. Test me."

"Test, huh?" He appears to think, although Feld predicted exactly where he'd go. "It's nothin to me, but since you didn't want to say, why don't you tell me what the latest developments are on Blanco and why the Feds are suddenly sure you had nothing to do with it. So that's your test. Spill. Why do you say it's a homicide investigation now?"

"Why does that matter to you, Ritz? I can't play spin the bottle with a murderer."

"It's not that it matters to me. It's that it matters to you. You want me to say, 'Okay, she's gonna be cool,' then be cool and answer the effing question. You want a chance for your thirty or not?"

In the back seat, Lucy falls back and sighs deeply. She is just flat-out wonderful, playing her part. Feld came up with the scenario: Start with the picture, come on vulnerable, and watch Ritz pivot to Blanco as soon as you mention the word 'homicide.' Dan figured that Vojczek was too exposed not to ask questions once he knew the investigators had established that Blanco's death was not from natural causes. But the plan, artful as it is, would fall flat if Lucy were less convincing.

"You know," the Chief says then, "the Bureau isn't really talking to me. This is what Tonya Eo, who's been working with them on Blanco—this is what she seems to know."

"Which is?"

"They did another chemical assay on Frito's blood. I don't know why. But they're sure now he died of an overdose of some drug I never heard of. Starts with a C and sounds like fentanyl but it's some super-duper form."

On-screen, the Ritz draws back just enough that we can no longer see his face in detail because of the shadows under the overpass. But he definitely seems to freeze from both camera angles.

"And how they thinking that happened?" he asks.

"Well, there are two injection sites on Frito's upper arm. But they're still not sure about why or who. Apparently, Blanco had some ugly little secret he needed to hide. He might even have killed himself, except there was stuff missing—his phone and the needles. And the needle marks are on the back of his arm, where he'd have a hard time reaching. So best thoughts now are either: One, he was shooting up with somebody else, who came out of their nod and scampered away with his phone and the syringes, probably to protect themselves when they realized Frito was dead. Or Two, someone offed Frito."

"Why would anyone else kill him?" asks Ritz. "You're the one who needed to get rid of the guy."

"How am I gonna zip-tie a guy with six inches and fifty pounds on me? But like I said, Ritz, for whatever reason, they don't think it was me, which I'm damn happy to hear. Beyond that, I'm not asking so many questions. Like you'd figure, I'm out of the chain on the investigation, so whatever I hear is limited and thirdhand. I do know that they're trying to figure out where that shit, the C-fentanyl or whatever, came from. There's some of it around, but it hasn't shown up in any of our cases. Then again, routine tox screen doesn't pick it up, so maybe there's more being used than we think. You got any ideas about that?"

"I have no ideas about any of this."

"You seem pretty interested."

"Me? I told you. I'll always be a police officer at heart. Someone kills a cop, I'm interested. Blanco? Nice kid, nice family, sorry for all of them, but I got no stake."

"Well, let me put it another way. Did I pass the test?"

"Maybe. You'll find out."

"Great. But I need at least one answer right now. You gonna back my story or not, Ritz?"

He waits, maybe thinking, maybe just to keep her hanging.

"Oh, sure," he finally says. "I get a subpoena, I'd say we did all kinds of kinky shit, you and me. But I dumped you. You were starting to sound serious, and to me, you know, you were just another hole to plug. I could say that, I guess. I dumped you and you cried like your mama died. Then they picked you for chief. I had to quit because I could see what would be coming my way then. 'Hell hath no fury.' But the photo? I never had it and had nothing to do with passing it to Blanco."

You can see on two camera feeds that they're staring each other down.

"Okay," the Ritz says, "I think you oughta get out now."

"Here?"

"Yeah, call yourself a fuckin Uber."

"You have my phone, jagoff."

He throws the various pieces and the hearing aids over the seat. She has to grope on the floor to pick up what Ritz has tossed in her direction.

"Get out, Lucy."

"I'll get out when I have everything put back together and I know it works."

You can see and hear her fumbling for most of a minute. Then she faces the phone toward herself and finally nods. "Okay," she says and opens the passenger door. "Oh," she says with one foot in the street, "one more thing."

"Yeah?"

"Smile, Ritz." She clicks a picture, then is gone.

38. SITTING ON MY RATTY LOVE SEAT

When I come back to my apartment around noon to walk Gomer, Koob is sitting on my ratty love seat. He's helped himself to a glass of water that's sitting on the table in front of him. There's no sign of his disguise.

"Sometime I'd like to know how you pick a dead bolt," I say to him.

"The same way you opened the locks on my storage cage," he answers. "Just a little more force."

"Point taken," I answer. I tell him he looks better this way and he shrugs.

"How did your client do?" he asks. "I thought she was excellent while I was with her. Was the FBI happy overall?"

I think about being evasive, but Koob would lose the benefit of his deal with the Feds if he tipped Ritz. And I still believe he wouldn't break his word to me.

"What made you so sure it was the Bureau?" I ask. "The hearing aids?"

"The two instruments were different weights. Very subtle. But I was pretty certain there was a transmitter in one. I assume that was a late addition to their equipment roster after we came to our arrangement. Also, I saw the closed-circuit camera on Madison moving down to focus on us. I had no idea that the FBI was able to share that feed. Very clever."

"It looked like you got your money?"

"We did. But you didn't answer. Was the FBI pleased?"

"They seemed over the moon. They were walking around high-fiving each other, and the Assistant US Attorney who was there wanted us to tell the Chief she was 'superb.' But I have no clue what they're planning now or how any of what the Chief got him to say fits in. Ritz asked a lot of questions about Blanco's death. Nothing Ritz said would convict him, but it would help corroborate other evidence, at least a little."

"Is there other evidence?"

I shake my head resolutely, deliberately unclear about exactly what I mean.

"As far as I heard," I say, "you're in the clear, if that's what you want to know."

"No, I took that for granted. I imagine they were delighted with me when Ritz tucked all that equipment in his pocket. I just came by to see you before I left."

"Okay," I say, but I finally sit down on the love seat beside him.

"You know," he says, "one reason I did not mind returning to Highland Isle was because I was not happy with the way I left things with you in Pittsburgh."

"And why was that?"

"Your remarks about Mel." He means his wife. "I think you feel I was lying to you while I was here."

"I don't know about lying," I say. "But I'm not sure you understand what you actually want. Men always say women are crazy.

You should hear what they've said about me. But if your wife is as off the hook as you claim, I'd think you would have realized a long time ago that you deserve something better. Which makes me wonder if deep down you like living that way."

"I would never deny that I feel guilty over the prospect of leaving. I have told you that before. But I will deal with it. She is a highly volatile woman. She lost her real estate license for a year when she poured a can of paint on another broker's car. She can be violent. And she refuses to get any help."

"Violent with you?"

"Frequently. And of course, I know that if I ever hit her back, who gets arrested. Right now, I need to protect my son. He gets into battles with her once a week that are so fierce I am never sure what is going to happen next, until I step in. A year from now, when he is in college, I will be freer to move on with my life."

"Well, I hope you get what you want, Koob."

"Clarice, I understand your skepticism about me. But our—" He waits for a word. "Our time together was very important to me. What did you say often? I do not know anyone like you. And it was a revelation in so many ways, that I felt so comfortable with you, that I looked forward so much to being with you. Call it a breakthrough, but I see my future very differently now. You are a remarkable person."

"Thanks, but that feels like a Participation Trophy."

"I truly mean it, Clarice. But what do *you* want?"

"From you?"

"From anyone."

"Well, I'm glad you were willing to talk. I wanted *that*. And don't take the wrong message from last night. I totally dug what happened between us, like you did, and I still feel passion for you and for being with you. But you know, for all my random hook-ups or circus sex, the one thing that's never appealed is being the sidepiece. That means one person is in control and the other one isn't. One person gets everything they want and the other one is settling for less. And I could never stand that.

"So, you know, a year from now, you get your life straightened out, if you want to call, sure, go ahead. I'll see where I am. If nothing else, it would be cool to hang out with you in public. But I won't be waiting for that. Because I don't think that's what's going to happen. If you actually split with your wife, it will take you a hell of a long time to figure out what you want next, that's just how it is. But I'll be glad if it turns out that I was part of your process."

"And have I been part of yours?"

"I guess. Yeah. Maybe I'm thinking about some things a little differently. I think it was net good, you and me. You know, disappointing in the end, but I haven't had a relationship that wasn't. Nature of the beast."

"Nature of the beast," he repeats.

He stands and so do I, and for a second we face each other in silence.

Then he smiles.

"Do you know what I was thinking about before you came in? Do you remember how you licked my face the first time I came over here?"

"Totally."

"That was so wonderful. Because it was so unexpected and different. I remember feeling this spurt of joy, genuine joy, because I had summoned the courage to knock on your door and was already experiencing something, small as it was, that was completely new to me."

He opens his arms and I rise to my toes to hug him again, a long embrace.

Then, before we entirely separate, he takes hold of my shoulders and leans in and touches his tongue quickly to my forehead. Then he goes out the door.

39. FOR A FEW DAYS NOTHING HAPPENS

For a few days, nothing happens. The Chief calls me frequently to find out if I have heard anything from Tonya, to which the answer is always no. Walter reported that the Ritz returned from his meeting with the Chief in a black mood and has barely spoken to anyone while he is in the office. When Walter, with Don Ingram's encouragement, asked Ritz if something was upsetting him, Ritz responded with a look that so terrified Walter, he became certain the Ritz somehow had figured out Walt had turned. For a day or two, Cornish was even talking out loud about being charged and entering custody immediately, but the agents settled him down, reminding him he would undercut himself by reducing the value of his cooperation.

Then on Friday a little before six a.m., my phone starts blowing up, rattling on my night table like there's something live inside. Just as I grab it, the screen darkens with a call from Toy.

"Turn on 4," she says. "Right now."

On the local TV, there is one of those nighttime scenes of dark figures teeming under the glare of several spotlights. I slowly take in that I am looking at people in blue windbreakers with the letters FBI on the back. The reporter on the scene says they are executing a search warrant at Vojczek Management, although no one is commenting on the purpose of the raid. I consider walking down there to watch from behind the police tape, but the news comes in so fast on various feeds, especially Twitter, that I never get out the door. Two other warrants are also being executed right now, one at VVM and the other at Ritz's penthouse across the river.

Eventually, I go down to the office to hang out with Rik, while the story continues to build. There is one local cable news station, and Rik and I do virtually nothing except stare at the screen. Every time we get ready to go back to work, the anchors break in breathlessly. First, there are unconfirmed reports that at least eight individuals are in federal custody. Then half an hour later one of those under arrest is identified as Secondo DeGrassi.

At noon, the biggest news breaks. Mona Thayer on Channel 4 announces, "WKCO-TV has confirmed that a federal arrest warrant has been issued for billionaire real estate developer Moritz Vojczek, who is reportedly still at large."

The Chief, who has called a couple times, phones again now, absolutely exultant. "Justice!" she shouts to Rik, loud enough for me to hear across his desk.

I check the website for the federal district court across the river, but none of the documents related to the searches or the arrests have been posted yet. I volunteer to go down and stand around to scan them when the papers are filed, which has to be soon.

As it turns out, my timing is perfect. After half an hour in the courthouse, I have made digital images of about two inches of records, including the criminal complaints against Ritz and Sid and several other people. The arrestees include the van driver— the delivery dude who's been running drugs and chemicals to and from VVM—two other nighttime employees of the company, and the three cleaners. I also pick up the inventories on the three search warrants, which hit the file while I am still scanning the last of the other documents.

As I'm about to leave the courthouse, I see reporters flowing in. One of them, Hanka Something, who I kind of know, tells me that the people who were arrested in the early morning are about to be arraigned.

The defendants appear before the chief judge here, Sonia Klonsky, in the grand Ceremonial Courtroom. The judge is a good friend of both Pops and my Aunt Marta, and she seems to flick a tight smile my way when she sees me in the gallery.

The eight men shuffle in, all in orange jumpsuits and handcuffs. I know from my years working for Pops that this is an otherworldly day for each of these guys, who, like all criminal defendants, did what they did because they'd convinced themselves they would never get caught. But now they have. And the charges against them are heavy: conspiracy to manufacture a Schedule II controlled substance, to wit, carfentanil, which carries a ten-year mandatory minimum sentence. The only chance to do less time is to, in the lingo, barf it all up and tell the Feds everything they want to know. Each of the lawyers—most from the Federal Defenders Office—informs the judge that his defendant is cooperating with the government. The attorneys announce this as part of their pitch for bail. No one gets bond, however, since the conspiracy charge carries a presumption against pretrial release. Sid DeGrassi takes this hard and is shaking with tears as the marshals herd the men back to the lockup.

Returning to Highland Isle, Rik tells me that the Chief is dying to get a look at the complaint the government filed against Ritz, which makes factual allegations to support the charges against Vojczek. As soon as I'm back in the office, I print out the document. Nothing is likely to please Lucy more than seeing the heading that spreads across the first page: United States of America versus Moritz L. Vojczek, beside a listing of the criminal statutes he violated. I run the papers over to the Central Station, where the Chief is literally waiting at the door. She takes them with one hand and uses the other to hug me.

Then I head back to the office to sit down with Rik while we both finally get a chance to read the complaint. Like the other defendants, the Ritz has been charged with conspiracy to manufacture carfentanil, but also with possession of controlled substances. When I look through the return on the search warrant, I see that among the items inventoried from both Ritz's home and office are "diabetic injection pens believed to have been repurposed and containing a controlled substance."

"Like the pens they used on Blanco?" I ask.

"Sure sounds like it," says Rik.

The lab, according to the complaint against Ritz, quickly confirmed that the pens contained carfentanil, leading to the possession charge.

I can also now understand what the Feds were waiting for, which was to see if the conversation between the Chief and the Ritz provided more evidence of the Ritz's connection to VVM. And it did. Once the Chief told the Ritz that the Feds were trying to source the carfentanil that killed Blanco, the twice-weekly nighttime van runs from the facility ceased immediately. The delivery guy, picked up by the Feds at his home, told the agents he had been instructed that they were going to lay off deliveries for at least a month due to 'possible heat.' One of the three chemists—the supposed cleaners—had a similar story. Ritz will claim that's merely coincidental and someone else could have gotten word about the Feds' suspicions. But that won't explain why he has automatic syringes containing the same stuff made in that factory in both his office and apartment.

"Notice anything missing from the complaint?" Rik asks me.

I'm stumped.

"No charges for the murder of a federal witness," he says.

"You think they're not going to charge him?" I find myself on the verge of outrage, and Rik smiles.

"No," says Rik. "They'll definitely charge him. They're just waiting."

"For what?"

"Well, for one thing, they'll want to do the spectrometry and other tests to confirm that the carfentanil at Ritz's house has the exact same chemical structure as the carfentanil that killed Blanco. That will do a lot to put Ritz in on the murder.

"But," says Rik, "my best guess is that the main reason for not bringing those charges yet is that Moses and Feld haven't given up hope of finally using Walter to record Ritz. If the G can arrest Ritz and hold him without bond, he's going to go into withdrawal. After a couple of days strung out, Ritz may be a lot less careful in what he says when Walter shows up at the MCC for a visit." The Metropolitan Correctional Center is the federal jail.

"And why haven't they arrested Ritz yet?"

"It sounds like they can't find him. Ritz probably went into hiding as soon as he heard about the search warrants."

"He has to own a hundred places in the area where he can stay out of sight. But do you think he's going to flee the country or something?"

"Not impossible," says Rik, "but he'd have to leave a lot behind. Best guess is that Junior," Rik says, referring to Melvin Tooley Jr., the pond creature who will likely represent Vojczek, "is going to call the US Attorney's Office soon to arrange Ritz's surrender. Having the FBI and the US Marshals hunting for you is an uncomfortable experience."

Rik picks up his phone off his desk.

"Right now," he says, "I need to call Lucy and get her permission to give a tip to a few reporter friends."

Because Moses and Feld are keeping Walter on the down low, the complaint gives the Chief the starring role, making several references to the Ritz's meeting on Tuesday morning with an unnamed 'Cooperating Witness.' Rik is guessing that by contrast the affidavit Don Ingram swore out before a federal magistrate judge in order to get the search warrants for Ritz's home and office made free use of information from Walter. Ritz and his lawyer won't see that affidavit until after Vojczek is indicted and Walter's role is revealed. But the complaint is public now. Due to Feld's crafty drafting, it leaves the impression that the main case the government has on Ritz stems from VVM. Without ever saying so, the complaint suggests that the FBI searched Ritz's properties, looking for additional evidence of Vojczek's connection to Vox VetMeds, and just stumbled on the injection pens loaded with carfentanil. The Chief, therefore, appears to be the principal actor in bringing Ritz to justice.

After Rik checks in with Lucy, he calls two different courthouse reporters he's on good terms with. I sit in his office to listen. Rik says he wants to provide information as an anonymous source concerning the bust of Moritz Vojczek. Both journalists are quick to agree.

"I can confirm for you," Rik says, speaking to the first of them, Stew Dubinsky, "that the 'Cooperating Witness' mentioned in the Vojczek complaint is my client, the Highland Isle Police Chief, Lucia Gomez-Barrera. Just like the brave cop she's always been,

Lucy put her life at risk to do this. She was completely unarmed, while Ritz had all his heavies a few feet away and probably was carrying himself. But what's going to come out, when you hear the recordings of that conversation, is that all the trouble the Chief's had recently, these lurid bogus charges against her, were part of Vojczek's plot to get rid of her as Chief, so he could install someone else who would allow him to run his drug operation out of VVM." Rik nods vigorously as he listens to Stew Dubinsky's response. "You bet," says Rik. "It's a great story."

When Rik finishes the second call, he points a finger at me.

"Big props to you, Pinky," Rik says. "This is going down just the way you figured. Amity and Moses will be giving the Chief a medal on TV by the end of the week. And Lucy will lead the local news for days."

"You know how it is, Boss. Once a year I get an idea that's not completely wacky."

"No, no," he says. "This was brilliant. You gave Lucy a real chance to save her career."

Whenever I receive any compliment, I experience a confused rush of feelings and Rik's praise brings on an extreme case so that right now I can barely breathe or move. I mutter "Thanks" to Rik and escape his office as fast as I can.

By nightfall, there is no further news about Ritz. Toy asks if she can stop by and she shows up about eight. I offer her a beer, but she says she has to work.

"On this case?" I ask.

"Yeah, Melvin Junior called Moses late this afternoon saying his client was willing to surrender, but only if Moses will agree to bail."

"Bail? When all the guys down the chain are in the cooler? Ritz is just desperate not to go into withdrawal."

"Agreed. But Junior is actually playing that card. Says he wants to get Ritz into a drug treatment program."

"Is Junior stalling just to give Ritz a chance to get away?"

"Could be. But hearing it thirdhand, it sounds like Moses played hardball with Junior. He reminded him, lawyer or not, that you get indicted for helping somebody flee prosecution." Melvin Tooley Jr. is in practice with his father, who is mostly in Florida these days. His father, Mel Senior, is, as Rik likes to say, so crooked that when he dies they will have to screw him into the ground. Melvin Junior is less oily but no more honest. You could fill an amphitheater with the prosecutors who'd love to bring charges against either one of them.

"Moses still thinks Ritz will end up turning himself in," Tonya says. "Moses and Junior are supposed to talk again tomorrow. But just to be on the safe side, we're covering all the points of departure. Train station, bus. The airport."

"I don't see the Ritz on a bus or a train," I say.

"Not his style?"

"Definitely not his style. But there are too many stops where law enforcement can board and search, and a long ride increases the chance that the other passengers will see something on their phones and maybe recognize him. I don't think the airport is much better, with Ritz's picture everywhere today."

"We sent it to TSA, in case they don't read the papers. And there's a brick on Ritz's passport."

"If Ritz runs, he'll probably drive, won't he? Go over the border. Mexico, I'd bet."

"Border patrol and ICE have the same photographs. And it's like what you said about a bus or the train. Driving gives the Bureau time to identify the car he's in and put out an APB."

"Sounds like if he takes off, Ritz would need a disguise and a phony passport. I'll tell you the truth. If I made bank like Ritz, I'd charter a jet. There's less security out at Greenwood."

"My colleagues don't think so. Since 9/11, CBP"—Customs and Border Protection—"keep pretty tight surveillance on private flights, what with the drug dealers and terrorists. A pilot who doesn't file an accurate passenger manifest at least an hour before he takes off can lose his license. CBP has got a tight eye on those lists now. Anything suspicious, like a pilot they've warned in the past, they'll sprint out there. And there's a Greenwood County deputy stationed there at all times who can hold the fort until they arrive.

"Net-net," she says, "Ritz is taking a big chance if he runs. The US Attorney would tie up every penny he has here, millions and millions, all his bank accounts and property, to secure the forfeiture of drug proceeds the government will ask for. That's why Moses thinks Vojczek will surrender."

I shrug. I don't really know the Ritz, but nothing I've heard about him fits with the word 'surrender.'

"I'll say one thing," Toy adds. "Everybody in the Bureau is happy they cut that deal with your guy. The Chief was a knock-out, but getting Ritz to stick all that gear in his pocket is why the recordings are so good, especially with the white noise extracted." Tonya kind of peeks up at me. "How was that for you?"

"What?"

"Seeing Joe Kwok again or whatever his name really is?"

It's a sign of where Tonya and I are as friends that I decide not to be evasive.

"Complicated," I say.

"Did you guys hang out?"

"We talked for a while. But you know, deep down I never believed he was The One, because basically I'm still not sure I want that. That was always a big thing between me and you back in the day, because you were looking for a full commitment and to me that's always felt like shackles."

She lets that pass, but it has to be comforting to her that even a dozen years later, I have the same hang-ups that came between us.

"But he was maybe a little closer to being the right person?" she asks, which is kind of a brave question.

"Maybe," I say. I'm liking the honesty of this conversation, getting down to a level we haven't quite reached before.

"What was it that appealed?"

"He's a grown-up. Very centered. And a real cool person. And calm. I totally liked that he's super interesting without trying to be. I'm not sure, maybe people want to link up with someone they'll never be. He's definitely not like me. And vice versa. But I guess the best thing was that he was really into that, how different I am. And that felt great."

"So that's what you want? A guy like that?"

"Or a woman," I add. It's kind of ironic, but I sometimes think Tonya has almost as much trouble imagining my yearnings as her parents do imagining hers. "I mean, who knows? What's the line? 'The heart wants what it wants.' Only it doesn't send out bulletins. You just have to keep living to figure out what that is. Like you and your college girl. Who knew? Right?"

"Right."

"That still going?"

"Definitely. Wanna meet her sometime?"

"Totally. I'm sure she's very cool."

We're still talking about Tonya's girlfriend when she gets a call. It has to be someone in the Bureau, because she looks hard at the phone and says she has to take it. She uses the bathroom to talk and is in there for a while. She's grim when she emerges.

"When Walter got home to his apartment today," she says, "he found a burner phone in his mailbox."

"From Ritz?"

"Just listen. Now that all these stories broke about Lucy being a government witness, Walter got a one-sentence voice message about an hour ago."

"Saying?"

" 'I'm going to kill that cunt.' "

"Nice," I say. "Do they think that's serious?"

"Well, nobody knows. You've got to warn the Chief for sure. But Ingram and Feld think that maybe Ritz's main goal is to test Walter, see if he's blabbing. Ritz will ask whoever his guy is in the Central Station to give him the word if Lucy suddenly has bodyguards. That will be the tell that Walter's talking."

"Meaning the Chief is supposed to protect herself? That's a little fucked. I thought the FBI always takes care of its witnesses."

"No, they definitely want her to have armed protection. Just do our best to keep the Ritz from realizing she's being covered. They're wondering if you'd look after her. Nobody would think twice at this point about you being with her. And I'd come at night and trade shifts with you, so you could get some sleep."

I completely spark to the idea. That's an old fantasy of mine, going back to when I was a kid, being the person to keep somebody safe.

"There's only one problem," I tell Tonya. "Lucy likes her space. She'll never agree to this."

40. BY 10:30
FRIDAY NIGHT

By 10:30 on Friday night I have moved in with the Chief. She was strongly opposed, but Moses personally talked her into this arrangement. He promised that it would last only until they grab Ritz, which could be any minute.

I spent so much time in this house when I was going through the video capture from the Chief's security system that this feels a little bit like a reunion. I admire and really like the Chief, and I know a lot about her habits, like how she always clears her throat before picking up the telephone, or how she and her older daughter talk every night for a couple minutes before the first of them goes to sleep, or how when she thinks she's alone, she picks at her fingers. But she's got her boundaries, and we're never going to be BFFs or anything like that. Still, I'm glad to have some time with her, to hear what she thinks about everything that went down this week.

When I get there, she's watching an old movie, *Unforgiven*, which is one of Pops's favorites. I've seen it at least three times but I sit through the ending with her again. After that, she offers me a nightcap. She pours herself a glass of white wine, and I ask for a beer, then don't let her uncap it, reminding myself why I'm here. I take a soft drink and we sit down together on the flowered sofa in her crowded living room.

"Ritz isn't going to kill me, Pinky. He wants me alive. He gets too much pleasure out of hating me and plotting revenge."

"Ritz just caught two federal felonies, thanks to you, one with a man-min ten. He's got to be pretty grumpy."

"I guarantee you he thinks he's getting out of this." Rik has already said that Melvin Junior, who'd want the fat fee for a trial, has probably encouraged Ritz to believe that he won't be convicted. The evidence that the Ritz owns VVM is thin and circumstantial, Melvin will tell him. And if they beat that charge, no one will put Vojczek in prison for simple drug possession. It's another reason Rik thinks Ritz will surrender. Not worth running from this rap.

"I doubt it's the charges that are the first thing on his mind right now, Chief. You saw the complaint. Ritz is a user."

"The diabetic pens? That's Ritz to a T. Smartest fucker he ever met. He can walk down the street with his shit in his pocket, or shoot up in the men's room without worrying about who sees."

"Right, but that's over. Now his big worry is going into withdrawal at the MCC. That's straight cold turkey. And you're to blame for that. Plus, nothing could burn Ritz more than the way you outfoxed him. If he kills you, he proves who's the smartest after all."

She shrugs. "You can never get completely inside a brain that twisted. But I still don't see him making his situation worse by trying to kill me. He still doesn't know that he's getting charged with Blanco's murder."

"Speaking of twisted and unanticipated, when you were in his car with him on Tuesday, I thought for a second that he was serious about telling the real story about that picture."

"I knew that was bullcrap. He could never admit what I was threatening him with, especially since getting down on his knees basically proved it was true."

"I understand, but for an instant, he made it sound like it would be worth almost anything to him to force you to tell the truth, because of how much it would hurt you."

"Well, it will. I won't lie under oath. And twelve years ago or not, I know I'll be real lucky if all I catch is some time off without pay after I tell that story."

Rik feels that by leveling with the FBI about the photograph and using it as the basis of her efforts to ensnare Vojczek, the Chief's done everything possible to turn a negative into a positive. But no one can predict what will happen with her job. The arguments will all be about what would happen to a guy who'd done the same thing, even if it was a dozen years ago and the so-called victim was actually an epic shit. One favorable development, though, is that Lucy won't have to testify for quite a while now, since Moses is emphatic that it would imperil Vojczek's prosecution if the Chief is forced to speak about these events under oath before she testifies at the Ritz's trial. Given how court dockets move, that won't take place until long after the election, perhaps as much as a year or even a year and a half from today. The length of time before the Chief's case could be formally resolved, as well as her celebrated status at the moment as a true hero, both weigh in favor of dismissing the P&F proceedings now. Rik keeps urging Marc to recommend that to the commissioners, and he says he has and expects them to agree, maybe as early as next week. That way, if the Ritz pleads in the end, the story behind the photo may never be told. But until then, Lucy's going to be baking in purgatory, a punishment that even I—and Lucy—know she deserves.

"I could never say I didn't know it was wrong," she says. "I did. I thought it was justice, too. But it was wrong. That's part of why I stopped." She gives me a long look over the rim of her glass. "I'm sure you were pretty disappointed in me, when I told you guys the story."

"Disappointed?" It's sort of heartening to me that the Chief would even notice or care about my reaction. Was I disappointed? My life every day is kind of a monument to the limited value of following the rules. "I guess. I mean, I know it was way against the law, an abuse of office and all that, and that's always a bad place for a cop to go. Would I have felt better if you thought about it but didn't do it? Probably. But you know, I was also amazed and kind of proud of you at the same time. Guys like Ritz have been getting away with that shit—what he did to those women on the street—since forever. And it's pretty satisfying to see the tables turned. So sometimes when I look at that picture, knowing the whole story, I'm kind of horrified. And now and then I've laughed my ass off."

She smiles wistfully.

"I stopped laughing a while ago. Like I say: Bottom line, it was wrong."

"I've always had a question, though. It's kind of personal."

The Chief nods. If Ritz could see her now, he might feel like he got his revenge, as she told him in his car. She carries a new weight and weariness. Worse, there's just less light in her face.

"What's your question?" she says.

"Well, here's what has never completely added up to me. You were trying to do Ritz like he had done those women. Right?"

"Definitely."

"Well, did you really stop as soon as you'd taken the pictures? Cause if it was me, and I was letting him know how it felt to be in that position, and I'd gone that far, against the law or not, I'd want to make damn sure the motherfucker took a little taste."

Lucy laughs in spite of herself, but then casts her eye down to the rug.

"Well, maybe it didn't end as soon as I hit the shutter button. But it didn't last very long. Because I started to get scared."

"Of what?"

"Myself. By how much I enjoyed it. Not the sex part. That truly left me cold. But I loved having so much power over him. It was an amazing rush. I felt limitless. Just huge. But then I heard the creep open his zipper, and that kind of woke up my conscience. Overall, it was a really strange moment. Because I hadn't known I had that power thing inside me. It never came out on the street. But it was a great lesson to get right before I became Chief."

Tonya arrives late, about three a.m., but lets me sleep almost to nine. It's Saturday, but the Chief is going to spend the day in the station. Like a lot of bosses, she uses the weekend to catch up on everything on her desk that wasn't an emergency. We've agreed she's completely safe inside Central Station. Like most law-enforcement offices, it has been fully armored with bullet-proof glass and steel doors with electronic bolts to keep out the crazies and terrorists. Besides, there are a dozen armed cops inside who'd draw on Ritz on sight.

Instead, I stop in to see Pops, who's been glued to his TV and wants all the inside poop about the VVM case. I tell him what I can, then go to my office to do my own catchup. About four p.m., the Chief calls and I drive her home, parking the CTS around the corner so that anybody Ritz might have watching doesn't see an extra car in the driveway. The Chief wants to prepare what she calls 'a good dinner.'

"You like Mexican?" I tell her about Ruben's, which she's never heard of. Not that she has any need—she's a real cook. She's making tamales, since her daughters are coming for lunch on Sunday, and she steams up several and also fries up some carne asada. I make a salad.

The tamales are amazing.

"Truly, they kill," I tell her.

"A lot of work," she says, "but always worth it."

Tonya arrives just at the end of movie time. Toy is going to take the early shift, which means that tonight I can enjoy a beer while the Chief is having her nightcap.

Seated in the wooden nook in the kitchen, the three of us have a great laugh over an old story about Sid DeGrassi. Apparently, the first time he applied in HI, P&F ordered a second test to support his application, without any explanation. Sid was devastated when it turned out he had failed.

'I musta been close,' Sid supposedly said to Stanley, the old Chief. 'That's why they gave me another chance.'

'Nope,' Stanley told him. 'They couldn't believe any human being could do that bad if it wasn't on purpose.'

I'm not a crazy laugher, but this gets me, and I'm still going when I suddenly see Tonya stiffen across the table. She grabs both our hands and moves her index finger to her lips. We listen, and my heart jumps because I definitely hear a stick break outside. Then Tonya, who's facing the kitchen window, yells, "I just saw someone," and flashes to the front door as she's shouting directions to me.

On Tonya's orders, I move the Chief to an interior hallway, close to the basement door in case she really needs to run for it, then I bolt out the back. This all takes only seconds. As I come flying out, I see a big guy on the gallop, looking over his

shoulder at Tonya, who is shouting after him. He's got a hat on
and dark clothes and he's holding something in his right hand
that instinct tells me is a gun. As he reaches the back edge of the
house, roughly parallel to the rear staircase, I am able to totally
blindside him, driving my shoulder into him at full velocity. He
goes down like fruit falling off a tree, and I land on him and
deliver a couple rabbit punches. But I immediately register that
something is wrong. Big or not, the guy felt completely soft
when I plowed into him. And he's immediately bawling, literally
whimpering and begging me to stop. There's no sign of what I
thought was a weapon.

Tonya cuffs him while he's still facedown. She uses the flashlight on her phone, and when she rolls him over, I'm sure this
is not any hit man Ritz would send. He's like eighteen, still with
pimples and big glasses and a wild head of hair. In the light, I can
see a big pizza stain on the front of his T-shirt. Everything about
him reads 'total goof.'

Tonya has pulled his wallet from his back pocket.

"Robert Gamal?"

The guy can't stop crying, so it takes a second to get his story.
He's a freshman at the U and enrolled in a photojournalism class.

"I thought, you know, there's all this coverage of Chief Gomez.
A candid of her at home with her daughters? That would be
worth something."

I search behind us and find his digital camera in the bushes.
No gun.

Then suddenly I yelp in panic as it strikes me: Robert Gamal
is not a hit man. He's a distraction. Total misdirection would be
just like Ritz.

I sprint back into the house with my Glock drawn.

"Chief?" I yell.

"Right here." She's still in the hallway, holding her own pistol.

I want to search around the house, but she's dead certain nobody came in.

"What's up out there?" She moves her chin to the yard.

"Jimmy Olsen, cub reporter," I answer. When I explain about Robert Gamal, she can't stop laughing.

"You're kidding. I have *paparazzi*? I have papa-fucking-razzi. I can't wait to tell the girls."

Tonya comes in a couple minutes later. Jimmy Olson is outside, handcuffed to the wrought-iron railing in front. She's already radioed the station. Robert has no sheet and no warrants.

"Charge him or let him go?" Tonya asks the Chief, who turns to me.

"I say book him," I answer. "He's got to learn better." Look at you, I think. But I know I'm right.

Tonya calls for a cruiser and it's there in five minutes. They'll book Robert for trespass, a misdemeanor, which means he will get to bond out at the station and avoid spending a night in the jail. That would definitely have given him something to write about for journalism class.

Afterwards, all three of us have a whiskey to settle down. When she's drained her glass, the Chief thinks she can sleep and goes up to her bedroom, but Tonya and I are still way too amped and hang together in the kitchen.

"We did good," Toy says.

"We did," I say.

"Maybe I should withdraw my application to the Bureau and we should open our own shop as PIs or doing security." She's sort of kidding, sort of not. Before now she hasn't said explicitly that she applied to the FBI, although I sensed it. She needs to stay on the DL, since everybody in HI would freak, maybe starting with the Chief, at the thought of her leaving.

"Neh," I say. "Cross my heart a hundred times, Toy, I'd love working with you. But I also love Rik, and the PI thing. Being independent is not an easy business. I'm not sure either one of us has the chops for hustling clients. Same with security. How much high-profile work you think there is out there? We don't want to be the rent-a-cops at weddings or bat mitzvahs. And besides, I think we're doing great as friends," I say. "Business partners, when they break up it's worse than divorce."

"Okay," she says happily. I think she heard exactly what she wanted. "Totally agree on working out as friends." Given her prior experience with me back in the day, she clearly appreciates the reassurance.

"Besides, how could you pass on the FBI without trying it?" I ask.

"I'm still going back and forth. HI will be a great department as long as the Chief's around. You'd have a friend in high places if you tried to get on the force now, you know."

Weirdly, the thought has never crossed my mind. But I know Tonya nailed it when she told me I'd be a shit cop. I'd always be in trouble for breaking rules I see as stupid or pointless. As she said, nobody changes that much.

On Sunday, while the Chief's daughters are there, I sit in my car, which I've moved across the street but down the block, still trying not to be too obvious.

Tonya shows up at four with big news.

"Moses just reached an agreement with Melvin. Ritz is going to surrender at the federal courthouse tomorrow at noon."

"Bail?"

"The government will object wildly. The only thing Moses gave Junior is that they'll take Ritz straight up for an immediate bond hearing. And Feld won't deny at the hearing that the Ritz is an addict."

We exchange a round of high fives.

"And bye-bye babysitters," adds the Chief. "Not that I don't love you guys."

"Love you too," I say. More laughs. We're a cheerful trio.

When the Chief goes off to watch the end of the Trappers game, Tonya tells me that Feld has a new plan.

"The Ritz will never get bail. Because to start the hearing, the government is going to file a new complaint adding charges for the murder of a federal witness. They can corroborate Walter now because there's an exact chemical match of the carfentanil in the automatic syringes from Ritz's house with what killed Blanco. But the new complaint will only mention the scientific evidence. Walter stays on the DL. After Ritz has been inside twenty-four hours, they'll send Walter over to the MCC. And you know what the pretext will be? This is so evil. Walter will say he wants to be sure that the Ritz isn't going to turn over on *him*. And Ritz will have to answer. If he doesn't, he'll know that Walter's only option would be to make a mad dash for the US Attorney's Office."

On Monday morning, the Chief leaves early for the station. She likes to get there for shift change at 7 a.m. The mayor's office has also texted her and asked her for a briefing on the latest with Ritz and several other issues, which Lucy will deliver to the mayor at 8:00.

"I'll ride along," I say.

"The hell you will."

"That garage under the Municipal Building is spooky."

"There's plenty of security, and I only agreed to let you guys shadow me until Ritz was accounted for. Now he has been. Not to mention that it would embarrass the crap out of me with the mayor if it looks like I can't depend on my own officers to protect me. And it's too hard to explain why they aren't there."

I still insist on following her to the station. In the parking lot, she leans in the window of the car to hug me again.

"Getting to know you, Pinky, has been the best part of a generally shitty experience."

"That's me all over," I say. "A little better than shitty."

We have another laugh, and she turns back to wave from the station's back door.

41. WE GOT A LITTLE BIT OF RUH-RO

We got a little bit of ruh-ro" is the first thing Tonya says when my phone rings at 8:30, about an hour after I get to the office. "Where's the Chief?"

"With the mayor, as far as I know."

"I may call her," Tonya says.

"She won't pick up. Not while she's with the mayor."

"And how long is the meeting?"

"Beats me. But the Chief has complained before that the mayor is always late. The text Lucy got made it sound like the mayor has a long agenda. I'm sure she wants to hear whatever the Chief can share about Ritz. His arrest has got to be a big boost to the mayor's campaign."

"Jinx."

"Even so, the Chief's got to be out of there by nine thirty, wouldn't you think?"

"I'm going to send a couple uniforms over to check on her. Just in case."

"Just in case of what?"

"Bureau business."

"Don't pull rank on me, girlfriend. If you're worried about my client, I'm entitled to know why."

Tonya thinks it through, then says, "Walter got a text half an hour ago."

"From Ritz?"

"Apparently. It said for Walter to go to Jewell's house at eleven and pick up a bag she'll have ready. Ritz said Jewell would be heading to the airport separately, but Ritz wants Walter to bring the bag to him at the cell phone lot near remote parking."

"Is Ritz burying treasure before he surrenders or is he skipping?"

"Skipping, it looks like."

"Fuck," I say. The misdirection, getting everybody to go to Center City to watch Ritz being cuffed, while he's actually taking flight, sounds totally like him.

"So surrendering was a complete head fake?" I ask.

"That's how it looks to us. I just got off the phone with TSA. They searched today's passenger manifests and found Jewell on a direct flight to Mexico City. Her first-class ticket was booked by the same travel agency that the Ritz uses, and she also purchased seats for her son and a third passenger, a male born in 1956, whose passport number comes back to a man from Waukegan, Illinois, who died two years ago. A connecting flight for each of them is on hold to Jakarta. Indonesia has no extradition treaty with the United States."

"And you think Ritz will stop to shoot the Chief on the way out of town?"

"I think I'm being paranoid. If you run, you run fast. Still."

"Still," I say. "What's the game plan now?"

Tonya says a dozen agents have been dispatched to KCO, the area's big international airport north of town. The FBI will cover all entrances, but their instructions are not to detain Jewell until the Ritz appears.

"And how would you feel if I just happen to be strolling around KCO near eleven?" I ask.

"I'd feel that you've just reduced your lifespan. The Ritz knows your face better than anybody else's. He sees that nail, he heads back out the door."

"So what am I supposed to do?"

"Nothing. I'm going back to the station. Keep calling the Chief and her daughters. Just let me know if the Chief answers before my guys get her."

I try the three numbers repeatedly for several minutes. But talk about FOMO! I can't stand just sitting here. There must be something useful for me to do. After a while, I start wondering if the bookings at KCO are the same kind of head fake as surrendering. In which case Ritz will depart via private jet. I understand that Ritz probably has a better chance of mixing unrecognized in the crowds at KCO than as one of a few passengers in a small waiting room. But at least I'd be doing something, if I make the half-hour drive out to Greenwood County Airfield, the private airport, for a look.

I ghost the nail and leave it on my desk. As I rocket along US 843 in the Cadillac, it dawns on me that if Vojczek is really escaping on a chartered jet, he's canny enough to drive a couple hours to another private airfield, maybe near Chicago or St. Louis. Meaning there's an even bigger chance I'm wasting my time.

Along the way, I finally reach both of the Chief's daughters. Neither has heard anything from their mom. I do my best not to alarm either of them, but ask each to have the Chief call me ASAP if they connect with her.

Twenty minutes later, Tonya calls again. She's way more amped than usual and is talking fast and I have to slow her down a couple times. Early this morning, Don Ingram instructed Walter to cruise by Jewell's to see if there was anything Walt could find out about Ritz's plans. Jewell's son, Tal, who Walter knows a little, was outside mowing the lawn. Tal said his mom is in Cleveland, because *her* mother is sick. The kid hadn't heard a thing about a trip to Mexico, and Walter is certain that Jewell would never make a permanent move without her boy. Tal checked inside to see if Jewell had left a bag of some kind, but after searching several rooms, the kid found nothing. Walter and the agents figure what Cornish has been afraid of for the last week or so is true: Ritz smelled Walt out somehow, or at least, is suspicious enough not to trust him.

"Ritz has probably been turning over his conversation with the Chief," Tonya says, "now that he knows it was an FBI setup. Everything he asked about the investigation of Blanco's death? Ritz can see he got played. And the most likely reason the government was already building a case on him for Frito's death was if Walter was blabbing. A lot of stuff falls into place, once you assume that. Which also explains why Ritz is running. He can see he's going down on the murder."

I tell her that I'm on the way to Greenwood.

"Good thinkin, Detective," Tonya says. "Keep going. I'll ask Ingram to have any agents left in the Greenwood field office to get over there."

"And what about the Chief?" I ask.

"I've been trading calls with the two patrol officers I sent over to the mayor's office. Wait," she says, "here they are again. Call you as soon as I get off."

When she does, about five minutes later, it's the worst news yet.

"My guys who went to the mayor's office found out there was no meeting scheduled with the mayor today. They just searched the parking structure underneath and found the Chief's car. No Chief."

"Oh, my fucking God." I shoot sideways to the highway shoulder, catching the finger from a woman I cut off. "I'll turn around. I want to help."

"Negative," she answers. "The best way to find Lucy may be to find Ritz."

"Fuck," I say. That is not a happy thought.

"You scout for Ritz when you get there. If you see him, call me. But don't confront him yourself. He's truly considered armed and dangerous."

Ten minutes later, I race into Greenwood County Airfield, where three private jets of different sizes are parked near the small terminal. The largest plane, a G-IV with twin engines at the tail, shows the wavy plume of hot fumes shimmering behind the motors.

I have actually been here a few times, since Pops represented a billionaire from Indianapolis who liked to send his jet to town to pick up Sandy for face-to-face conferences. It's a pretty laid-back operation, whatever Toy says. You wait in the lounge until the pilot calls for you. There is a magnetometer, but I never saw it used. What are you going to do? Hijack your own plane? They check ID's, but only to be sure you're who you say you are. But TSA is not assigned to private facilities. Instead, the closest thing to airport security is the Greenwood sheriff's deputy who's outside the front doors, currently sucking down a cigarette while he talks on his white earbuds. The Greenwood deputies wear Smokey the Bear hats, but he apparently left his in his vehicle. He's a paunchy guy in his fifties with old-fashioned muttonchop sideburns. He definitely does not look poised for action, unless it's picking up a runaway doughnut. This is the kind of assignment you accept if you've burned out on the street.

I rush past him into the terminal, which is no more than a large waiting room, with framed posters on the walls, basically advertisements for the various private jet companies that operate here. A bright-looking young woman in a blazer is at the short counter, with a guy dressed the same way poking at a computer behind her. Otherwise, there are only a few passengers in the small lounge, all seated in overstuffed black leather easy chairs, where the 1 percent get to park their tushies while they wait for their flights. My quick take is these folks, all seated together, are signs of a better America, an African-American family: a mom, a dad, two kids, and Grandpa in a wheelchair, asleep. They are apparently a fuck-ton richer than any people I actually know—leaving aside Pops's client—since I'm not on speaking terms with anybody who could even think about flying private. It makes it better, though, that they're Black.

I have already headed back out the door when Tonya calls.

"Is Ritz there?"

"I sure as hell don't see him. Unless he's disguised as an African-American woman a lot shorter than him or her husband who's a lot taller. Tell me what's going on."

She says two agents from the Greenwood County FBI field office and several sheriff's deputies are about ten minutes away.

"It looks like they're wasting their time," I tell her. "Maybe they should go to the bus or train station. Or call other private airports within a hundred miles."

"Well, that's not good," she says, "because I'm pretty sure Ritz has got the Chief."

With that, my heart jolts so hard it actually hurts.

"Oh fuck," I say. "Alive or dead?"

"I wish I knew."

Tonya has now had a fuller briefing from the two HI cops

who went over to the mayor's office. Once they established that there had been no meeting between the mayor and the Chief— the mayor, in fact, was campaigning at the ferry port, shaking hands with commuters—the officers checked the footage for the security camera pointed toward the section of the garage where Lucy's Camry was parked. You could see the Chief exit the car and stroll toward the elevators, speaking on her cell. The video captured by one of the two cameras above the elevators showed the Chief approaching. What happened next was largely hidden by a square concrete pillar, which was why it was chosen as the point of attack. Lucy was caught completely by surprise. An arm was suddenly thrown around the Chief's neck from behind, and she almost immediately wilted, like she'd been unplugged from an electric socket, sinking from the bottom of the frame. The last video the officers had reviewed was from a camera at the exit, which showed a Chevy Suburban without a rear license plate, flying up the ramp to the street.

"And it was Ritz who grabbed her?"

"You can't see for sure."

"And you say she just collapsed?"

"I asked," Tonya says, "if it looked like she was drugged, maybe injected with something, and they said that's exactly how it looked."

"Oh fuck," I say.

"And you're sure Ritz isn't there?" Tonya asks.

I look back through the glass entry to see if anybody else has come in another door. The family is still chatting, except for Grandpa, who's now slumped to the left. He was wearing those big wraparound shades for macular degeneration before, but now his hat has slipped down over his face. I study him from the distance.

"Hey," I say to Tonya, "while we're on the phone, can you have your buddies at Customs and Border Protection check the passenger manifests for any plane due to leave here in the next thirty minutes."

"Sure, hold on."

She's gone about three minutes.

"They're still looking for the rest of the flights," she says, "but there's a Gulfstream scheduled to take off any minute that's carrying a family named Green."

"Like Yolanda Green?"

"Exactly. She's the first name on the list. How did you know?"

"That's Jewell's niece. The lawyer for VVM."

"Shit. And what about the Greenwood deputy out there? What's he doing?"

"Waiting to retire from the looks of it." The guy has never set foot in the terminal in the time I've been here. I suggest to Tonya that she call the Greenwood officers headed here and have them direct their guy to do what he can to keep the Green family from boarding.

Sure enough, within two minutes he picks the radio off his belt. He throws aside another cigarette he just lit and nods emphatically while he stares down the sidewalk toward me. He hitches up his trousers and starts my way quickly.

"You the PI working with Highland?" he asks me. He says he couldn't understand what they were trying to explain over the radio. He's filling in for someone named McGonnigle who called in sick. "They said I should just follow your lead. Something about a fugitive?"

As we head in, I tell him to ask the Green family to show their IDs. Just as we arrive, their pilot emerges through the security door, with a small window, that leads to the aircraft. The pilot is a middle-aged white guy, lean and completely bald-headed, dressed in a white shirt with epaulets. He makes a wide beckoning motion to the Greens, who all stand, except of course for the old man in the wheelchair. The deputy—Wronka, according to his nameplate—and I basically block the way between the family and the door.

"Need to check your IDs again, folks," Wronka says.

Yolanda speaks up. She's closing in on forty, in a fashionable lime dress with a contrasting yellow belt and low heels. Very professional and collected.

"They already checked them at the desk," she says.

Wronka shrugs, nothing he can do. "My lieutenant wants me to double-check everybody leaving for the next hour."

Yolanda and her husband, who has the staid well-groomed look of a banker, both produce their driver's licenses. After rooting in her ostrich handbag, Yolanda also pulls out copies of the children's birth certificates.

"And what about him?" I direct this to Wronka, gesturing to the old guy in the wheelchair, who's seated no more than two feet from where I stand. I have been checking him out, and he appeared to stir when Wronka mentioned IDs, but I still can't see much of his face. His tweed hat is all the way over his nose. And below that, his mouth is covered by a blue surgical mask, the COVID precaution you'd still expect for an old person traveling.

"My great uncle?" Yolanda asks. "He's asleep."

"Where's his ID?" I ask.

"I don't know," she answers. "I think he's got it. No, wait. Here." She finds his driver's license in her purse and hands it to Wronka. It's expired—a nice touch—but looks real enough, which is what I'd expect. It identifies the man in the wheelchair as Morris Sloane.

"Can we see his face?" I ask.

"He's *asleep*," Yolanda repeats. "He's a sick old man. Leave him be."

I turn to Wronka, who backs me and repeats that we have to get a look at the old guy.

"I'm not putting up with this," Yolanda Green says. She points at the pilot behind us and tells him, "Let's go."

Her husband and kids immediately slide a couple steps toward the runway exit, while she grabs the stainless-steel handles on the wheelchair, preparing to push it herself.

I quickly lift Mr. Sloane's hat from his face.

"What are you *do*ing!" Yolanda yells. "That's illegal."

Whoever he is still appears to be sleeping, and even now, I can't see much of his face behind the shades and the mask. There are several days' growth, the start of a whitish beard, around the edges of the light blue material. Then again, there's one thing for sure I notice, looking at his forehead. He's white.

I ask Yolanda to please remove his glasses and mask.

"I'll do no such thing. We're leaving." She motions the pilot forward to help her with the wheelchair.

"Arrest them all," I tell Wronka.

Wronka looks at me dubiously.

"At least him," I say, and with no more said, I reach down again and pull off the sunglasses. It's definitely Ritz. I bend forward from the waist and say, "Sorry to disturb you, Mr. Vojczek, but there's a federal warrant for your arrest."

"That him?" Wronka asks me.

"That's him."

"Okay, then. You're under arrest, sir." Wronka to his credit starts reciting the Miranda rights. Ritz's gray eyes spring open, fixing me with that inhuman look Koob warned me about.

"Where's the nail?" he asks me. "Did you grow up?"

"Don't rush me," I answer. "But if it ever happens, I'll come see you at Marion. You heard the deputy. You're under arrest, Mr. Vojczek."

He laughs once, a brief arrogant snort, and slowly comes to his feet. Wronka steps back but puts his hand on the buckled holster to his service weapon.

"You can't arrest me," he tells Wronka. "You just saw my ID. My name is Sloane. Whoever she thinks I am, this is a mistake."

I can see a qualm pass through Wronka's heavy face.

"Let's go," Ritz announces to the four Greens, who are watching in silence. Vojczek steps up to the pilot.

"Grab him," I tell Wronka.

"I did see his ID," he answers.

"For Godsake. He was posing as a sick old man in a wheelchair. Do you want him to carry a sign, too, that says 'I'm a fugitive'? Use your cell phone and look at the front page of the *Tribune*. His picture has been there for four days."

"Okay, just hold on," Wronka answers, addressing all of us. "That's a good idea. Let me get a look at the paper."

Ritz slides past the pilot and opens the door to the runway. The huge noise of the engines and the smell of exhaust flood into the lounge.

I reach under the open blouse I am wearing over a tank top and remove my Glock. Yolanda Green's daughter, nine or so, shrieks at the sight of the weapon.

"You're under arrest," I repeat to Ritz in the doorway.

"How I remember," Ritz answers, "you're not sworn. You flunked out of the academy, didn't you? This gentleman, he's the police officer, and he's not arresting me. Let's go," Ritz repeats to the pilot. "She's upsetting people."

"Stop," I say, "or I'll shoot."

"You can't shoot me," Ritz answers. "My name is Sloane. The officer isn't detaining me. And nobody's life is in danger. You shoot me, you're the one who'll end up in prison."

He waves to the Greens and steps around the pilot and out onto the tarmac, walking deliberately toward the stairs of the Gulfstream, about a hundred feet away. I push past Yolanda and run until I can position myself between the plane and Vojczek. I assume a shooting posture, knees slightly bent, bracing my wrist with my left hand.

Ritz smiles faintly. As part of his disguise, Ritz even lost his sport coat. He's wearing a blue blazer instead, but I see his right fingers drifting down toward its hem.

"Stop!" I scream. "Hands in the air, Ritz. Get down on your knees."

He shakes his head confidently.

"Get down," I say again. "If I have to shoot you, I will, Ritz. I can't let you get on that plane."

"Neh," he says. "You're not shooting me and I'm not shooting you. I got something you want. So you're going to let us go."

I feel a wave of shock. With all the adrenaline flowing and the way I have been concentrating on Ritz and the Greens, I lost any thought of the Chief.

"Where is she?" I ask.

"Now, why would I tell you that, when you're trying to arrest me? You step aside and let us board, and before the door closes, I'll tell you what you want to know."

"I don't think that's how this works. After you're in custody, you can try to bargain with the prosecutors. Unless it's murder. That'll be the needle for sure."

"She's alive," he says. "For now. I wouldn't wait long, if I were you."

"You're under arrest," I repeat. "Get down on your knees." I'm basically vamping, because I truly have no idea what to do. The FBI agents are trained for these situations. They can't be more than a couple minutes away.

"You're killing her that way," he says. "Your choice."

"Get down, Ritz."

"Tell you what," he says. "I'll give you something right now. Sign of good faith. And I'll tell you the rest when I'm on the top of the stairs, right before the door closes."

His right hand moves back again slowly, now creeping under his coat.

"Don't!" I scream. "Don't, Ritz!" My finger tightens on the trigger. Then I hear the reports of a gun, an enormous sound that feels absolutely shattering—two quick shots, *bang bang*, their force tearing apart the air. I am astounded as I look down, wondering how I could have been so fucked up that I fired. The Glock has no safety, but when I touch the barrel gingerly, it's cool. Meanwhile, the Ritz is completely still—then I see him waver, like a wheat stalk in the breeze, and fall face forward onto the tarmac before rolling to his shoulder.

At that point, I finally notice Walter Cornish, at the chain-link fence that secures the runway area from the parking lot. He's about thirty feet away, and his pistol, a silver revolver, is extended in both hands. He kicks open a locked gate in the fence and quickly reaches the Ritz, who lies within a swelling circle of his own blood.

With the toe of his shoe, Walter nudges Ritz's foot, which, in response, shows no movement. Walter looks up at me with that greedy smile.

"How's that for fucking cooperation?" he asks.

42. THE GREENWOOD SHERIFF'S POLICE ARRIVE

The Greenwood sheriff's deputies arrive—one cruiser with lights spinning—before the ambulance does. My gun has been holstered for several minutes, while Walter immediately identifies himself as the shooter and surrenders his weapon before he's handcuffed. As that's happening, he adds with considerable pride, "I'm a cooperating witness for the FBI."

"Better be, for your sake," the senior of the two Greenwood deputies answers. She's around my height and solidly built like me, with sergeant's stripes over her delts. "Their agents are about one minute away."

The little airport has come to a total standstill. The field personnel, the luggage handlers and the runway workers, have crept closer, and almost everyone inside the terminal is surrounding the open door to the runway to watch, including Yolanda Green, who is weeping. I don't know whether she's mourning dear old Uncle Ritz, or is simply reacting to the speed and drama of the way things unfolded, or if she's realized her life has just taken a very dark turn.

As everyone in law enforcement is trained to do, Walter aimed for the thorax—the biggest target—and I can now see signs of the exit wound, as blood wells from the center of the back of Ritz's blazer. Every couple minutes, I take a step or two away, trying to avoid two thick lines of Ritz's blood that are running down toward my boots.

I beckon Wronka, who finally eased outside through the doorway after the other Greenwood officers arrived. Lowering my voice, and without pointing at Yolanda, I tell him, "You better detain the lady who was giving us all that back talk. The FBI will be taking her into custody for aiding and abetting unlawful flight, and somebody will blame you if she disappears."

Wronka nods gratefully and heads inside with his left hand on the cuffs on his belt. Even with all of this going on, I am stifling an urge to scream and beg everybody to stop so we can all concentrate on the Chief.

In the meantime, Walter is explaining what happened with Ritz to the sergeant.

"He was reaching for his weapon," Walter tells her. "I know this guy, I know him too well. He was going to kill that girl there," Walter says, apparently referring to me. He delivers a lingering glance in my direction, clearly beseeching me to support him. The sergeant also turns my way.

Whether or not I should be, I'm grateful to Walter. He didn't save me the way he thinks. I'd have squeezed the trigger at the first sight of Ritz's gun, but I had no idea what to do if he didn't draw, if he just kept giving me a line about the Chief and headed up the stairway to the plane. Walter probably thought a 'girl' would never have the guts to fire, so maybe he believed he had to shoot to save me.

"I definitely thought Vojczek was going for his weapon," I say. "And Walter knows a lot more about the man than I do. So yeah," I add.

The three FBI agents from the field office, all in their dark suits, have finally appeared. I tell them about Yolanda, and two of them head in to take over with her, their creds already in their hands. When Wronka returns, the second deputy takes him aside to get his version about the shooting.

"What about the Chief?" I ask the third agent, a woman, Latina from the look of her. We know one another by sight from the occasional meetings with the Chief I've attended at their field office. The Greenwood sergeant is beside us, and I try to make sure I'm talking to her, too. "Ritz said he was going to give me some information about her, the Chief. I thought he meant a bullet, frankly, but maybe he was reaching for something else, instead of his gun."

The sergeant nods and double-times to their cruiser. It's parked very close to the spot at the fence where Walter shot from, and no one has bothered to turn off the car's spinning lights. She returns with blue rubber gloves and hands a pair to the male officer she arrived with. Everybody, inside and out, gets a little closer as the deputies turn the Ritz slightly to his side and roll up his sport coat with extreme care to avoid disturbing anything else. They find the back holster and the weapon he was carrying, which looks like a .32 Beretta, like the Chief's.

Walter is nodding the whole time.

"I told you I know this guy," he says to the deputies, then he turns to the FBI agent and me, about ten feet from him. "Once I was at Jewell's, I knew just where that fuck would be heading. He always talked about how great it was, flying private, even though he'd done it maybe twice. And it suddenly hit me, you know, while I was driving out here. My insides have been in a knot for weeks about diming him out, and this motherfucker was going somewhere to live off the zillions he's got in crypto, while he let the whole weight for Blanco fall on me. Loyal, my aching ass."

He smiles again, but he's the same dumb Walter who's just said more than he should have. He made it sound like maybe he raced out here intent on smoking Ritz the second he saw him. The prosecutors can figure it out.

The ambulance, siren blaring, finally comes to a screeching stop before the terminal doors. I can hear a second siren getting closer. It has the pitch they use in Highland Isle. The EMTs sprint over to the small group encircling Ritz. Gowned and gloved, the two medical technicians do a quick exam. Ritz has no pulse, and I guess his pupils aren't responsive either. They put an oxygen mask on him but one of the EMTs just shakes her head. The other one dashes back to the ambulance and returns, pushing the rolling stretcher. While the EMTs are scraping up the Ritz, Tonya arrives.

She looks at Ritz's pale body strapped to the stretcher and says, "Holy fuck. Did you have to shoot him?"

"Walter," I say.

"No shit," says Tonya.

The Greenwood sergeant, who clearly knows Tonya, walks up with something in her gloved hand.

"You think this might be what he was reaching for?" she asks me. "They were in his back pocket."

It's two brass keys on a ring. I fill in Tonya quickly on what Ritz said about the Chief.

"You think he has her tied up in some apartment?" Tonya asks. It will take forever to search every Vojczek property in Highland Isle.

I ask the sergeant to step closer so I can get a better look at the keys without touching them. They're shorter than house keys but somehow familiar. Then the nodes connect—I saw keys just like this when I was trying to figure how to get into Koob's cage in the basement at the Archer.

"They're for a padlock," I say. "I think the brand is called Superlock."

"A padlock?" Toy asks. "So she's in like a storage locker?"

"He said we didn't have much time," I tell Tonya.

"Because of the drugs, I bet," she says.

I didn't completely believe Ritz when he said the Chief was alive. But once Tonya says that, I see his plan. He gave the Chief a dose, probably of carfentanil, as a Fuck You farewell note to all of us. I'm guessing it was enough to kill her, but not at once. He wanted her alive for a while, but not because he felt any sympathy for the Chief. If he got nabbed before his plane took off, he was going to swap Lucy for his freedom, which is exactly what he was trying to do with me.

As I am thinking this through, I suddenly register what I was seeing but not really taking in while the EMTs were attending to Vojczek. The movement was strange, because all the other activities at the airfield have paused. Even though the Greens are still inside—watching from a distance while two agents continue interrogating Yolanda—what must be their luggage was wheeled out on a handcart and then raised on a mechanical lift into the hold of the G-IV. There was a big brown steamer trunk—Louis Vuitton, I'm pretty sure—and searching my immediate memory, I want to believe I saw a padlock on it. But the plane now is in the initial stages of taxiing, having been pushed back from the terminal area by one of those power carts with the long white arm.

As the jet begins slowly turning toward the runway under its own power, I scream, "Stop it. Stop it!" and draw my gun again as I dash toward the aircraft.

Nobody seems to pay any attention, except Tonya, who's a step or two behind as I sprint straight at the plane.

"Shoot his tires," I tell her, looking back.

"Why?"

"Shoot," I tell her again.

"You shoot. You're twice as good as me."

And I do. Six tires, two on each landing gear. I don't miss, although the smaller tires under the nose gear seem to be losing air only slowly. The four under the wings go flat almost at once.

Don Ingram and his team from Center City have appeared—I have no idea when they got here—but with Tonya shouting suggestions, Don and two others surround the plane, weapons in hand, while Don stands below the front window showing his credentials. A minute later, the hatch stairs come down again and the pilot appears in the doorway with his hands raised. He looks thin in his mock uniform—a short-sleeve white shirt and navy trousers with silver piping—and what little hair he has on the sides stands straight up in the jet exhaust. Stammering, he descends, his arms still in the air. Ingram asks him directly if he was trying to escape, but the pilot insists he was simply following the customer's written instructions to the charter company, which were to board all the baggage and take off on time, even if there were no passengers. Amid the pilot's babbling, he says that their flight plan's ultimate destination was Taiwan. Ingram tells me that that's another country without an extradition treaty with the US.

"But one where the Ritz speaks the language," I answer. Don nods.

My brain goes back to the padlock I believe I saw before, and I suddenly get the point of Ritz's instructions to fly, even if there was only baggage aboard.

"The Chief's in that luggage," I yell to Don. That way, the Ritz would ensure Lucy died even if he was taken into custody.

I tear off toward the restricted area behind the terminal, but Tonya is already racing out with two of the baggage handlers. I get the attention of the Greenwood sergeant and yell at her to bring the keys she was holding.

By then, all the luggage is on the lift and halfway down. The brown trunk, close to four feet long, is there, and even while it's still aloft, I recognize the Superlock on it.

With the baggage inching down, there is too much time to think. Life or death. It's the fundamental binary code. Then I rush forward as soon as the bags reach the ground, screaming at the handlers not to take the time to remove the trunk from the lift.

It's so strange, I think. It's just like at Blanco's. Even from first sight, you know the difference between living and dead. As soon as I lift the trunk lid, I process the tiny signs that Lucy is alive, especially her color. The Chief has been folded into the padded interior, with her legs, still in her short heels, bent demurely beneath her. But she is also in trouble, completely unconscious, eyes shut and breathing shallowly. She's unresponsive when one of the EMTs shakes her arm. The phony insulin pen Ritz used to deliver the carfentanil has been tossed inside beside her.

The EMTs complete a hasty exam and then inject naloxone, to reverse the opioid overdose, into the Chief's thigh. It's only seconds before she stirs a bit, but she seems trapped behind an invisible wall, and after two minutes, they give her a second shot. This time all her limbs begin to move more freely, and her lids rise slightly over her dark eyes, which remain unfocused. The EMTs and Tonya and I help pull her out of the trunk and lay her on a second folding stretcher the EMTs have produced. Now she'll really like me, I think.

Without much discussion, the two medical technicians run the Chief to the ambulance and take off for the hospital with the siren wailing. Ritz's body, still strapped to the first gurney, waits forlornly in the traffic circle in front of the terminal. His shirt and coat and pants are painted in blood, and the stain reaches down to the top of his cowboy boots. For the ten minutes it takes for the second ambulance to arrive, no one goes near him.

ACKNOWLEDGMENTS

My heartfelt thanks to everyone who helped me with this book: my perceptive first reader, my wife Adriane, and my agent, Gail Hochman. I had great assistance at Grand Central from my publisher/editor, Ben Sevier, and Elizabeth Kulhanek, who gave this book that rarity in today's publishing world, a patient line editing. Although they are often unsung heroes, I want to thank the copy editor, Rick Ball, and the senior production editor, Mari Okuda, who, as they have before, once again scrutinized every word and did their best to respect my idiosyncratic style. Deep thanks also to other early readers, including my daughter, Eve Turow-Paul, and my stepdaughter, Lily Homer, who tried to help me get Pinky right, and to Julian Solotorovsky.

Despite the great efforts of all the people mentioned above, a lot of mistakes of all kinds will probably be discovered by alert readers. The blame for any remaining errors belongs entirely on me.

ABOUT THE AUTHOR

Scott Turow is the author of twelve bestselling works of fiction, including *The Last Trial*, *Identical*, *Innocent*, and *Presumed Innocent*, as well as two nonfiction books, including *One L*, about his experience as a law student. His books have been translated into more than forty languages, sold more than thirty million copies worldwide, and have been adapted into movies and television projects. He has frequently contributed essays and op-ed pieces to publications such as the *New York Times*, *Washington Post*, *Vanity Fair*, *The New Yorker*, and *The Atlantic*.

For more information, you can visit:
www.ScottTurow.com
Twitter: @ScottTurow
facebook.com/scottturowbooks